CALAMITY

The Spirit of the Trees: Volume III

Shane L. Coffey

N
W E
S
BURN THE MAP
PUBLISHING

To my dear and loving wife, who accepts me

Contents

Chapter One: The Hunter

Joseph sat down and panted after heaving the ten-foot ridge beam into place. Being the only human in a village full of elves made him the biggest and the strongest by default. That had its advantages, but it could also be a burden, launching him to the top of everyone's list when it came time to lift heavy things, especially when they had to go into high places. All in all, though, Joseph couldn't complain. Rescuing the Windrider elves from the clutches of the evil Baron Turov had convinced many of them Joseph was, in fact, Azrith, a prophesied savior out of their legends. Making a harrowing journey to thwart the Baron's attempt to find the fabled Hoard of Dalviir, a dangerous collection of magical artifacts, had only cemented the Windrider clan's belief in Joseph's mythic position.

Legends were never meant to be seen up close, though, nor especially stood downwind of after days-long hikes through the forest without a bath or change of clothes. In the months that had passed since those portentous events, the elves had come more and more to treat Joseph as a person, as one among them and not above them. He still had their trust and respect, but now he had their affection as well, and he was less surprised each day to find that he returned those feelings, he who had lived as a virtual hermit for years after his wife had fallen to illness. That solitude had shattered on the day Kaillë Windsong, young chief of the Windriders, had interrupted his morning hunt to beg help escaping the Baron's men at her heels, the event that had catapulted Joseph into so many battles. Yes, Joseph knew his mettle in a fight, but he much preferred heaving timbers to slaying men, and he was glad the elves had grown familiar enough with him to ask for the former.

Familiarity aside, applause for his feat of strength mixed with the rustle of wind through the spring leaves as Joseph sat recovering his breath, and Kaillë was beaming as she ran across the grass to sit next to him. Dona and Redel, the young couple whose house Joseph was framing, followed close behind. "Our hero again, as always," Kaillë said as she put her arm around Joseph, her head too low to lean properly on his shoulder on account of her shorter, elven frame.

"Thank you, Joseph," Redel said, and Joseph was pleased to hear no hint of hesitation before using his proper name. He had finally broken the lot of them calling him "Azrith" sometime while they had wintered in a temporary camp down in the foothills where the snows were less brutal.

Joseph nodded up at the young elven man. "Don't mention it."

"This is it, Joseph," Kaillë said. "The last house. The Windriders are home again."

Joseph did catch the note of apprehension in her voice, thanks in no small part to Kaillë's long instruction on how to read people better. Joseph had always considered himself a good judge of character and courage, but the subtleties of mood and tone were largely beyond his ability, or at least his interest, until recently. Once he noted Kaillë's concern, he needed no special instruction as to its source: It was *him*. He had promised to stay with the clan, and by extension with Kaillë, until they had established a new home for themselves, their last having been destroyed by Baron Turov's mercenaries just before Kaillë and Joseph met. Now that the new village was all but complete, Kaillë feared Joseph would return to his own forest, to his wife's grave and his solitude.

Some stubborn part of him still longed to do just that, and this resistance had kept him silent, kept him from announcing to Kaillë he had made his mind up to stay at his new camp a mile or so from the village. It even kept him from expressing deeper things to her that occasionally tugged at his heart when they were apart, during rare moments to himself when his thoughts and pulse would quicken of their own accord, even as they quickened now while she sat beside him. He had learned other things from the elves, though, some small measure of their talent for being at peace with things as they are, not as they would have them, and in that spirit he accepted the battle within his nerves, the war between pulling Kaillë close and pulling away. Content with the conflict, he simply sat resting, enjoying the camaraderie and closeness that were so new to him. "You are home," Joseph finally replied, "and a beautiful home it is." The rush of the stream that bent along their northern and western sides reached his ears as a growing breeze wafted the scents of trees and earth and wildflowers through the alpine clearing. "I pray you are never uprooted again."

As if in answer, a shadow fell just before a buffet of air tossed their hair and clothes. A giant owl, large as a horse, landed nearby, and its wiry elven rider leapt down from its harness, a bow and quiver on his back. Military form was not the elven way; the rider gave only a slight bow of his head by way of salute before stating, "I've concluded my patrol, Chieftain. There is nothing out of the ordinary to report."

"Good, Ten'venni," Kaillë replied. "I am glad to take your report, but why make it to me and not to Tal'onë? He is the captain, after all."

"I passed him on my way back," the young owl rider explained. "He asked me to relay a message as well. He took an owl to scout some smoke that had been reported on the northern patrol."

Though they conversed in elven, Joseph had become fluent in the words over the past months, and he tensed at them now. "He didn't tell me. Does he need help? How much smoke was seen?"

"He knew that you would ask," Ten'venni answered. "I'm to assure you he will return for help if it is needed."

Kaillë smiled at Joseph. "You worry too much, as always."

"I'm not worried," Joseph rebutted with a scowl. "Tal'onë is sorely needed here, though. He shouldn't put himself in harm's way." That much was true. The Baron's attack last autumn had cost the Windriders many of their warriors, and Tal'onë's efforts at training a new cadre of guards were in their infancy. Joseph had led men in the past, and elves as well of late, but *teaching* elves to fight was another matter. With their smaller size and lesser strength, they required different techniques that could only be properly learned from one of their own kind.

"Tal'onë knows his worth, and he is wise," Kaillë answered. "He will not endanger himself unless the need is grave, and if it is, he will not fail to warn us of it."

Joseph stood and walked back toward Dona and Redel's house, where a number of elves had gone to work attaching rafters to the new beam. "If you're so sure there's nothing to worry about, then I guess I'll get back to work," Joseph called over his shoulder. He heard Kaillë dismiss the owl rider and knew she would be coming to work alongside him for as long as she could, until some Windrider called her away with a question or concern. The day's work had been good, but Joseph was eager for it to be over. His muscles were weary, and, more importantly, the clan was preparing a celebration for the evening meal.

Tal'onë returned in the afternoon to report that all was well. A small group of trappers was in the woods, but they were lightly armed and, at least from a distance, didn't appear to be doing any harm. Joseph set aside his worry and continued his work on the last Windrider cottage.

~ * ~

The inside of the house was dark, lit only by a single candle on the rough and wobbly table. In fact it wasn't really a house at all, just the back quarter of a carpenter's shop located in the low-class quarter of the capital city of Onderburg, screened off from the working and selling by a thin wall of clapboard. The only door creaked open, and the little bit of gray dawn that reached the ground in the alley outside crept softly into the hovel. A lithe form slid inside as well, covered only with close-fitting pants and a vest of canvas that worked with tight-cropped hair to mask any hint of the wearer's femininity save the delicateness of her features and the feline grace with which she used her body.

"Rook," said a voice in the shadows at the table, "where have you been?"

"Out, big brother," the entering woman replied, her voice an uncivilized alto. "Bringing home silver for to buy bread for our bellies and wool for our blankets. But you knew that already."

"I make enough fixing our landlord's tools and doing his detail work to keep our heads dry and our bellybuttons off our spines, like I've told you a hundred times. I hate you going out on your 'jobs'; what am I supposed to do if one morning you don't come back? It was bad enough before, but now there are rumors of rebellion from the north and the mountain tribes picking up their raids. It's getting dangerous out there."

Rook sighed. Adler, her older brother, worried too much. Not that she hadn't had some close calls over the few years she'd been treasure hunting...as she called it. Just the previous autumn she'd ended up traipsing through the mountains with a bunch of elves and a hunter looking for the Hoard of Dalviir. That had been a total waste. Well, maybe not a *total* waste. Joseph, the hunter she'd met, was a tall, stiff drink of whiskey if ever she'd seen one, and no mistake. Rook shook her head at the memory. The power of the Hoard was the best chance she'd had of healing her crippled brother, so she still half-hated Joseph for denying her the prize, even though failing to destroy the Hoard and Turov, the Baron wielding it, would have resulted in her certain death. On the other hand, the half that didn't hate Joseph *really* didn't hate him, but she knew she'd missed her chance for any fun on that front. Even if they ever met again, which seemed unlikely, chances were good that elf maid, Kaillë, had domesticated him by now and ruined him for carnal pursuits altogether.

"Necessary risk, Adler," Rook finally replied. "Food and clothes aren't what we really need. We need to get you back out on the street, playing for the crowds, not stuck in this shack dragging yourself between the bed and that chair." Rook looked at the rough, homespun blanket that covered his legs, useless and atrophied since Adler had taken an ax to the back during the war. A cruel enough fate for anyone, especially an unwilling conscript, but for the best acrobat within a week's travel in any direction, a man who'd tumbled for kings and peasant children and everyone in between, the tragedy was beyond words. Rook closed the door behind her, knowing Adler was likely to get loud any moment, and busied herself lighting another candle.

"I am *not* my legs!" Adler shouted, confirming Rook's suspicion. "Dammit, girl, how many times do I have to tell you, I don't *need* the crowds or the kings. When mother died, I swore I'd take care of you, and I can do that in my own way, but not as long as you're running off to fates-know-where getting up to your hips in trouble! I might even be able to save up enough for some proper rooms if you'd stop 'investing' everything on your hopeless capers."

"And there it is again," Rook shot back. "Hopeless. Just because you've given up doesn't mean I have to!"

"Since when is playing the hand you're dealt the same as giving—"

The argument was interrupted by a light knock on the door. Both siblings stopped talking, and Rook's hands strayed toward the daggers she always wore on her belt. Though she'd carried them for years, they were mostly tools and partly show, or had been until her battles for the Hoard. It was only since then she'd developed the habit of preparing to draw them when startled.

"Excuse me, am I interrupting?" came a voice through the thin wood of the door.

"Charlie?" Rook asked without turning. Still facing Adler, she saw her brother grimace. Of all her acquaintances, it was no secret Adler disliked Pockmark Charlie the most.

"Indeed it is I," Charlie responded with his customary false sophistication. "May I—"

Rook cut him off by opening the door and stepping back outside. "Best we talk out here," she told her contact. "He's in a mood."

"Far be it from me to impose," Pockmark Charlie replied. Charlie was a man of average height, though like virtually everyone, next to Rook he looked tall. His black hair was turning to gray, not just on top of his head but through his scraggly beard as well. He tried to grow it to cover the fever scars that had given him his moniker as a youth, but it didn't help, and as far as Rook was concerned, it sometimes hurt, depending on the light. He was dressed as Rook always saw him: in black and in a style that might be called "last year's fashion," but only as an act of charity.

Rook leaned back against a stack of crates then decided to hop up onto them to sit, putting her on a level with Charlie. The man always liked to trade pleasantries or gossip before getting down to business, so Rook asked, "What do you make of these stories circulating the past few weeks, trouble brewing in the north and the mountains?"

"All true, I'm afraid," Charlie answered, "at least as far as my sources can tell. Could turn out to be lucrative, but there's always a cost. Supply lines compromised, smugglers arrested or pressed into honest service, stealing from the wrong noble suddenly becomes high treason."

"Not to mention lots of people dead and crippled." The levity had left Rook's voice, its absence heavy.

"Of course. Forgive me; I didn't mean to be flip."

"I didn't expect you here this morning," Rook said, changing the subject back to the matter at hand, whatever that was.

"I didn't expect to be here," the fence and fixer replied. "I came straight from a meeting with a most prestigious client. Normally he has been unwilling to meet your somewhat unusual fee requirements, but in this case he insisted that he could only accept the best, and so...here I am."

Rook didn't blush or bow. She was the best, and she knew it. No human alive had picked the locks on a dwarven vault, save Rook, and she'd done it under threat of immediate bodily harm at that. It was a level of skill that allowed her to name her price, but it wasn't in coin alone she took her remuneration. Rook worked for information, the older and more potentially powerful the better. "So what's the job?" she asked.

"A book," Charlie replied.

"A book?" Rook echoed, skeptical. She had frequently appropriated books for herself in the hopes of finding magic to heal Adler, but when jobs came down from "prestigious clients," it usually meant one noble wanted to nick some bauble or trinket from another. Books had been key status symbols for a time back when literacy first became all the rage amongst the nobility, but that had been before Rook was born.

"Indeed, a book," Charlie confirmed. "I have the title and other particulars here; they'll help you locate it within the collection." He handed her a scrap of paper.

"Alright, so I have the What. I still need the When and the Where."

"It has to be tonight, I'm afraid," Pockmark Charlie said, his voice trailing.

"Tonight? One day to prep a job is no way to do business, Charlie."

"I told him you could handle it. I'd hate to—"

"I never said I *couldn't* do it. Where is it?"

"It should be a smooth job. The client has guard schedules and a line on a secret entrance by the tournament green, and—"

"Tournament green?" Rooks eyes narrowed. There were only a couple things by the tournament green. "*Where, Charlie?*"

"...Ulfmann's vault."

"...Ulfmann?" Rook answered, almost choking. "Ulfmann, the private sage to King Dieter. Ulfmann, who's vault is *in* the royal palace, *that* Ulfmann?"

"That's the one. No problem, right? You're not the best for nothing."

"If you thought it was no problem, you'd have led with it."

"Be that as it may," Charlie continued, "it's worth the risk. I haggled him up to a small fortune, and as for your special payment needs, you can take as much from the vault as you can carry for yourself. Your pick of the most varied store of arcane knowledge on the continent."

Risks aside, Rook nearly salivated at the prospect, to say nothing of the prestige she would earn by pulling off the job. Cracking a dwarven vault was a solid bona fides, but only amongst those who had the foggiest notion of how impossible a task it was, and that was a small clique to say the least. Hoping against hope her brother hadn't heard the name Ulfmann from his seat inside, Rook looked Pockmark Charlie square in the eye. "Tell me about this secret entrance."

~ * ~

The long twilight of the forest cast the trees in deep shadow, but all in the Windrider village was light and laughter. Candles and lanterns hung from every bough, bathing the central green in a warm, yellow glow. The winter stores had been turned out, creating a makeshift feast laid out on a line of blankets running down the center of the open space. Windriders sat in groups around the green or strolled between them with their food in bowls. Children ran about laughing and tagging one another, though calling their play a "game" would have assumed some form of rules were in force. Stitch and Yowler, the dogs Joseph had liberated from some of the Baron's footpads, dodged and cavorted along with the young ones, adding to the wholesome chaos of the gathering.

Joseph stood to one side of the lawn, eating a salad of tender, spring greens as he leaned against a narrow maple. The peace of the tableau contented him, but his eyes were especially on Kaillë as she moved amongst her people, ensuring everyone had a chance to share the celebration with their chieftain. Her grace, both physical and social, had grown more and more to captivate him over the winter.

Tal'onë, the captain of the Windriders' guards and the second member of the clan Joseph had met, ambled across the green to where the hunter stood. "Are you enjoying the celebration, Joseph?"

"I am, Tal'onë, thank you."

"Why do you stand here alone? If you don't mind my asking?"

Joseph looked down at the elf. He wasn't one to speak of his feelings, but he had come to trust Tal'onë. "I guess I'm just not sure where I fit. It's been a lot of hard work over the last few months, but I've never celebrated with elves before."

Tal'onë nodded. "I understand. Just know that you are welcome. And don't stay over here too long; there's at least one elf I know that will be eager to speak with you." The elf nodded his parting and walked away, angling toward a knot of older elves sitting on stumps a little way around the green.

Joseph continued his observations of the festivities until his salad was gone then headed back toward the dried meats and fruits to continue his supper. Kaillë appeared at his side as he was filling his bowl. "You've kept your distance this evening, Joseph. I hope everything is alright."

"It is," Joseph said. "You know I'm not much for socializing."

"Of course. We've kept you a long time from your forest and your solitude." Her tone was more formal than

Joseph had become used to, and Joseph found it somehow frustrating.

Other elves were waiting for space at the food, so he and Kaillë moved away to continue their conversation in private tones. "Staying has been my choice," Joseph said.

"Under the circumstances, I suppose. Not that any of us *gave* you much of a choice. Now that the village is built, I expect you'll want to get back home."

Joseph was surprised to hear Kaillë speaking so obliquely. It wasn't the way of elves, nor of Kaillë in particular. He decided to be direct. "For me to go back home...is that what you want?"

Kaillë met Joseph's eyes, but only for a moment. "No," she said after a pause.

"I thought I might stay in my camp upstream. For a while, anyhow. Make sure you're all getting on alright before I go too far."

"Oh," Kaillë said, the corners of her mouth tugging into a smile as she blushed. "It will be nice to have you close awhile longer." She brushed Joseph's arm before moving away to speak to more of her people.

Joseph watched her go before moving to the edge of the clearing and sitting on the grass, his divided heart beating fast.

~ * ~

Rook held her breath as she hid in the shadows and waited for the guard down the corridor to turn his back. The secret entrance to the palace, an old and forgotten escape tunnel on the north side where the royal quarters sat once upon a time, had been as advertised: dusty and half collapsing, but unguarded and passable for a skilled infiltrator. By covering her customary trousers and vest in a serving girl's dress, making her way from the secret passage to the door of Ulfmann's private library had been easy. There were always folk coming and going in King Dieter's palace, and going unseen in plain sight was as important in Rook's profession as picking locks.

Now, however, her servant garb was tossed into a corner, her pack hanging off her shoulders instead of hidden under her skirt. The time for disguise had passed, and the time for speed and agility had come. Rook could approach the guard on some pretense, but then his attention would be on her, and any number of things could go sideways when she moved to subdue him. Better to take him completely unawares. The wait made her mind wander to the best way to locate the specific knowledge she sought amidst such a treasure trove of other arcana, the proverbial needle in a needle-stack.

At last the guard turned away, so Rook snapped her mind back to the immediate task and sprang forward, crossing the distance in a few leaping strides, silent as a hunting cat. The man-at-arms was a head taller than she was, but she'd felled larger. Holding her breath, she uncorked a glass vial and reached around from behind the man to hold the open end of the tube to his face. He coughed once as his knees wobbled, then buckled completely, before he could turn around to face his attacker. Rook caught him as he fell and eased his bulk to the ground as gently as she could before corking the vial and returning it to the pouch on her belt. No doubt her job would be easier if she had fewer compunctions, but she was no killer. Indeed, she had only killed a man once in her life; it had been half an accident and in defense of that same Joseph that plagued her thoughts. Even still, it didn't sit well with her. Some might have questioned the strength of her conscience, but she did have one, and there were some things she didn't need weighing on it.

The lock on the room she was infiltrating was no match

for her, and within seconds she stood inside the personal record store of Ulfmann, chief amongst King Dieter's private sages.

King Ludvarch, who had started the war in those parts a few years back that had taken Adler's ability to walk, had been obsessed with the Mad Sorcerer Dalviir and anything he might have left behind. That had sent him and his armies searching after many rumors concerning magical treasures of all stripes, just to be sure. Some of these rumors led him to his neighbors' lands, which wasn't inconvenient for Ludvarch, since he was hungry for land and power anyway. It was, however, rather inconvenient for his neighbors. King Dieter had led the coalition of smaller kingdoms banding together against Ludvarch's aggression, and when the megalomaniacal king was eventually defeated, Dieter had taken possession of his libraries and passed them on to his sage, Ulfmann, for study.

The collection was vast, and some documents of lesser value, thought to be apocryphal or to represent only dead ends, were known at whiles to find their way onto the illicit market thanks to the larcenous entrepreneurship of some subordinate scribe or other. It was by piecing together clues from those and more accessible historical sources that Rook had discovered Dalviir's raided tomb and the directions it contained to the Hoard, which in turn had caused no small amount of death and trouble for herself, Joseph, and the Windriders. Now that prize had slipped from her grasp, but here she was only months later on a job that led her straight to Ulfmann's private library, the most concentrated trove of knowledge said to exist, where the most sensitive and potentially dangerous of Ludvarch's secrets had been locked away.

The vault door now breached, Rook realized the most critical work was only beginning. She followed Charlie's instructions to her client's target in a trice, a smallish tome bound in red leather with no mark on the outside save the word "MALICE" stamped vertically down the spine. The book took barely a quarter of the space in her pack. Deciding what else to take would be the hard part. After all, she could hardly expect to find an ancient tome with the title *Healing Artifacts* or find a master index containing *Restoratives - War wounds - Crippling, see also: Saving your brother*. She was lucky to be able to read at all, but that she did only in her native tongue, which covered perhaps a quarter of the titles she now saw on book spines and scroll cases. A non-trivial portion were in languages that didn't even use her alphabet. The guard would only be out for a few minutes, so she had to move quickly.

Half the storeroom contained shelves so dusty and cobwebbed with inactivity that nothing could possibly have been added to them in the last few years; Rook skipped those over entirely. Other sections showed signs of more activity but had the opposite deterrent. They were so worn and dog-eared they must have been the go-to reference tomes for Ulfmann and his research staff for decades. In the back corner of the room, though, she found what she sought, an area still only half organized, stacks of tomes and scrolls still in the process of being fully identified and catalogued. Wasting no time, she set down her rucksack and scanned the largest tomes for one written in her language. The need for a translator opened a treasure hunter up to deceit and betrayal, as Rook had recently learned the hard way. After jamming in the largest book she could read, the pack had a bit of room left, so she grabbed scrolls that would fit vertically down the space on either side of the book, then closed up the bag and heaved it onto her back. She turned to leave and stopped in her tracks.

In front of her, at the end of a row of bookshelves so it had been out of her eye-line on the way in, sat a wooden pedestal topped with a glass case. Inside the case hung a necklace suspended from a wood cross-piece. Its chain was silver of medium weight, and it flared at its front into a network of silver and gold links and leaves about a hand-span wide at the top and tapering to a sizable, blood-red ruby that would have rested at the very top of Rook's cleavage if she'd had any. Any eye could see by its size and weight it was crafted to accent a body more voluptuous than Rook's, and for a rare moment she doubted her own beauty, wishing she met the feminine ideal of whoever had fashioned this stunning jewelry. It was the most beautiful object the treasure hunter had ever seen, and her heart longed to take it, to have it for a time, and then to sell it and live like a queen off the proceeds.

She chided herself. She had taken up treasure hunting only to heal her brother, and that the skills the occupation required lent themselves so easily to thieving was no fault of her own. She'd taken a number of contracts to keep her and Adler warm and fed since then, but her cuts were only enough to get by, and what did she care if one noble just couldn't live without a bauble from the vault of another? She had never coveted anything for herself, nor even profited from her ventures in any meaningful or lasting way. She stole only to save her brother and to survive while doing it, that was all.

And yet, there was the necklace, hanging almost at her eye level, begging to be had. Chances are it had come from Ludvarch's hoard most recently, and it had probably been stolen ten times before that in order to arrive there. Why shouldn't the better thief wind up with it in the end? She could even claim to have found it later on, turn it in for a reward instead of selling it. It would end up right back here, but she with some coin in her pocket—fair compensation for pointing out the gaps in their security, when she thought about it.

She shook her head. Rook had always had a knack for

justifying what she wanted, but this was getting flimsy, even for her, and she'd wasted enough time gawking that the guard would be waking up soon. She adjusted her pack and hurried to the door, locked it behind her, and slid off into the shadows to make good her escape.

At least, that was her intention. In fact, she got only two steps past the glass case before she found herself stopping and turning back to it. Her hands shook as she reached for the case and eased it off the pedestal, leaving the silver chain exposed before her. She had the glass halfway to the floor when a series of crystals set high in the wall flashed a brilliant white, nearly blinding her. She started, and the case slipped from her fingers to fall the last foot down to the floor. The glass was sturdy enough not to shatter, but it made a clear and resounding bell tone as it struck the flagstones. She grabbed the necklace and stuffed it into her belt pouch then bolted for the door. The great tome's weight in her pack threw her off balance, and, still trying to blink the spots from her eyes, she stumbled into a stack of crates and knocked the top one onto the floor with a clatter. She heard the guard outside struggling to rise.

Rook darted out the door. The guard, now on his hands and knees, lunged for her. She felt his fingers latch around her ankle and hurtled toward the ground, the shock of impact slamming through her hands and arms as she caught herself with the heavy pack falling on top of her. Rook pulled her free foot out of the guard's reach as he scrambled to improve his hold. She turned onto her side and drove her heel down into the man's face, smashing his nose. He cried out and let go of her foot, and Rook jumped up and ran as pounding footsteps and the clank of arms seemed to resound up every hallway.

She had studied the layout for hours before the job; she had to sweat through a few tense moments, but in the end, Rook gave the guards the slip and made her way back to the tunnel. Safely in the shadows, she sat hard against the stone wall, her lungs heaving with exertion. The minutes passed, and with it her adrenaline, slowly giving way to realization the job was done. Her prize of knowledge cushioned her back from the stones even now, but it was to her belt pouch and the necklace inside that her hand was first drawn. She couldn't see its metal and ruby in the dark, but she ran her fingertips over its contours, drinking in the cold smoothness of its surfaces. She longed to put it on, but she resisted. Even if there had been light, there was no looking glass in which to see herself, no one else present to describe how beautiful it made her, so why bother? Besides, she had gotten away, but she hadn't gotten away clean; the necklace would attract too much attention for a time yet. Best to keep it hidden.

Finally hunger and thirst overcame exhaustion, and heaving the heavy pack, she rose to her feet, feeling her way forward in the dark. She yearned to find a place to hole up and study the tome and scrolls she had won, but first she had to hand the contracted book over to her client.

Chapter Two: The Hunted

Rook took a cautious step onto the ladder leading up to the haymow of a little-used barn near the river docks of south-central Onderburg. The barn looked out of place among the storehouses and other buildings keeping more static wares. Occasionally, however, an animal would come into market too thin or sickly to remain and risk driving down the price of the whole lot. Pockmark Charlie had devised a system wherein he would purchase these animals for a shamefully low price, though still higher than the "nothing" that the drovers were likely to get anywhere else, then house and feed them for a few weeks. After some fattening up to make the stock appear more appetizing, Charlie could sell them at a profit, or at least that was the plan. Rook wasn't sure Calarlie ever made money on the deal, though it was her understanding he'd won the old barn in a card game, so he didn't have much in the way of overhead to recoup.

On her approach, Rook had seen the twin lanterns

hanging from the jib over the upper door of the mow, the signal it was safe to proceed to the meeting, but she still felt uneasy. She had only a description of the man she was to meet to hand off the book, and while she doubted the noble client would come himself, her contact would almost certainly be someone comfortable in those circles. She had always felt anxious around the upper classes, and no less lately since the last noble she'd spoken to had thrown her into a dungeon. Eager to add some sense of status to her plain trappings, she reached into her belt pouch and pulled out the necklace then clasped it about her neck. Even in the dim light of the lanterns that filtered down from the haymow, the central ruby sparkled, and on a whim she pulled a small lamp from her own pack and kindled it, the better to see the prize around her neck. Rook knew the act was foolish, as the piece might be recognized, but as soon as she donned it she felt her apprehension lessen, and with a steadying hand she reached for the next rung of the ladder, and the next, until she had reached the top.

There were bales of hay, some still tied and whole, others loose and fraying, stacked all around the attic-like space, but a room-sized area at the top of the ladder was left clear. A path between the bales led to the upper door that was open to the night air, the two lanterns Rook had seen from the ground glowing just outside. The hanging lanterns meant her contact should be there, but she could see no one. Then her canvasing glance fell on a pair of legs sticking out from behind a pile of hay, and a shift in the breeze alerted her to a subtle odor of blood. A whisper of rustling hay sounded from behind her.

Rook whirled around and whipped a dagger from the sheath at her thigh, the only weapon that had ever shed blood in her hands. "Who's there!" she demanded.

A short man stepped into the light of her lamp, his bulk impossible to guess under layers of clothing but bearing no resemblance to her planned contact. He wore boots and gloves of soft leather with oversized, turned down cuffs. His attire was voluminous and all in shades of crimson and scarlet: pants and jacket with a wide belt and sash, and a heavy cape hanging about all. A wide-brimmed hat shadowed his face, but Rook was more focused on the stout crossbow pointed at her chest, loaded and spanned, ready to shoot. "I've no wish to kill ye," the man said, "but kill ye I'll do if it comes to it. I'm come for this afternoon's haul."

Rook would sooner *eat* that crossbow bolt than give up her treasure without a fight, but she'd neither seen this man before nor knew him by description. She wanted to get the measure of him before making her move. "How did you find me?" she asked, stalling.

"Ye need to associate with a better class of people, lass. Yer friends are more motivated by greed than loyalty."

"Damn you, Charlie," Rook hissed. She slowly sheathed her dagger, fearing any false move could cost her life. "Alright, stranger. Nobody needs to get killed here. Especially me. I have what you want." She crouched to the floor and set the lamp on the ground then shifted her weight to let the pack slide off one shoulder. She raised up slowly as she slid off the second strap as far as her elbow, then with a jerk swung the pack in a pendulum arc to slam into her lantern, sending the small, clay vessel to shatter against the wall. The oil splashed into a sunburst pattern across the rough floorboards and ignited instantly, the flames licking at the piles of hay.

Rook rolled toward the flames and knew the direction had taken her enemy off guard as she heard the crossbow twang and saw the bolt fly wide just as she came out of her roll. Uncoiling from her crouch, she pressed the balls of her feet against the floor, springing forward in three long bounds as the stranger cast aside his crossbow and scrambled to follow. Another bound and her attacker was left farther behind, his eyes likely dazzled by the brightness of the sudden flame. Rook's final stride took her through the opening of the haymow, launching her out into space. That final leap kept her rising for a few feet, then she felt the relentless grip of gravity dragging her earthward with ever increasing speed. As she heard the man in red curse her foolishness, for a sickening moment she thought she'd overshot her target then suddenly she was landing, smashing into a full hay cart a few yards in front of the barn.

It took her longer than she would have liked to pull herself from the billowing hay and cart wreckage, but as soon as she had her feet, she spun back toward the barn. The enemy had not jumped after her, but as she looked up at the open haymow, she didn't see him silhouetted before the spreading flames.

Knowing she needed very quickly to get gone, Rook plunged her arms into the hay pile, searching for her pack, which had been knocked from her grasp by the impact. In a few seconds she smacked her hand into it and quickly tucked it under her arm, not wasting the time to put it back on. With that she darted into the shadows and was gone, a glint of firelight from the stolen necklace the last trace of her passage.

~ * ~

The sun dawned upon the Windrider village, and Joseph awoke to Yowler licking at his hand. Even as sleep had overtaken him where he sat on the green, he'd expected to doze an hour or two then wake to find a better place to pass the night, but as it turned out the spot had worked just fine. He sat up and stretched, then ruffled the dog's fur between his ears. "You can't *possibly* be hungry," he said, "I saw all the scraps you got last night." The dog gave a short, whimpering snuffle, so with a scowl Joseph reached into the pouch at his belt and gave the dog a piece of dried meat. "You'll earn it soon enough. Back to camp this morning, and then in a couple days it'll be time for another hunt." Joseph smiled in anticipation. Work on the village had kept him occupied, but his bow had sat unbent far too long.

Joseph retrieved his gear from where he'd left it by the maple tree the night before. A few Windriders were up and about, seeing to various needs or duties, but most still slumbered, the celebration having gone late into the night. As Joseph prepared for his short hike, he toyed with the idea of staying long enough to say his goodbyes, but he decided against it. He wouldn't be going far, and it would be better not to make more of his departure than it really was. He settled his pack, whistled for the dogs, and started the mile hike to the north.

Joseph's camp was simple; only a fire pit at the bottom of a large oak and a rough platform in its branches, roofed over with hide and canvas to keep out the wind and rain. Before winter he would need to harvest furs to have any hope of surviving the cold, but there was ample time for that. For all the lack of amenities and inherent risks of Joseph's little home, it was *his*, and for that above all else he valued it. Even still, he had to admit that as the spring had passed, he had spent less and less time in his camp and more and more time in the village, often opting to spend nights in a warm spot by a campfire rather than back in his tree. He told himself the work had grown too great the longer they left behind the first thaw, but now he realized how quiet his patch of forest seemed.

Nevertheless, it was a good quiet, and anything else would see to itself in time. Joseph climbed the rope ladder to the platform and pulled it up behind him, taking an unnecessary rest to drink in the birdsong and wet leaves and all the other sounds and scents of the forest.

~ * ~

A few hours had passed since the escape from the barn, and Rook was spent. The stocky man who attacked her had dogged her steps all night and into the next morning. Well, him or someone just like him. She'd never actually seen her hunter, but every time she stopped to breathe, there were sneaking footsteps not far behind. Each time she tried to turn the tables, lying in ambush or working to lure her enemy into danger, no good had come of it. It was as though the foe knew her thoughts. She couldn't risk going home, leading a dangerous killer straight to her helpless brother, so she was forced to improvise. At last she had found a tavern with enough patrons to discourage a confrontation and slipped inside, remembering at the last second to remove the necklace and stow it again in her pouch. Her shoulders ached from the straps of her pack and the weight of the thick tome on her back.

She made her way to a dark corner with a good view of the door and sat down, easing the pack off her shoulders. A few moments passed before a serving wench approached Rook's table. Rook spoke to the lass before she could offer anything. "I'll take a pint of ale, a meal and a room." She placed a silver coin on the table as she spoke and didn't let her hand stray far from it. When the wench reached for it, Rook grabbed her arm and pulled her close. "Who would I talk to around here about getting some information?"

The girl pulled her arm free but didn't back away. "No need for rough hands, girl. Just say what you want, and I'll see to it. I serve a lot more than drinks hereabouts."

"Fine then," Rook said. "I need to know where to find a man, a fixer who runs a piece of this neighborhood."

"You have the silver?" the serving girl asked.

Rook jangled her coin pouch.

"I'll send someone back with your food who can see to your other needs," the wench said and left for the kitchens.

A few minutes later a man emerged through the swinging doors carrying a board of food and a foaming flagon. He was of middling height and wore a red tam and a white apron; he was solidly built but had a belly that betrayed his tendency to sample his wares. He laid the food and drink before Rook and sat down as she picked up a farl of bread and a chunk of greasy mutton.

"I hear you're in a spot of trouble...or looking to start some, mayhaps," the man opened.

"That's my own affair," Rook said after washing down her first bites with a swig of ale. "Do you have what I need?"

"I know most of the players hereabouts and where they comes and goes," the proprietor answered. "Put your silver on the table and tell me who you're lookin' for."

Rook placed another coin. "Pockmark Charlie."

The man didn't bother feigning forgetfulness or any other coy quips usually used in such circumstances. He shook his head. "Gonna take more silver than that, luv."

Rook grimaced and put two more coins on the table, then cinched her coin purse in signal that the inn-keeper would get no more.

"Pockmark's holed up in an inn called the Hobnail," the man revealed. "You know it?"

"I'm a bit off my usual spread, but I know the place. A little rougher living than Charlie's used to. Enough to make a girl doubt you know your stuff."

"There's a reason it's called 'laying low,' ain't there? The whole idea's being other than where you're thought to be."

"What's he hiding from?"

"Dunno. Just took up in there last evening and ain't moved an inch since. If you're who I think you are, rumor out on the streets is that it's got summat to do with you, though."

"Charlie got the usual mob watching over?"

"Far as I know."

Rook stood and hoisted her pack, balanced the flagon on the board of food then picked up the board in one hand. "I'll take the meal in my room. Key?" She held out her other hand.

The man placed a key in her palm. "Second on the left from the top o' the stairs." The innkeeper returned to his more usual duties, and Rook headed to the steps. The owner's comment that rumors were identifying her rattled in Rook's mind, and she grimaced. She could count on the man to be forgetful only until someone could produce a tall enough stack of coins to jog his memory, as she'd just proven herself: there was no way she could stay in one place for too long. Still, she needed rest and time to form at least the start of a plan. Then it would be time to pay ol' Pockmark Charlie a visit.

~ * ~

Rook awoke from uneasy sleep as the lazy hours of afternoon were hanging stagnant and thick over the city. The cover of darkness was the best condition for her trade, but Charlie would be most vigilant after nightfall. Her best bet to catch his boys napping was to get to the Hobnail without delay. Rook scowled at the heavy pack on the floor at the foot of the bed; she would prefer to leave it behind and stay unencumbered, but she couldn't risk coming back to the inn after confronting Charlie. She took up the pack once more and headed down into common room, wary of the many eyes that were sure to be gathered there. At this point she had to assume all her movements would be marked by observant opportunists, but after satisfying herself that none of the inn patrons paid her any undue attention, she stepped out into the street.

The way was narrow and winding, this district of the city being older and not situated for heavy wagon movement. Craftsmen of various stripes plied their trades or barked their wares, but there was little traffic, no crowd where Rook could lose herself. Feeling naked before the eyes of the city, she made her way by indirect and shadowed paths to the Hobnail.

An hour passed before she was in sight of the place, a central common hall and tavern with wings of rooms thrusting forward to the street on either side, forming three edges of a square. The fourth side was open to the street, allowing access to a great courtyard of flagstones between the wings with tall iron braziers marching in a pair of lines toward the main entrance at the far end of the court. At night they would be kindled, but now they stood cold, black, and ashy, each surrounded by a circle of soot and cinders from countless nights of burning. The property must have been grand once, the city manor of some high lord or merchant prince, but that was before the capital had grown in another direction, leaving this area to laborers and thieves, the outcast and forgotten. Now the Hobnail was a rough alehouse with a rougher reputation, a place folk didn't go unless they were looking to keep their deeds or their persons hidden, or, as in Rook's case, looking for something that was. Still, its diminished grandeur harmed not its great size, and the population and rate of comings and goings now must be many times greater than they were when the manor served as a private dwelling. To properly case the Hobnail would take days, and days Rook did not have.

At last she was able to derive some benefit from her insistence that she was a treasure hunter and not a thief; she worked closely with Pockmark Charlie but did not associate with many in his broader circle of miscreants.

Some might recognize her by description if pressed, but a lithe young woman in the Hobnail would always strike the eye as a very different profession at first glance. She undid the top two buttons of her vest, not that she had much to show for it, and stowed her daggers in her pack, the better to play into those assumptions. Within moments she had slid through the back doors and across the kitchens, taking a seat at an empty table too close to the kitchen doors to be popular but within earshot of the bar. For the best part of an hour she sat there, catching veiled comments suggesting that Pockmark Charlie was indeed on the premises, but nothing to help narrow down his location within the extensive wings of rooms. Finally, a serving girl approached the bar and caught the barman's eye. He hurried over to the girl, cocking an ear her way. "Our special guest in East 303 has requested another bottle of Andullan port," the girl stated.

"That's well and good," the tall barkeep replied, "but he already drank the last of the '07. What's his next favorite?"

"Just give him what you want. I doubt he could really tell the difference."

Rook smiled to herself. Pockmark Charlie's tendency to put on airs had finally betrayed him; Rook was well aware of his favorite drink and vintage. She slipped back out through the kitchens.

~ * ~

The east side of the Hobnail was falling into shadow as the sun sank in the west. Rook had hidden her pack as carefully as she could and rearmed herself. She crouched on a ledge three stories up, preparing to make her entrance and ruin Charlie's evening. Once again she had donned the necklace, knowing what a striking image she would cut when confronting Pockmark and figuring by now he must know she'd taken the thing anyway. She could hear him joking with three of his thugs, but his tone sounded forced. He wasn't paying particular attention to his surroundings, but something had him rattled. Rook drew one of her daggers and popped the lock on the window then stepped through like she owned the place.

"Pockmark Charlie!" she shouted. "Give me one reason I shouldn't gut you like a fish right here." Charlie and his goons went quiet, the guards shifting their weight and letting their hands stray toward their weapons.

"Because we're friends, ain't we?" Charlie responded, his voice matter-of-fact and bereft of his usual affectations.

"I thought we were," Rook said as she finished moving to the table where he sat, Charlie's guards easing away while subtly encircling her, "but friends don't sell each other out to bounty hunters after sending them to a meet."

"Damn that red-hatted bastard," Charlie grunted. "Fine, so he gave me up. But you're alive, and he's dead, and you burned down my barn, so why not just call it all even, eh?"

"He's dead?" Rook asked, surprised. She'd known the haymow would go up quick, but a man of the bounty hunter's skill should have had ample time to escape.

"Well, I," Charlie stuttered, "I don't know what you must have done to get him to talk, but sure you didn't leave him alive to suffer after. I never figured you for cruel, Rook."

"You think I tortured him?"

"Man has a reputation. If you didn't torture him, how else did you get him to snitch on me?" Charlie asked, the question clearly rhetorical.

Now Rook was puzzled. "Uh...I asked him."

"Hmph. Guess he doesn't live up to the advertising. So you didn't kill him?"

"I set the fire for a distraction and got the hell out of there."

"Alright, like I said, we're even, then. Friends." Charlie extended his hand.

"Not so fast, Charlie," Rook said, leaving the rogue's hand hanging awkwardly in space over the table. "You broke faith, so not friends, but first you owe me the information. How bad is it? How many people did you sell me to?"

"Just the red hat, I swear."

Somehow Rook knew he was telling the truth. "Why now? Or if I've outlived my usefulness, why not offer me up to everybody looking for info on the library score? Why just the one bounty hunter?"

"I didn't want to do it. He was the only one I was told to expect," the fixer said.

Rook was stunned to silence for a split second, then her eyes narrowed. "What do you mean, 'told to expect'?" she demanded.

"Rook, I don't know how somebody with your skill managed to leave a trail, but you've attracted some frightening attention. A man came to my place to talk to me yesterday, not long after I gave you the job. He told me the red hat would be coming to me to buy information, and I was to give it to him. And then he gave me this." Charlie set something on the table and slid it across to Rook, then removed his hand.

Rook picked up the large coin and examined it. The color was like pewter, but it was harder somehow, and warmed less quickly in her hand. On one side was a simple crown, and on the other a slavering wolf's head. Rook gasped for a moment then scowled, throwing the coin back down on the table with force enough that it bounced off and hit Charlie in the shoulder. "Horse shit, Charlie. The Wolfsguard? You want an excuse for selling me out, you're going to need a better one than tavern tales and guttersnipes' myths."

Charlie looked affronted, and one of his men piped up. "Nah, but 'e's tellin' ya troof, miss."

Charlie waved his hands for silence before continuing. "I wish I was lying, Rook. If I never see a man like that again, it'll be too soon. He scared the stuffin' out of me, an' that's sure. I never put much of any stock in those tales myself, but he was threatening enough to start with, and then when he handed me that coin..." Charlie shuddered. "Made a believer o' me, and let's jus' leave it at that."

Again, Rook somehow sensed Pockmark wasn't fooling, and she had to suppress a shudder herself at the implications. If even the least frightening quarter of doings ascribed to the Wolfsguard, the king's supposed cadre of spies and assassins, was true, then they were a force not to be trifled with. In a flash of insight, she smiled at their brilliance. She had never seen a coin like the one Charlie had showed her, but she'd heard tell of them many a time, never quite believing it. But a calling card was precisely what their order needed, something just tangible enough to add fuel to the legends. After all, even a mostly-secret group had many benefits, and they could wield a weapon that a completely secret group never could: fear.

"Alright, Charlie," Rook finally said. "Call me a fool, but I believe you. This'll be the last time I trust you. Stay out of my business from here on out."

Charlie nodded, and his men pulled back from the window, allowing Rook to leave the way she came in.

She climbed back out the window, fear of what she'd just learned preventing her from leaving through the increasingly crowded taproom. Dusk was fully on the alley as Rook climbed down, her mind walking back through her conversation with Charlie. In her anger over his betrayal, her heart had demanded to look him in the eye and get answers, but now that the encounter was over, she realized confronting him directly had been reckless. Pockmark

Charlie could have had her killed, and she couldn't have stopped him. That didn't seem in his character; however, Charlie held great influence over much of the city's underworld, and he retained that position largely through reputation and bravado. It was dangerous for him to brook offense, so to have Rook beaten and tossed out into the street was well within the realm of possibility.

Quite the contrary, however, the fixer had answered her questions without resistance or evasion. Why? Guilt? Not likely. True, Charlie was known to develop a soft spot for a dependable asset, but soft enough to speak openly about the Wolfsguard? And what of the bounty hunter? It was true he hadn't mentioned Charlie by name, but his meaning had been clear enough. Why give anything up?

These questions were so nagging that Rook almost missed a critical statement in her exchange with Charlie, but suddenly it flashed through her mind. "A man came to my place to talk to me yesterday, not long after I gave you the job." With the alarms going off the moment she took the necklace, and its absence so obvious to anybody investigating the scene, Rook had taken for granted its theft had been the cause of her trouble. But now it was revealed she was being hunted because of the job she'd actually been hired for: the book. Charlie was wrong; Rook hadn't left the trail, *he* had, or someone else on the front end. So the Wolfsguard knew the book was a target, then why let her steal it in the first place? Rook's sharp mind gnawed on the problem for only a moment before arriving at the only plausible answer: they knew the book would be stolen, but not who it would be stolen for. Apparently neither did Charlie, or the Wolfsguard could have gotten that information directly from him, meaning the supposed client was really just an intermediary. People were going to an awful lot of trouble to steal something nobody should have wanted to begin with, and the palace had let at least one man be killed in order to get it back. It was about time Rook found out precisely what she'd stumbled into.

By the time she'd made that resolution, Rook was less than thirty feet from where she'd stashed her pack in a side alley north of the Hobnail. It was black and quiet, silent but for a sudden footfall behind Rook, soft leather on the hard-packed earth of the alley. The thief whirled and put her hands on her daggers.

The red-dressed man stood staring at her, his crossbow once again pointed at her chest. "Don't move," he ordered. "If I didn't need to know where ye'd stashed yer prize, ye'd be dead already, but if ye pull those daggers...I don't have to kill ye to stop ye."

"Don't shoot!" Rook begged, instinct overriding her guile. To her surprise, the bounty hunter pulled the quarrel from his crossbow and pointed the weapon toward the ground. Rook looked over her shoulder, wondering if the man had allies behind her. There was no one she could see. "Well," she continued after a moment, her tone lame with confusion even to her own ears, "I'm glad to see you've decided to be reasonable. Let's be civilized about this."

"Course," the man answered, doffing his hat to reveal a bald head. "My name's Archibald the Red. I do tend to make me livin' by bloodshed, but there's naught that's civil about tha'. Me employer's adamant the book be returned, but I c'n claim to ha' laid hands on it while ye were in yer palaver with Charlie. It's like as not they won't believe ye know enough to be a threat an'll call off the hunt."

"Why so accommodating?" Rook asked, her eyes narrow with suspicion.

Rook couldn't see his face in the dark, but Archibald cocked his head as if pondering for a moment. "Not rightly sure. Ye said we should be civilized and tha' seemed like the best idea, that's all."

"And what about this?" Rook asked, taking off the

necklace and holding it at arm's length, the better for Archibald to see it in the dim light without moving her body any closer.

Suddenly the stocky man's demeanor changed. "There's quicker ways t'make ye talk!" he growled, dropping his crossbow and pulling a broad cutlass. His advance was slow but menacing.

Loathe to drop the necklace in the dirt, Rook slipped it back over her head as she backed away. For all her speed, she knew it was unlikely she could take the man in an armed confrontation, so she held her hands forward, palms out, desperate to stall for the time she would need to escape her dire situation. "What happened to civilized?" she quipped, hoping to move the confrontation back toward talking and away from cutting or stabbing.

"Changed me mind," the man replied, still advancing.

"Just back off!" Rook demanded.

Archibald the Red took three steps backward and stood still.

Rook was stunned once again, but an idea began to form in her mind. "Sit down," she said.

The man sat.

"Throw your cutlass behind those crates," she ordered, pointing toward a stack of boxes to her right.

The cutlass clattered against the clapboard wall of the building bordering the alley before falling down behind the crates.

"Why did you do that?" Rook asked.

"'Cause ye asked me to," Archibald replied, his tone making clear that Rook might as well have asked why the sun rose in the east.

"Who hired you?"

"Nobleman called Gage, but I think he was dealin' fer someone else."

"Who?" Rook demanded.

"Dunno. Somebody in the palace, I'd wager, but that's only speculatin'."

"Go back to Gage. Tell him you saw me near the Hobnail but that I gave you the slip. Add that rumor has me leaving the city and heading west."

"A'right," Archibald assented, standing up and leaving the alley. He stooped to pick up the crossbow that lay directly in his path but made no deviation to retrieve his sword.

Rook watched him go, one hand resting on the necklace as her head spun in awe, and not just a little fear, at this thing she had stolen.

~ * ~

Rook hoped her orders to Archibald the Red would ease the pressure on her, but a nagging feeling still pricked the back of her mind, fear of her new enemies making her reluctant to return home and risk leading them to Adler. Instead, she returned to the inn where she had rented a room, ordered the innkeeper not to tell anyone she was there, and returned to her chamber, already tempering her dismay at the necklace's power with an appreciation of what it might do for her. When she asked a question, she got a straight answer, and a complete one. When she gave an order, it was immediately obeyed. Nor was there any great struggle of wills as the tales always told, no unsettlingly slavish devotion—her desire simply became everyone's instinct. Such a power could open many doors.

But then there was the Wolfsguard, a virtually unknown enemy, the most dangerous kind. One thing, at least, was sure: the more powerful the magic, the more likely someone had studied and developed a counter for it, and unlike Archibald and Charlie, any agents of the Wolfsguard would know what they were after. The book may have been the original focus of their attention, but there was no way her theft of the necklace had gone unnoticed; if there was a way to prepare, they'd be prepared. A quiet, but deep, paranoia crept into her thoughts as she climbed onto the bed. Why had she worn the necklace so brazenly in her meeting with Charlie? It had worked out to her advantage in the short run, but she had also ended their association; he no longer had any reason to keep her secrets. Even now she could almost hear the whispers, voices running down dark alleys and up back staircases to where the infamous, fabled Wolfsguard waited in the shadows, safe behind a web of fear and skepticism, ready to pounce as soon as they had her scent.

There was no choice now but to leave the city, just as she had told Archibald the Red she would. Rook told him she would head west because it was the most obvious choice. The port cities were easy places to disappear, and the trade roads could get her there quickly, so no one would doubt reports that she'd headed that way. Now she had only to decide which way to actually go. There remained one unanswered question that might help her with the choice. At last she opened her pack and removed the book, lifting it onto her lap as she sat on the bed and ran her fingers over the blank cover and the capital letters running down the spine. Something in these ancient pages was important enough to justify the deployment of the most lethal agents in the king's arsenal, important enough to commit murder for. With one hand resting on the necklace to bolster her confidence, she eased open the cover and turned her attention to the title page. Her brow creased. She turned to the next page. She turned another and another.

She couldn't read a damn word of it. Couldn't even pronounce the alphabet.

But she knew who could, and now she knew where to go next. South-southeast, to the lands of the Windriders.

Against all odds, it appeared she would be meeting Joseph the hunter again, after all.

Chapter Three: Friends and Foes

Joseph had spent a day and a night in the solitude of his camp with only the dogs for company. Even they were often absent, straying off to hunt or, as Joseph thought more likely, back to the Windrider village to beg for handouts. The quiet had been a refreshing change of pace, but not the utter relief he'd imagined, and he'd found himself reluctant to stray too far on his first day away from the village. If something happened, he wanted to know the Windriders could find him quickly. He had no idea what such an emergency might be, but it nagged at him just the same until he had to chide himself for acting so much the mother hen.

The following morning Joseph was re-stoking his fire when he felt a sudden breeze that carried the scent of owl. He looked up to see one of the great birds making a gentle landing a few yards away, and as its rider dismounted, he saw it was Kaillë. She was smiling as she walked toward him. "Welcome, chieftain," he said. "What brings a person of such importance to my humble camp?"

"I wanted to visit," Kaillë replied as she looked around at the fire pit and platform overhead, "but there is some business as well. The trappers Tal'onë surveyed a couple of days ago have been edging closer, and he wondered if you could approach them and ensure they aren't dangerous."

"Of course," Joseph agreed. "Best you don't reveal yourselves if you don't have to. Why didn't Tal'onë just come himself?"

Kaillë turned towards him, and the evasiveness he'd seen at the celebration was gone. He suspected his staying nearby had calmed her somehow concerning the whole matter. "It had been over a year since I'd ridden an owl," she answered, "and I wanted to see you. The village seems too quiet without you."

"Are you saying I'm loud?"

"Hardly. You're as stealthy as any of us and speak less than most. But something is different, and I couldn't think of a better way to say it."

"Well, the camp is brighter this morning since you got here," Joseph said, surprising himself. Kaillë lowered her eyes, the picture of modesty. "I haven't had breakfast yet," Joseph continued. "Can you stay awhile, or are you needed back?"

"I could eat," Kaillë answered.

Joseph climbed to the platform and lowered some food down to Kaillë. They had taken many meals together over the months, but few alone, and Joseph found himself enjoying the company but unsure what to say.

Soon after they had eaten, Kaillë excused herself, knowing Tal'onë would begin to worry if she stayed away much longer, and Joseph walked her back to her owl and gave her a boost up she didn't need before saying goodbye. "I'll come to the village to make my report on the trappers," he concluded, "but it will probably be tomorrow by the time I'm there and back." After Kaillë was gone, he packed his gear for a hike of several hours and a one-night camp, then set out for the area where the smoke had been sighted.

The hunter didn't require a precise bearing, knowing he would come across the party's trap lines if he could get anywhere near their camp. After a few hours at an enjoyable pace, with Stitch volunteering to follow him, he was proven correct, spotting a muskrat trap below the waterline of a clear stream flowing across his path. He inspected the trap, followed tracks to two more, then away from the stream to a few rabbit snares outside a thicket. So far Joseph was encouraged by what he saw. The death of animals was the reality of trapping and hunting, and the idea of a perfectly painless kill was almost entirely a myth, but the traps he'd found were set with skill and not to cause undue cruelty or take more than the forest could bear.

Afternoon wore on into evening as Joseph worked his way toward the camp, approaching from downwind through the scent of wood smoke.

"Hail to the camp," Joseph called when he was a few yards away.

"Who's there?" challenged a burly man with a wild black beard as he reached for a hatchet.

"Just a hunter," Joseph said as he stepped from behind a fir, his hands raised and clear to see. "Well, a hunter and a spoiled old hound," he corrected as Stitch jogged into view.

The trapper started at how close Joseph had managed to approach undetected then whistled as he looked up at the hunter's height. "You just go up a mile, don't you?" The man hung onto his hatchet but didn't make any threat with it. "My friends aren't far," he offered in caution.

Joseph nodded, wary as well. "A man can't be too careful," he agreed. He knew the trapper had two compatriots, one in the woods on the opposite side of the camp and the other to the right, both within earshot and unarmed save for the tools of outdoor living. "How goes the trapping?"

"Well enough so far. I see your bow, but you don't look kitted out for a proper hunt. What brings you to the woods then?" The implication was clear enough. Bows might shoot men as easily as animals.

"I live hereabouts," Joseph answered. "Just saw your smoke from a ways off and thought I'd come and see who my neighbors are."

A voice called from the trees to Joseph's right. "Everything alright, Ralph?"

"Seems so for the moment. Come on out."

Another man, a bit taller than Ralph and just as stout, came out of the trees carrying a heavy stave and keeping his eyes trained on Joseph.

"Well, we don't mean any trouble," Ralph continued, "and we won't be neighbors, not for more than a couple weeks anyway. We're just going to get what we can and head back to town. Sorry if this is a spot of yours, but you didn't have any traps or sign down."

Ralph seemed to be gearing up for a verbal defense of their claim on the area, so Joseph headed him off. "I range all through here, but I don't know if any of the spots are 'mine.' I've seen a lot of trappers come and go through these woods over the years, but I don't recognize you. You're new to these parts?"

"Came down from the north, past Oskar's Gap," the taller one said.

"That's a long way. I hear trapping's better up there too. What brings you south? If you don't mind my asking."

"Trouble brewing up that way. Tribes are making raids more often, and some of King Dieter's lords are getting downright neglectful in keeping the peace."

Joseph scowled. "Any of the raiders pushing down

south of the gap?"

"Not that we've seen or heard," Ralph offered. "Why else do you think we came down here?"

The tall one eyed Joseph a bit closer. "You ever meet any other hunters out here? Ones living out here, I mean."

"Not in many a long year. Why?"

"Talk of the fighting back north just made me remember some rumors we heard. In the town down on the flat, folk said a great hunter lived up in these parts, supposed to have been some kind of big hero during the war, scouting for King Dieter or some such. Think his name was Jo-something. Josiah, maybe."

"That ain't it, idjit," came the voice of the third trapper entering the far side of the clearing. "Peter, when it ain't yer ears it's yer mem'ry. It weren't Josiah, it were Jonah."

"Well, people talk," Joseph said. "I wouldn't put any stock in it. Sure I've never met anybody like that out here. Seen some strange things in the woods, but never a war hero."

"Well, we're getting ready to throw the stew pot on," Ralph said. "Care to trade some stories for a bite of supper, friend?"

"No, I'll be moving on I think. Mostly I'll be well clear of here, but if I have reason to come back around, I'll leave the small game alone for as long as you're trapping, save you don't hunt any deer or elk that wander down. Fair?" The men nodded, and Joseph turned to go. "Oh, one more thing," he added, stopping, as if an afterthought. "I'd take it as a kindness if you didn't head any farther south. There's plenty of room north and east for all the trapping you could want."

"Any particular reason?" asked the last trapper, who seemed to be in charge despite his less refined dialect.

"My own affair. You seem like decent folk, and I'd like to stay on friendly terms. Best you don't go farther south."

There was nothing in his words or tone that would threaten their pride, but the warning was clear enough.

Ralph and Peter looked to the third trapper, who eyed Joseph for a moment, rubbing his jaw, before answering. "Alright. Like you said, there's more'n enough room for everyone, an' we don't want no trouble."

"Thank you. If I can ever do you a good turn, I will." Joseph raised his hand in salute and was gone. Stitch lingered for a few moments, watching the trappers, then Joseph whistled once and the dog hurried after him.

~ * ~

Joseph made it most of the way back to the Windrider village before nightfall, but he decided to make camp rather than pressing on the two more hours to his destination, enjoying the unhurried nature of his hikes. He climbed into the fork of an old hornbeam and slept the night as comfortably as a prince on a feather bed.

He rose early and entered the Windrider village about an hour after dawn, there finding that Yowler had made himself an uninvited but welcome guest in his absence; Stitch trotted over to the other dog in reunion. A few elves spotted Stitch's return and looked up, then saw Joseph and hailed his coming. Kaillë stood in the center of the green with Tal'onë and a pair of the clan elders, but whatever they discussed seemed not to be urgent, for she excused herself and walked over to Joseph when she saw him. Her unbound hair blew in a light breeze, and Joseph found it lovely.

"Welcome back," she said. "How was your hike?"

"Good. It was nice to stretch my legs after staying so long in one place, remind myself what a bit more of my forest looked like."

"And what of the men who've come?"

"Nothing to worry about, I think. Living off the land

takes a certain amount of roughness," and Joseph thought he caught a twinkle in Kaillë's eye at his statement, "but they seem peaceful enough. Keep an eye on them from above. If they start coming farther south than chance would warrant, then they've broken their word and might be trouble. I don't think that's likely, though."

Kaillë seemed pleased at the news then quickly offered the village's hospitality to Joseph. "Can we entice you to stay awhile? We don't want you to forget you're always welcome."

Joseph considered for a moment. "I'd hoped to go on a hunt tomorrow, but I suppose I could leave from here just as easily. I don't have all my gear, though; the loan of a few things would save me a trip if you're that set on having me hang around."

"I'm sure that can be arranged." Kaillë smiled, and Joseph found himself glad his answer had pleased her.

~ * ~

The hunter was up before dawn the next morning, setting out for the higher slopes to the east. He'd hunted the woods up and down the mountain range since he was a boy; it never took him long to find game. On his way out of the village, though, he was surprised to see a young elf wife out on the central green. He struggled to recall her name, then called out when he remembered. "Onahnë, what brings you out so early?"

"Have you seen my husband?" she asked. "He had the last eastern foot patrol of the night, and he hasn't returned."

"Did you alert Tal'onë?"

"The last patrol runs late into the night; he is only just now an hour overdue. I've visited the house of his partner on patrol, and he is gone also. I was just on my way to inform the captain."

"When you do, tell Tal'onë that I'm already on my way to the eastern patrol route. He should bring a flight of owls and catch up."

Onahnë nodded and ran off toward the tree that held Tal'onë's home, and Joseph turned and hurried into the woods, his hunt immediately forgotten. As he ran he called out, "Yowler, you're on duty today. C'mon, boy." Then he let out a long, high whistle. By the time he reached the edge of the forest, the faithful hound, though less disciplined than Stitch, was loping alongside him down the patrol trail.

They had gone less than a mile when Joseph heard the slightest rustling of foliage to his left. Tal'onë appeared from the brush. "Joseph," he said, "we made a wide circle and saw nothing from the air. The canopy here is too dense to be sure of anything without a foot search. I've sent the other three guards back to rest the owls; they'll catch up when they may."

Joseph and Tal'onë continued forward on the trail, with Yowler up ahead sniffing intently at nothing in particular. Joseph favored care over speed as they moved forward; there was no sense in outpacing the three elves still coming to join them, and if something indeed had happened to the night patrol, it wouldn't help them to miss a vital sign or stumble into an ambush. The other elves caught up in half an hour, and Joseph ordered the group to fan out to cover the ground on either side of the trail.

After another mile, Joseph hissed to the others to halt and be silent, for a shift in the wind seemed to have brought a new scent to Yowler, who was whimpering and pawing at the ground. This was his signal, a behavior Joseph had, after endless hours of work, trained into him to break the incessant habit of premature baying that had earned the dog his name. After a moment, the wind carried a voice to Joseph's ears. "Ten'vohnë!" it called, "Ten'vohnë, where are you?"

The band rushed toward the sound, calling back to Tes'sael, Ten'vohnë's patrol mate and comrade-in-arms to Joseph during their quest to destroy the Hoard of Dalviir, a journey that had earned him a promotion to lieutenant among his people. In a matter of moments they found one another; Tes'sael was grimed with dirt and sweat, and dried blood caked a cut on his head at the locus of an ugly, swollen bruise.

"Tes'sael, are you alright?" Joseph asked.

"I'll be fine," the elf replied, "but I fear for Ten'vohnë. There is something in the woods, Joseph, something neither man nor beast, and many of them. We heard them in the dark, but before we could investigate, we realized they were headed right for us. I sent Ten'vohnë back toward the village and tried to draw off the pursuit. I made as much noise as I could, but the greater part seemed to be going after him. I shot blindly behind me as I ran, but I must not have hit anything. I lost my bearings in the chase and went down an embankment and struck my head. I never thought to awaken, unless it was in the clutches of whatever was chasing me, but... I went looking for Ten'vohnë as soon as I came around, but I have not found him. Did he make it back to the village?"

Joseph shook his head, fearing the worst.

Between Tes'sael's memory and Yowler's nose, they were able to trace the elf's trail back into the woods to the point where he and Ten'vohnë had split up. From there it took some effort to follow Ten'vohnë's path, for elves leave little trace even when on the run, and whatever had chased him seemed also to move with an uncanny grace. An hour of careful tracking passed before they found Ten'vohnë, or rather, all that was left of him.

Joseph stepped into the area of thrashed undergrowth that surrounded Ten'vohnë's remains, careful not to disturb anything. His clothes were torn and bloody, and much of his flesh was absent; what was left was ripped into pieces as by wild beasts. Several of his bones lay a pace away from the corpse, all gouged deeply with gnaw-marks, though not of wolves, the only large predators in the region. Joseph took a step back and surveyed the wider carnage. It was clear from the trampled brush that Ten'vohnë had put up a fight, but no enemy bodies were in evidence, nor, Joseph realized after a careful search, any blood trails leading away from the battle. It seemed unlikely Ten'vohnë could be felled without so much as drawing blood from his enemy, but the facts were undeniable.

The band gathered around the body, and Tal'onë spoke the words that comprised an elven funeral. "As Vohnë came into this world, so Ten'vohnë leaves it, unburdened by the trappings of life and surrounded by those who love him. We will sing his song and wait for him to greet us in the next world." With no further ceremony, the group turned back to the trail and began the long walk home.

"I don't understand," the youngest elf spoke up after a time. "He left the patrol path far east of the village. If he'd stuck to the path and kept his speed, he might have made it home to safety."

Joseph could guess the answer, but he stayed silent. It was Tes'sael who replied on behalf of his partner. "When he realized the majority followed him, not me, he must have known he couldn't shake the pursuit and chose to lead the beasts away from the village. It was brave."

Joseph stopped. "It was. As brave as we are foolish." The rest of the group looked at the human in surprise. "Why else would these creatures leave Tes'sael alive, but to follow him back home? They could be dogging our steps even now. All of you, disappear into the brush. Be silent and watchful; make sure I am not followed. I'll run back to the village and send a rider with owls back to retrieve you. Unless these creatures can fly, there is no way they can follow you home through the clouds."

Tal'onë nodded his assent, and the elves hid themselves in the underbrush, silent as a feather falling on snow and so quick Joseph couldn't mark all their hiding places, though he stood only feet away. After that he took off into the brush with Yowler trotting behind, taking a long, knotted path through the forest while using every trick he knew to disguise his trail. He stopped often to watch and listen for pursuit, but no one followed...unless he had finally met his match in woodcraft. That thought paired with the memory of Ten'vohnë's savaged remains made him shudder.

It was nearly midday when Joseph finally came into the Windrider village, and Onahnë was at the eastern edge, standing vigil for news. She caught Joseph's eye with a questioning look, and the hunter shook his head. Her eyes went bright with tears instantly, but with typical elven stoicism she crossed the distance to Joseph and placed her hand on his arm. "Thank you for finding him," she said. "Whatever happened, he will have peace knowing his final moments might save others from a similar fate."

Joseph wasn't ready yet to spread word that trouble was afoot, but he sought to comfort the young elf wife, or rather, elf widow. "Ten'vohnë was brave. His sacrifice was not in vain. It won't be forgotten."

Onahnë smiled at him a distant, hurt smile. "I can see you came here in haste," she said then. "You must have important things to see to. I will leave you to them." She turned and went into her cottage. Even its place was a reminder of her pain, for most elves lived in dwellings built into the canopy of the trees. Only those most in danger of falls lived on the ground: the old and families with small children, or planning for them. Now those children would never be. Onahnë's neighbors were aged elves, and Joseph saw two women move from nearby homes to comfort the widow. He turned away from the scene of grief and went looking for Tes'voran, the other of Tal'onë's lieutenants and the master of owls. The hunter found him where he expected to, on the high platform where the owls made their nests.

"Tes'voran," he said without greeting, "there is trouble. You must take four owls to Tal'onë and his party; they are a few miles away on the eastern patrol path. And spread the word that all the foot patrols are to be recalled immediately, and to be sure they aren't followed and leave no trace. All patrols will be from the air until further notice. Go now." Tes'voran gave a curt nod, mounted the nearest owl, and took to the sky, the wing-buffeted air forcing Joseph to squint and shield his eyes as the great bird climbed aloft. The immediate need met, Joseph went next in search of Kaillë. As soon as Tal'onë returned, the chieftain would need to convene her council. Joseph grimaced. Whether in solitude or in company, it seemed he was never to have peace for long.

~ * ~

Kaillë had called the Windrider elders to council. "Elders" had become something of a relative term in recent months; many of the oldest Windriders had been slain in Baron Turov's attack, leaving numerous council positions to those little past middle age. Joseph sat on the village lawn with Kaillë and Tal'onë. The lieutenants were present as well, though they were customarily silent. The nearby brook still laughed across its bed of stones, and birds still sang in the trees, but a pall seemed to have fallen across the village and everyone in it. The winter had claimed a few older elves whose time was known to be upon them, but Ten'vohnë's loss had been the first violent death since Tes'oriv had been slain in the effort to destroy the Hoard of Dalviir. The killing forced a sense of quiet foreboding onto the stoic elves.

Tes'sael was giving his report. "We heard crashing in the brush higher up the slopes. At first we thought it was just a wild goat or some larger game trying to escape a wolf pack, but in a few moments we realized that more than one creature was present, and we were directly in their path. The wind shifted and picked up, a breeze in our faces that we knew would carry our scent right back to whatever was in the woods. Suddenly, the creatures went silent, and we knew that, whatever they were, they had gone on the hunt.

"I sent Ten'vohnë back to the village straight away and made off into the woods in the hope of drawing off the pursuit. It didn't work. The few that did come after me were quiet, and I could see shapes enough to realize they walked on two legs, and they navigated the darkness as surely as we move in broad daylight. I made a few hasty shots behind me, but the number chasing me never reduced. I thought of climbing but had no way of knowing if I could do that any faster or better than my hunters. Even if they couldn't, I had no desire to be treed, trapped at bay. Eventually, I tumbled down a ravine and struck my head. I did not expect to awaken. That is all I know."

"You said they walked on two legs," Tal'onë began, "but you don't think they were human or elf?"

"No," Tes'sael confirmed. "They were too big to be elves but did not move the same as humans, and when they were close enough, I caught a strange smell, something fetid but also strangely musty. Even the most unwashed humans I have come across do not smell that way."

Something in Tes'sael's descriptions sparked a memory in Joseph, but even after considering the rarest forest creatures he had heard of, some of which he couldn't even be sure were real, still nothing matched. The memory, or at least the sense of one, settled in the back of his mind and nagged him there, worrying at his thoughts.

"What of their number?" Tes'voran asked.

"From the churning of the ground where Ten'vohnë was killed, I figure a dozen in this band. There could be many more elsewhere," Joseph replied.

"There might," suggested an elder, "or there might not. Of course we should prepare for the most dire possibility, but let us not fuel fear with speculation."

Joseph nodded at the elder's wisdom as Kaillë entered the discussion. "Tal'onë and I must formulate a plan," she said, standing, "but first I would know the minds of those gathered here. We have heard what little we know or can deduce of the danger. What do you counsel for our response?"

Joseph smiled inwardly at how far Kaillë had come in the last few months from the frightened waif he found in his forest to the chieftain before him now. Her heart was light, but she did not shrink from duty.

"We know of the trappers in the woods," one of the elders pointed out, "trusty enough by Joseph's report. Let Tes'sael wing out to them, approach them in friendship. Perhaps they have seen some sign as well. If not, since they have done no harm to us, we are duty-bound to warn them of the dangers."

Joseph would have preferred to go himself, but it would take too long, and ground travel had to remain restricted. "Say I sent you," Joseph suggested, "but don't use my name. Just describe me and Stitch." He caught an odd look from Tal'onë and shook his head. "Long story."

Tal'onë agreed to the plan. "Go, Tes'sael. Only take care they do not see your owl. They are still strangers, after all."

Tes'sael stood and left the council.

"What about the patrols?" another elder asked. "Joseph has halted the ground scouts, but does that not leave us with less warning of danger?"

"As always, Joseph speaks with my voice in matters of the guard," Tal'onë answered, "and he was wise to recall the foot patrols. You are right about the risk, but the danger of leading these creatures back to the village is simply too great. Starting now, I order the owl patrols to be doubled as well, or as close to it as the birds can endure. I fear these creatures will keep to the deeper forest where we cannot see through the canopy, but this is the only way we can attempt surveillance without leaving a trail for the enemy to follow."

"Spare the birds during the day," Joseph suggested. "So far the beasts seem to be most active at night, and the owls may sense things in the dark that even elves in the daylight could miss, if the riders are attentive to their birds' reactions."

"Wise advice, as always, Joseph," Kaillë said. "You might have been among us always, you know our ways so well."

The elders murmured agreement, then Tes'voran spoke up. "It goes almost without saying, but elders, please assure the people that all the foot patrols not reassigned to flight will be guarding the perimeter of the village all day and night without interruption."

Kaillë spoke again. "I believe we have made all possible preparations until we know more. Thank you for your wisdom, my people. Tal'onë and I will confer in private now. Is there anything else?"

"What of Joseph?" an elder asked.

"Tal'onë and I will welcome his insights in our discussions, as always," Kaillë responded, a tinge of confusion in her voice.

"Not that," the elder responded. "What I mean is, we do not claim the right to give orders to Azrith, begging your pardon for use of the title, Joseph, but should we not advise that he remain in the village until this crisis is resolved? I know your camp is not far, Joseph, but you are alone when you stay there."

"I have Stitch and Yowler for sentinels," the hunter responded.

The elder smiled. "Of course, but they are trackers, not guard dogs. And besides, for all your woodcraft, you still might leave some sign for these creatures to follow. We have no idea their powers of scent, for instance."

Joseph grimaced, but he assented. "I don't worry for my own safety, but I would never forgive myself if I led anything back here. I will stay." Joseph could all but feel the tension drain out of Kaillë as he spoke, yet when he looked over, there was a strange apprehension in her gaze, and she would not meet his eyes.

The rest of the council returned to their duties, and Kaillë, Tal'onë, and Joseph continued their private conference. They had no need to remove to a more secluded spot; none of the passing elves looked in their direction or strayed to listen. It wasn't their way.

"I didn't want to cause a panic," Joseph said, "but we can't just wait to see what we can see. The elders are wise not to speculate, but if there's a whole host of these creatures on the higher slopes, by the time we know for sure it may be too late to react."

"Surely if there are that many, one of our riders will spot them from the air," Kaillë suggested.

"You don't know that any more than I do," Joseph countered. "There was no blood but Ten'vohnë's in the woods, Kaillë. I don't say that he was our best fighter, but he was certainly not our worst, and he was battling for his life. How could he have failed even to draw blood on one? I hate the thought, but we have to stay open to the chance that these creatures aren't completely natural. If that's the case, we can't predict our chances of spotting them any more than of fighting them."

Tal'onë spoke. "I'm not sure I agree on that last point, Joseph, but I do concur that sitting and waiting is not safe for the Windriders. What do you think we should do?"

"We will wait for reports, but only for tonight. If the owl riders don't spot the enemy, you and I will go out tomorrow, at midday, with the dogs. Tes'sael said he smelled them, and Yowler caught a strange scent this morning as well. Whether natural or mystical, a smell can be tracked. Maybe we can catch them where they sleep."

"But Joseph," Kaillë answered, "what if you don't find them? The danger of them following your trail back will be greater than ever."

"Tal'onë can take an owl most of the way, and I'll stick to the trees as much as I can. The ugly fact is that they're bound to find us eventually if we don't find them first, and they're free to roam while we're stuck here, on edge. Trying to wait them out is good for them and bad for us. I say it's worth the risk. I'll stand with whatever you decide, Chieftain."

"As will I," agreed Tal'onë.

"Thank you. I will take time to consider your proposal. If Tes'sael brings knowledge back from the trappers, or air patrols see anything tonight, the matter may be moot. Tal'onë, you should go and attend to scheduling the increased patrols and perimeter guard."

Tal'onë rose; Joseph started to stand to accompany him, but Kaillë stopped him with a hand on his knee. She stayed silent for a few moments as Tal'onë strode away, her eyes on the ground, her posture strangely demure, but finally she met Joseph's eyes with the resolute gaze he'd come to expect from her when she meant to be serious.

"Joseph," she said, "you should know that you are free to sleep in my home while you are here in the village."

He almost declined, offering that he would be perfectly happy to sleep under the stars, as he always did, but he sensed her words were not merely a polite offer. His chest grew tight. Though his wife had been half-elven, he knew nothing of elven courtship customs, and his wife's elven parentage had come from a completely different clan, in any case. It seemed naive, almost childish, to assume too little in Kaillë's offer, but it seemed churlish in the extreme to assume too *much*. He hated the thought of going into such a situation not knowing what to expect, but as he looked back into Kaillë's eyes, he saw a tenderness there, tenderness married to a burden whose easing was long overdue. Most of all, he felt a strange sense he was standing on a precipice, that if he refused her offer, then for the sake of their friendship and her vast respect for him, she would never offer it again. Whatever spark might hide in his heart, he couldn't trust it to burn hot enough through his grief and stubbornness and isolation to take the first step if she withdrew. Her eyes twitched almost away for the barest instant, and he knew if he hesitated any longer, it would be too long.

"I would be honored," he finally said, his throat suddenly dry.

There was nothing stoic about the grin that spread across Kaillë's face, and Joseph saw the glow of carefree youth that never completely deserted an elf even in their gray and aging years, and which burned fiercely in the bloom of Kaillë's womanhood, despite the tragedies that had befallen her. "Whenever you tire then," she replied, "or have need of shelter, my house is yours. I hope you will enjoy my hospitality."

Joseph nodded as Kaillë stood and returned to her duties. When Kaillë had first stopped him, he'd intended to hurry after Tal'onë and help with the preparations when she'd finished, but now he found he preferred to sit for a time. He couldn't decide if his head was more confused or his heart, and there were enemies at the doorstep, as always, but the sun was shining, the stream ran in flashing ripples over the rocks, and the breeze was sweet with the smell of honeysuckle. Stitch wandered by and flopped down on the grass next to Joseph, who obliged him with a quick belly rub. Living off the land required careful planning and constant preparation; Joseph had not lived fully in the moment since he was a boy. Something as simple as Kaillë's decision to delay, though, paired with the requirement that he remain in the village, had now cast him into a limbo in which he had no immediate responsibilities, nothing constructive he could do until reports started coming in or he received some new order.

Joseph leaned back onto the green, letting the sun warm his weathered features, and waited.

Chapter Four: Unions and Reunions

Tes'sael returned a few hours later. The trappers had seen nothing, and after Tes'sael's warning they had decided to move to the lower slopes where they could make a quicker escape if anything dangerous did threaten. His rest ended, Joseph busied himself assisting with finishing touches on Dona and Redel's house, and soon the afternoon patrols were landing and the dusk patrols were launching. Joseph was anxious. The hour wasn't late enough to retire, but he'd noticed Kaillë going into her house in the branches of the village's central tree, and she hadn't emerged. Wherever he went, he felt as though every elven eye was on his back as he left.

Finally, Joseph wandered to the stream and sat at its edge, watching the ripples in the twilight. Only moments had passed when he heard someone approaching from behind. "Hello Tal'onĕ," he said into the dusk without turning.

"Good evening, Joseph," the elf said as he sat down to the hunter's left. "You seem troubled today. Why?"

"Savage packs of beasts killing our people and menacing our woods isn't reason enough to be troubled?"

"For you, no."

Joseph grappled with how to respond. The matter was too private for discussion, and yet he was eager for the advice of another man, though he had made it this far in life without it. Finally, he spoke. "Tal'onĕ, what do the Windriders really think of me? Am I really one of you, or am I still something apart?"

"It is a poor tailor who cuts every sleeve the same length, Joseph. The Windriders are many voices; I cannot answer your question as though we speak with only one."

Joseph looked sidelong at the shorter elf. "Let's speak of you and me then. Certainly we're allies. I would never overstep your authority, but we lead the guard together. I think we mostly see the world in similar ways. Is that all? Or have we become friends?"

Tal'onĕ furrowed his brow as though thinking of something for the first time. He leaned toward the water, and Joseph followed his gaze to a school of minnows sheltering in an eddy behind a protruding rock. "Do you suppose that one minnow likes the neighbor on his left better than the one on his right? And if he did, would the minnow on his right be troubled by it? Elf clans do not draw circles within circles the way human villages do; your question strains my context, I admit. But you *are* my friend, Joseph. That much I can tell you."

"I haven't had many friends," Joseph replied. "I've been alone since I was young. There were other families in the woods who helped me survive until I could fend for myself, but they're all gone now. Delia and I kept ties with a few other families; they were decent folk, but we were motivated more by survival than friendship on both sides. I do believe I have friends here now, though, and I wouldn't want to jeopardize that...much to my surprise. For the first time in my life, I'm facing a decision and worrying what others might think of my choice."

Joseph saw Tal'onë smile wanly in the failing light. "This is about Kaillë, then," the elf said.

Joseph grimaced. "It's that obvious?"

"*You* are not obvious in your inner self, hunter, but Kaillë is very much so, at least to me. I've known her since she was born, after all."

"Then I'll put a finer point on my first question. Maybe the Windriders see me as one of them, maybe not. Even if they do, do they accept me enough to see me paired with their chieftain? If the many voices were boiled down to one, I mean."

"Joseph," Tal'onë replied, "whether they would agree or not, the most common musings on that score, not gossip, you understand, but innocent curiosity, are why you didn't take Kaillë to wife sometime during the winter. The nights did get awfully cold for anybody sleeping alone, after all."

"I didn't think anybody *took* a chieftain of the Windriders to wife or to anything else. Besides, if it's just a matter of keeping warm, I recall you sleeping alone all those winter nights too. Why don't the people wonder of you what they wonder of me?"

"Well, in the first place, there's taking and there's taking. If I take a fish out of the river, nobody would think the fish enjoyed the arrangement. But if I then offer you the fish, and you take it, that's something else. There's no shame in taking what is freely given."

"Not to be crass, but I'm not sure Kaillë would appreciate us comparing her virtue to a fish," Joseph said.

"How will Kaillë be any less virtuous by joining with

you?"

"Never mind. Just a human term. It doesn't translate."

"As you wish, then," Tal'onë replied. "As for me, Kaillë is like a daughter to me. True, she is not my blood, and so I didn't completely overlook her coming into womanhood. Perhaps my heart would grow less paternal if she cast the same longing eyes at me that she does at you. But she does not, and I am content."

"So what you're saying is that you can't think of any reason I shouldn't present myself at Kaillë's threshold tonight?"

Tal'onë didn't often gesture when he spoke, much less reinforce his point with a touch, but in that moment he pressed a hand on Joseph's shoulder. "You are a good man, Joseph. If you're looking for some excuse or threat from me, you won't get it. What I'm *really* saying is, this isn't between you and the tribe or you and me. This is between you and her...but there are other young elves in this clan who would make a good match. She waits to know your heart. If you cannot give what she needs, then speak honestly to her. Let her move past the disappointment and find happiness with another."

The sun had nearly disappeared beneath the horizon, so Joseph only saw the barest glint of Tal'onë's eyes as he turned to meet the elf's gaze. "Thank you, Tal'onë. You are a good friend."

"Likewise, Joseph." Tal'onë released Joseph's shoulder, rose, and melted into the twilit forest, leaving Joseph to his decision. The hunter looked over his shoulder to Kaillë's house, where lantern-light glowed warmly from within.

~ * ~

The last trace of sunlight had receded from the Windrider village, and Joseph stood on the platform outside Kaillë's door, his pack, quiver, and bow resting against the wall just to the right of it. He reached for the latch, then hesitated and let his hand fall back to his side. He shifted his feet and cleared his throat, trying for once not to be quiet. The lantern light still glowed through the shutters, but Joseph heard no movement within. At last he knocked on the door as softly as he was able, still heavy with the sense that every elf in the village was staring at him, though as far as he knew they had all retired to their own separate dwellings.

"Please come in," he heard Kaillë respond from inside. Her voice was light and pleasant, though he'd feared she might be upset he had kept her waiting so long. He lifted the latch and opened the door.

The sight that greeted him was one of infinite welcome and peace. The lantern bathed the house's single room in a golden glow, and Kaillë sat, smiling at him, at a table laid out with a late supper of bread, nuts, and dried venison. Kaillë wore a simple smock that just covered her knees, and her hair was unbound, flowing in waves across her shoulders. An early cluster of lilac blossoms was tucked behind her left ear, and her eyes were more content than inviting. Joseph had expected anxiety as he stepped across the threshold, but instead his body was loose as he closed the door behind him. Kaillë watched as he unclasped his outer cloak and hung it on a peg next to the door. When he turned around, Kaillë was gazing at the cloak as if measuring its place there, in her home.

Joseph sat across from the elf and took a few nuts from the wooden bowl at the center of the table, ignorant of the pre-meal etiquette for such an intimate supper. Kaillë lifted an ewer from the table and poured a glass of clear spring water she placed before Joseph, and he took that as an invitation to begin the meal. His companion ate as well, and Joseph noted as he hadn't before that Kaillë ate with a practical grace, keeping the decorum of her station without seeming reserved or dainty. "You don't need to knock before you come in, Joseph," she said after a few bites of bread. "I want you to feel free to come and go as you please."

Joseph swallowed. "I wasn't sure. I know you expected me, but I didn't say when I'd be here, and I didn't want to intrude on your privacy."

Kaillë hesitated for a moment before she spoke. "There will never be anything in my home that is not open to your eyes, Joseph. Where you are concerned, privacy is the last thing on my mind." Only at the end of her words did her eyes finally flick up to meet Joseph's, but apart from that hesitation, there was nothing coy in her manner. She spoke plainly in the usual elven way, so Joseph knew, though her phrasing hadn't been indecent, she meant her meaning to be taken clearly.

In a sudden flash Joseph realized how senseless his indecision had been. After all, if he wasn't one of them, he shouldn't be here. If he was, he shouldn't beat around the bush; he had never been known for restraint even when dealing with other humans. "Kaillë," he said, putting down his venison and looking into her with an effort to keep his eyes gentle, "are you in love with me?"

Kaillë's smile grew. "Of course I am, Joseph. Even you should have been able to read that."

"I was," the hunter replied, "only...only I didn't know what to do about it. And the embarrassment of being wrong would have been too much."

Kaillë chuckled, then her face became serious. "You didn't know what to do about it? You've lived a solitary life, Joseph, but I know you were wed before, so I'm sure you *know*...unless you don't feel the same way."

Joseph stood up, and he saw pain shoot through Kaillë's eyes, so he paced toward her instead of away, though that was not his instinct. Moving past her, he stopped at the far corner of her dwelling, looking at the pallet of down the tribe had spent all winter putting together for her, taking twice as much time in order to make it wide enough for two...and longer than any elf was tall, and indeed many humans. He hadn't noticed as he'd watched them stitching it, but it was obvious enough now how it dwarfed much of her other furniture. Looking back across the home, he saw his cloak hanging and realized how high the peg was. He turned back toward Kaillë and saw she still sat, but had turned in her chair to keep her eyes on him, her look more patient than any human could muster in like circumstances.

"I wouldn't be here now if my feelings for you weren't deep," he finally said. "I just... Earlier tonight I asked Tal'onë something about friendship, and he said my question strained his context. I think your love for me strains mine. My first love came when I wasn't much more than a boy; it was heady and all-encompassing and confusing and...and wonderful. I have never been so drunk in my life on spirits as I was on that anticipation. You are young. I see that kind of love in your eyes, and it frightens me. When I buried my wife, I never thought to find any kind of love again, though I know she wanted me to. But age and tragedy and the knowledge of how fragile life can be have robbed me of the kind of love that you feel. I could trust you with my life, and even my heart, but I've learned through much pain that many things aren't yours to decide, or mine. Even now there are beasts nearby that may kill us all even this very night...or worse yet, kill you and leave me alone again." Joseph's chin fell to his chest, and he sank to the floor, suddenly overcome by emotion as he had rarely been. He shed no tears, but he hung his head in his hands as realization swept over him of the true cause of his reluctance: pain and fear. The longing to share his life surged over him, followed immediately by the terror of losing someone he had allowed himself to love so deeply, so uniquely, all over again.

He heard Kaillë's chair scrape back, and in a moment she was at his side, her lean arms reaching as far around him as they could. "Did you think I would hope to share with you everything I am and not want the same from you?" she whispered. "Did you think I would demand any kind of love that you couldn't give me? Did you think any of this would surprise me? I know the man you are. I know your heart and its scars. I only want you to know mine."

Joseph looked over at her. "Alright. Then let me ask you something else. There are many young elf men in this clan that would give much to court you, and yet your eye fixes on a human widower, too old and dour for you by half. Is this something you want, or is this some attempt to court destiny? Have you fallen in love with the man, or with the prophecy? The hunter, or the savior?"

Kaillë blushed, a sight Joseph rarely saw but which made her beauty bloom all the more brightly in the golden light. "I suppose I worshipped you a bit at first," she admitted. "I do still think the prophecy was true, and that it spoke of you, and that you still might do much for my people. But I learned long ago I didn't need to offer myself to keep you here, and once I realized that, I found that my thoughts dwelt on you all the more for it. You are a hero, Joseph, and that is part of what I love about you, but how could you fault me for that? I also love your strength and your wit and your cynicism and your temper. I love your eyes and your words and... I even love the calluses on the fingers you use to draw your bow." Kaillë's passion mounted as she spoke, her devotion rushing out of her through every word. "I am young, Joseph, but no younger than you when you first wed, and not some foolish girl. There is no threat here. If you cannot love me, I will not pine away or ply you with guilt and flirtation...but I love you to your very soul, and have for some time, even in the face of the danger that you might not feel the same. The only way that might change is for you to stop being the man you are, and I know that won't happen." She paused and smiled. "You're too stubborn for that."

Joseph smiled back at her. He felt he should make some proclamation of his heart, but his words failed him, and so much thinking about his feelings was exhausting. He enjoyed being with Kaillë, enjoyed the care and affection he felt for her, and why shouldn't that be enough now, as it always had been before? "I suppose we should finish our supper," he said. He expected Kaillë to look disappointed or defeated somehow, though he knew he shouldn't have. Instead, she only stood and said, "I suppose you're right." She extended her hand down to him.

Joseph took it, though he relied on it but little, knowing he would drag her back down if he tried to force her to take too much of his weight. The idea of doing just that flashed briefly through his mind's eye, and the down pallet was just inches away, but he cast the thought aside. There was still too much unsettled in his heart.

Joseph was determined to enjoy his evening and return to the feeling of welcome he had first experienced when he saw how Kaillë had prepared the home for him, and as was almost always the case when Joseph was determined to do something, that was precisely what he did. He asked Kaillë how she felt about the dangers in the woods, and she told him, and within moments they were speaking once more as intimate friends without confusion...or, he realized, *he* was; Kaillë had never been confused in the first place. Their inability to solve much of their immediate problem forced the conversation to other things, and soon they were debating the merits of the different seasons in the forest as the food disappeared down to the last nut from the wooden bowl between them. Joseph looked down and realized he and Kaillë had taken one another's hands during the conversation, and her skin, smooth and cool under his weathered fingers, felt vital and exciting and natural. He was overcome with admiration and comfort, and in that instant considered such things, perhaps, could be love, too; perhaps the queasy bellies and pounding hearts were only stuff for wide-eyed boys and minstrels' songs.

Kaillë yawned. "It's gotten late. I think I should like to go to bed."

"Of course," Joseph said. "I can move the table and chairs to make room—"

"The bed is big enough for two, as you must have noticed," Kaillë pointed out. "The ladies of the clan weren't particularly subtle in their craft."

"I, uh," Joseph began.

"Joseph," Kaillë interrupted, "if I thought you were eager to bed me, I wouldn't discourage you, but I can see you're still wrestling with your heart, and I am not impatient. Still, there is no lack of affection between us, and no sense in either of us sleeping on the hard floor. Please, come to bed."

Joseph swallowed a sudden lump in his throat as he stood from the table. "As you wish, Chieftain," he quipped, hoping to break his sudden anxiety. It didn't work.

Kaillë rose and blew out the lantern. Only a little moonlight filtered through the shutters, so he could just make out her lithe silhouette as she lifted her tunic over her head and tossed it to the foot of the pallet. She reached to the collar of Joseph's shirt and undid the lacings, reaching under it to raise it off him, her hands soft and light against his skin. Joseph helped pull the shirt off and dropped it more or less where Kaillë had dropped hers. He was still in fine condition, but he wasn't as young as he once was, and it was known elves saw far better in the dark than the most night-eyed human; he suddenly felt himself at a disadvantage, and even more than the weight of time he became aware of the scars of war across his body. Before he could do aught else, though, Kaillë had stepped into him, wrapping her arms around him, her head against his sternum as she pressed her body into him. Joseph returned her embrace, one hand stroking her hair, and if she sensed his desire, she made no reaction. After a few moments she pulled away and, taking Joseph by the hand, led him through the dark to the pallet.

Joseph laid down on his back, and Kaillë nestled against his side, one arm draped across his chest, the scent of her hair filling his breath. He trailed his fingertips up and down her back; his body thrummed with need, but she was young, and Joseph was unselfish. Their months together had been no kind of courtship, and Kaillë might change her mind when they started spending time together as more than friends. At the very least he intended to give her the opportunity, allow her to make that decision without regrets or having lost anything she couldn't get back. He nodded inwardly, the path before him finally clear. His mind at last made up, he turned toward Kaillë and wrapped his other arm around her.

~ * ~

Joseph could not remember the last time he had slept so soundly or so long. The tree cottage was alight with sun through the shutter cracks when he finally opened his eyes. He had returned to his back in his sleep, and Kaillë was half on top of him, her head on his chest and one leg straddled over his. For a moment his heart thumped with blind panic at having spent the night with her, but he took a breath to steady himself, to remember his wife was gone and had all but asked him to love another one day. He supposed, on reflection, it was natural at first to need time to remind himself he was a widower, not an adulterer, when he woke up in Kaillë's bed. His stirring, subtle as it was, woke his partner, and Kaillë looked up at him through sleepy eyelids, her hair unkempt from slumber, and smiled. "Good morning, Joseph," she said, putting one hand to his cheek. She stood then, and everything that had been suggested in moonlight was now made clear in the sun, and her beauty was even more stunning than Joseph had expected. Kaillë paced to the shutters, opening them a crack to let in more light, and stretched. She was as graceful as a lynx and as soft as a doe, and every bit as unashamed before his eyes.

Joseph sat up and picked the sleep from his eyes. "I meant to be up and about before the dawn," he said. "There's enough to do, and I'm not sure I'm ready for everyone to realize I'm spending my nights here, the clan ladies' lack of subtlety notwithstanding."

Kaillë found a ribbon and tied back her hair. "You worry too much, Joseph."

"You aren't afraid folks will talk?"

She paused and looked to the ceiling as if considering the idea for the first time. "No."

"You think they won't talk, or you don't care what they say?"

"Both. It isn't as though—"

Kaillë was interrupted by a knock at the door, followed by Tal'onë's voice. "Chieftain, are you awake?"

She grabbed her simple dress from the foot of the pallet and quickly pulled it over her head before tossing Joseph his shirt. The hunter knew the Windriders were a close and pragmatic people, but Kaillë's urgency reminded him casual nudity was not the norm for them. Kaillë's easy manner in the last few moments had been for his eyes alone, and that thought warmed his heart.

Joseph stood as Kaillë opened the door. "Good morning, Tal'onë," he said, not just a little self-conscious but trying not to be.

"It is not, Joseph," the guard captain replied. "Chieftain, may I come in?"

"We've only just awoken, Tal'onë," Kaillë replied. "Can you wait for us on the green? We'll only be a moment."

"Of course," the elf replied. "When you've prepared yourself then." He made a slight bow of the head and began to climb back down as Kaillë closed the door.

She turned back and crossed to where Joseph still stood, then placed her hands on his hips. "I slept wonderfully last night, Joseph. Thank you." Her hazel eyes were soft as they looked up into Joseph's.

Seized by a sudden impulse, Joseph leaned down and kissed her lips, a soft pressing that lingered only for a moment, drawing Kaillë on tiptoe as he pulled away. "You are most welcome," he replied. "I'll leave you to make ready for our meeting with Tal'onë." Joseph gathered his cloak and gear and headed down the ladder.

~ * ~

Joseph hurried to the stream to refresh himself for the day ahead. It still felt strange to start his daily routine with the sun so high, a sense of disruption that warred over his mind with reflections on his time with Kaillë and apprehension at Tal'onë's foreboding manner. The stream water was cold, shocking his senses back into some semblance of focus on the matters at hand. He finished his morning rituals and rushed back to the green, determined not to leave the guard captain waiting.

As he rounded the corner of Dona and Redel's house, Joseph saw Tal'onë pacing on the village's central lawn as Kaillë hurried up from the other direction, now in a flowing dress the color of the sky with her hair worked into a tight braid down her back. "Tal'onë," Joseph called, "tell us the news. What's the matter?"

"Tes'sael's owl came back moments before I came to see you. Tes'sael was not with her."

By then both Joseph and Kaillë had arrived at Tal'onë's side. "Tes'sael has been pushing himself hard since his ordeal in the woods," Joseph reasoned, "heading out to find the trappers, then taking his usual patrol after only a little sleep. Is it possible he nodded in the saddle? Fell off in mid-flight?"

Tal'onë and Kaillë both simply looked up at him, and Tal'onë raised an eyebrow.

"Alright, I had to ask," Joseph replied.

Kaillë looked into Joseph's eyes, and he sensed she was drawing inspiration from him, remembering the many lessons in planning and tactics he had taught her over the winter. "This is a problem," she said. "Wherever Tes'sael went, he went by owl, so there is no way to track his outward travel, nor any way to know what route the owl took back. We are too few now to dismiss the loss of even one, and the risk that Tes'sael may give up some information as to our whereabouts, even unwittingly, is too high to ignore. Tal'onë, Joseph, yesterday you proposed to go out with the dogs at midday and seek the enemy by scent. I was reluctant. Now I am left with little choice. Take the dogs and go now. Find these creatures, gain what knowledge you can, and if Tes'sael is in their clutches, bring him home."

"It will be done, Chieftain," Tal'onë assented. "I will make the preparations. Joseph, meet me at the head of the eastern patrol path when you are ready." The warrior turned on his heel and walked away.

Joseph looked down at Kaillë. "If Tes'sael lives, we *will* get him back," Joseph assured her.

"I'm worried for you more than for him," Kaillë answered, her eyes downcast. "That doesn't seem right."

"You can't help how you feel. You didn't stray from the right path. You didn't try to hold me back to protect me."

She smiled a smile laden with grim humor. "I might have, if I thought it would have done any good."

Joseph put a hand on her cheek and looked into her eyes. For a moment she held his gaze, her eyes deep with longing, but the moment passed, and she looked away. "Go," she said roughly. "Go quickly, and come back safe."

~ * ~

Joseph met Tal'onë and the dogs at the eastern edge of the village, and without a word they were off. Even given the danger and urgency of their mission, Joseph couldn't completely suppress the exhilaration he felt when making a hard run through the forest with a skilled companion, and Tal'onë was possibly the best woodsmen Joseph had ever met. The dogs raced out ahead of them, and Joseph and Tal'onë sprinted behind, taking fallen logs and brooks in stride, skirting thickets and bounding into the lower, spreading branches of the trees for an occasional look farther down the path ahead. Sometimes the hunter took point, sometimes the guard captain, and either might disappear to search a side path or some sign before rejoining the other, always moving eastward and upward.

After the better part of two hours, the men stopped at a stream to breathe, and the dogs loped back, tongues lolling, to drink deeply from the babbling water. "We make good time, Joseph," Tal'onë said, still working to regain his breath, "but it still takes too long. I would rather have taken an owl out, but I had little hope that any signs would be visible through the canopy."

"I'm disappointed that the patrols didn't find anything last night," Joseph said. "The owls often sense things in the dark."

"Perhaps one did. Tes'sael may have found more than he could handle alone."

"That wouldn't be unlike him. He might have—" Joseph stopped short and cocked an ear to the east. The dogs were also perking up at some sound, which Joseph quickly resolved as a rustling through the brush, growing louder by the moment.

"That is not Tes'sael," Tal'onë muttered. "Even injured or in a panic, he would not make such a racket."

Joseph nodded then glanced up at the trees. Tal'onë took his meaning and scrambled up the nearest trunk as Joseph ducked behind a larger bole and readied his bow. "Stitch, Yowler, down," Joseph hissed. The dogs obeyed, hunkering as low as they could by the edge of the brook, but Joseph noticed an odd tension in Stitch's manner, an occasional twitch as he scented the air.

The crashing through the brush grew louder and nearer, but before Joseph could peek out for a look, Stitch leapt up from his hiding place, barking loudly. Joseph silently cursed the dog before he realized that the barks were not the throaty sounds of challenge, but high and playful, and Stitch's tail wagged. The dog's prior tension, Joseph then understood, was not anxiety, but repressed playfulness. Puzzled, Joseph stepped from hiding just in time to see a great black-and-white-striped head burst from the nearby brush south of the trail, followed by a furred body as long as a horse's but not half as tall.

At first glance, the giant badger could have been any inhabitant of the dwarven caves Joseph had visited last fall in his quest for the Hoard of Dalviir. By the familiar triple scar running down his left flank though, as much as by Stitch's easiness as he sniffed the huge beast's muzzle, Joseph knew the badger to be Steva, companion of his dwarven friend Dorav the Restless. The dwarf had still been unconscious when Joseph and his company left the dwarven city, wounded nearly to the point of death in the battle over the Hoard, and, alas, his animal friend now seemed to be in little better condition. The badger's hide was a patchwork of scratches and bites, and he sank to his belly as soon as Stitch's greeting stopped his mad dash. He looked up at Joseph and plied him with urgent, mewling grunts.

"Tal'onĕ, come down," Joseph called. "This beast is a friend."

"Thank the spirits for that," Tal'onĕ sighed as he dropped from the branches. "I would not want to face him as a foe."

"No, you wouldn't, but he's badly injured. I'm not sure we have enough herbs in our packs, but we can see to the worst of his hurts."

"Do we have time for this, Joseph? I know your tale and guess who this badger is, but surely even your dwarven friend would agree finding Tes'sael is precedent."

"I don't disagree, but he shouldn't be here at all. Something is amiss, more than I'd imagined, something we may not learn if he dies."

Tal'onĕ nodded and began to search his pack. Stitch had stopped his playful bounding as soon as Steva collapsed, and now his eyes were tight with worry as he licked at his friend's wounds. Yowler had approached as well and was sniffing at the badger, unsure what to make of things.

"I believe you have the better herb-craft, Joseph," Tal'onĕ said, handing the human a handful of bandages and a small clay jar. "Give me your pack; I will set to grinding the herbs that aren't yet prepared."

Joseph nodded and took the items from Tal'onĕ's hands, then broke through the beeswax sealing the jar and scooped out a dollop of sharp-smelling poultice. He spread it on a bandage and knelt by Steva's side, but the moment the cloth touched the badger's skin, the beast surged up and snapped at Joseph, missing his hands by inches. It was clear the badger had not intended to injure the hunter, but his point was clear enough and made more so as the badger gathered his rear legs under him and stalked over to the brook. Steva drank noisily for half a minute, then turned and shambled back up the way he had come. After a few feet he stopped and looked back, then made a pointed grunt at Joseph.

Joseph looked down at Tal'onë. "Let's go."

Chapter Five: Homecoming

Steva set off at a brisk trot, but he was not on his home terrain, and his injuries told heavily on him. After several minutes it was clear Joseph and Tal'onë could follow his trail just as easily without him, and more quickly.

"This slows us down, Joseph," the elf called, "and it does him no good."

Joseph nodded grimly. In a few long bounds he overtook the badger, then whirled around in his path. Steva snarled and kept forward, seeking to bowl the human over, but Joseph braced his feet and set his hip against the badger's shoulder. At Steva's full strength, Joseph knew he'd have been trampled down without a pause, but so profound was the badger's exhaustion that he finally came to a stop after forcing the hunter back only a few steps. "Easy boy," Joseph soothed the beast, stroking the striped fur between his ears. "We'll find Dorav," he added, for Joseph had long since concluded that nothing but peril to his companion could urge Steva to such lengths of determination. "Don't you worry, Steva. Just rest, now." Joseph stood. "Stitch, stay with Steva. Stay." Stitch continued his earlier ministrations to the badger's wounds as Joseph and Tal'onë started moving again, Yowler streaking out ahead.

No longer slowed, the runners surged forward even more quickly than before, driving into the ground to make each stride count. Soon it was clear Yowler had picked up a familiar scent, and Joseph urged him on to greater and greater speeds. Nearly half an hour had gone by when shouts and growls reached Joseph's ears from up ahead, loud enough now not to be drowned by the sounds of their mad rush. Apprehensive, Yowler slowed a pace, sticking closer to Joseph and Tal'onë as they continued to charge ahead, now with even greater urgency.

Rounding a bend in the path, Joseph nearly stopped short at what he saw. Tes'sael stood over a body on the ground, his bowstring twanging in blinding repetition as he emptied his quiver at three beasts snarling down the trail toward them, their pebbly skin and thick black manes looking blacker than black against the surrounding colors of the forest. Joseph knew them at once: Trolls. He had fought those savage inhabitants of the deep underground once before, knew the armor-like strength of their hides and the contagion carried by their ragged claws and the sharp, bony ridges that served them for teeth.

Tes'sael was too preoccupied to hear help coming from behind, and Joseph saw him reach over his shoulder for one last arrow that wasn't there. The lieutenant dropped his bow and drew two long knives as the trolls closed the range in long, loping strides.

"Eyes and throats," Joseph shouted to Tal'onë as the captain drew alongside him and stretched his bow. Though the trolls had no true eyes, just atrophied patches of taught skin where it seemed eyes used to be, Joseph's point was clear, and Tal'onĕ's aim was true. Two of the snarling beasts were felled by a shot from each of the rescuers before the final troll slammed into Tes'sael, his tough hide turning aside the elf's knives that would have impaled any other creature. Joseph knew from his past encounter how intent trolls remained once they latched onto a target. His motions were swift but calm as he drew his knife, stepped behind the troll, and slit its throat, spilling its black blood over Tes'sael and the body he had fallen onto when the troll struck.

Joseph helped Tes'sael up as Yowler, who had practiced the better part of valor during the battle, ran up to the elf, tail wagging, and began pawing the ground at his feet. At last Joseph was able to take proper stock of Tes'sael's condition, and though he was grimy, bruised, and clearly exhausted, under the circumstances things could have been much worse.

After regaining his feet, Tes'sael, in turn, reached down to the body that had previously been beneath him, and only then was Joseph certain the man was still alive. As the elf bore his burden up, pulling the form's left arm across his shoulders for support, Joseph realized the body was a dwarf, and this dwarf was, indeed, Dorav the Restless. His tan skin and black beard were caked with sweat and blood, and a light cloth was tied around his head to protect the cave-dweller's all-black eyes from the harsh, midday sun.

"Tes'sael," Joseph said as Tal'onĕ, now finished ensuring the deaths of the first two trolls, drew up behind, "are you hurt?"

"Not enough to worry over," the elf replied.

"Joseph?" Dorav asked even before Tes'sael had finished speaking. "Could that be my human friend I hear?"

"It is, Dorav," the hunter replied. "What happened to you?"

"No worse than happened to most of my people," Dorav said, a shudder in his voice. "The trolls swarmed up from the lower reaches like ants. Never seen anything like it; they were so fierce and so many. I got cut off from the city; I don't even know if she still stands. The rest of my Irregulars are dead. The best I could think of was to make my way to the surface, see if I could find your people, or anybody else that might help us. We're desperate."

"What about the other clans?" Joseph asked, speaking of the neighboring dwarf regions. Dorav was of the Ninth Clan, and Joseph knew of a Fourteenth Clan far to the northwest. He assumed the areas nearer by had their own numbers.

Dorav just shook his head. "We tried to send out runners, but I have no idea if they got through. Near as I can tell, there isn't a foot of tunnel for leagues in any direction we can be sure is safe."

"Captain," Tes'sael interrupted, "we need to be moving home. Many of these trolls are pushing out onto the surface. Seeing them now in the light, I'm sure they are what killed Ten'vohnë."

Joseph had suspected as much as soon as he saw Steva on the path, but given a moment to think he cursed himself for not making the connection sooner. Troll hides were remarkably difficult to pierce, explaining why there had been no blood trail leading away from Ten'vohnë's body and how Tes'sael had failed to fell any with his arrows as he ran. Even though Tes'sael had been underground, he wouldn't have recognized the creatures, since of their band only Joseph had seen them. If trolls were the enemy, though, they might at least have one advantage... "Surely they won't move by day," Joseph said, considering the improvised veil Dorav wore. "They live in total darkness; the sun must be terrible to them."

"You forget, Joseph," Dorav objected. "They have no

eyes to be bothered by the light. Steva managed to start a rockslide upslope of the tunnel I left from, but they're bound to have found other ways up here. Your lieutenant here is right; we need to move."

Their disparate heights made it difficult for Joseph to support Dorav, who limped on a cruelly twisted left leg, but Tal'onë took over the job, allowing Tes'sael some rest as they moved off.

"Have you seen my badger?" the dwarf asked after a few minutes.

Tal'onë said nothing, and Joseph hesitated long before he answered. "We saw him," he finally said. "He was bad hurt, Dorav, and he wouldn't let me salve his wounds until you were found. Your badgers aren't immune to troll poison as you are. He was very weak when we left him."

Dorav didn't answer, and he stayed silent as they walked.

~ * ~

Nearly two hours had passed when finally the band returned to where Joseph and Tal'onë had left Steva on the path. Stitch had curled up on top of him, but the hound wasn't asleep, and his eyes, set in a brow wrinkled with anxiety and confusion, stared up at Joseph as they approached. Joseph looked down at Steva; his eyes were closed, and his flanks were deathly still. He dropped down in front of the badger as the elves looked tensely on, placing his face before the great muzzle, desperate to feel even the slightest puff of breath. He waited there for long moments, longer than he knew would do any good, before standing. "I'm sorry, Dorav. He's gone."

The dwarf drew a deep, racking breath before dropping to his knees. "No," he wept. "Oh, please, no." As he sobbed, Dorav crawled forward the last few paces to his fallen friend, resting his head against the great badger's cheek. Stitch had jumped down from Steva's back, and the dog licked at Dorav's left hand and whimpered. Dorav wrapped his arm around the hound and pulled him close, his sobs coming harder and more choking with each moment.

Joseph turned away, heartbroken at his friend's suffering, steeling himself for the callousness he was about to commit.

"Dorav, midday has passed, and we still have far to go."

"Just leave me," the dwarf cried. "It's bad enough poor Steva died for my sake. Don't waste your lives on me too."

"No lives are wasted unless you stay here. Come on, Rover, on your feet. There's more at stake here than just your life...or your pain."

Dorav turned his head toward Joseph, who could sense the dwarf glaring at his silhouette through the cloth over his eyes. "Fine, hunter. I'll go with you." The dwarf climbed to his feet with the help of the elves and staggered a few feet before stopping again. "What about Steva? He'll be food for the trolls if we leave him here; I can't let that happen."

"There's nothing else for it, Dorav," Joseph answered, his misery clear in his tone. "We don't have the time to bury him or the fuel to burn him. I don't know what else we can do."

Dorav nodded, turning back to Steva, but only briefly. "I'm sorry, old friend. You deserved better from me. Don't hate me when we meet again one day in the Great Cavern. An eternity of that I could not bear."

Joseph pushed the band only as far as the brook where Steva had first appeared before calling a halt for food. The hunter motioned Tal'onë some distance upstream for a quiet discussion.

"At this pace," he began, "we won't make the village by nightfall. Dorav's leg is getting worse, and Tes'sael is exhausted."

"That has occurred to me," Tal'onë replied. "I can run back if you wish, but I'm not sure what it will solve. The dwarf is surely too heavy to bear out on an owl."

"I know," Joseph grimaced. "Do it anyway. An owl can at least get Tes'sael home before he collapses, and we could use proper supplies to treat Dorav's leg or, better still, a litter to carry him."

"You take a risk, Joseph. Dorav cannot move without proper help. You are too tall and Tes'sael too weak. If I go, you won't be able to move at all. Not quickly enough to matter, anyway."

Joseph nodded. "You'd best hurry then."

Tal'onë nodded back and lifted the strap of his food satchel over his head, handing it to Joseph. His main pack and quiver he had already removed when they stopped at the brook. "I'll go light." With that, the elf was off into the woods, and within moments Joseph could neither see nor hear him.

The human wandered back to Dorav and Tes'sael. "Rest easy," he said. "I've sent Tal'onë back to the village for help. We'll have you out of here in no time. In the meanwhile, you might as well relax and get your strength back."

The pair protested, but their arguments were weak, and Joseph could sense their relief at having time to take their ease. He ordered the dogs to watch over the pair and moved into the forest, gathering brush and deadwood as he moved east. He continued scouring the woods for the best part of an hour, and when he'd finished, Steva was buried under a mound of dry wood as high as Joseph's head. He emptied an oil lantern over the pile, holding back the last to soak a patch near the ground, and took flint and tinder from his pouch. In moments, the pile was caught up in a roaring blaze. "You rest easy, too, Steva," he whispered. "The trolls will get no more of you."

Joseph was solemn as he returned to the brook, and before he could even speak to his companions, his attention was pulled skyward by a downward buffet of wind. A giant owl alighted on the ground to his left, guided by Tes'voran. "Chieftain Kaillë expected you back," he said as he dismounted. "We've patrols fanning out over the forest, and I spotted Tal'onë on his run. He told me what happened. I am to send Tes'sael back on my owl and help you splint Dorav's leg." The elf's nostrils flared. "I smell smoke."

"Our friend here lost a comrade," Joseph said, nodding to Dorav. "I was able to build a funeral pyre while we waited."

Dorav nodded thanks to Joseph as Tes'voran looked down at the dwarf then gasped and stumbled back a pace. "By all the winds and stars," he muttered, "it's real!" During his sojourn to destroy the Hoard of Dalviir, Joseph had been shocked to learn the Windriders considered dwarves to exist only in children's tales. Of all their people, only the survivors of that journey, Kaillë, Tes'sael, and two other elves, had ever seen one.

"As real as you or me," Joseph replied, "and 'its' name is Dorav. Dorav, this is Tes'voran. He didn't mean any harm."

"It's alright," the dwarf grunted. "I'm the stranger here, after all, not him. What's this I hear about splinting my leg?"

"More importantly, what's this I hear about being sent back?" Tes'sael protested. "I'm not just going to leave you all out here."

"That's exactly what you'll do," Joseph rebutted. "Tal'onë gave orders, and so am I. You've done more than your part, and you're all but dead on your feet. Time for a nice owl ride back home."

Tes'sael scowled as he climbed into the harness on the owl's back but didn't argue any further, his eyelids heavy.

Joseph smirked at the realization that he'd questioned whether Tes'sael's disappearance might have been caused by falling asleep in the saddle, which the lieutenant was now almost certain to do with no danger. Before Tes'sael took off, Tes'voran untied his supply packs from his owl's harness and started removing bandages and jars of salve. He began treating Dorav's cuts as the owl took to the air. "Getting your friend fit to walk is just a contingency," Tes'voran explained. When Tal'onë reaches the village, he will send back more elves with a litter, and I've advised him to set up a rotation of owls to bring fresh guardsmen throughout the evening. We'll carry your friend out of here well before dark, if everything goes to plan."

"If," Joseph answered, and Tes'voran nodded his concern as Joseph looked up at the sun-bright patch of sky shining brokenly through the canopy. Sunset was still some hours off, but his first battle with trolls had taught him to be wary of their savagery and toughness. Out in the forest, with little hard cover, it would take them mere seconds to overwhelm any force the Windriders could field, and if Dorav was right about their indifference to light, their prior activity at night was little more than coincidence...meaning they could appear at any moment.

~ * ~

The sun was setting over the Windrider village when Joseph and a band of elves broke out of the brush with Dorav on a stretcher. The dwarf had resisted being carried at first, but he relented when Joseph got stern and reminded him how many lives were in the balance if he insisted on slowing them down for the sake of his pride. The moment Joseph lifted one end of the litter, though, he'd almost regretted winning the argument, for the dwarf was incredibly dense. Joseph had guessed Dorav would be heavy, but even so he was off his guess by nearly half. Still, with a steady rotation of elves ferried back and forth by a steady rotation of owls, they'd managed to keep up a respectable pace and return to the village before proper nightfall.

Kaillë was waiting at the eastern edge of the village when the band emerged. "Is everyone alright?" she asked Joseph, her brow tight.

Joseph nodded. "Dorav will need care, but I think he'll mend."

"Course I'll mend," the dwarf insisted as he stood from the stretcher, supporting his splinted leg with a crutch they'd cut from a forked sapling. "Kaillë Windsong, wasn't it? You're as lovely as I remember."

Joseph smiled briefly as Kaillë flicked her eyes down. "Thank you," she replied. "I wish I could say that you are looking well, but you will be soon enough. These elves will lead you to our best healers." Two elves had approached from the village, and they led Dorav away as he thanked Kaillë.

Kaillë met Joseph's eyes, and with a subtle motion of her head led him a few steps away from the crowd. "Dorav's news was most dire, Joseph. Tal'onë told me all that has happened, and I convened the council while we awaited your return. They're frightened. Half are speaking of packing up and moving somewhere else; I am not so quick to abandon our new home, but I understand their fear. After all you've told us of the trolls you fought..."

"I wish I had wise counsel for you, Kaillë," Joseph answered. "I can't guess whether the trolls have some end in this attack beyond destruction. I know nothing of their temperament outside of battle. We need Dorav to speak."

"First thing tomorrow, then, the council will hear him."

"There's a problem," Joseph said.

"You mean *another* problem."

"Yes. We did our best to leave little trace and cover what we left, but carrying Dorav and trying to hurry back before dark, it's impossible we didn't leave some signs, and anything we did leave will point straight back here."

"Perhaps the trolls will be too ignorant of the surface world to follow your trail," Kaillë hoped aloud.

"Maybe. Speak to Tal'onë. I recommend he pull the patrols in for the night. Rest the owls and put as many men as we can on watch at the border. If the enemy wants to rampage around the tunnel entrances, let them, but if there's so much as a stray wind within a mile of the village, we need to know it."

"I will tell him," Kaillë agreed. "I suspect he was thinking in the same direction, as usual."

"I'll try to join the group by the third watch," Joseph said. "For now I need food and sleep. Carrying a dwarf is a hard afternoon's work."

"Of course. Retire to our shelter and help yourself to the larder. I will join you when I may. There is still much to see to this night." Kaillë squeezed Joseph's hand before leaving to attend her duties. Joseph headed to the ladder up to Kaillë's platform, noticing how easily she said "*our* shelter."

~ * ~

It was some hours after dark when Joseph began slowly to come around. It was still dark outside, but he was warm, and a sense of contentment draped over his mind as surely as the blanket covering his form. He also didn't remember Delia coming to bed, but she was with him now, wrapped up safe in his embrace as he slept, her hair in his face. His bleary mind wondered if she had created some new flower-water concoction for her hair, for the scent was different than he——

Joseph's eyes snapped open as he awoke with a start, suddenly remembering reality as it truly was and not as he had dreamt it. He pushed Kaillë's sleeping body to arm's length, somehow dizzy in his soul. Only with great difficulty had he begun to open his heart to her, but to awaken like this, holding her against him and thinking she was his lost wife, was too much to bear. Kaillë woke at his abrupt movement and blinked open her eyes as Joseph raced out of bed and started to dress.

"Joseph?" she asked, her voice hoarse from sleep. "What is it? Has there been an attack?" Her words grew stronger as the danger of their position crept into her mind.

"I slept too long," Joseph answered, his tone brusque. "I need to join the patrol."

"Tal'onë rested most of the day in anticipation of a long night. He and the guard were quite fine when I—"

"I have to go," Joseph insisted, and with that he left the house, still fastening his cloak as he went.

The night was chill, and Joseph was breathing into his hands to warm them when he found Tal'onë. "How is everything?" he asked. "Any sightings?"

"Nothing at all," the captain answered. "What are you doing out, Joseph? You should be resting at home."

"Home? You mean Kaillë's home."

"I...I understood that was no longer a distinction."

"Well, it is," Joseph corrected.

"I see. I'm dismayed, Joseph. When we spoke of this, I thought if you chose to be with her, you would remain with her. Does Kaillë understand your feelings on this? Don't misunderstand, she's a woman grown, and wise with the hearts of people, but if you've misled her—"

"What?" Joseph interrupted with frustration. Realization dawned as he watched Tal'onë's face in the torchlight. "By the seasons, Tal'onë, what do you think of me? I've seen and felt more than I meant to, but only by invitation, and I surely haven't taken a husband's leave with her."

"Oh," Tal'onë replied, his voice as confused as it had been defensive a moment before. "Why not?"

Joseph was taken aback by the sudden reversal in Tal'onë's interrogation. "Wha... Why *not*? Tal'onë, I came out here to ask about the patrols. I don't—"

"The patrols are fine," the elf said, cutting Joseph off. "Nobody's seen or heard a thing; everybody has been accounted for at each rotation, and dawn is only two hours off. What's more, you know all that, since you know I'd have been at your...*Kaillë's* doorstep if anything was otherwise. I don't know why you're here, but it isn't to ask about the patrols."

"Fine," Joseph spat. "I'll go have a look around for myself, then, someplace with better company."

Joseph started away but felt Tal'onë's hand grip his elbow. He wrenched his way free and rounded on the elf, ready to fight if the need arose, but Tal'onë just looked up at him. "You said that we were friends," he stated.

Joseph took a deep breath. "Yeah."

"And among your people, friends...do they sometimes speak their minds to one another? Even if they believe the other may not want to hear of it?"

Joseph could see where Tal'onë was heading, but he refused to be dishonest. "Sometimes," he replied. "Sometimes too often."

Tal'onë nodded. "I thought so. Joseph, you have placed yourself in an endless in-between because, for all your fierce protection of life, you show more reverence to the dead than to the living. Your wife is gone, Joseph. You love her still, you will love her always, but wherever her soul is now, she is not here."

Joseph fumed at the elf's blunt words but held his tongue for the sight of Tal'onë's steadfastness. "Come to your point quickly, Tal," he said, his voice low and not without foreboding.

"We all come and go, Joseph. We are in this world for a little while, and then we aren't. Some passings are more cruel than others to those left behind, but it is not given to mortals to live a set of beautiful days over and over again. Even if your wife forbade you to love again, which I doubt, what would you owe to the memory of one gone? The dead collect on no debts. *You* are still alive, Joseph. At least on the outside."

"I know that, Tal'onë. It's how to live the life I have left that concerns me."

"It concerns you too much, as most things do," the elf rebutted. "Joseph, for a man to earn the love of even one great woman is a rare thing, but you have been so blessed as to earn the love of *two*. If I thought you did not love Kaillë, I would say her favor placed no rightful hold on you, but I believe that you do love her...and I believe that you're simply biding time, waiting to act on your heart until you can somehow feel less guilty about it. You, of all people, should know how little time we have for waiting in this world, and yet you force Kaillë to wait for your conscience to ease, even though you've decided deep down that being with her is your chosen path. You wouldn't have gone to her if you hadn't."

Joseph stared at the torchlight crackling in Tal'onë's pupils as he considered the captain's words. It was true - there was no version of the future he envisioned that saw both he and Kaillë alive and yet not together. Indeed, he realized, they'd come to rely on one another so much over the past months that the idea of letting her go to find and wed another made his heart burn. What business was it of Tal'onë's, though, to dictate the terms of his relationship with Kaillë? Only a day before he'd said he needed time, and she'd been only too understanding. Of course, he thought, there was no doubt she would accommodate his unease to the ends of the earth, regardless of her own feelings. Her compassion knew few bounds, and none, perhaps, where Joseph was concerned. And maybe it wasn't Tal'onë's business, but he did speak as a friend, and it had never been Joseph's habit to refuse wise counsel. It was rare enough to get it. "What are you suggesting?" the hunter finally asked.

Tal'onë held Joseph's gaze for a moment before answering. "There are still two hours of darkness left. I suggest you go back and put them to their best use. And if having Kaillë at your side, truly at your side, at last, doesn't help ease your troubled mind, then you've something other than a man's living blood in those sour, old veins of yours."

Joseph started to turn away, his pulse quickening but his mind unsettled to have received such advice. He stopped at a passing thought before Tal'onë could also start away. "Tal'onë," he asked, "have you ever been wed?"

"I have not," the elf replied, "but I have loved, and I know something of pining and doubting and waiting too long. I am more cautious than bold, though, and I carry my past lightly when I carry it at all; I can live with such regrets. For a man like you, who carries so many burdens, I fear this one would be too heavy." The shorter elf turned back and reached his hand up to Joseph's shoulder. "Go now, Joseph, before you concoct some reason to change your mind."

Joseph's heart was hammering his ribs by the time he reached the top of the ladder to Kaillë's platform, but he did not hesitate before he opened the door and crossed the threshold, flush with the desire to make the home his. He crossed the dwelling to the bed, where Kaillë sat upright at his sudden entrance, and while the darkness lasted, he was far less cautious than bold.

Chapter Six: Abomination

Joseph awoke from a brief, light sleep just as the sun was peeking over the mountain slopes. He and Kaillë were still on her down mattress, tangled together, and the hunter fought down his guilt for long enough to enjoy her warmth and allow himself a smile at the memories of their recent hours together. Joseph knew the time for duty and action was at hand and wished to rise, but he knew just as assuredly there was no way he could extricate himself from Kaillë's embrace without waking her. Hoping to rouse her more gently, he stroked her hair and whispered her name.

The elf also slept lightly, it seemed, for at this soft encouragement she raised her bleary eyes toward Joseph and blinked. She smiled, and in her sweet expression and mussed hair Joseph saw something of the girl she must have been before the cruel world had made her a chieftain. "Good morning," she purred, arching her back to stretch.

"That remains to be seen, I think," Joseph replied. "The council will be convening soon; we're to hear Dorav's report on the troll attack."

Kaillë nodded. "There's never enough time, is there?"

Joseph shook his head, and the two of them rose and began to dress. The hunter started to speak, then hesitated as he ordered his thoughts. "Kaillë," he said after a moment, "I wanted to ask what needs to be done in your clan to...seal our decisions with one another over the last two days."

Kaillë looked over her shoulder as she adjusted her robe and reached to where a belt hung from the back of a chair. Joseph met her eyes and saw that she was blushing. "I'm afraid I don't understand," she said.

"Among my people," Joseph explained, "there are ceremonies to perform when two people have...pledged themselves to each other. Vows, blessings, that kind of thing."

Kaillë crossed the dwelling to where her heavy outer cloak hung on the wall, for the chill of the night before had not yet lifted from the forest. "We have no such ceremonies amongst the Windriders," Kaillë replied. "There is no misunderstanding in the clan of the commitments we have made here, and they are commitments not easily broken. Saying words over them has never been our way." She crossed back to stand before Joseph. "What needs to be done is only between us, and all those things have been done...now." She laid her hand on Joseph's chest and looked up at him, a hint of sheepishness in her eyes.

Joseph bowed his head to kiss her brow, but she stood on tiptoe and kissed his lips instead. "As you wish," Joseph said, moving toward the door.

"As *you* wish, too," Kaillë responded then shook her head as though flustered. "I mean, I wasn't trying to put you off. If it's important to you that we have a human ceremony, then we will...though you'll have to direct the arrangements. None of us will know what to do."

"No," Joseph said, "I just didn't want to leave anything

undone or to give any of your people cause to think ill of either of us...or of my motives here. If you are content, then so am I. Except...I want you to know, to hear from me in so many words, that even though I might never leave my past completely behind, I will care for you always and do everything I can to keep you safe and make you happy, no matter what." Joseph suddenly looked away and cleared his throat. "I, uh...I just wanted you to know that beyond any doubt."

Kaillë took her lover's hands and brought his eyes back to her own. "I did know that, and knew it beyond any doubt. And I hope you know just as surely that I will be a good wife to you and devote myself to your happiness. Even my duty to the clan will not come before that, for without family and home there can be no clan."

Joseph's pulse quickened to hear Kaillë call herself his wife, and the lack of ceremony in the Windrider culture somehow made the commitment seem sudden, even jarring, though he recognized in many ways it had been a long time in the making.

"Is that the kind of thing your people say when they wed?" Kaillë asked into Joseph's hesitant silence.

"That's the sense of it," Joseph replied, donning his cloak. With that, he opened the door and held it for his bride.

After visiting the stream to make ready for the day, the couple presented themselves on the main village green, watching as the council members approached from various directions. Tal'onë appeared and gave Joseph a wink in greeting, a mannerism that struck Joseph as surprisingly human. Dorav shambled up to the gathering circle as well, wrapped in two blankets and a fur cloak, looking utterly miserable in the morning chill, though his limp was much improved. "This is where I'm supposed to be, then?" he asked Joseph as he approached.

"That's a deeper question than I can answer," Joseph

said, "but this is where the council meets, if that's what you mean."

"Funny," the dwarf replied, his tone making clear he thought Joseph was anything but. "How can you be so quick with your tongue while you're freezing to death?"

Tal'onë cocked an eyebrow. "Joseph led us to believe your people were a hardy race."

"Look here, tree-dweller," Dorav snarked, "a dwarf can march for days with no food, hardly any water, and sleeping on his feet without breaking stride. I've lived for months at a time with nothing but what I can pack out and the fungus and critters I find in the tunnels. But where I come from, only a few of us with duties taking them once in a while to the surface know even a thing about the cold, and for my part, they can *have it.* Why anybody would choose to live up here with drafts and chills cne minute and sun and swelter the next is beyond me."

"See," Joseph said to Kaillë, responding to her disbelief before meeting dwarves that any race would live willingly underground, "I told you they'd think our way of living was as daft as you thought theirs."

Kaillë didn't respond, but instead addressed Dorav. "I'm sorry for your discomfort, my friend. Shall we start a fire for you?"

"No, you shan't," Dorav replied, mimicking Kaillë's more formal speech, "I'll manage. I'm led to believe I'm a member of a hardy race." Dorav thrust his bearded jaw up and out, taking a haughty stance, but his teeth chattered a bit as he did.

"You must already be adjusting," Joseph said. "Your tongue's getting quicker."

By then the council members had all arrived, so the group sat on the grass in their customary circle and commenced their deliberations.

"Friends," Kaillë began, "this is Dorav, a rover from the

dwarven city of the Streets of Twilight. In our clan we would think of him as a scout, more or less. As we've told and retold over the long winter nights, Dorav is a hero of the quest to destroy the Hoard of Dalviir. He nearly lost his life in that battle, and there can be no doubt that without his stalwart defense, the rest of us might only have thwarted the Baron at the cost of our lives, and maybe not at all. Moreover, he comes before us today despite being in his period of mourning for many of his people and for the badger Steva, his dearest friend, so we are doubly in his debt."

Joseph recognized Kaillë's slightly more ritualized speech and use of dwarven phrases she'd learned during their quest last fall, noting, largely thanks to her instruction over the months, how she blended her styles of speech to bring Dorav and the council together rather than painting the dwarf as an outsider. The council, for their part, placed hands over hearts and bowed their heads to the rover, the elven manner of greeting someone in times too somber for applause.

"Dorav," Kaillë continued, "would you explain what has transpired in the dwarven realm over the last few days."

Dorav didn't stand, and Joseph wasn't sure whether that was a cultural difference or he simply wanted to stay better cocooned in his blankets and furs. Even so, he spoke with more confidence than the hunter expected from one who spent most of his days alone in a subterranean wilderness, far from his own Council of Elders, and that very much by design.

"I understand your people don't know much truth about dwarves," Dorav began, "so I should tell how we're always fighting with the trolls that live in the deeper caverns. They're savage beasts, dark as an unknown tunnel with claws and bites riddled with plague. For all their fury and numbers, our better organization, defenses, and arms usually stand us dwarves in the better stead, and the battles have been down to occasional skirmishes for generations now. Joseph was unlucky and generous enough to fight beside me in one of those, and he can tell you that, nasty as they are, they retreat quickly.

"Then four days ago they were all over us. Somehow they got past our patrols and our outer gates, slaughtering their way through the city in numbers we haven't seen since the times of our great-grandfathers' great-grandfathers. As usual, I was away from the city, and I'd met up with a few other rovers I know, trading reports on the sections we'd been mapping. The lot of us crossed paths with a hret-dialt, ah, that is to say, a guard troop, who'd been driven back by sheer numbers. They told us what had happened to the city, and how all the tunnels that might give us a path to our neighbors were choked with trolls. None of us knew the surface, but I knew that you all were nearby and could probably be convinced to help us find an overland route past the trolls to other dwarf clans that could send reinforcements.

"We fought a running battle with trolls for two days, and I'm afraid all I accomplished in the end was to lead them to your doorstep. The other rovers gave their lives protecting me, since I was the one with the best chance of finding your camp, and the last of the hret-dialt died holding back the trolls while Steva demolished the tunnel behind us. I barely got out alive, and Steva... Then to make matters worse, when I get up here and find you all, I learn the trolls had already boiled out of some other tunnel at least two nights before. I'm sorry if my people somehow shoved our mess up to yours. I doubt that was anybody's intention, and it surely wasn't mine."

"I know I speak for all when I release you from any blame for this," one of the elder council members said. "Regardless, our eyes now must be forward, not back. How are we to respond to this threat? We have suffered one travesty only months ago, and our numbers are few, less than six-score now. We must preserve the clan, first and foremost."

Joseph knew well the thought behind those words. The desire for flight was growing slowly among the Windriders.

"Are we sure they will continue to harass us?" a councilwoman asked. "If the trolls who attacked the first night were also on the heels of dwarves who escaped, perhaps they won't return."

"What say you to that, Dorav?" Joseph piped up. "Will the trolls return to their tunnels, or will they turn their sight, or whatever they have instead, toward the surface?"

"You should know my answer to that, Joseph. As I told you once before, I can make no guess at a troll's plan, since they have no plan to start with."

Joseph nodded as Tal'onë responded, "No plan, perhaps, but there is certainly *something* driving their behavior. They were fearless in their attack the night before last, but since then we've seen not so much as a sign of them, save the three that followed Dorav out of the tunnel yesterday. It's as if they disappeared completely."

"Well, they didn't go back the way I came out," Dorav said. "I wouldn't be standing here if they had; we'd have been overrun." A breeze cut through the clearing, and Dorav shivered and wormed his way a bit deeper into his furs.

"That's it," Joseph realized aloud.

"What's what?" Dorav asked.

"You said the trolls lived even deeper than dwarves," Joseph explained. "I considered how dark their home must be, so at first I thought the light must be discouraging them...but I wager there's something else they don't have that far down: cold."

"You're right," Dorav confirmed with a nod. "Actually,

in some of the deeper caverns we've found sulfurous vents and liquid stone. The fumes are choking, but the trolls don't seem to mind, and they give warmth to spare. They're known to be thickest in those places."

"So as long as this cold snap keeps hold, they'll stay underground," Tal'onĕ reasoned.

"Which gives us time," Joseph added, "and with Dorav's help, a course of action."

"Name what you need," the dwarf said, perking up at Joseph's renewed zeal.

"You've blocked one tunnel; I say we block another. Show us the way to the most likely tunnel, or tunnels, the first wave of trolls probably used, and we'll make sure they stay underground, where they belong. Help us do that, friend, and I'll lead the overland party to get you to the other clans myself."

~ * ~

Preparations for the mission were made in haste, but sussing out the destination took some time. The Windriders kept no maps, and Dorav was unfamiliar with the surface. Still, after repeated description of the location of the first troll attacks and much scratching in the dirt and with charcoal sticks on bark scraps, all while Dorav checked and rechecked his subterranean charts, the band managed to merge their collective knowledge to determine the tunnel the trolls must have used. It was mid-morning by the time they were ready to set out, and the rising sun was warming the forest...a bit too quickly for Joseph's taste.

"If we don't return," he told Kaillĕ, "you need to pack up your clan and get out of here while you can."

"Don't say that," Kaillĕ argued, her eyes bright with tears that didn't flow. "You have to come back."

It was with a deep ache that Joseph separated from

Kaillë's embrace and turned toward the trees, passing Tal'onë as he did. He glanced over his shoulder to ensure Kaillë was out of earshot before speaking in low tones to the captain. "If the worst does happen," he said, "see she gets to safety. Promise me that."

Tal'onë nodded then Joseph left him behind as well and moved to where Tes'sael was marshalling the picked force that would accompany Joseph and Dorav to the tunnel mouth.

"Are you certain you're rested enough for this?" Joseph asked Tes'sael.

"I'll have to be," the elf replied. "Tal'onë and Tes'voran will be too sorely needed here if we fail. Besides, I've slept long enough. Are you ready to move out, Joseph?"

Joseph looked to Dorav, and the dwarf grunted his assent. Tes'sael made a motion to two owl-riders that sent them scouting aloft in a downdraft of buffeting wings, then the band set off into the trees.

With Dorav along, the going was slower than Joseph would have liked, but he needed the dwarf's knowledge of stonecraft to block the tunnel, especially as the Windriders were painfully light on tools. The hunter brought the dogs along as well to alert the band to any strange scents, and Stitch barely left Dorav's side. The dwarf often complained about the dog being too close and getting in his way, but Joseph noticed the old rover dropping his hand to scratch behind Stitch's ears when he thought nobody was looking.

It was midday when the band reached the tunnel mouth. The owl riders had reported nothing unusual, but Joseph was cautious as he led his company on their final approach. He sent the riders to trees farther up the slope to keep watch and fly back to the village with warning if anything should go wrong. Dorav he kept in the cover of a thicket with Tes'sael and another elf guarding him, his ability to work the stone making him the only indispensable member of their mission. Joseph crept forward with the six remaining elves, peering into the shadows of the tunnel; Yowler was next to him, sniffing the air and ground but not showing any alarm. Joseph spotted some scat that matched no natural creatures of his forest, giving him confidence the trolls indeed had come this way, but by Yowler's lack of reaction, he hoped they had retreated as the cold descended and were nowhere near. Still, the day grew warmer, and he resisted the urge to doff his cloak as much for wishful thinking as anything else.

At last they reached the shadows under the tunnel, and Joseph motioned for the elf to his right to light a torch. The orange glow drove back the darkness, and Joseph saw a few fresh bones gnawed too clean even to stink, but otherwise the tunnel was deserted. A motion to another elf sent the scout hustling noiselessly back to the trees, bringing Dorav and the rest of the band to their side a moment later. The dwarf spoke no words before setting to his work, placing an ear against the stone wall before tapping it with a hammer, then creasing his forehead in thought before moving to another spot and repeating the process. This was interspersed with running back and forth from the tunnel to the overhead slope with a string that was knotted at regular intervals and wrapped around a stone cylinder, about the size of a hand drum, with a spiral groove and dwarven characters marking each turn. Before the first trip he motioned the closest elf over to the spot where he was standing and pressed the free end of the string into the elf's hand with an order to "hold the dumb end." On future trips he would just point to an elf with the measuring device and expect to be understood. Finally, after marking several locations on the slope overhead with his chisel, Dorav ordered some of the elves to boost him up to the tunnel roof, which took more of them than he seemed to think right, then repeated his hammer soundings on the ceiling.

Satisfied, he returned to the outside slope, measured an offset from each of his prior marks, and marked the new location.

"Alright," he said, pulling a long, steel gouge from the side of his pack, "who's got a decent mallet?"

One of the elves stepped forward with a large, wooden hammer.

"Give that to Joseph," the dwarf grunted. "You're too damn small."

"They're stronger than they look," Joseph assured the dwarf.

"Stronger than you?"

"...No."

"Then get over there and start pounding. I need a channel running from the mark on that far end to the one over here, passing through each of the ones in between. That's the new marks, mind, the old ones were just for setup."

"How deep?" Joseph asked.

"'Bout a hand-span. The rest of you lot, find some good clay soil and start making piles next to the trench. Understand?"

Tes'sael translated for about half the band whose human speech was still rudimentary, then they all set to their work, Dorav using hammer and chisel to start at the nearer mark with the intention of meeting Joseph in the middle.

The going was slow for Joseph, but Dorav's arms and tools chewed through the stone like a hungry wolf chewing through tallow. He met up with Joseph's trench only a quarter of the way from Joseph's end, finishing triple the work of the human in the hour they had both spent. Joseph wiped his brow, his cloak long since discarded, and shook his head in amazement at the dwarf's speed. "I suspected you were stronger than I," Joseph said, catching his breath, "but I hadn't thought so much stronger."

Dorav eyed the sides of Joseph's narrow trench. "I'm not sure it's a matter of strength. I've been working with stone my whole life, after all, and...well, you seem to be working *against* it."

Joseph was expert enough in his own craft to understand precisely what Dorav meant, but as for applying it to the unyielding stone he'd been sweating over for the last hour, he had no idea.

Dorav paced over to his pack, a few feet from the far end of the new channel, and put away his tools then removed a coil of rope, or at least something that looked rope-like. Unraveling the coil, the dwarf counted off a number of turns that looked to Joseph to about match the length of their trench. As he looked more closely, the hunter realized what he had first taken for rope was actually a fine mesh of something like wool, with crabapple-sized bulges every hand-span or so down its length.

"What's that?" Joseph asked.

"Blast rope," Dorav answered. "Each bulb is a little charge, all with staggered fuses so you just light one end of the rope and they all blow at once. 'Course, the longer you're into the coil, the faster you get the 'Boom', so you don't want to lose track of how much you've used. But they're made to a standard length, so it's pretty easy to tell."

Joseph had seen firsthand the dwarves' advanced knowledge of crafts and strictly-structured society during his sojourn there the previous autumn, so nothing Dorav said surprised him, but seeing such precision in action again, he couldn't help but admire it. Living in that kind of culture would have smothered Joseph nearly to death, but he respected it for its own merits.

Starting at his end of the trench with the freshest-cut end of his blast rope, Dorav laid the explosive into the newly dug seam of stone. Once he was a few feet down, he motioned for the surrounding elves to start filling the trench with the clay soil they'd prepared. "Pack that down good, now," he instructed. "The better the pack, the more force will—"

Yowler, standing nearby, was pawing at the ground, and Stitch, nearer the cave mouth, let loose a throaty, growling bark.

"Stay here!" Joseph ordered the detail he had left to guard Dorav before approaching the cave. He motioned for the rest to follow, unslinging his bow, which he'd kept strung all day.

Joseph and the elves bounded down the slope to the tunnel mouth, peering into the dark. The sun was only a little past its zenith, lighting but a few feet into the westward-facing cave. Joseph saw that the elf to his left was lighting a torch, and as soon as it was burning well he took it and heaved it into the darkness. The elves gasped and cursed at what it revealed.

Seething from the deeper reaches of the caverns were half a dozen trolls scrabbling abreast up the tunnel, and behind them half a dozen more, and a like number beyond that, farther back than the torch could show. Their black fur seemed to catch and hoard the meager light, bringing the darkness with them from the depths; their bat-like noses and ears flared in recognition of nearby food.

"Eyes and throats!" Joseph ordered in elven as he stretched his bow. A handful of arrows hissed out on either side of Joseph, and trolls fell screaming to be trampled by the ranks behind.

"Blow the tunnel, Dorav!" Joseph shouted up the slope. "Blow it now!"

If the dwarf replied, Joseph did not hear it as he loosed arrows at the trolls in lightning succession. The elves Joseph had selected were the best in the camp; one or two even rivaled his own skill with the bow. Trolls fell in waves, arrows sticking out from their faces, but there always seemed to be more to replace them, and Joseph's quiver was getting light.

Still, Joseph noticed the onslaught was slowing. With each rank of dead trolls to climb over, the rest seemed more reluctant to charge forward; it was the only hint of reason Joseph had ever seen in them. In another few moments the mob had halted altogether, milling about as if waiting. The archers, eager to conserve what arrows they could, stopped their counter-attack.

"Half a minute more, Joseph," the hunter heard Tes'sael shout in the elven tongue. Joseph eyed the rippling trollish mob and gritted his teeth.

"On my mark," Joseph growled, pulling a shaft from his quiver and nocking it to his bowstring. He had only four or five arrows more. He raised his bow and took aim. "Stretch!"

The line of archers pulled their bows, loosing at the end of their reach. At this less frenetic pace, every arrow found its mark, and seven trolls fell dead. The horde pulled back a little. Joseph gave the order to repeat the salvo, but even as arrows were drawn, a path opened in the crowd of trolls and a tall figure strode into the torchlight. Ragged, purple robes hung from his frame; the hair was missing from the right half of his head, replaced with a shiny burn scar, and a black eyepatch hid his right eye. His lips were pulled back in a wolfish grin as his one-eyed gaze pinned Joseph.

Joseph's jaw hung agape, for the thing standing before him could not be. The man he saw was dead, killed, more or less, by Joseph's own hand. Yet the eye, the grin, the robes were all unmistakable: Baron Turov, murderer of the Windrider elves, thief of the Hoard of Dalviir, and sent by Joseph to his inevitable death at the fiery bottom of the dwarven Well more than six months ago.

Turov, if indeed the thing was him, reached to his face and tore off the eyepatch, revealing an empty socket underneath, the blackness of its depths seeming to reach back forever, broken only by a single point of bilious, pallid light in its center. Revealing that light seemed to dispel some sort of glamor that masked the baron's true face to reveal a grinning death's head, cracked and charred as by intense heat. The wan twinkle flared into a hideous green flame, and suddenly the bow fell from Joseph's hand as his arms went numb. He gasped for breath, but his ribs were being squeezed as by cords of steel, letting no air in. The sensation of constriction inched upward to his throat; the hunter scrabbled meekly at his neck with enfeebled arms, but there was nothing tangible to pull away. Seeing his distress, elves launched arrows with renewed vigor, but those striking the Baron seemed to do no harm, drawing only a hideous cackle from his immolated face, and the trolls surged forward once more.

All the elves dropped their bows and drew long knives or axes; the four nearest Joseph stepped forward to protect him as he dropped to his knees, his lungs burning, while the other two leapt forward, hurling themselves into the seething, black horde. Joseph tried to scream for them to stop, but he could no more force his voice out than he could draw air in.

Suddenly a low *whumpf* sounded from the stone overhead, and a shower of small rocks and dust rained down on the melee, not heavy enough to obscure the sight of one of the elves being slashed across the face with ragged claws while another, his arms pinned by two trolls, had his throat ripped out by the razor maw of a third. Barely a moment later, a series of piercing cracks sounded from the stone, followed by a shake and rumble as the whole hillside slid down on the cavern, burying troll and elf and revenant alike. The last thing Joseph saw before a massive stone slab blocked the cave mouth was the sickly flame of the Baron's eye, and even after Joseph's breath returned in a *whoosh* and silence settled over the forest, he could still hear that awful cackling in his mind. Whatever vile craft preserved the Baron from the hellish flames of the deepest earth, Joseph knew a few tons of rock would give it no pause. The contradiction was impossible to reconcile, but he couldn't deny the facts: Baron Turov was surely dead, and just as surely walked the earth once more.

Chapter Seven: Hospitality

$\mathfrak{R}$ook's journey to the mountain forests took more than four days, first heading south from Onderburg on river barges. Rook had not forgotten her days helping Adler as a street performer, so between busking for coins and occasional help from the necklace, brokering passage was easy. The barges ran day and night with the current, and after three days she was more or less parallel with the place she'd last encountered Joseph and his elves. She jumped ship at the next stop and struck out overland, sticking to a road that headed east for a day to a village in the foothills where hunters, loggers, and millers lived or crossed paths. There she purchased or otherwise appropriated the supplies she would need for the two day upstream trek to the pass where Baron Turov's keep stood, where she'd spent unhappy time in the Baron's dungeons the autumn before, after his double-cross. Somewhere between the village and the keep she hoped to find signs of the Windriders; she knew they had abandoned their previous village, and where they were now she had no clear idea, though she assumed they had not gone far.

Luck was on Rook's side even before she left the village, for while taking some salt pork from a tavern on the main road she overheard a group of trappers warning friends of a danger in the upslope woods. They in turn had been given this warning by an elf Rook thought matched the Windriders' description perfectly. Leaving the tavern with her prize of cured meat, she returned by the front way and plied the men with liquor and feminine wiles until they were willing to divulge details of their trapping grounds, even to a stranger.

Rook left the tavern feeling proud she had achieved her aims without using the necklace, though a deeper part of her itched to wear it again. Early in her trip she had come even to rely on it, and each time she used it she felt more comfortable in the doing, but the longer the journey ran, the more she grew sure she was being watched. On the barges, quiet men in corners seemed to keep their eyes on her too long. Even in the solitude of her walk to the village, in the long shadows of dawn and dusk she would swear to a dark form paralleling her movements at the edge of her vision, but when she turned to look it was gone. Once she even left her path to investigate but found nothing. Still, if she hadn't managed to shake off pursuit, then the more she kept the artifact hidden, the better. The following morning she began her hike into the forest.

Within a couple hours of dawn, Rook had entered the fringes of the wood. Buds were beginning to open on the trees, and the scent of spring was in the air, the smells of wet earth and fresh-flowing sap and growing things. Rook breathed in the fragrance, so much cleaner then the pungency of close habitation she was used to in the city. She knew life in the wilds would never be for her, but it was refreshing to visit now and again. Still, the cover in the forest was deep for those who knew how to use it, and she didn't. If her pursuers were skilled enough...

Around midday Rook's ears and heart were pounded by a sudden shout, the voice clear but hard. "Stop there!"

She stopped, one hand moving for her dagger even as the other went outward in a warding gesture. In another heartbeat she mastered her surprise and took her hand off the weapon's pommel, raising it likewise until both hands were held out at either side. She looked around but could see no owner of the voice that had called. "Who's there?" she asked.

"I will ask the questions, for now," the voice replied. Hearing it again, Rook knew it was ahead on the trail, not behind, and possibly up in the trees, but she could still make out no speaker. "It is not our way to be suspicious with travelers," the voice continued. "Usually we leave them to their business. But we are beset by enemies and must be cautious."

"I am not your enemy," Rook answered. "If you're who I think, then I have met only a few of you, and after I did we parted in peace."

"Who are you?"

"My name is Rook. I am a friend to Joseph and Kaillë of the Windriders." Rook heard murmurs from the trees to her right and left, but the voice gave a sharp command in the elven tongue and the murmurs stopped.

"Can you prove this?" the voice asked.

Rook considered for a moment. "Not really. I can tell the story of my time with your people, but I could have heard it from the real Rook. Or I could give you something to show to the ones who know me, but I could have taken it from the real Rook. Apart from Joseph and Kaillë, I also met Ten'daren, Ten'sael and Ten'vahlë. Any of them could vouch for me."

Another voice sounded from Rook's left, no quiet murmur this time but a clear call, once again in elven.

"Who are the men following you?" called the first voice.

"Damn," Rook hissed. "I didn't mean to lead them here, I swear."

"You'll lead them no farther!"

Rook turned to run, but instead of arrows whistling past or, as she knew was much more likely, *into* her, a net dropped onto her from tree branches above. She struggled for but a moment before its edges were drawn up, and in the next moment she was pulled upward swinging and twisting as she surged into the air in a downdraft of wind. Within seconds she was above the canopy, watching the upper leaves of the trees skim by beneath her. She was curled up and face down in the net; she could not see above her to know how she was being made to fly through the air, and though she had the dexterity to move herself so she could see, she feared any such motion might send her tumbling back to the earth and her certain death, or at least certain fracturing. "Please, set me down," she cried. "By all the gods and fates and powers, set me down!"

A moment later and the face of an elf was looking up at her from scant inches below. Her flight had smoothed out considerably, and the elf matched speed and position with her perfectly from the back of a giant bird, an owl by the look of it. She had overheard conversations of such things during her time with the elves, but she'd never actually seen one, and it took her breath.

"These men following you," the elf shouted over the wind in her ears, and Rook knew it was the same voice she had heard on the ground, "are they evil men?"

Rook knew a word from her would end all her trouble with being followed. The Wolfsguard, for she was sure it was they, might be masters in Onderburg, and while she suspected they had talent even in the wilds, they could be no match for the stealth and archery of the Windriders. For a moment fear and anger roiled within her and she considered giving that word. Nevertheless, she wouldn't have their deaths on her hands if it could be avoided. "Ruthless," she said, "and dangerous to their master's enemies. But not evil, no."

The elf nodded once and then banked away, his owl tucking its wings as it slipped back beneath the upper canopy.

~ * ~

Rook lost all sense of time as she flew through the air in her net, but at last she was set down, and when she rolled onto her back in the now-slack mesh, she saw the sun and figured her ordeal had been less than an hour. There were elves gathered all around, and it seemed someone had come ahead to warn them of her arrival, because before she could even stand, a familiar voice said, "Yes, that's her." The tone was not entirely complimentary.

"Kaillë," Rook called, turning to locate the Windrider chieftain. "It's so good to hear your voice. I need your help."

"Really? I'm so surprised to hear it." Kaillë didn't use sarcasm often, but when she did it was scathing.

Rook went on the defensive. "Maybe you've forgotten. I was promised one stone of the Hoard of Dalviir last autumn. Did you deliver? You *owe* me."

A strong-looking elf stepped forward from the encircling crowd and looked Rook level in the eye. "Do not speak to our chieftain that way again. We know very well the tale of your quest. You played as much a part in the losing of the stones as the finding of them. You must decide if you are here to ask for help or demand it."

Humility did not come easily to Rook. Her eyes scanned the faces around her, but not one was friendly. And one was missing. "Where is Joseph?"

"Away for the time being," Kaillë answered. "Tell us what you want...and what kind of trouble you've gotten yourself into in order to get it."

Now Rook eased. She was disappointed not to deal with Joseph, but she knew elves were straightforward in their speech. Kaillë wouldn't ask what Rook wanted if she'd already made her mind up to refuse. "I just need you to read a book for me, that's all. It's in the same language Dalviir used in his messages."

"Why come here?" Kaillë asked. "It's a long journey to get a service you could have contracted for in your home. There are many scholars in the city, I understand."

"Many. I can't trust a one of them."

"And you trust me?" Kaillë asked.

Rook's eyes went to the ground. "Until my brother can walk again, I can't forgive the loss of the Hoard," she said, her voice thick, "but under the circumstances you treated me fairly. You've given me no reason to doubt your honesty."

Kaillë laughed. It was not a kind laugh. "You value honesty, then? You might try using some of your own. I know you haven't lied, but that's not the same as being really truthful, is it? You 'just' need me to read a book? Why are men following you? Where did you get this book you need me to read?"

Rook's eyes smoldered. Her hand went to her belt pouch as she felt tempted to use the necklace to get what she wanted, but she had no idea how the other elves would react if their chieftain suddenly began acting differently. "I stole it," she finally spat. "Is that what you wanted to hear? The men following me want it back. That's not so surprising, but they're agents of the king himself, and they've had one man killed already and meant to do the same to me to retrieve it, but they didn't. Or at least they haven't yet. That much bears some more explaining, and I need somebody who can read the damn thing in the first place to make even a guess. I got nothing else to say. Look down your nose at me all you want, but I ain't done you any wrong, so either help me or let me go to find someone who will." In her frustration Rook's cultivated diction slipped back into the unrefined dialect of the streets of her upbringing.

Rook continued to glare at Kaillë, and indeed the elf's expression was haughty for another moment before suddenly it softened. "Of course we'll help you, Rook."

The strong elf stepped out from between the pair, and the gathered crowd began to disperse.

"Please forgive my rudeness," Kaillë continued in private tones, "you came here in good faith, and I have no right to judge you. The moment I saw your face again, I just...I found myself sparring in a match long over."

Rook looked down at Kaillë with a glimmer in her eye. "And a match I never stood much chance in if you mean what I think you do. You mean Joseph."

Kaillë opened her mouth as if to say something, then closed it and nodded quickly as though she was nervous.

Rook caught something in her manner and laughed a raucous, unladylike laugh. "You really have won that match, haven't you? Out, out, out with it, princess, tell us longing losers what the big man is like when he's at home."

Rook's euphemism was obviously transparent even to Kaillë, for the elf blushed scarlet from the bottom of her chin to the tips of her upswept ears, elven stoicism be damned. Rook laughed again. "*That* was worth the trip. But I suppose we'd best get down to our business so we can each get back to our own."

Kaillë nodded and led Rook to a sheltered place where she could read.

~ * ~

The translation went slower than Rook liked. Kaillë explained the book was written in a high style that defied easy reading. Moreover, unlike the straightforward instructions they had read in their quest last year, this book was a form of epic poem, riddled with idiomatic expressions and cultural references that didn't easily yield up their true meaning. After the better part of the afternoon, Kaillë had managed only a few pages and a partial translation of a few more. She then took her leave from Rook and explained that her regular duties would prevent any more work on the text that day.

Rook thanked Kaillë and sat with her back against a tree on the village edge. She was frustrated at the slow progress and Kaillë's departure, but she swallowed her tongue. She had come to the Windriders hat in hand, after all, and offending them would solve nothing. Worse still, her experience with Pockmark Charlie had highlighted how easily her associates in the city would play her false if their backs were against the wall. With a sinking sense of self-loathing that drove her to a brusque, sardonic chuckle, she realized Kaillë Windsong might be the closest thing she had to a real friend.

In answer to her laugh, Rook heard someone clear their throat to her left. Looking in that direction, she saw three elven women standing at a slight remove, a younger woman in front and two older behind and at either side. Two bore trays while the third held a pitcher and wooden tumbler.

"My name is Onahnë," the lead elf said. "Our chieftain explained that your errand here may take several days, and you are welcome to stay in my home while you are with us. We've also brought food and water for you."

"Oh," Rook said, standing and brushing the dirt off her

pants while she mastered her surprise. "I have a little silver I can spare..."

The two elder elves' eyes remained kind but vacant, leaving Rook to suspect they didn't understand the language, but Onahnë smiled. "We have no use for your metal coins here, Rook. Even if we did, we would not accept them. We are glad to provide for your needs for as long as you remain our guest."

"I...I mean, thank you," Rook said, taking one of the trays and setting it down on the grass. Such rustic hospitality gave Rook pause. There were few in the city that would give to a stranger without expectation of something in return, but here she was given help and food and lodging, even though her benefactors knew at the outset she had nothing they valued. The other old elf set down her tray, then they both nodded and took their leave, but Onahnë with her pitcher lingered for a moment. Rook surveyed the fare set out before her, simple but plentiful. "There's more than enough here for me," she said. "Could you, I mean...would you care to join me?"

Onahnë cocked her head to one side as though pondering the question, one that a human would have anticipated and been prepared to decline with an appropriate excuse if they didn't wish to stay. After a long moment Onahnë replied, "I think I would like that."

She sat, and the two ate the meal together.

~ * ~

Joseph allowed himself only a few minutes to catch his breath and ensure his ribs weren't broken before insisting they press onward. He trusted Dorav's stonecraft as far as it went, but he had no idea if the Baron could be kept down by such a rockslide, and even if he could, Joseph had no desire to remain in the place of carnage. The hunter pushed the team two miles north before allowing a brief rest.

As Joseph sat with his back against a tree, Dorav ambled over and bumped down next to him. "Most of the boys are talking in that elfish talk, but I picked up a thing or two. That Baron Turov fellah, you say he was alive and walking?"

"I don't know about alive," Joseph answered, "but he was upright, and he seemed to be commanding the trolls."

"Bah," the rover protested, "now I know something's gone fault-slipped. Alive, dead, Baron, or badger, nobody and nothing *commands* trolls."

"I wish you were right, Dorav, but I know what I saw. Maybe he survived the fall somehow, used the power of the Hoard to keep himself alive, I don't know."

"Power of the Hoard," the dwarf scoffed. "Magic again? I may not be as close-minded as a lot of my kin—a man goes roving the tunnels and sees a lot more of the world than the elders and their type locked up in debates in high towers—but magic? Surface-dwellers use that excuse for everything."

"How do you explain it, then? What did I see?"

"Peering into a dark tunnel with the sun overhead, pack of seething trolls coming up out of it. A man might see all kinds of things in that blackness. I've seen some things myself in the dim light, but the sounds and smells never turned anything up. Just part of life in the tunnels."

Joseph allowed himself the luxury of doubt for just a moment, replaying the scene in his head, the inky ranks of trolls and the appearance of the Baron in his robes, the growing surge of power in that horrible, sickly light. Joseph shuddered. "I know what I saw," he concluded.

"Alright, so you saw it," Dorav assented. "Doesn't mean much now. My people never did know what was at the bottom of the Well, so there must be something the Baron used to survive and escape. But we just buried him under half a hill's worth of rock. Even if he survived, he ain't getting out again."

Joseph looked over at the dwarf. "You know this doesn't change anything, don't you? I'm still leading you to the Tenth Clan, just like I promised."

"I do know that, Joseph," Dorav replied, and that's just exactly why I'm trying to ease your mind about what you're leaving your people in the middle of while you're gone."

"You're doing an awful job," Joseph quipped without thinking.

"Well, I never said it was a specialty," the dwarf said, rising and brushing dust off the back of his pants. "I'll rouse the rest of the troupe. I assume you'll want to be moving them out soon."

"You assume right. The sooner I get you where you're going, the sooner I can get back h...the sooner I can get back."

~ * ~

The next morning, Rook awoke to the sound of someone knocking on Onahnë's door. "Rook," Kaillë's voice came through the thin panels, "are you awake? I can spare a few hours if you want to get back to the book."

Rook jumped up from the pallet of furs Onahnë had made up for her. "Yes, I'm awake. Time we got back to work."

Once outside, she asked Kaillë, "Where is Onahnë? She wasn't inside just now."

Kaillë laughed. "Off attending to her duties, I expect. She's been up for hours, Rook. The sun is high, and the morning wears on."

"Sorry," Rook mumbled, feeling stupid.

"Your apology isn't needed," Kaillë responded. "You

are ignorant of our ways, just as we would be ignorant of yours if we were visiting you in the city. Of the two, I suspect you will acclimate the more quickly.

"So, though we didn't accomplish much, let's review what we read yesterday," Kaillë continued as they walked to their previous spot under a tree by the stream. "The book began describing the earliest creation of the world, the separation of the land into different races and tribes of men, and how those tribes became jealous of one another's resources and began to build weapons and practice warfare."

"Certainly nothing worth stealing, much less killing over," Rook said.

"Not as yet," Kaillë agreed, sitting down beneath the tree. "Let's continue."

They worked for the best part of an hour, barring two interruptions by elves asking Kaillë questions, and Kaillë's speed was picking up somewhat as she became more familiar with the style of writing. Still, during that time Rook was struck more than anything by a sense of her own uselessness. One idiom that was easier to understand for one accustomed to city life was all Rook contributed to the project in the entire hour, and she suspected her hanging around distracted Kaillë's focus far beyond what that meager tidbit had provided. Rook had planned to get the translation, or enough of it to understand her present circumstances, and get back out just as quickly. She had many times in her life accepted a coin or a crust, but she had never been the recipient of ongoing hospitality, and to look people in the eye from whom she was receiving charity grated on her sense of self-reliance.

"I'm not really helping here, am I?" Rook said with a huff.

Kaillë looked up at her. "Not very much," she answered, her tone neutral.

Rook bristled at the bluntness before remembering that

she was talking to an elf. "Is there something I could be doing? I'd rather be useful than sit around bored."

Kaillë's eyes returned to the book. "We don't have any vault locks to pick if that's what you mean."

Rook shouted back, affronted. "Like that's all I'm good for? I'm not a thief!"

Kaillë looked up and cocked an eyebrow.

"Alright," Rook relented, "so I am a thief, by definition anyhow, but you know why I do it. It isn't the life I'd choose if things were different."

"What is?"

Rook started to answer then instead she paused, unfastening her dagger belt and dropping them to the ground. With that, she launched into a series of flips and handsprings that carried her past Kaillë, almost to the stream. She flipped her legs forward over her head and walked back to the Chieftain on her hands, then bounded into the tree's lower branches before dropping down with a flip directly in front of Kaillë, landing in an elegant bow. A few elves passing by within sight of the display stopped and offered applause before going about their way.

Kaillë was smiling. "Impressive, Rook. You must have been quite a prize to your troupe before your brother's injury."

"I was getting there," the girl responded.

"Alright," Kaillë said. "I don't know that we have an immediate need for an acrobat, but find anyone going about their tasks. If they speak your tongue, they'll give you something to do. Tell them I said so; we don't normally ask guests to work for their keep."

Rook had never been called "shy" in her life, but she was strangely self-conscious about approaching any of the strange Windriders and asking them to show her a task where she could contribute. Fortunately, in only a few minutes she saw Onahnë moving across the green, and the human hustled over to intercept her.

"Good morning, Onahnë," Rook said.

"Hello, Rook. How does your work with Kaillë go?"

"Um, well enough, but I'm no help. I asked if I could be useful someplace else, and Kaillë said I could ask someone to put me to work."

"Alright," Onahnë replied. "I have a little more packing to do. You can help."

"Packing?" Rook asked as she followed the young elf. "Are you going somewhere?"

"No." Onahnë offered no additional information, so Rook stayed silent until they reached the house. Once there, Onahnë put Rook to work climbing on a small stool to reach a number of tools and short spears that were stored on high pegs. Rook looked down as she worked and saw Onahnë moving the contents of a wooden chest into a wicker basket; they were clothes, too large for her and appearing by cut and style to be for a man.

"Do those belong to your husband?" Rook asked.

"They did."

Rook took Onahnë's point, but now that she had opened the subject, it felt ruder to leave it than to continue. "What happened?"

"He was killed a few days ago."

"I'm so sorry," Rook answered, taken aback. She had recognized the man must have died but assumed much more time had passed. "How did...? Never mind."

"It's alright. There are vile creatures that live underground, trolls."

"I'm familiar with them, at least by reputation," Rook said. She had been fortunate enough not to cross paths with any during her subterranean sojourn, but she knew by stories how awful they were.

"Of course," Onahnë continued. "Something happened underground, something that made the trolls come up here.

My husband was the first casualty. Well, above ground, that is. Before they reached the surface, it seems they sacked the nearest dwarven city."

Rook's shock was redoubled by the thought of the beautiful Streets of Twilight overrun by trolls, but she kept her focus on the more immediate tragedy of the woman right in front of her. "You must be in such pain."

"I was, for a time, and at whiles I expect I will be again. But all things in this life are temporary. I will treasure the time I had with Ten'vohnë, and I will sing his song at our campfires. I may wed again, and if I do not, the clan will care for me just as I support it. I could keep these things of his, but I choose to pass them on. I have no use for them, and others will."

Rook stepped down from the stool, her arm's laden with Ten'vohnë's tools and weapons.

"You just move on?" Rook asked. "Accept things as they are?"

"What else can I do? 'Who remembers the past builds foundations for the future, but who clings to it makes it a binding chain.' Ten'vohnë would not want that for me any more than I want it for myself."

Rook's brow was creased as she set down her burden on top of the wicker basket.

"Did something I said upset you?" Onahnë asked.

"No," Rook answered, shaking her head and smiling. "No, I'm fine. Let's take these to...to wherever you were taking them."

~ * ~

Rook learned many other things that day. She learned the extent of the troll threat and of Dorav's emergence. She learned how to clean fish and small game, how to mend nets and scrape the hair off a deerskin. She was terrible at all of it, but she never gave up at anything she was shown, and though by the end of the day she had produced more laughter than anything else, the elves welcomed her help.

Kaillë found Rook resting on the green at the end of the day to give an update on what she had learned. Once again, she hadn't the luxury of a full day's work on the project, but the time she'd spent had been fruitful.

"The story continued," she told Rook, "explaining some entity, a being or force of will, that was attracted to the bloodshed of men. It fed off their hate and misery, and once made aware of the existence of mankind, it stayed always among them, advocating for war. At first it appeared in the form of a man, offering arguments in favor of conflict or shaming peacemakers among the tribes as cowards. As time passed, the being shed this guise more and more often and invaded the minds of men, whispering words of lust for power and blood and planting the seeds of war. That's as far as I got today. Does this tell you anything about the danger of this book?"

"I hope not," Rook answered, her face concerned. "Fighting has been boiling among the northern kingdoms. It's bad enough as it is, but I would hate to think of it happening because of this...force. If that was the reason, how would the war ever end?"

"We hadn't heard of this strife. We don't go out of our way for news of the outside lands, and little of it ever finds its way here of its own accord. It points to a connection between the past the book is explaining and the present desire for it, though. Enough to keep reading."

Rook agreed, but the day's work had tired her. Kaillë also was ready to retire, so they went their separate ways. Kaillë left Rook with a promise to bring news the moment she translated anything more of note.

~ * ~

Joseph and his band had trekked northward for the last few hours of light after their confrontation with Baron Turov, then for all of the following day, and so far there were no signs of pursuit. Their quivers were refilled from bundles of arrows packed in the supplies, and they did not unstring their bows. As they went they also moved to higher elevations where cover was sparser, so Joseph felt confident in one owl's ability to scout from the air. In the afternoon he sent the second back with its rider, Ten'toma, to the village to report on the situation: the loss of two elves at the cave, the rest of the group's continued safety, and, most importantly, Baron Turov's infernal rise.

As the owl winged away, Joseph made a silent prayer that Kaillë and the village were still safe.

Chapter Eight: Western Front

The next morning, Rook awoke at the first sounds of Onahnë stirring in the cottage. "Good morning, Onahnë," she said from the floor, stretching her stiff muscles.

"Rook," Onahnë answered, "you're up early this morning. Good day to you too." The elf opened her shutters, letting dawn light and air into the house. She turned to Rook. "You are small for a human?"

"Yes," Rook answered, already growing accustomed to elven frankness and learning not to read judgment into it.

"I thought so. I think we are close enough in size that some of my larger clothes might fit you. If you like, I can loan you some for a day, and we can give your garments to the washer women to be cleaned in the stream."

"Are you saying I stink?" Rook asked.

"You had a long journey here," Onahnë replied, skirting the line between frankness and rudeness, "and I suspect spare clothes were a luxury you couldn't afford when you packed."

"That's true enough," Rook agreed. "Let's see what you have."

Rook was quite petit, so Onahnë's clothes were short on her, but not snug. She chose a pair of light blue pants that hung to her mid-calf and a maroon shift that fit her like a long shirt.

"Come on," Onahnë said after Rook had changed, "after seeing you bounding through the air yesterday, some of us got together and arranged a special treat."

"What is it?" Rook asked.

"Just come on," Onahnë said, taking her by the wrist and pulling her out into the green.

The elf called Tal'onë, who had challenged her when she spoke to Kaillë, was there waiting for her, his expression less stern than she had seen it earlier, though she read in his face that he didn't often smile. "Good morning, Rook," he said. "The women you worked with yesterday tell me you are keen-eyed and clever, though a bit ignorant of their kind of work."

"I was starting to get the hang of it...wasn't I?" Rook looked sidelong at Onahnë.

Before Onahnë could answer, Tal'onë continued. "We have a different assignment for you this morning."

Suddenly, two giant owls landed next to them on the green with flapping crow-hops. An elf dismounted from one, but the other was rider-less. Tal'onë led Rook to this owl, and it nuzzled Tal'onë's hand. He handed it something from a pouch on his belt, and the great bird gobbled it down. "Rook, this is Pinion. He is the oldest owl in our flight. He has not many summers left, I fear, but in the meantime he is a good bird to train our young, calm and easy on his rider. There are few grown humans who are small enough to ride an owl, and even those we do not allow to do so except in the rarest of circumstances. I hope you enjoy this opportunity."

Rooks eyes were wide with fear. "I'm sorry you went to all this trouble, but I couldn't. Flying in that net was horrifying, there's no way..."

Some of Tal'onë's stern aspect returned. "I didn't say I hoped you would come with me, I said I hoped you would enjoy it." A few other elves had gathered around, and Rook felt the pressure of their eyes. Her feet were still on the ground, and already she felt she was freefalling through the sky. She swallowed the lump in her throat and moved to the owl's side, then paused before trying to climb on.

"Does it matter which side?" Rook asked, though she had already chosen the left. She knew nothing about riding any beast, much less a giant owl, but she understood as a matter of common knowledge that many horses would only take a rider from one side.

"Which side?" Tal'onë echoed. "No. Should it?"

"Not as far as I'm concerned."

Tal'onë furrowed his brow in confusion but didn't inquire. "Put your foot in the stirrup, there," he said, pointing.

Rook did as she was told.

"Now take hold of the handles on either side. Good. Be light as you throw your leg over; an owl isn't as sturdy as a land animal."

Rook sprang up as gently as she could, and Pinion didn't seem to notice her weight.

"Now," Tal'onë explained, "you have to pull up the stirrups and hook them on the back of the saddle there so they aren't in the way of his wings. Like that, right. Now lean forward a bit and hook your knees behind the bars on either side."

Rook settled into position, then looked to Tal'onë with unspoken question in her eyes.

The elf nodded in answer. "Quite good for a first timer. Now just hang on. Pinion will do all the work; you're just a passenger on this flight. Understand?"

Rook nodded, her fear still running high. Tal'onë leapt to the saddle of the other owl and made a clucking noise with his tongue. With that, his owl leapt upward and beat his wings, surging up and forward one great flap at a time. Pinion followed.

At first Rook's nervousness dissipated as she rose. Her position in the saddle was far more stable than the net had felt, and the ascent much slower. That trend violently reversed when they cleared the canopy. The trees seemed to spin beneath her, and the sky didn't stay above them where it belonged. Rook's eyes squinted shut against the sense of vertigo so she couldn't see her knuckles turn white from their grip on the saddle.

Perhaps a minute passed, then Rook heard Tal'onë's voice on the wind. "Open your eyes, Rook. You're safe."

Rook marshalled her courage. Heights did not trouble her, or at least they never had. It could only be the owl she feared, handing over control to this creature powerful enough to lift her bodily into the sky. She opened her eyes.

They had perhaps tripled their altitude. The treetops no longer rushed below her, but only rolled gently by in lazy circles as Pinion rode currents of air. Slowly her grip loosened, and Rook allowed herself to look about as Tal'onë led them on a straight path southward. To her left, the mountains spread out next to her. She still flew well below the tree line, but she could look down in wonder into clefts and valleys that ran between peaks, and even the craggy summits still towering above them seemed close enough to reach over and touch, to grab a fistful of the snow that still blanketed their stony heads. North and south the forest ran to either horizon like a river of green. And to the east the plains stretched out like a carpet, vibrant green closest to the forest fading to a dun expanse broken by ribbons of brush where the mountain streams flowed down and watered the dry earth. Rook's eyes were most drawn, however, by the moving shapes in the vault of blue overhead, birds of every kind, and here and there another owl and rider sharing the sky with them, some passing near enough at whiles for her to make out the elf's face, others little more than specks in the distance.

"Tal'onë," Rook called, "how do you keep the owls secret with so many in the air?"

"From the plains they appear as no more than vultures seeking food in the wood below. The canopy hides us from eyes in the forest, save that we do not fly directly over clearings if there has been sign of any strangers about. Our greatest risk of discovery comes from the mountains, but we are aware of the settlements and most common paths and keep our distance. You are right to question what you see, though. We normally keep far fewer in the air, but our present need is great."

Tal'onë led his owl in a steep eastward bank, and Pinion followed, though at a gentler curve. Her fear much reduced, Rook held on and surrendered herself to the thrill of acceleration as Tal'onë conducted his canvas of the area south of the village, sweeping west to east and back again with a southward jog between each pass. At the end of one eastward traverse, Rook thought she spotted movement in the forest fringes to the south, but Tal'onë showed no reaction, so she held her tongue. On their next pass, though, she could still see the brush shaking, now directly below them, as well as a few men moving some fifty yards out into the plain. "Tal'onë," Rook called over the wind in her ears, "what is that?" She pointed.

"Well spotted," the elf replied. "Let's have a closer look." Tal'onë led them on a long, looping path southward, approaching from behind the movement and figures Rook had spotted. The owls were utterly silent, and Rook found herself holding her breath, though she had no cause to believe the people she saw were anything but hunters or trappers from the villages of the flats.

As they moved closer, however, Rook saw that these were not humans at all, but elves, though their gear and attire were quite unlike anything the Windriders carried or wore. Each elf she could see was dressed in armor of hide or boiled leather, scattered with bits of mail or metal bracers. Most had steel caps or helms, and each one wore a simple sword at one hip and some other weapon, usually an ax, at the other. If there were women or children, they must have hidden in the forest fringes, for Rook saw only men. On the whole, she did not like the look of them.

After a few moments' observation, Tal'onë turned back to the west, flying until the band was out of sight, then hastened northward, back to the village.

~ * ~

When they landed, many elves had gathered on the green, and there was a smattering of cheers and applause as Rook dismounted. Her legs wobbled when her feet hit the ground, and only at that moment did she realize how tightly she had gripped the saddle with her knees. Tal'onë smiled and congratulated her on a successful flight, but Rook read the concern behind his eyes, and he rushed away from the crowd as soon as Rook had all their attention.

The morning wasn't yet half gone, and Rook turned her hand once again to whatever tasks she could find to occupy her time. Onahnë pressed her for details of her flight, but Rook restricted her narrative to the general fear and wonder she had experienced and stayed silent about the traveling band they had seen.

Kaillë approached Rook after the midday meal. "I'm sorry, Rook. I've had little time for your book today. After Tal'onë brought news of your sighting, I've spent hours in debate with the council." She sighed.

"Not good?" Rook asked.

"Have you ever *known* hours of debate to be good? No, not good. Half say we must find out what the elves you saw want, but the other half say we shouldn't risk revealing ourselves. To resolve the deadlock, I suggest the only possible compromise: to keep a careful watch and wait. *But* this is seen as a tacit endorsement of the second half, which draws objections from the first, and the whole argument starts over."

Rook pondered for a moment. "What if I could solve your problem? Find out what these traveling elves want?"

"...How?"

"I have ways. I can approach them and learn what I can, then take a roundabout way back. Better still, use an owl to get most of the way there. No trail leads them here, in fact nothing even hints to them that you exist, and if their intentions are good, then my suspicion won't reflect on the Windriders when eventually you meet them."

"And if their intentions aren't good?" Kaillë rebutted. "This could be very dangerous, Rook."

"I'm not worried. Besides, I don't intend to be beholden for all your hospitality, and I'm not good enough at normal things to earn my keep by gutting fish or skinning rabbits. *This*, I can do."

"You don't need to pay us back for—"

"Oh, yes I do."

Kaillë was silent for a few heartbeats. "In truth, your help would be an asset. Certainly it would break the deadlock in the council."

"So you could get back to my book."

Kaillë smiled. "Potentially."

"So we both win."

"Very well. I will give orders for Pinion to be saddled again and an elf to guide you there and back."

~ * ~

Tes'voran volunteered for the assignment, allowing Tal'onë to resume coordinating the patrols and receiving reports while still providing Rook an expert guide. In less than two hours they had approached the strange elven band and landed the owls in deep cover. Tes'voran helped Rook down to the lower branches of their tree then remained as Rook dropped to the ground and began the mile-long trek to the north. She waited until Tes'voran was out of sight before donning the necklace. As soon as its cool metal touched her skin, she felt a rush move through her body that matched the anticipation in her heart. She had missed the sensation over the last few days, the intoxicating power of command.

Rook knew there was no way she would see the elves before they saw her, so she used no stealth, leaving the heavy brush for the sparser cover at the edge of the plain. Soon she had overtaken the position of a few of the skirmishers she had seen from the air, spotting them as they took a brief halt in a grove of silver maple, a last gasp of the forest before it yielded completely to the rolling grasses.

As Rook approached, she heard a bird call in the trees. Certainly she hadn't the experience to differentiate a true call from that of a skilled mimic, but the only other sound had been wind rustling through the brush, so the whistle alerted even Rook that she had been spotted. When at last she entered the ring of trees, she found a half-dozen armed elves waiting for her. None showed open hostility, but her eye noted their swords were loose in their scabbards.

For good measure, Rook met each of their eyes before saying, "Everybody just be calm. No need for weapons."

The elves visibly relaxed their stances. "Who are you?" one asked.

"Just a traveler," Rook answered. "And yourselves?"

"We're the Blood Clan," the same elf replied.

"Where do you come from?"

"South of here," answered a different elf. "Across the river."

Rook heard rustling in the treetops above and behind her. "Order your men to come down," she said to the biggest and best armed of the elves.

"I don't take orders, girl, I give 'em out," came a voice from overhead. Rook knew then she had made a miscalculation, potentially a grave one. It hadn't occurred to her a leader might be keeping watch in the trees while his men took their ease. She had no firm notion of the necklace's power. Would it work against so many underlings if they were given conflicting orders from one in authority? Her previous uses of the necklace had suggested she needed at least some form of rapport with her target for the power to work, direct eye contact or enough prior conversation to engross the subject in her words. The best plan was to get her eyes on the leader and dominate him now, but how to do it? If she moved too quickly, he might shoot her, and no doubt he had already noted his men being too accommodating to her brusque questioning.

"My apologies," Rook called over her shoulder, thinking fast. "I thought I was speaking to the man in charge."

"Now you are," the voice in the trees answered.

"You should come down so we can speak face to face." She phrased it as a request, but it was still a gamble.

"No interest in your face, and I'm very happy up here. No need to speak either, for that matter, except to tell you to turn around and go back the way you came."

Damn. In her attempt to get immediate control of the situation she had overplayed her hand, and the leader had ordered her to leave. Even if such an order didn't shake her hold on the elves on the ground, of which she couldn't be confident, she was all but certain there were other elves in the trees who were still beyond her sway. Leaving immediately was no option, though; while she had established the group was militant, she hadn't gained the answers she sought.

"I'm happy to leave," she answered, her eyes on as many elves as she could keep in her field of vision, "but your men want me to stay. Don't you, boys?"

Several of the elves closest to Rook voiced their assent, and the one who had spoken first called back, "Come on, Captain, let her stay. She's just a harmless girl."

"Seems my men are pretty smitten with you, considering you've only just met."

"I make a good first impression," Rook answered, using the flow of conversation as a natural excuse to turn toward the voice in the tree and try to spot him. She was unsurprised when she could not. Still, she had to be gaining more of his focus, more purchase for the necklace to play upon. She just needed to cement his attention. Rook held her arms out to her sides and tilted her shoulders in a playful pose. "What about you? Do you like what you see?"

"I'll admit, it's not often to see a human so trim."

"Then you should probably come down for a closer look."

The elf in the tree was silent. Rook could feel the eyes of the other elves on her, and her heart began to hammer at her ribs. Her tone had been too solicitous; if the necklace failed, she would have dispelled any remaining doubt she was up to some deceit. She heard a rustle in the branches above. If the elf captain meant to shoot her, she couldn't hope to avoid the arrow without seeing the angle or timing of the shot. She sidestepped toward the nearest elf, desperate for any kind of cover.

The elf captain dropped out of the tree, landing in a crouch with his gaze glued on Rook's, and in that moment she knew she had him. "So you give all the orders?" she prodded.

"I do."

Rook dropped her voice to a near whisper. "Order the rest of your elves down for me."

The captain shouted in elven, and three more elves jumped out of the trees at the other three points of the compass.

"So now I know who you are and where you're from," Rook began again. "All I need to know now is why you're here."

"Plunder," the elf said. "Others of our kind are content to grub in the earth for their livelihood, but we take a less miserable path. Others may grub if they will, and we will relieve them of some of their worldly burden."

"You steal even from your own people? From elves, I mean."

"We prefer to when we can. Humans hoard too many worthless things, coins and trinkets of metal."

"Not to mention their men have fifty pounds and a foot of reach on the biggest of you," Rook said, her tone sardonic.

"That has an influence, but we don't like to talk about it."

"So why come plunder up here? Did you kill and steal everything in your own land?"

"The southern tribes, human and elf alike, have broken out into war. We had the best of it for a while then three of our enemies banded together against us. It was flee or die. Rumor has it there are clans here in the northern forests that will be easy pickings."

"How many are you?"

"Of warriors we have five-score and ten. Some women

and children besides.”

Rook had heard enough. “Captain, you will go back to your chieftain and tell him there is nothing here for your people worth the taking. Tell him strange creatures came from underground and the weak clans of the north could not stand against them; everything in the north is eaten or destroyed. Go west or take a pass over the mountains or go back home and take your chances in the wars. There’s nothing here for you.”

“As you wish,” the captain replied, bowing his head.

Rook turned and left the circle of elves and trees. She doubted her sway would hold long enough for the elf captain to reach his chieftain, or that the superior would be deceived in any case, but it was all she could think to try.

~ * ~

The way back to Tes’voran was quicker, and within less than half an hour Rook was at the base of the tree where their owls were hiding. The elf helped her up to the lower boughs then they both started to climb.

“Where did you get that necklace?” Tes’voran asked.

Rook cursed herself under her breath for failing to hide it. “It doesn’t matter,” she said aloud. “Just forget about it.”

“Alright,” the elf replied.

As soon as she knew her command had stuck, she paused in her climb to remove the jewelry and stow it back in her pouch.

“Did you learn anything?” Tes’voran inquired as they mounted their owls.

“Yeah,” Rook answered. She didn’t have the heart to give the lieutenant any more details, and he didn’t ask.

~ * ~

Once back on the village green, Kaillë and Tal'onë were eager for Rook's report. Rook followed the elven leaders to a slight remove from any passing Windriders, and once the others realized privacy was desired, they gave a wider berth. "The danger is real," Rook began as soon as they were out of earshot. "A hundred armed men, and their tribe is built around war and plunder. They call themselves the Blood Clan. Not a very imaginative bunch, I guess, but it gets the point across."

"If they keep their current course," Kaillë speculated, "they'll pass us by on the west, won't they?"

"They've heard there are elves in the area and think you're ripe for pillaging. Unless they've forsaken every shred of elven woodcraft, you'd best assume they'll find you eventually."

"Rook is right," Tal'onë agreed. "We need to start boarding the ground dwellers in the trees, and I'll have to pull back the air patrols."

"I leave it to your expertise," Kaillë said. "Tell me if you need anything from me. Go now. I will report to the council later. Right now I must speak to Rook alone."

"What's wrong?" Rook asked as Tal'onë left.

"What I learn from your book and what I learn from the outside world continue to run together. It troubles me. You already told me of war brewing in the north, and now we hear that things in the south are likewise. Meanwhile, powerful men kill over a book describing a being that fans the flames of war."

Rook shared Kaillë's fear but refused to acknowledge it. "We have no way to be sure the book's story is true, and even if it is, I'm not naïve enough of human nature to think they need some god-like trickster to get into wars with each other. Most likely this is all just a coincidence."

"I hoped so, too, at first, but after what I translated while you were away, I can no longer be so hopeful. I'm familiar enough with the style now to parse through the poetic verse more quickly and get to the relevant knowledge, so I'm neglecting a lot of detail, but here is the sense of it: Over time certain sages learned of the existence of this entity, but they were powerless to oppose it. A cabal was formed, and for generations they worked toward creating a power to destroy the thing. They never succeeded, but in time they did devise a way to bind it, to hold it in a magic prison that would seal away even its influence over men's thought. And bind it they did."

"Alright. What does that have to do with what's happening now?"

"Not what, Rook. Where. They needed a place of power around which to build their cage of magic, and only in such a place could the thing be held. It was the Well, Rook. They trapped it in the Well."

Rook shuddered at the very mention of the place where she had come so close to her death. The last thing she wanted was to speak of it, but Kaillë didn't stop.

"A force of will bent on fomenting warfare is magically imprisoned in a place of magic. We cast into that very place the most powerful collection of magical objects ever created, and just months later every place west of the mountains starts down the path of war. Still believe this is a coincidence?"

Before Rook could answer, an owl dove into the green, unfurling its wings in a hard landing. It's rider leapt from the saddle, jogging to Kaillë and bowing in salute. "Chieftain, I bring news, a report from Joseph."

"Is my husband well?" Kaillë asked.

Husband, Rook thought. *As bad as I thought, maybe worse. Domesticated him, through and through. Son of a bitch.*

"He is...as well as can be expected," the rider answered. Kaillë's face betrayed her fear, which the rider seemed to note. "He is unhurt," the elf clarified, "but the whole band is daunted. The blocking of the tunnel was successful, and the rest now proceed to the lands of the Tenth Clan, as we promised Dorav. During the blocking of the tunnel, though... Chieftain, Baron Turov is alive, or at least not dead in the natural sense. Joseph saw him in the tunnel, and he was assailed by powerful magic. The Baron is buried under rock and likely stuck underground for now, but Joseph does not believe him defeated. He sent me back to warn you."

Rook was struck dumb. She looked to Kaillë and saw the Windrider chieftain was similarly speechless. Rook couldn't be certain she was the first to find her voice, but she was the first to use it. "That's impossible. The Baron fell, we both saw it. The Well went on forever, and there was fire and...and lava and...he couldn't have survived. He's dead, he has to be."

"I'm not sure he did survive, in the strictest sense," Kaillë said after a few moments in silent consideration. "After the journey last year, right after you left us, Rook, Joseph said he still felt uneasy. He usually feels uneasy, so I gave little consideration to his concern, but knowing what I do now, what seemed at the time a simple coincidence now seems far darker. Joseph was suspicious of the timing of the troll attacks; how they distracted the dwarven guard enough for the Baron and his men to reach the vault that held the Hoard of Dalviir with minimal opposition. Even allowing that such a thing could be possible between a human and those savage beasts, which I doubted, I couldn't see any means by which the Baron and the trolls could have been coordinating; for that matter, neither could Joseph, so we let the matter rest.

"What we failed to see was that the Baron was not the mastermind of his own search for the Hoard. Somehow the entity imprisoned in the Well learned to extend some small measure of its influence, some faint whisper of its voice, beyond the boundaries of its prison. Or perhaps the magic began to wane in strength with the centuries, or both. To the trolls, a race so near and so given to fury, such influence wreaked great effect. Or perhaps the thing has murmured to them bit by bit down the generations, making them as they are now. Whatever the case, it seems others fell under the entity's sway as well, probably in much more subtle ways: a greedy baron goes searching for magical treasure and brings it to the nearest place where he can attune it...or an ambitious noble contracts a desperate thief to steal a book of lore concerning its imprisonment."

The thief shook her head in disagreement. "No. You can't think what I did played into this thing's plans; what would it want with this book. It doesn't need a lesson on its own history."

"I'm only a quarter of a way through the translation. There could be more dangerous information in its pages, even a description on how the sealing ritual was performed."

Rook was silent for some time, running events over in her mind. She knew Kaillë's reasoning was sound, and it explained the vital importance of the book. It led to other questions that Kaillë couldn't answer, though. How did the Wolfsguard know about the book's importance? And had they killed to retrieve it in order to protect it, or on the orders of one among their own ranks who had fallen under the ancient being's sway?

"I have to go back," Rook said suddenly. "There's nothing more I can do here. Knowing any more about what's in that book is going to put me in *more* danger, not less. It's time for me to go."

"But I'm not finished with the book," Kaillë protested. "Its information could be critical."

"It probably is. Keep it. It's safer here anyway, and you can finish finding out what it says and do whatever seems best. You're a much better judge of these things than I am."

"Then what are you going to do?"

"I'm going home, collecting my brother, and getting as far away from this supernatural insanity as possible, and if you have even half a lick of sense, you'll do the same thing," Rook spouted, her city accent creeping through again in her discomposure.

"I haven't got a brother."

"Funny."

"Rook," Kaillë pressed, "do you think this is really the kind of problem you can just outrun?"

"Only one way to find out. Listen, Kaillë, I appreciate you helping with the book and letting me lie low for a couple days, and I'm glad I could help with those Blood Elves. You and me, we're square now. But I gotta look after me and mine."

Kaillë nodded slowly. "You must walk your own path. I wish you would stay, but that is not for me to decide. We part as friends, and you are welcome to return whenever you wish."

"Thank you. I'll just get my gear and be on my way."

"Not quite. The men following you when you arrived were led quite a miserable chase back to the plains, but we can't risk them spotting you and backtracking your trail to the village, especially not with all the dangers surrounding us. Tes'voran will take you back to the place where we found you, and you can hike back down from there."

As Rook walked toward Onahnë's house, a realization struck her mind like a hammer. The last time she'd seen the Baron, plummeting to his apparently-less-than-certain death, he'd had the entire Hoard of Dalviir strapped to his back. And now that he'd returned, *some* force of magic had to be keeping him alive... She started to turn back to ask the scout if any of Dalviir's artifacts had been spotted on the Baron, but he was gone, and Kaillë was hurrying away. She shook away the thought, reluctant to betray her curiosity to the Windriders in any case. Besides, it sounded like the Baron was no longer one to be trifled with, making her desire moot. Her original plan of headlong flight was still the best option. For now...

Chapter Nine: Into the Dark

Rook was sent on her way with a full pack of supplies that would see her through most of her homeward journey with careful rationing. Fear had begun clawing her as soon as she learned how blindly she had stumbled into what was likely to become the great struggle of the era, and it only increased its grip now that she was alone in the woods with nightfall just hours away. Only one thought gave her comfort. As soon as Tes'voran took off on his return trip, she dug into her belt pouch for the necklace and settled it around her neck. She knew the world was erupting. She knew the Wolfsguard were after her. But a sense of the artifact's power rooted in her heart, supplanting her fear with confidence and a sense of control.

That night Rook sheltered in a thicket between three closely-spaced oaks. The night was chill but she couldn't risk a fire, so she snugged under her pack as best she could and passed the dark hours wishing she had brought warmer clothes.

Rook was awakened by sunlight filtering through the thicket and immediately felt the grip of fear that the necklace was gone. Her hand flew to her throat, but there it was, right where she had left it. She shook off what must have been the remnant of a dream and crawled out of the thicket, stranding and stretching her limbs. The rising sun brought warmth, and Rook set off without delay, eager to reach lower elevations where it would be warmer still.

The hike downhill was pleasant, but the farther she walked, the more she feared the Wolfsguard. What had they done after she gave them the slip? Obviously they had not found the Windrider village or continued their search in the forest, but where *would* they have gone? She had no idea save one, that it was not in keeping with their elite reputation to go back to their king emptyhanded. Somewhere, probably nearby, they almost certainly sat in waiting.

Her supplies still holding out well, Rook bypassed the village on the plain entirely and headed northwest, making for the nearest town directly on the river. This was the most dangerous gamble. The river was her most obvious choice of returning route, but for good reason—it was also by far the fastest, even traveling upstream. Would the king's agents expect her to return to the city? The answer to that question was simple: of course they would. And the reason just as simple: because they had worked their way to Pockmark Charlie, which meant by now they had used him or others in his rogues' gallery, and probably both, to learn everything that could be learned about Rook, which meant they knew she had a brother.

Rook gasped even as the thoughts tumbled through her brain. Adler. If the Wolfsguard had sent word back to Onderburg they'd lost her, then they could already have put plans into motion to apply the right leverage to convince her to give herself up. For all she knew, Adler could be rotting in a dungeon, never to be released without her cooperation. How would she react if that proved true?

Her growing paranoia fractured and multiplied her fears like a kaleidoscope held up to the light, spinning her thoughts out of control. By the time she reached the plain, every wind through the grasses seemed an enemy ready to spring up and capture her, or worse. The sun was before her, bathing the plains in amber and blinding her to the west. Her legs exhausted from the hike, she sank to the ground, her pack heavy behind her, put her face in her hands, and wept.

Rook's descent into self-pity was powerful, but brief. After a few minutes of wracking sobs that left her face wet and slimy, Rook took a shuddering breath and looked up. Emotion would never be her master. She had her skills and her wits. And she had the necklace, so she had more than she'd ever needed before. Pulling a cloth from her pack, she blew her nose and scrubbed at her face, then set out enough food for a passable supper. After eating she resumed her northwestwardly trek, striking a stream course and following it more or less due west until dark, ever watchful for a hollow in its banks where she might shelter for the night.

~ * ~

The overland journey to the lands above the Tenth Clan took two more days, and Joseph saw no sign of enemies, either trolls or undead noblemen, in all that time. Were it not for the urgency of their purpose, the hike through the woods would have been a pleasant diversion. One other thing did tug at the back of Joseph's mind: traveling north would take him closer to Delia's grave than he had been since joining the Windriders. He thought about leaving the party for a detour, as a few hours would take him there and back, but in the end he decided against it. Part of his reluctance still stemmed from guilt over loving Kaillë, but a larger part was the desire to leave his old life in the past, a desire which fueled his guilt all the more. Still, he had more pressing matters to attend, so justifying his avoidance was simple.

Even after arriving in the Tenth Clan's region, it took a day of searching to locate an entrance. Dorav's unfamiliarity with surface navigation, combined with his minimal knowledge of the tunnel layout outside his own clan, made for a worthy challenge, but at last they located a narrow fissure in a protruding outcrop of gray bedrock, just large enough for the party to fit through one at a time. Once they had filed in, Dorav sat, encouraging the band to do the same. Joseph could see the elves were already anxious, cut off from the wind and sky, but they obeyed, staring at one another with anxiety etched into their expressions as the setting sun glowed through the fissure, holding the chamber in a weird, umbral light.

Sympathetic to the elves unease, Joseph looked at Dorav. "What do we do now?" he asked.

"We wait."

"For how long."

"As long as it takes," the dwarf replied. He crossed his legs under him and closed his black eyes, sitting with his hands on his knees and taking on the impossibly still posture of a dwarf settling in.

The elves inched away from his eerie immobility, and Joseph was struck by the contrast as the elves shifted left and right, forward and back as if caught in a breeze only they could feel. It occurred to Joseph for the first time that in all his months with them, he'd never seen an elf completely still unless hiding or aiming. To a dwarf the slighter beings must seem utterly frenetic.

The sun finished its journey beyond the western plain,

casting the small cavern into pitch darkness. Yowler, who at first had been as anxious as the elves, had finally taken his cue from Stitch and curled up to sleep. Joseph heard one of the elves mutter something about the folly of staying so long "buried" under rocks, but the hunter paid it no mind. Already most of the elves were surrendering to the needs of the situation and nodding off with their chins on their chests.

The moon did not rise, offering Joseph no way to mark the time that passed. He, too, nodded off for a time before a gentle, nighttime storm brewed outside, thunder rolling between the mountains and the foothills in unending peals. The wind and rain were soft, though, and the group sat sheltered from the weather; Joseph allowed the muted rage of the storm to relax him, and once again he slept.

He awoke sometime later to see Dorav now standing, his head cocked to one side as if listening for something. A few moments after, only a slight current of air, and no sound he could note, signaled the opening of a portal at the back of the chamber, a door previously invisible to all but the most experienced investigation.

As soon as the back wall of the cave swung inward, Dorav called out a few phrases in the dwarven language, a greeting if Joseph correctly read the rover's stance and bearing. Even as he spoke, a dozen dwarves, identically dressed and armed with halberds, marched in perfect step into the cave, and for the third time in his life Joseph found himself in the fascinating presence of a dwarven hret-dialt.

The hret-dialt, or "stonebound troop" was a squad of dwarves raised together from birth. Using a talent unique to their species, dwarves so raised soon began to share in one another's thoughts whenever they were in proximity, and sometime before full adulthood this constant mental communion gave rise to the dhor-zabh, a new mind and personality greater than the sum of its parts. That, at least, was the best Joseph could understand it. What he knew with greater certainty, and from firsthand experience, is that such a unit could act in perfect concert, timing movements with precision as though each dwarf was a limb on a single body, which in a sense they were. Perhaps what awed Joseph most of all, however, was that this blending was accomplished without any noticeable diminishing of the self of any of the members; when the hret-dialt broke apart for rest or to attend different duties, each resumed his own identity without apparent difficulty or sense of loss.

Now such a troop all but surrounded the elves, though their spears were kept pointed at the ceiling and their stances betrayed no concern. If that was true, Joseph knew, it was only because Dorav had already spoken for him and his companions.

A brief exchange in dwarven followed, then Dorav spoke to Joseph. "I have asked them to use the speech common to this region so you can understand. It's rude talking about people when they don't know what you're saying."

"Thank you," Joseph said to the dwarf closest to him, knowing that speaking to one was the same as speaking to all.

A different dwarf spoke to Dorav. "Rover, what news of the Ninth Clan? We were told by the eighth patrol that they expected to exchange reports with the twenty-first patrol of your clan as regularly planned three days ago, but the Ninth Clan patrol did not appear, and there has been no news since."

"I offer grave news," Dorav replied. "The Ninth Clan has fallen. Trolls overran our defenses the best part of a ten-day ago, and the Streets of Twilight at best are sacked, possibly worse. I have no news of the situation there, or to where any survivors have scattered."

The dwarves reacted as one to Dorav's report, gasping

and shuffling. The speaker then resumed. "None have come to the Tenth Clan, I'm afraid."

"That's no surprise," Dorav said. "All the connecting tunnels were thick with trolls. Only by great fortune and my chance friendship with these surface-walkers was I able to come here with my warning. Surely you have seen signs of the trolls yourselves on your southern borders."

"The southern patrols have reported an increase in troll skirmishers, but nothing to herald these fell tidings. We must conduct you at once to the Council to tell all you know."

"Of course." Dorav turned and spoke to Joseph. "You have done more than your duty, my friend, just as you did in my city last year. This good hret-dialt will see me safely to the Council; our ways must part again."

Stitch seemed to sense the shifting of the mood and sidled up to Dorav, pressing against his leg.

"I would offer my bow," Joseph said, "and those of these brave elves, were it not—"

"Azrith!" called Ten'marden, his best archer keeping watch at the fissure. His bowstring twanged. "We are in peril."

Joseph leapt to the opening and peered over the elf's shoulder, then grimaced. The night was still black, but in the starlight he could just make out something, or rather a great many somethings, seething across the southern hillside in their direction, moving like a great carpet of utter blackness against the dark. A breeze stirred, and the scent of troll reached Joseph's nose, acrid and mangy. He could not begin to guess their number.

Ten'marden shot his bow twice more, his night-honed eyes probably finding their marks, but no meaningful change could be made in the writhing mass outside. "That way lies death, Azrith," the elf told him.

It seemed that by scent or uncanny hearing the dwarves

had come to understand the nature of the threat outside. The hret-dialt made a collective curse or exclamation in dwarven, then the dhor-zabh's speaker cried, "Trolls moving over the surface?"

Joseph suspected the question was rhetorical, at any rate giving no answer.

"Joseph," Dorav urged, "you must come with us. Hurry!"

Joseph's face was grim. His elves had their own people to protect, and going underground and east was altogether the wrong direction to get back to them. The elves were divided; some moved toward the deeper tunnel entrance, albeit with hesitation, while others edged toward the fissure, readying their bows. Joseph suspected horror at going underground motivated them as strongly as the desire to fight their way back to the village. His eyes flicked to the trees. In time the owl would return home riderless to her nest; the Windriders would have no idea what happened, but on the heels of Joseph's news of the Baron they would likely fear the worst. Kaillë would not know if he was alive or dead. That was bad, but he knew her mettle and her mind. She would not give up on them and would send scouts to find the lost party, scouts that would only be going to their deaths for no reason. That was worse. The trolls drew nearer with each moment; even now Joseph could hear their snarling.

"Ten'venni," Joseph barked to the remaining owl rider, "I need your eyes. Can you get to your bird?"

Ten'venni leapt to the fissure and looked out. "I must," he answered and started to move.

"Wait," Joseph commanded, holding the elf's shoulder. "Tell them we're safe. Don't let them send anyone, you understand?" The elf nodded. "And...tell the Chieftain that I love her." He removed his hand, and without further signal Ten'venni sprinted down the slope, quickly lost to

Joseph's eyes in the darkness.

"Joseph," Dorav called again, "please follow now." Already the hret-dialt was situating itself to move back into the tunnel.

"Not yet," Joseph argued.

"He's at his tree," Ten'marden reported. "Only three yards to spare, but he's above their reach."

"Do they follow?" Joseph demanded.

"Three are trying..."

"Tes'sael, get the rest into the tunnel now," Joseph ordered. "Don't let those dwarves shut us out." He heard motion behind him but didn't turn, still straining his eyes vainly on the darkness ahead of him as Ten'marden continued speaking.

"...they are not swift climbers, these trolls, at least not in trees. I think they have only little hope of catching Ten'venni."

"Make it none," Joseph growled.

The elf's bow twanged twice, and shrieks and crashing thuds sounded over the general clamor outside. "The third is on the far side of the tree, but Ten'venni is almost there."

"Joseph," Dorav yelled, "come on! This dhor-zabh is getting impatient. You know how they are."

A long, warbling whistle pierced the night from on high, cutting through the sounds of crashing and snarling below. Ten'venni was away. Joseph grabbed Ten'marden and half-dragged him through the dwarven door even as it began to swing noiselessly shut.

"Dammit, you dwarves," Joseph hissed. "You couldn't wait one—"

"Silence!" ordered the dhor-zabh. Joseph sensed his tone was one of urgency and not of anger. He immediately obeyed.

Less than a minute passed before sounds of scrabbling could be heard on the other side of the door. The trolls were searching.

On Joseph's side, the darkness was absolute. The dwarves kindled no light, having no need of it for moving around their tunnels. Joseph knew only that they somehow sensed the location of things by hearing, but he didn't fully understand the ability. Not even breathing could be heard around him, his every sense was starved but for the scent of unwashed bodies and the sounds of the trolls clawing at the door.

In a moment Joseph felt a hand come to rest on his shoulder, and by its breadth and weight he guessed it to be Dorav's. The dwarf then passed a rope around Joseph's waist and knotted it. After that he crept away. Two minutes passed, perhaps three, then Dorav was back, his hand at Joseph's elbow pulling him up. Joseph stood, then a pull on the rope at his waist signaled him to move. He felt resistance from the opposite direction and realized he was a link in a chain, a human and six elves being led through the utter darkness by the dwarven rover, followed by two dogs Joseph knew were still there only by an occasional pant or sniff or bump against his leg.

Joseph kept a silent count in his head, though he wasn't sure why. His rope connection to the bodies in front of him made it easy to sense the turns, but without any visual cues he doubted he could translate that back into any sensible memory of their path should he need to make a quick exit. Nevertheless, by the hourglass in his head he estimated twenty minutes at a fast walk before the dhor-zabh called a halt, and audibly now.

"We are now out of earshot, even for troll ears," he said. "We have matters to discuss."

Joseph heard Dorav mutter something under his breath, but he couldn't make it out.

"You should not have invited the surface-walkers down here, Dorav of the Ninth Clan," the voice continued. "Such is beyond a rover's authority even in his own lands, which you are not."

"Trolls rampage on the surface," Dorav rebutted. "You find yourself in a peril not covered in your *rules*. They happen more often than you might think when you get away from your cities and your regular patrol routes. Reminding you of that *is* within a rover's authority, in any land."

"What trolls do on the surface is no concern of the dwarves. Surface-walkers are to be forced out of our tunnels."

"But all who venture under the earth, even strangers, are to have our protection from trolls."

"This is a moot debate," Joseph interrupted. "We're here now, which means we must be presented to your council. Unless you mean to kill us?"

"...No."

"Then let's be off from here," Dorav argued. Joseph felt the dwarf guiding him to his feet again.

"Can we not make a light?" Joseph asked. "Time is not our friend here, and we could move much faster if we could see."

"Out of the question," the dwarven speaker shouted.

"Pick your battles, Joseph," Dorav murmured.

In a moment they were up and moving again, but only minutes passed before Tes'sael whispered, "Do you hear that?"

Joseph heard nothing, but one of the other elves affirmed that he did. The dwarves didn't respond, but given how little Joseph understood of their "seeing with their ears," he would take the word of two elves as fact against the denial of an army of dwarves. "Hold," Joseph ordered. He felt a momentary jerk on his line as Dorav tried to continue another step, then nothing.

Seconds passed. One by one the remaining elves began

to mutter about strange sounds, then Joseph heard the dwarves shift their stance as one. Only a moment later did the noises become loud enough for Joseph to hear: scrabbling and clawing and snarling. The sounds came from behind them and echoed back from up ahead. Or was it the other way around? His hearing was confused in the twisting tunnels. Then a sharp shriek stood out from the noises ahead of him, and he listened for its echo, desperate to get his bearings. A few more seconds passed, but the echo of that shriek never came. He gritted his teeth. He wasn't hearing echoes. He was hearing two different forces of trolls that now had them surrounded.

"Run!" cried the dhor-zabh.

Joseph heard the hret-dialt break into a fast jog, and a hard yank on his rope told him Dorav was following. Joseph reacted quickly and kept up, but he felt a pull on the line behind him, then a cry and jostle that told him the elf at the back of the line had been taken off guard and fallen.

"Enough!" Joseph growled, coming to a stop, which forced Dorav to do the same. He heard the hret-dialt jog on ahead. "Dorav, make a light. I don't give half a damn what those stubborn bastards think." Joseph heard Dorav scrambling in his pack, then a soft, blue-green glow filled the tunnel. Its brightness could have been the noon sun after so long in utter darkness. Dorav held in his hands two bowls of glowing lichen topped with glass, perfect hemispheres that Joseph guessed fit together to make a ball and hide the light, but he wasted no time on such consideration. Dorav slipped the bowls into mesh pouches at either shoulder, freeing his hands and giving the appearance of misshapen, glowing pauldrons on his jacket. As he did so, Joseph's knife was already out and slashing through the lines holding his people together, then they were moving again, sprinting now to catch up with the dwarven patrol that had started to leave them behind.

"That may not have been the best idea, Joseph," Dorav chided as they caught up to the hret-dialt. "What if somebody gets separated? And there are deadfalls in places through the tunnels—"

"We aren't getting out of here without a fight, Dorav. We can't fight all tied together."

They came to a fork in the tunnel. The sounds of trolls reached their ears from the right; the dwarves went left. Without any outward order, half the dwarves fell back behind the elves to form a rearguard, and half of those turned to face behind them, their halberds leveled, to trot backwards without any noticeable decrease in speed. The troll noises grew closer behind them.

They passed a tunnel opening on their right, and snarls and scratching echoed down that tunnel as well. Dorav cursed. "So many."

They jogged on. The sounds behind them were getting frightfully close, and Joseph hazarded a backwards glance. Dorav's light didn't reach far, but Joseph thought he could make out movement in the shadow just beyond its radius. After a few moments Joseph convinced himself his eyes were playing tricks on him, then two trolls leapt from the darkness, suddenly screeching at ear-splitting volume. Prior they had been silent, giving no indication they had outpaced the hoard behind them. The trolls leapt high in their attack, and for a split second the noise seemed to stun the dwarves, but not for long enough. The two rear-facing guards on either side thrust up with the heavy spear points atop their halberds. The attacking trolls fell to the ground kicking and twitching, one pierced through the throat and the other through the heart, its own weight and momentum allowing the set spear to pierce the pebbly hide of its chest. The party trotted on.

They were approaching another side passage when the situation completely fell apart.

The front ranks of the hret-dialt passed the intersection just as a band of trolls surged in from the right. The dwarves turned to face the threat, and those in the back halted, the whole unit silently redeploying to block both the right and rear passages with a double-rank hedge of steel. Joseph had fought with dwarves once before, but that had been with a squad of Irregulars, rovers like Dorav who shared thoughts with no stonebound unit. The hunter stood in awe as he unslung his bow, watching the perfect coordination of the hret-dialt in action, the combined will of the dhor-zabh directing the actions of twelve men as easily as he walked or climbed or shot his bow.

Trolls dodged left and right as they came forward, trying to avoid dwarven spear points, but everywhere they turned another angled to defeat their attack. One slipped between the points of the firsts rank of halberds only to have an axe-blade hook his neck from behind and drive his face into a spear point in the second rank. Two dwarves in the center of the rearguard had their weapons drawn outward by disparate attacks, but just as another troll tried to exploit the gap their ax heads swung back, slicing off its head like shepherds' shears. Assists and set-ups Joseph had heard human soldiers brag about, but never believed for a moment, the dwarves carried out second by second, grinding the troll assault to a halt as the enemy was forced to climb over piles of their own dead.

At first the elves had worked to do their part, loosing arrows into the enemy ranks, but the margin between Dorav's light and the dwarven line was narrow, leaving them little opportunity. After only a few volleys Dorav called out to them, "Save your arrows, hunters. You may need them, but not here."

Joseph confirmed the order, standing ready but shooting no more. Stitch and Yowler stood behind him, anxious; they were trackers, not fighters, and knew it well.

Two minutes went by, then three and four, and though the dwarves' combat was brutally efficient, by then even they were beginning to tire, with no end to the trollish horde in sight. Fortunately, the onslaught had slowed, and suddenly the dwarves fell back by a quick two-step. A few trolls surged forward, mistaking the move for weakness, a mistake that proved to be their last. The guards repeated this motion several times, pausing after each move, never coming off balance. In this way they moved past the intersection to the next straight section of tunnel, interweaving their ranks so they were now three deep and four abreast. The hedge of halberds was all the more dense, and the trolls seemed content to let the dwarves retreat for a time, licking their own wounds.

The hret-dialt moved to a somewhat quicker, rolling retreat: the second and third ranks would turn slightly, allowing the first rank to fall back through them and become the last rank. Reset and repeat, each repetition moving the unit back a precious couple of yards. The going was slow but safe, no troll daring to challenge the wall of ax heads and spear points. Joseph was sure, from a sense of tactics more than anything he saw or heard, that troll scouts were hugging the walls somewhere outside the range of Dorav's lights, but if indeed they were there they gave no sign.

After retreating about a furlong, the dhor-zabh suddenly said, "Run." And run they did, suddenly beginning a mad dash through the darkness of the tunnels. Joseph's guess about following trolls was proven right as their sudden change of pace invited a trio of nearby snarls, but these were cut off as quickly as they started, and the hunter did not look back to see what exactly had befallen. Passages yawned open on the right and left, but they passed them; whether they were dead ends or simply clear of trolls, Joseph heard no snarling or shrieking coming up from them.

Without warning the tunnel they traversed opened into a massive cavern, Dorav's light touching no walls or ceiling, only the floor below. Veins of quartz ran through the floor under their feet, polished smooth by some dwarven craft, and as they ran on Joseph saw that some of these veins had been allowed to survive, thrusting up from the softer stone of the floor until they made a low wall on his left. Dorav jogged close to it, so Joseph fell in behind him to see what he could on the other side. Craning his neck, Joseph saw as much nothing as he could ever remember seeing in his life, the cavern floor falling away into a chasm of unfathomable depth. A moment later he was distracted as the sounds of pursuit began to echo into the huge chamber. The trolls must be less than a hundred yards behind.

At first the party put on an extra burst of speed, but within moments the right-hand wall of the cavern swung back into their view, rising up like a cliff face on their right hemming them in as surely as the sheer drop on their left. Only faith in the dwarves kept Joseph moving forward as the rail of quartz disappeared and the path on which they ran grew ever narrower, finally allowing only two dwarves to pass side by side. A rough wall suddenly loomed up before them barring their way but for a narrow cleft. The party was forced to slow to a virtual halt as the dwarves ushered first Dorav, then Joseph and the elves, through to the other side, then filed in after then. The troll sounds grew ever nearer.

Joseph found himself in a tunnel not unlike the one they had left just minutes before, save that the walls and floor of this one were smoother, worked by dwarven tools rather than eons of water.

"Here we part ways," the dhor-zabh said. "Two of us will continue to escort you, the remainder will hold here. You must reach Lun'rool-Carrig'ach and warn the guard."

Joseph had gathered in his travels that each of the

dwarven clans was built around the central hub of a large city; it seemed the Tenth Clan's was this Lun'rool-Carrig'ach, though he did not know what it meant.

Dorav was reluctant to leave the guards against such grim odds. "Stick with us; we can outrun those trolls."

"Perhaps, if we are very lucky, and even then we would reach the city with them at our heels, providing no warning. We must assume there are other hordes moving to attack from deeper in. The city must have time to mount its defense."

The two dwarves designated as their escort were already moving down the tunnel, and as the distance opened one began to call over his shoulder. "We, er, *they* can hold that fissure for hours; the trolls' numbers do them no good there, and in minutes they'll start clogging it with their dead, giving the defenders time to rest. Come on. You don't have the right arms or training to do any good here, but we're leaving to warn the city with or without you."

Joseph could see that was true. Already the pair of dwarves breaking off from the hret-dialt was nearly out of sight. He gave Dorav an expectant look. The dwarf scowled but made no further argument, and in a moment the group was jogging after the two dwarves down the tunnel. A chorus of snarls and yelps sounded the first clash at the fissure behind them, but soon even those noises were lost to the twisting forks and tunnels of the Tenth Clan's domain.

Chapter Ten: Glowing Rocks

The second morning of Rook's homeward journey dawned, and she surveyed the land about her. All was empty in the broad land between the river and the forest, and no prying eyes seemed to be about. Now that light had returned, she saw smoke curling upward in a blue haze to the north, but after closer scrutiny she realized a house lay in that direction just at the edge of her sight, a small cottage surrounded by gardens and animal pens. A hundred such dwellings scattered across the lands in these parts, growing thicker as one reached the north and the safety of King Dieter's lands. Simple folk carving their life out of the wilderness beyond the reach of a king's orders, in fact if not in name. Rook wondered what would become of these people if the whole world erupted into war, but she quickly shook away the thought. If that happened, they would look to their own needs, just as she was looking to hers. Their fate was not her problem. She refilled her canteens in the stream she'd been following, then set out across the plain, once more heading northwest. She had lost an exact idea of her location, but by late morning she should strike either the river or a major trade road, and either of those she could follow to the nearest town where she could catch a barge heading upriver. The realization that Adler was in danger was enough to convince her the fastest route back home was the only one worth taking, no matter the risks.

In mitigation of these risks, and against the assailing fear that grew by the hour, Rook wore the necklace constantly now, and even the thought of taking it off made her feel naked and alone. She struck the trade road and followed it west to the river town exactly as she had planned, and this time she cast aside all subtlety and commanded passage on a northward barge, demanding a private room where she could pass the trip away from prying eyes.

~ * ~

Joseph and his band had jogged for nearly two hours with only a brief halt for water when at last they came to a checkpoint, a wall of wrought iron bars across the tunnel with only a small gate in the middle. A pair of guards stood on each side of the barrier. At first they eyed the surface dwellers with suspicion, but the dwarves accompanying Joseph exchanged a few rushed phrases with the guards, and very quickly the gate was opened. At the same time, one of the dwarves on the outside of the checkpoint moved to a space on the wall where Joseph noticed an animal skin was stretched. The dwarf pulled a small baton from his belt and beat out a rolling tattoo on the skin. He cocked an ear toward the strange drumhead, and though Joseph heard nothing, a moment later the dwarf nodded as if satisfied he had received an answering call. Joseph hadn't yet seen this form of dwarven ingenuity. He was sure there must be a passage in the wall behind the skin, too small for foes to use but suitable for relaying signals. He couldn't guess where the passage might lead, but he suspected the sensitivity of dwarven ears would let them relay messages that way by miles at a time.

After another mile of quick walking, they passed another checkpoint, but this one was open to them, the guards trading words with the party's escorts as they walked through without stopping. Dorav translated for Joseph's benefit. "They say they've passed the message on ahead, but our guides have to report to the council before they commit too many men to any planned defense."

"Is there time for that?" Joseph asked as they passed through the second checkpoint and once again picked up speed.

"There has to be," Dorav answered. "Trolls are unpredictable at best. The generals will need all the details they can get before they deploy, otherwise they could get outflanked or drawn into a thousand ambushes."

Joseph nodded. "The fog of war."

"Hm?" Dorav asked. Then, seeming to pick up Joseph's meaning from context, he said, "We call it 'battle echoes.' Can't tell where a thing is really happening."

The dogs had been surprisingly obedient during the entire run through the tunnels, but Joseph recalled the last time he tried to bring a "long-legged badger" into a dwarven city and knew they would need to be harnessed. Time being of the essence, he pulled the remains of Dorav's safety rope from his waist as they walked and leashed Stitch. Ten'marden copied the move for Yowler. Stitch's nose began to twitch, and soon enough even Joseph could smell the scent that interested the dog: giant badger, the musky, mammal odor carried to his nose by the subtle breeze that always flowed through dwarven tunnels. They were approaching inhabited areas, and soon Joseph began to notice differences between the Tenth Clan and the Ninth, the only other he'd seen.

The area surrounding the Ninth Clan's Streets of Twilight, or in the dwarven tongue "Tra'id-Stie'che," was a maze of tight tunnels with individual dwellings cut directly into the walls. Instead, the Tenth Clan's surrounding "pastureland" consisted of a series of progressively larger chambers, filled with trickling streams and pools, around which every manner of mushroom and lichen was cultivated. Some areas were pungent, and Joseph chose not too carefully to consider what living matter was used as a base and food for the fungus. Still, on the whole the approach was pleasant, with each chamber containing its own small village that would not have looked out of place in human farmlands, save that it had a smaller population and was constructed entirely of stone. Giant badgers were everywhere, hauling carts of tools, fungus, or rock. None took much notice of the travelers, but even Stitch was wary and Yowler, who had never been in dwarven settlements before, kept his tail tucked and wouldn't stray from Joseph's heel.

"What is the city called, Dorav?" Joseph asked as they walked. "In my language, I mean."

"More or less, Glowing Rocks," the dwarf answered. "You'll see."

At last the group passed through an archway into a cavern immeasurably vast, and the city of Glowing Rocks spread out before them. Its name was, perhaps, less poetic than the Streets of Twilight, but what it lacked in word craft it made up in pure accuracy. Great stalactites hung from the ceiling as far as Joseph could see, and every one glowed with a blue-green light cast by a layer of phosphorescent lichen. The color was unnatural to a surface walker's eyes, but exotic and beautiful in its way. In a half-dozen places that Joseph could see, a stalactite had grown into the mirroring stalagmite beneath it, forming a vast column from floor to ceiling, and these seemed to cast the brightest radiance to the homes and buildings at their feet. Water dripped down almost everywhere, carrying the glow with it so it carpeted the roofs and cavern floor wherever traffic did not wear it away. The Streets of Twilight had been a tall city, tier upon tier of dwellings in the cavern walls and central buildings thrusting up a hundred feet or more from the cavern floor. By contrast, Glowing Rocks was low and flat, with the tallest buildings Joseph could see standing only fifteen or twenty feet. The same bustle of activity was present, however, with dwarves and their badgers moving this way and that on errands Joseph couldn't estimate.

Their dwarven escorts kept them moving quickly, sparing no time to take in the sights of their home. After several minutes, they arrived at a building that had been lost in the dusky light upon their arrival to the cavern, but which could be seen on the approach to beggar the size of any other structures in the city. The hall stood in four dwarf-sized stories from the cavern floor and stretched easily a hundred feet in either direction from the central entrance to which Joseph and his friends were being guided. Outside the main doorway was a statue so perfect in likeness to a dwarf Joseph half expected it to climb down from its pedestal and start speaking, save that it was triple a real dwarf's size. The carving depicted regal clothing and a crown on the dwarf's brow; he leaned on a great hammer that looked equally suited to crushing stone or skulls, and a patch was over one of his eyes. "Who is that?" Joseph couldn't help but ask.

One of their dwarven escort replied, "Dalvinav, the founder of Lun'rool-Carrig'ach." The dwarf continued speaking as they passed the statue and entered the great building then passed through hallways and up staircases. "Our earliest histories are lost, but legend holds that when the first three clans grew too numerous for their caverns, nine expeditions set out to find new tunnels to settle. Dalvinav was chosen to lead the seventh of the colonies, which would one day become the Tenth Clan. He was a great warrior, and it is said that he and his kin had to slay many trolls in order to make these chambers safe for habitation."

"Not only trolls, some will say," Dorav cut in. "In the Ninth Clan we have other tales of Dalvinav, tales of some creature that dwelt in our ancestors' tunnels. It never strayed far from the Well, that place you know, Joseph, but fear of it lay on all our dwarves, and trolls seemed drawn to it. The council asked for help from the Tenth Clan, and they sent Dalvinav and his band of Irregulars. They say he killed the beast, and when it was cut open they found it to have a heart of stone, which Dalvinav brought back to the Tenth Clan as a trophy."

"I thought to give a lesson on history," the dwarven guard quipped, "not on mythology."

"See the problem with being brought up hret-dialt," Dorav said to Joseph. "Best fighters you'll ever find, but ain't a one of 'em has seen anything they couldn't pound into one of the little boxes where they pack the whole world. No imagination."

By then the band had reached a massive set of doors with armed guards on either side. The guards seemed to expect them and pushed the doors open without speaking. Dwarf and surface-walker alike strode through, and as the doors shut noiselessly behind them, Joseph had an opportunity to take the measure of the Tenth Clan's council of elders.

His immediate impression was a lack of formality or ceremony; few of the elders wore any kind of insignia or uniform, and two had their badgers with them. Their stone seats, eighteen of them, were arranged in a single circle centered on a glowing stalactite that ended just above head level. Below it, instead of a growing stalagmite, lay a small depression carved into the floor, filled with glowing water. Most of the seats were empty, with the elders gathering in knots around the room.

No one announced the travelers' entrance, but as soon as the doors started swinging shut behind them, the elders began finding their seats. The escorting dwarves didn't await permission to enter the circle, but Dorav stopped short, so Joseph and his elves did the same. For several minutes the guards gave their report in the dwarf tongue, the various elders asking questions in turn. Joseph thought he caught his name, modified heavily by the dwarven accent, and Dorav's, but apart from that he had no idea what was said. Once all was done, three of the elders, sitting together on the right side of the circle, motioned to alcoves set into the wall behind them, and three younger dwarves emerged. Joseph still knew only a little of dwarven culture, but the uniforms and bearing of the younger dwarves marked them to the eyes of any army scout, on the surface or below it, as dispatch runners.

At last one of the elders stood and beckoned Dorav and Joseph into the circle, and the rest of the elves followed. Joseph could feel the dwarves' eyes on him and mentally prepared himself, as best he could, for an encounter as frustrating as his last appearance before dwarven elders had been.

"You are Dorav the Restless," one of the elders said, a female dwarf with a husky contralto. For a moment Joseph was taken aback. He had seen many female dwarves coming and going both in the Streets of Twilight and during his brief time in Glowing Rocks, but the dwarven council he had addressed in the Ninth Clan last fall had been exclusively male. He knew that in elven and some human lands, women were accepted as leaders just as easily as men, either by heredity or consensus, but he realized once again how thin was his frame of reference for dwarven customs.

"I am," Dorav replied, saying no more. Joseph noticed by his body language the dwarf was nervous; these were not his people, after all, and even in his homeland he had crafted his lifestyle largely upon avoiding entanglements with the bureaucracy of the councils.

"Welcome, Dorav," the woman continued. "I am called Zallah. My seat is no greater or less than any here, but you'll find me doing most of the talking since I am the most comfortable with surface-walker languages. The marshal of our guard recalled your name from patrols on our southern borders. You've spent some time mapping the tunnels between our clans."

"I have."

"The marshal recalls the mentions of your name as routine but favorable. He believes you are one to be trusted by the Tenth Clan unless reasons present otherwise."

"Thank you, elder," Dorav mumbled, his eyes on the floor.

"And you," Zallah continued, her all-black eyes now on Joseph, "are Joseph, the surface-walker."

"Yes," Joseph answered. He followed Dorav's lead in keeping his answers short, but unlike the dwarf he held Zallah's gaze.

"You are known to us as well. Those with you are Windrider elves, yes? Those who have made an agreement with the Ninth Clan to provide herbs and poultices that can draw troll contagion from wounds to their badgers."

"That's right," Joseph answered, but he wanted to ensure there was no possibility of offense. "I was not directly involved with the negotiations, but I am...an advisor to the Windrider Chieftain. I don't think either side meant for the agreement to preclude working with any other clan—"

Zallah smiled and interrupted Joseph's self-conscious explanation. "Be at ease, human, you are in no danger for your dealings with the Ninth Clan. We have received samples of your medicines and are eager for more, but these things can be discussed later. Dorav's news to the patrol was grievous. We mourn deeply the loss of our cousins in the Streets of Twilight, but alas we can spare no time to honor them properly, for that same danger that shattered them so cruelly speeds now to our own gates."

"Elder," Joseph responded, "that danger threatens our home as well, and we need to get back to it. We don't know if there is a safe passage anymore, and of course you can't spare an escort until your own people are safe. So, it appears that for the time being I and my people are stuck here, and it isn't my way to sit by when defenseless folk are in danger. Our bows are yours." Tes'sael nodded his agreement.

"Thank you," Zallah replied, "but for now it is not your bows I need but your knowledge."

With that Zallah launched into a string of questions covering every detail of the troll hordes' movements, both above and below the surface. Dorav had the most information to provide, but Joseph and the elves were questioned as well concerning when the trolls had appeared in the forest, the best estimates of their number, and any other fact they could remember concerning their locations and actions.

Soon it became clear something was inciting the trolls to aggression in the borders of the Ninth Clan. Joseph did not mention the risen Baron, knowing the dwarves' disbelief of any supernatural powers in the world would prevent their believing the Baron's involvement and bog down the investigation. Still, it was clear enough to Joseph the Baron's resurrection and the troll attacks must be related, and the hunter sensed a larger hand moving behind the scenes, orchestrating events; he just didn't know what that force could be. Indeed, a suspicious part of him had suspected this very thing after the expedition last fall: The trolls had attacked the Streets of Twilight at the perfect moment to draw focus away from the Baron's target, the city's vault and the Hoard of Dalviir that lay inside, but there was no way the Baron could have coordinated with the trolls directly.

The Baron's rise now pointed even more strongly to some greater force, for though the Baron had desired the power of the Hoard, Joseph believed him to be nothing more than a pretender to real magic, not able to work the incantations needed to orchestrate his resurrection beforehand. Even less likely was Turov's ability to tap into the power of the Hoard in the instants between tumbling into the Well by Joseph's hand and meeting his inevitable death in the magma and flame that pulsed below. Joseph knew little enough of magic, it was true, but apart from old tales about battlefields or scenes of great tragedy returning up their dead as mindless destroyers, he had never heard a story of a man being brought back from the dead, or of a body being restored from complete incineration. The nature and identity of this orchestrating power was the knowledge Joseph so desperately needed, and it was the one piece of knowledge that was sure to elude him as long as his investigation was driven by skeptical dwarves.

What the council of the Tenth Clan *could* determine, however, by piecing together reports from Dorav, Joseph, and their patrols, was a general idea of where the trouble with the trolls had originated. Other elders spoke in detail in the dwarven tongue, seemingly referring to landmarks or locations that Zallah didn't know or couldn't translate, for she offered Joseph no insight. In this case, however, her help was not required, for Joseph could see Dorav's brow furrowing as he reached down and patted Stitch's head as if to reassure himself.

"What is it?" Joseph asked when the elders had finished speaking.

Dorav scowled. "It's the Well, Joseph."

Joseph nodded slowly. "The place where we thought we defeated the Baron. A place the Baron went because there was a focus of power there that drew the Hoard. Now you mention it was also the site of an ancient battle between some unnamed beast and the hero of the Tenth Clan. Are you seeing what I'm seeing, Dorav?"

"I don't know for sure *what* you're seeing, but I don't like it. Something is very wrong here. More wrong than I can explain."

"What are you two discussing?" Zallah asked. Her voice was urgent but not accusing.

"The location you're geographers are describing," Dorav answered, "is a place we've had to deal with before. I bow to no superstition, but I've seen enough in my travels to figure that there are things under the world that I can't understand, and bad things are drawn to that place or I'm no rover."

"Even supposing that's accurate," Zallah replied, "how does that help us now?"

Joseph wasn't sure if her question was rhetorical, but in any case he couldn't see that it did help, at least not immediately, so he stayed silent.

"Based on the movements of the trolls over the past week," Zallah continued, "we have begun ordering the defense. So far the patrols have reported no enemy contact other than what your hret-dialt already experienced." Now she was speaking to the two dwarves.

They exchanged more dwarven words with Zallah, and Dorav whispered an explanation to Joseph. "They've asked if there has been any further word from their unit. Zallah informed them that reinforcements were sent to the location along with masons and supplies to set up a temporary fortification at the choke point."

Joseph nodded his appreciation. He knew it was really for Glowing Rocks the ten dwarves stayed behind at the risk of their lives, but he and his people benefitted from it just the same, and he hated to think of them forced to make a stand to the bloody end without help.

Zallah now looked at Joseph and Dorav. "We are in your debt," she said. "Our situation is grave, but it would be far worse had you not made such a hard journey to warn us. It pains me that the Streets of Twilight have been sacked, but I make this pledge: If any strength remains in us after our own battle, we will devote every measure of it to finding the survivors of the Ninth Clan and rebuilding what has been sundered, in honor of your bravery and of the ancient bonds between our cities."

"Thank you, Elder," Dorav replied.

"Now, we may have need of your ax and your bows before all is over, but for now you need rest and food if you are to be of any use to yourselves, much less to anyone else. Follow my maidservant to chambers that have been made ready for you while we've talked. Take your ease for a while, and in peace if you can. Only if all else falls will trolls find their way into this place."

Joseph and the elves offered thanks while Dorav bowed with respect, then they followed a young female dwarf out of the meeting room.

~ * ~

A few minutes later the party was led into a large sitting room from which nine other arches opened. As in his prior visit to a dwarven city, Joseph had to stoop to go through doorways, and even in rooms themselves he could feel his hair brushing against the stone ceiling at low points. The dwarven handmaid spoke just enough of the human tongue to get her point across, explaining that the group was free to use the central room to gather, and each doorway led to a private bedchamber and lavatory. Food would be brought within the hour.

The party disbanded to refresh themselves. Two of the elves were showing obvious signs of claustrophobia in the close dwarven quarters, but they bore their burden in stoic elf fashion.

Joseph headed into the leftmost chamber in case there was trouble; its entrance being closest to the outer door in the sitting room, and inside found a laver and pitcher of water on a low table. He used these to clean up as best he could. In the Ninth Clan there had been an assortment of scented powders, but the Tenth had no such amenities, only a bar of rough, gritty soap that burned a bit when he used it. Joseph found this refreshing and was glad to strip off the sweat and grime of his travels. There was nothing to be done for his clothing but to change into a light set of breeches and shirt he kept rolled up in his pack and leave the more rugged travel clothing to air out on the floor.

By the time Joseph returned to the central room, Dorav and half the elves were already there, and a selection of food had been laid out on a stone shelf on the right-hand wall of the chamber. Joseph identified several kinds of mushrooms, but apart from that he couldn't tell what he was looking at, including the contents of three crystal decanters off to one side of the shelf.

Joseph looked to Dorav before picking up a plate from the near end of the shelf. "Is this all safe for us to eat?"

"It's true we dwarves aren't the most welcoming to guests from the surface," Dorav said, "but they wander down more often than you'd think, and we aren't in the habit of poisoning them for it. We know what you can eat, not that it's so different from what we can."

Joseph was hungry and needed no more urging. The remaining two elves arrived as he filled his plate, and after that they all ate with wordless gusto. The food was mostly bland, but it was filling, which was welcome to the travelers' growling stomachs. Even had he not been so eager for the meal, Joseph would have been silent. The need to get home, and back to Kaillë, was pressing on him, and he expected the thoughts of the others around the table were much the same.

After eating, the party retired to their separate chambers to rest. Unsurprisingly, Joseph found the bed too short for him by more than a foot, but he set his pack at the end of the bed to support his feet and was more than content.

~ * ~

The hunter was unsure how long he'd been asleep when he opened his eyes, the eternal twilight of Glowing Rocks dispelling any sense of time. The area was quiet, and Joseph's instinct was to go back to sleep while he could, but after lying still for what felt like a few minutes, he knew slumber had escaped him for the moment. The ceiling in the sitting room was slightly higher, so he paced out of his room in the hopes of getting a proper stretch. Joseph was somewhat surprised to see Dorav sitting at the far end of the table with his feet propped up on a second chair.

Knowing the harrowing week the dwarf had endured, Joseph asked, "Did you sleep?"

"A bit," the dwarf answered, pouring Joseph a glass of the mild, beer-like beverage they had drunk with their meal.

The hunter sat and sipped at the drink, then leaned back and looked toward the ceiling, sighing.

"What's the matter, Joseph?"

"I'm tired, Dorav."

"Well, that's easily fixed. Someone will call if you're needed, why not finish your drink and—"

"Not that kind of tired," Joseph interrupted.

Dorav chuckled. "You're still a young man, Joseph. Too young to be any other kind of tired."

"I don't *feel* young. I've lived alone off the land, I've fought in wars, buried a wife—"

"Rocks and tunnels, Joseph, I had no idea."

"Well, that's no surprise. I count you a friend, but it's a friendship forged more by fighting and bleeding together than by trading words."

A minute passed before Dorav spoke. "I couldn't help but notice back in the village," Dorav began. "You and Kaillë? I didn't pick up on it last year."

"Last year she and I had only just met, really. I stayed with the clan over the winter and we...became close."

"That's good news. Isn't it?"

Joseph nodded.

"Don't be so enthusiastic," Dorav quipped. "I don't know much of surface standards, but if that lass had more meat on her bones—"

"Easy there, Rover."

"No disrespect," Dorav finished. "In honesty, though, what kind of damn-fool notion would make you leave that woman and come here?"

"The imminent threat of troll slaughter was a bit of motivation. And glad as I was to see you alive—you were still unconscious when we left you last fall—frankly, I thought I'd be rid of you and on my way back home by now, not surrounded by trolls in the bowels of the earth."

"It's not a position I'd hoped to be in again so soon, myself," Dorav replied, his voice rough.

For a moment Joseph imagined the Streets of Twilight overrun with trolls, slaughter running rampant in the streets, and he felt a tug of guilt for emphasizing his own problems to his friend. "I didn't mean to compare miseries."

"Hm? Eh, I didn't take it like that. It's just...well, it's just been a shitty week."

In spite of everything, Joseph laughed. Dorav chuckled in response, and the burdens of the moment lifted, if only a little.

"Still," Dorav continued, returning to the subject, "you don't seem as overjoyed as I'd expect for a man in love."

"I'm still trying to work it out, I guess. I'm a very different man than the boy I was when I met my wi...I mean, my first wife. And the Windriders aren't much on ceremony, which I respect, but the human in me feels a bit strange not marking such a big change somehow. Not to mention all this coming together during another catastrophe."

"But you're happy, yeah?" Dorav prodded.

"I will be, when I'm home and my people are safe, Kaillë most of all."

Dorav regarded Joseph for a moment. "Me, I'm a loner," he said. "I mourn hard for Steva, but I didn't need much in the way of other company. I know you lived a long time alone, Joseph, but to hear you talk I'm not too sure you were ever a loner. Just a man waiting for the right family to come along, maybe."

"Maybe," Joseph said, his brow furrowed. It was a challenge to a long-held image he had of himself, and he wasn't sure the dwarf was right, but there was more truth in the statement than he might have realized just a few months ago. "So, what about you," Joseph asked after a moment. "Loner or not, no pretty young dwarf lass ever turned your head?"

"Well, I wouldn't go as far as that. Dwarf passions don't seem to burn quite as hot as you surface folks', though, and our families work a little different, too. Dwarves really only pair up for children, and since I never wanted to be a father, I didn't have much to offer the ladies. It's the roving life I chose."

Mention of children gave Joseph pause. Kaillë had never discussed it, and, stupidly, Joseph hadn't given the matter any consideration before committing himself to her. The issue had been moot when he was a younger man; Delia was half-elven, and those of mixed parentage couldn't have children. Joseph considered then that even if he and Kaillë did have a child, that child would have none of its own, ending the hereditary line of the Windsong family as chiefs of the Windrider clan. He felt like a fool for not bringing these matters to Kaillë much sooner. Finally, he reined in his train of thought and met Dorav's eyes again.

"I noticed you didn't say anything about the Baron in your report to the council."

"Aye. And neither did you."

"No reason to try to explain something they'd never believe anyway."

"Just what I was thinking," Dorav agreed.

"It eats at me, though. Suppose the Baron does come, wielding magic. How will the dwarves stop him?"

Dorav shook his head. "I don't know what you saw at the cave, Joseph. I trust your eyes, and I'm more open minded than a lot of my kind, but it's still hard to swallow the idea of that man still being alive, or alive again, or however you'd say it. Even if he was, he's buried under tons of rock, now."

"I hope you're right, but I doubt it. There's something else in play here, some power, and it seems to know what happens in all places at once, and to have influence somehow over the trolls, and to have pulled the Baron's strings even last year, or before. I don't know what it means, but so far I have only one clue. Dorav, what more can you tell me about the Well?"

"Some. I'm not sure how much help it'll be, but I'll tell

you what I know.

"The original settlers of the Ninth Clan came upon the place before the colony was even established. Some of our people in those days still held to a less rational view of the world, and they claimed a sense of darkness about the place, a feeling, they said, of something old and evil. Most had already come to disbelieve such things, and they set up expeditions to sound out the depth of the Well and explore whatever was at the bottom. Legend has it they never did find the floor of the thing, but the attempts attracted unwanted attention. Trolls began to attack the area, and a huge beast, a giant lizard, of sorts, with claws and teeth like steel and a hide as hard as stone."

"You mean...a dragon?"

"A giant lizard by another name. Whatever the case, some legends say it issued from the Well itself, but others suggest it came from somewhere else to put off any intrusion. Nobody really knows. That's when the leaders of the Ninth Clan sent for help from the Tenth, as I mentioned before, and the Tenth sent Dalvinav."

"And Dalvinav killed the giant lizard."

"So he did."

"And cut it open and found a heart of stone?"

"That's what the legends say."

"What else?" Joseph pushed.

"Nothing else. The expeditions hadn't turned up anything of value, and the attempts had caused enough trouble, so the council declared the place off limits, and that was that. Young dwarves would go there sometimes to prove their courage, and every rover worth his salt visits the place at least once, along with every other 'off-limits' spot. I guess the Well must have found its way into some surface-walker legends, 'cause humans have come down two or three times over the years looking for it, or something that sounds like it. That's all from the records, though, before my time."

"Any humans ever find it?"

"If they did, they got in and back out again without crossing paths with any patrols."

Joseph was silent in thought for a moment. "There's something in that Well, Dorav. I know it. I don't know what it is, but it's dangerous and up to no good, just as sure as I'm sitting here."

Dorav yawned. "Maybe you're right, but that doesn't give us much to work with. I think I could sleep again, and I mean to. I'll see you later on, Joseph."

Joseph nodded to Dorav as the dwarf got up to leave then the hunter sat alone for a few minutes in thought. The rover was right about at least one thing; there was nothing much they could do from where they sat. Convinced as he was that the risen Baron was only a servant of something greater, it was the Baron himself, or itself, that still posed the gravest immediate threat. Without a wizard, Joseph had no idea how he might be stopped. And the trolls would likely arrive at any time.

Chapter Eleven: Things Buried

When next Joseph awoke, it was to the sounds of two of the elves entering the room as two dwarven maids set another meal on the wall shelf. Joseph stretched and rubbed at his face with dry hands, then wasted no time in filling another plate. By the elves' appearance of energy, he suspected they had slept several hours in total, meaning that he had as well, albeit with a break in the middle. Dorav wandered into the sitting room just as Joseph was sitting down and likewise moved to the buffet.

"Dorav," Joseph called, "have you been up? Is there any news?"

"I popped out for a bit about an hour ago. The trolls took longer to get here than I'd have thought, but it seems the fighting has started up here and there, mostly in the northern tunnels."

"Northern tunnels?" Joseph asked. "That's odd, isn't it, since they're coming up from the south?"

Dorav shrugged. "You never can tell with trolls."

Joseph scowled. He respected Dorav, but sometimes he wished he wasn't such a dwarf. "Well, what's on the north side?" the hunter asked. "Anything strategic or that trolls would want? Does the terrain favor them more?"

Dorav considered for a moment. "Not that I can think of. It isn't going to matter much, though, Joseph, the trolls aren't going to get within two miles of the city. The Tenth Clan put the time we bought them to good use preparing their defenses, and even now they're reinforcing the north side to make sure there are no breaches."

"Reinforcing the north side with *what*?"

"They pulled in the patrols and skirmishers from south of the city. Don't worry; the real defense is still at full strength, or near enough. They won't get caught napping if the trolls test them there."

Joseph knew Dorav was well experienced in troll behavior, but he was convinced his friend was underestimating the enemy. His experience, the experience of all the dwarves, came exclusively from times when the trolls had been working only on instinct, attacking wherever their lusts and savagery led them. This attack was different; this time they had a strong will guiding them. "Just humoring me," Joseph continued, "what's south of Glowing Rocks, outside the defenses."

"Nothing, really. Some empty tunnel complexes, the farms we saw on the way in—they've already been evacuated—what else?" Dorav's all-black eyes went to the ceiling, exposing the faintest line of white around the bottom to betray his mental activity. Suddenly his gaze pinned on Joseph again, and the hunter saw his face go slack with something very much like dread. "The vault, Joseph. Glowing Rocks' vault is southeast of the city."

"Damn," Joseph hissed. "Men, we're moving out," he said to his elves, standing up from his half-eaten meal and heading back to his room to change his clothes and gather his gear.

"What are we going to do?" Dorav asked.

"We're going down there," Joseph answered, exasperation edging his voice at what he considered an obvious question.

Dorav followed him into his room, still speaking, and more quickly than was his custom. "It's just like last year in the Ninth Clan; the trolls attacked to pull our attention away while the Baron and his men broke into the vault to steal the Hoard."

"I know, Dorav," Joseph answered as he began re-stuffing his pack.

"We'll be on our own; the defenders already have their orders and we can't change the council's—"

"I know!" Joseph paused and took a breath. "Dorav, I don't know what we'll do when we get there; if I'm right, there might not even be much we *can* do, but I won't just sit here while the enemy gets exactly what it's after with barely so much as a fight. Even if all we can do is report back to the council on what they take, it's better than nothing." He put his hand on Dorav's shoulder. "If you want to stay here, I understand. You've already been through hell and done more than anybody could ask."

Dorav pulled his shoulder away. "Don't be stupid. 'Course I'm coming. And it's a square bet there'll be at least one rover band between here and there, and I ain't met a one of 'em yet that wasn't itching to buck a few orders if it'll show they're smarter than the councils."

Within a few minutes the company was ready to set out again. The maid who had been instructed to look after them was not amused by their intention to depart.

"You must not just go wandering," she was insisting, "I'm responsible for you."

Joseph was a step back, deferring to Dorav's better understanding of the culture in this argument.

"We ain't prisoners, are we?" Dorav snapped back.

"Of course not."

"Then we must be guests, and guests are allowed to come and go, and that's that. C'mon, Joseph."

"Even guests can't just have the run of a place," the maid answered, her formal composure falling a bit. "Tell me where you want to go."

"Listen, your councilwoman Zallah said our axes and bows might be needed before all was over. Well, now we've rested, and we've ate, and we're gonna go pop around a bit and make sure those axes and bows aren't being missed anywhere on the defense. Is that alright with you?"

"...I...guess so," the maid said, picking at a hangnail that suddenly needed her attention.

"Sounds like a 'yes' to me. I said come on, Joseph, we're going." Dorav left the room before the maid could argue further, and Joseph followed him out, his elves and the dogs just behind.

"Is she going to get in trouble?" Joseph asked after a few steps.

"How should I know?" Dorav answered. "Would that have changed your mind?"

"No," Joseph admitted. They passed down the hall and onto a staircase before Joseph added, "One thing's a lot more clear to me now."

"Which is?"

"Why you never got on with women."

~ * ~

Dorav's better head for dwarven architecture and brief exploration of the building before Joseph and the elves had woken served them in good stead, and in several minutes they were out of the council building and back on the streets. Dorav had led them out by a side entrance that avoided the full force of guards at the main doors. The few dwarves they did pass definitely looked their way, but lacking any orders concerning this party, which didn't seem hostile in any case, they gave no challenge.

The streets of Glowing Rocks were wide and straight, making navigation easy. They passed a few guard squads and carts of supplies heading north, but the traffic in this part of the city was light.

After several minutes of moving steadily to the southeast, Dorav spotted a group of dwarves and badgers crossing their path. "Hai! Tuvdahl!"

One of the dwarves looked in their direction and called, "Dorav?" This meeting was followed by a series of shouted dwarven phrases, falling to a more normal volume as the dwarf squad turned from their course and moved closer to Joseph and his friends, their two giant badgers bringing up the rear. At last the two groups came together and Dorav and the lead dwarf clasped hands.

"Joseph," Dorav said, turning, "this is Tuvdahl. He's a rover from the Tenth Clan; we meet up a time or two each year to trade tales and such. Ugly as the hind end of a troll, but a good man otherwise."

Joseph couldn't see any discernable difference in attractiveness between Dorav and Tuvdahl's leathery skin, though his blonde and gray beard was long and unkempt beneath his bald head. Tuvdahl, on the other hand, creased his brow for a moment then grunted something in dwarven before backhanding Dorav across the shoulder as the dark-haired rover laughed.

"Boor," Tuvdahl said. "My surface talk..." and here he scrunched his face and shook his head, "...not too good. Dorav plays unfair."

Dorav stopped laughing in a moment and resumed his conversation with the dwarven group in their own tongue.

After a few exchanges, Joseph noted a shift in their body language and a few nods of assent. He suspected Dorav had just secured the help he had anticipated back in their quarters.

The rover turned and confirmed Joseph's assumption. "Tuvdahl and his friends have agreed to go with us. I'll spare the introductions since we're in a hurry. Let's keep moving."

The two parties now joined and continued their way at a brisk walk. Joseph reflected for a moment on what a motley bunch they made: one human, head and shoulders taller than all the rest, six lithe elves looking like they expected the roof to fall in on them at any moment, nine stocky dwarves with an assortment of weapons and gear, and in the midst of all two giant badgers sniffing at two playful dogs all trying to figure out what each other were.

After walking what felt like a mile, leaving the center of Glowing Rocks well behind, the group approached a checkpoint where no trolls were in evidence. It seemed one of Tuvdahl's companions knew the dwarves on guard, for after a brief conversation the group was allowed passage out of the city despite the state of emergency. Joseph noticed the guard beating a quick message on the drumhead on the wall as they left, and when they arrived at the second checkpoint, they were allowed through without incident.

After this Tuvdahl took point, leading the group through a section of winding tunnels that thwarted even Joseph's sense of direction. The tunnel forked and switched back on itself several times, and Joseph found himself hoping he didn't have to find his way back without dwarven help.

Judging distance was difficult now that they had left straight, clear paths, but Joseph guessed they had traveled another two miles, with Dorav once again providing light, when the badgers bared their teeth and snarled, sending Stitch and Yowler skittering back. Tuvdahl held up his hand, signaling the party to halt. He crept forward with one of his fellow rovers, approaching the next bend in the tunnel. The dwarves had only poked their heads and shoulders around the corner when suddenly they were thrown back by dark shadows bursting forward. The shapes snarled in rage, and as they threw the dwarves backward, closer to Dorav's light, Joseph was able to make out the form of two trolls.

Ten'marden had not been idle while the dwarves moved forward, and his bowstring twanged twice. Two thuds sounded from the scuffle ahead, and the trolls fell back, kicking and thrashing, each with an arrow sticking out from an atrophied eye socket. The dwarves nearby muttered and nodded in appreciation of his skill. Tuvdahl and his friend stood and finished the trolls with ax strokes to their throats.

Immediately afterward they urged the rest of the party forward, and there they were greeted by a site of destruction. Another checkpoint had stood there until recently, but it had been blasted back as if by a great explosion, leaving only twisted iron on either side of the tunnel. The nearer gate had even been ripped from its anchors in the stone, leaving ragged craters in the tunnel walls and splinters of rock strewn across the floor. There had been four guards, but all were dead, their bodies mangled, and the one nearest the party had clearly been used as food for the two trolls left behind, ostensibly, to keep watch.

"Always too late," Dorav groaned, moving forward along with Tuvdahl to do what little he could to compose the bodies of his people.

"Maybe not," Joseph replied. "As far as we know, they have no master thief to pick the locks. By the damage to the gates, we have to assume the Baron is here, but we don't know the extent of his powers. Your vault doors may give even him pause."

Dorav nodded. "Either way, no time to dally. Time to

move."

Tuvdahl gave the order, and now the band was off at a brisk trot, making up time as best they could while still conserving energy for the inevitable battle ahead. Two dwarves went in front, each wielding a long spear, and Joseph ordered two elves to run behind them, arrows nocked.

They passed another checkpoint as ruined as the first, and again two trolls sprang to the attack. Spears and arrows made quick work of them, but Joseph was sure he heard scrabbling motions going before them down the tunnel: other trolls retreating to warn the main force ahead.

"They know we're coming," he muttered, and Dorav, at his side, nodded, leaving Joseph to assume the other dwarves had already noticed what he had. Tuvdahl, running a little ahead, turned and spoke to Dorav.

"We're almost there," Dorav told Joseph. "Tell your archers to fall back. And be ready."

Joseph gave the order then nocked an arrow to his bowstring. The dwarves pulled to either side, allowing the two badgers to surge forward to the front of the squad. Stitch and Yowler sensed the change in mood and sheltered behind the legs of Joseph and the elves.

The band turned the corner, facing a mob of snarling trolls not fifteen paces away.

The badgers hit them like battering rams, slamming several trolls a piece to the ground. Their long claws and savage teeth flashed all around, ripping into the seething mass that now surrounded them. The dwarves gave a battle cry and ran ahead, the spearmen working with grim efficiency as the rest hewed with ax and hammer. Dorav's twin axes sang and glinted in the cold light of his glowing bowls, and Joseph saw his pent-up rage unleashed upon the trolls. Joseph gave no order, knowing the elves needed none. Arrows whistled through the cavern, passing around the dwarves on all sides to fell any troll seeking an entry into the fray, denying them rest or opening. One of the badgers was overwhelmed, and Joseph merely pointed. The elves concentrated their arrows, and suddenly the knot of trolls was thinned to only a pair of survivors that were quickly dispatched by the other badger.

Perhaps twenty seconds had passed, and the troll mob was wavering. Openings began to appear throughout the mass. Up ahead Joseph saw a faint, orange glow illuminating a sheer wall with two large mechanisms at about chest height—the vault door. Dorav saw it too.

"Joseph," he shouted, "go! We'll hold here."

"Windriders! On me!" the hunter commanded, slipping his bow over his shoulder and drawing his long knife. The elves did likewise as all five began their mad sprint through the chaos of battle. A troll reared up to block Joseph's path, it's tooth ridges snapping and dripping, but Joseph lunged forward with his knife, raking through the creature's neck and spraying black blood over his face. He could hear grunts and shouts from behind him as the elves reached out to either side, thinning the troll horde as they rushed through. Another troll barred Joseph's path and he put on speed, lowering his shoulder and hoping to bull the beast to the side, but suddenly there was a second snarling enemy and Joseph was stopped dead. His knife slashed at arms and hands as they clawed at him, but his blade could find no chink in the armor of their thick hides. The left-hand troll strengthened its grip, holding Joseph as the right troll raised a now-free hand to swipe at his neck. Joseph tucked his chin and tried to spin out of the hold, but before the strike could land the top of the troll's head suddenly disappeared in a gout of black blood as Tuvdahl's hammer crushed its skull. The dwarf gave a quick salute before returning to the fight, and the second troll, now alone, found his grip on Joseph a marked disadvantage as the elves caught up and went to work with their knives.

At last the group was through the melee, standing just feet behind the resurrected Baron Turov as he chanted and waved his hands at the vault door. Joseph had come to the point of final conflict and had no notion of what to do. The Baron seemed to pay them no mind, if he even yet knew they were there.

Joseph clenched his jaw. He wasn't confident, but one thing was sure: the simplest plans were usually best. He caught Tes'sael's eye and nodded, and the group sheathed their knives and readied their bows once more. When Joseph stretched his bow, the elves did the same, and seven arrows thudded into the Baron's back almost simultaneously, driving him forward with the impact.

Turov turned and faced them, his scarred face and eyepatch as Joseph had remembered them from the cave. For all his courage, Joseph's heart quailed at the Baron's gaze, knowing there was no imminent cave-in to save him if the Baron employed sorcery again.

Instead, the grinning revenant merely reached behind him, placing his palm against the vault doors, and pushed.

A deep cracking, grinding sound issued from within the stone, and the seam where the doors met, invisible a moment ago, glowed with pallid light. The doors swung inward, and the Baron snorted at the elves in contempt.

More out of frustration, even spite, than hope it would do any good, Joseph stretched his bow again, inspiring another volley from the elves. More arrows now riddled the Baron, but rather than counterattack, he rolled his good eye and waved his hand, turning away as elf and hunter alike cried out in consternation and fought to hold their springing bows as all seven bowstrings snapped in unison.

Joseph could do nothing but watch as the Baron entered the vault, turning his gaze this way and that. All Joseph could see was row upon row of crates, but the Baron peered intently at each one as if seeing through the metal of their construction.

The sounds of battle were dying down behind Joseph, the trolls killed or driven off. He hazarded a glance over his shoulder to see Dorav helping one of Tuvdahl's friends up off the ground while Tuvdahl himself knelt over the form of another, his head bowed as he closed the fallen dwarf's eyes.

It seemed the Baron had found the crate he was looking for. He stepped toward it, taking the lock in his right hand. The metal flashed hot and broke, and he cast the slag aside absently as he lifted the lid of the box.

Joseph stood transfixed, watching impotently as this remnant of a dead man, arrows piercing him front and back, reached into the crate and drew out a deep brown stone two or three hand-spans across. The Baron turned toward Joseph and the elves, a hideous grin slashing across his face, raising the stone in both hands. His mouth moved, forming words too quiet for Joseph to hear, and a sudden glow, starting deep red and flashing white hot as it moved, shot from his chest, up through the veins of his arms, and into the artifact he held now above his head, kindling a fire in the depths of the stone.

Now Joseph could see it clearly, shaped like a great heart, and as the glow pulsed within it, the hunter could swear it was beating. "You have caused me no end of trouble, hunter!" the Baron cackled. "Upon a time I'd have killed you for it, but for now you will live. From darkness and hate this heart was forged, and it goes now back to whence it came. The master comes forth, and he has his own plan for your miserable life."

The Baron lowered the heart, cradling it against his body, and walked back toward the defeated band. Joseph stepped aside, his eyes silently ordering his elves to do likewise. He had been called a hero by more than one people, but there was nothing brash in that heroism. If there was a difference between courage and valor, he knew which he would choose, and if his enemy was foolish enough to let him live, whatever cruelty might have inspired it, Joseph would do nothing to change his mind. Still, he knew he was beaten, and his survival tasted like gall.

The dwarves, for their part, were too overawed by the display they had just witnessed to do anything but shrink against the cavern walls, cowering from a power they could no more confront than understand. Joseph's jaw clenched as the Baron moved away, his knife-hand flexing and relaxing as he fought to control his rage. Ten more steps and the Baron would disappear around the bend in the tunnel. Five more. Two.

And he was gone.

Joseph sprang into action. "Tes'sael, help tend the badgers." He flung his pack to the ground, kicking it toward the elf so that he could access any of the poultices inside if his own pack ran light. "Dorav, I'm sorry for the man you lost. Are any of the others bad hurt?"

"No, Joseph. Nothing that won't mend on its own with time. Nothing that will slow us down."

Joseph nodded. "Good."

Tes'sael had already delegated the dressing of the badgers' wounds to Ten'dalla and Ten'harnë, the elves with the best herb-craft. "Where are we bound, Joseph? And what are we to do when we get there?"

"We're going to the Well," Joseph answered, "as for the plan...we should have a couple days to figure that out."

"Take all the time you want," Dorav spat, "what can you do against that?"

Tuvdahl growled something and dug into his pack, holding forth a small cask.

Dorav translated. "He says we just need to intercept the

enemy somewhere he can use that without killing us all." Joseph believed the dwarf's next comment was an addition rather than a translation. "The Baron may not technically die, but it's bound to slow down his plans a bit if he's blasted into a million pieces."

"Best bet so far," Joseph agreed. "Ask Tuvdahl to pick two of his dwarves to go back and tell the council what's happened here, as much as they'll believe, anyway. See if they'll send all the dwarves they can spare to the Well. If we fail, maybe they can do something."

Dorav explained the request to Tuvdahl, who sent two of his dwarves heading back up the tunnel.

Tes'sael had already anticipated Joseph's next intention and started collecting arrows from dead trolls. Some were ruined, but most could be reused, and with little hope of getting more underground, they were precious. Everyone's quivers were refilled from the backup bundle in the supplies, but now that reserve was spent. Equally important, Joseph and the elves dug spare bowstrings from their packs and repaired their weapons.

As the preparations to move out continued, Joseph turned to Dorav again. "Supposing you decided to believe in legends and myths, really believe in them, what would you suppose the Baron took out of that crate?"

Dorav grimaced. "The stone heart of the...dragon...that Dalvinav brought back to the Tenth Clan."

Joseph nodded.

"And you think he's going to bring the beast back to life from the depths of the Well, by some magic?" Dorav guessed.

"Based on what I've seen, that's what I think," Joseph said. "Only I think the dragon is no mere beast, but something of great wits and power."

"Figures," Dorav grunted.

"I know myth of Dalvinav," Tuvdahl grunted.

"Dalvinav killed great lizard. If robed man brings it back," Tuvdahl paused, thumping his chest, "then *I* kill great lizard. My hammer crush bones, no matter how thick hide is."

"And thank you for that," Joseph said, nodding. "I owe you my life. Your hammer may match the great lizard." Joseph turned to Tes'sael and spoke in elven. "Then again, it may not. One important thing has changed since Dalvinav killed the beast in the past."

"What is that, Joseph?" Tes'sael asked.

"When Dalvinav slayed it, I hadn't sent the whole Hoard of Dalviir tumbling into the well to feed it."

Preparations were completed, and the band moved out, heading back down the winding tunnels toward the main thoroughfares that connected the Ninth and Tenth Clans. Joseph knew they were doing little more than biding their time, but as they walked he tasked Dorav and Tuvdahl with devising a shortcut or remembering a secret way that might allow them to ambush the Baron. Until then they could only move south, keeping their distance from the sorcerous wight without allowing him too great a lead.

They were almost due south of Glowing Rocks again when Joseph knew something had gone terribly wrong.

A great clamor echoed down the main tunnel leading back to the city. Joseph had trouble associating the sound with well-ordered dwarven society, but there could be no mistaking it, as he'd heard it more times in his earlier life than he cared to remember: the sound of a city gripped in the chaos of war.

A general rumble of pounding footsteps, creaking cart wheels, and panicked shouts wove together down the tunnel to his ears, punctuated by occasional sharp noises that rose above the din before being swallowed up just as quickly: a baby's scream, a badger yelping, a cart crashing or shattering.

Joseph looked sidelong at Dorav, wondering if the rover had enough experience with open warfare to interpret the sound. Dorav was looking back up at him, and Joseph read his eyes: the dwarf had guessed correctly but was silently begging Joseph to disagree. The hunter could only clench his teeth and shake his head.

The party passed within sight of the second checkpoint they had exited to leave the city, looking back to the north and straining their eyes for some sight of the blue-green glow of the great cavern, though they knew it was around too many bends in the tunnel. The guards at the checkpoint met their eyes, resolute but hopeless as they held their post. Tuvdahl shouted to one of the guards in his language, and Joseph thought he caught two dwarven names he'd heard since pairing up with Tuvdahl's Irregulars. The guard pointed toward the city and shook his head, and Joseph understood. The dwarves Tuvdahl had sent back had been permitted through the checkpoint before the battle erupted, and now they were somewhere in the maelstrom.

Suddenly a seething mass of shadows surged in the tunnel behind the farther guard, his screams drowned in the snarling of trolls as they tore at him. The nearer guard, on Joseph's side of the checkpoint bars, gripped his halberd and shouted a word in dwarven, then caught Joseph's eyes. "Go!" he repeated in the surface tongue.

"Come with us!" Joseph shouted back, straining to be heard over the horrible, rending sounds of the trolls on the other side of the gate. Those not sating themselves on the flesh of the fallen guard were already tearing at the iron, and Joseph knew their unstoppable strength when they moved en masse. The gate would hold, but only for a time. "Come on," the hunter repeated.

"I will not leave my post," the guard argued.

The party couldn't afford to stop, but Joseph turned and jogged backward as they moved, still hoping to convince the dwarf. "Your post is lost, and we need every ax we can get."

"You have my ax," the guard shouted back, saluting. "You have it right here." With that the guard turned and began thrusting the pike head of his halberd through the bars, wounding or slaying as many trolls as he could.

The gate creaked and bowed inward in a great lurch, driving the guard back as Joseph turned away, no stomach to see what he knew would follow and needing all his focus on the tunnel ahead as the party picked up speed.

They had increased to a dead run when they heard the gates crash in their final collapse a furlong behind them. The tunnel was a straight shot to the trolls now on their scent. "Dorav," Joseph called, "can you see them?"

"Not as you do, but yes," the dwarf replied.

"How many? How many got through?"

"The guard did his duty well. Not many. Four, I think, no, five."

"Drop a torch," Joseph ordered to Ten'harnë.

He did as he was bid, lighting a torch from his pack as they ran and dropping it behind them in the tunnel.

Joseph then turned his orders to Ten'marden and Tes'sael. "Drop back. When the trolls get to the light, see they get no farther."

On the party ran, Joseph easing the pace just slightly so his men could catch up when the job was done. For the best part of an hour they jogged on, but finally even the dwarves were forced to rest. They all leaned against the walls, sipping at their canteens, resting only a minute or two when the last two elves caught up.

"We're light on provisions," Joseph told Dorav. "We packed for a fight, not a journey. We can tighten our belts and do without food, but is there water between here and there?"

"Maybe, depending on the rains up above. We dwarves

can do without and give our shares to you and the elves. It's the badgers that will suffer the most if the stream isn't flowing."

"We can only hope it is then." Joseph poured some of his water into a low spot in the tunnel, giving Stitch and Yowler at least enough to wet their tongues, but the journey so far had not taxed them, being bred and trained for tracking all day through thick woods. "How far to the Well?" Joseph asked.

"Much shorter than traveling overland," Dorav answered. "The tunnel we're in runs arrow-straight to Tra'id-Stie'che...or whatever's left of it, and it's just a short detour around it to the Well on the west side. You guessed aright before—two days."

Joseph sensed an unspoken "but" in Dorav's tone and prodded him for it.

"When the Streets of Twilight fell," the rover continued, "these tunnels were choked with trolls. Even with the main horde moving around Glowing Rocks to the north, it's beyond hope that we won't come up against some on our way south. There's no way to know if we have the numbers to fight our way through. Not until it's too late."

"Are there narrower tunnels?" Joseph asked. "Somewhere we could nullify their numbers?"

"There are, but they're a roundabout way and will slow us down too much. We go that way, we abandon any hope of catching up to the Baron."

Joseph confided in the dwarf. "It was no secret I didn't have much of a plan to start with, but even with that I've left too much to chance, haven't I?"

"I don't see that you had much choice."

Joseph exhaled a mirthless laugh. "It seems I never do. Or a choice between two bad options, if a choice that can be called."

~ * ~

Soon they were moving again, this time at a more sustainable pace. Joseph's mind churned as they walked, but no plans came any clearer. Dorav pointed out shortly after they began to move again that they had no way to know the extent of the Baron's knowledge of the tunnels, so the only sure place to set an ambush was at the Well itself. Dorav would lead them there by the best routes he knew, but it was impossible to predict whether they would beat the Baron to the finish, his powers being unknown and unknowable.

Their first day of travel came to a close, though Joseph had lost all sense of whether this was evening or morning or anything in between, up on the surface, and at last they caught a small break. The underground stream Dorav had mentioned before was indeed flowing full, filling a semicircular basin a dozen or so feet across against the left-hand wall of the tunnel, then continuing on in the direction they were heading in a channel running like a gutter where the tunnel floor met the wall. They drank their fill and, since their way ran with the stream, declined to fully fill their water skins to save the weight.

Joseph and Tuvdahl set a rotation of watches, and the party was able to catch a few hours' sleep. Joseph knew they couldn't do without it but begrudged every minute, assuming the Baron to be sleepless in his undeath.

Chapter Twelve: Prisons

Four or five hours later they set out again, and for the first half of the day the only enemies they faced were fatigue and boredom. Troll sign became more and more frequent as they went, though, gnawed bones and scat and occasional patches of matted fur or dried, black blood.

Joseph was about to call a halt when the dogs started acting skittish, catching some unknown scent on the subtle currents of air. The badgers, too, perked up their ears and sniffed the air heavily. Tuvdahl ordered the party against one wall of the tunnel as they moved forward toward a major intersection, the great ceiling supported by a groin vault of dressed stones.

After several minutes they saw no movement, so they stepped into the open, facing the blind side of the intersection with weapons at the ready.

They were immediately stopped short by a dense hedge of spears. As quickly as the steel points were offered in challenge, however, they collapsed into disarray as their bearers dropped their stances and leaned against the tunnel walls or each other. It was a hret-dialt, but in a state Joseph had never seen one, exhausted to the point of failure, their faces slack with broken will.

Even Joseph recognized the uniforms and arms of the Ninth Clan, and Dorav clearly did likewise, rushing forward to minister to his clansmen as best he could. A long exchange in dwarven ensued, and Dorav summarized. "They were away southeast of Tra'id-Stie'che when the attack fell. They've been fighting through the tunnels ever since, cutting their way to what they hoped was safety, trying to make Lun'rool-Carrig'ach."

"I don't think there's any hope for them that way," Joseph said.

"I've told them," Dorav assented. "They want to come with us. I told them how dangerous our way is, but they're desperate."

Joseph wasn't surprised. Now that their spear points weren't in his face, he could get a proper count of them. There were only six, putting the unit at half strength, and they were caked thick with troll blood, as was all the rest of the hret-dialt's gear. "We could use them," Joseph admitted, "but not like this. They're barely fit to stand, much less to travel or fight."

"It was time to halt. Yes?" Tuvdahl interjected.

"Yes," Joseph agreed.

"They have reached stream. They drink. We give them our food. They recover. They are dwarves, hret-dialt. You will see."

Joseph knew his elves could part with the food they'd brought, though they hadn't much left. Ten'vahlë and Ten'dalla did credit to elven generosity, though, taking from their packs a great store of the dwarven food they had managed to squirrel away while preparing to set out the day before. The hunter was amazed at how much they had packed, and how efficiently, shaking his head as they pulled out one container after another as if their packs had false bottoms. Tuvdahl's dwarves opened their meager stores as well, including some from the gear they had stripped from their fallen comrade.

The hret-dialt set to with vigor, devouring all they were given without modesty or apology. Knowing the dwarves' martial bent, Joseph supposed the guard was accustomed to receiving the best of any provisions when commons got short. In any case, he was surprised to see their spirits rising as they ate, true to Tuvdahl's prediction. After eating, they set their backs against the tunnel wall and their short legs straight out before them and fell instantly to sleep, heedless of the world around them.

Reluctant to question their fitness again, Joseph likewise settled down to rest, closing his eyes and relaxing his muscles but keeping far from sleep. He was conscious of the time and knew in a matter of minutes he would have to insist that the band move on, at least any he could still convince to continue, even if the hret-dialt continued their sleep.

Joseph's concerns proved groundless. After what felt like fifteen minutes, he heard Dorav say his name. Joseph looked up and threw back his hood to see the dwarf standing before him.

"They're ready to move," the rover said.

Joseph looked across the tunnel to where the stonebound unit had slumbered and saw they were indeed up and arrayed, standing at attention as rigid and disciplined as any dwarves he'd seen.

"Are they really alright?" he asked.

"For long enough," Dorav explained. "Another day or two, no more, and they'll have to sleep for a week, but until that time comes, they'll be as sharp as ever."

"Fair enough," Joseph said, standing. "Let's move out."

~ * ~

They'd been marching for three more hours when the trolls attacked.

Joseph never knew for sure how they set such a perfect ambush, but twenty minutes after they left the main tunnel for Dorav's chosen route to the Well, with only the barest hint of warning from the dogs, they launched a pincer from both sides of a four-way intersection, washing over the party like floodwaters in a storm surge.

Ten'marden went down under an assault from two trolls only feet from Joseph, but before the hunter could come to his aid, he himself was beset by one of the largest trolls he'd seen. One of the hret-dialt, marching at his side, speared the troll cleanly through the throat, only to be dragged backwards by two more of the black-furred savages. The badgers clawed and bit, but the trolls had weighed them down with their heaviest assault, and it was more than they could handle just to tear the trolls free from one another. Dorav had been bringing up the rear and was on the fringes of the ambush, if fringes they could be called, and again his axes did heavy work. Joseph saw him cutting his way into the thick of the melee as he knifed the first two trolls and helped Ten'marden up from the ground; blood flowed from a cut above his eye and a ragged chunk had been bitten from his left shoulder.

"Joseph," Dorav called, "they're lined up both tunnels. There's too many; we have to fight our way clear!"

The news was grave but unsurprising; however, Dorav's advice was easier said than done. Joseph's elves had managed to disengage and rally to him, their nimble frames and training to fight in wood and thicket doing them good service in the tight-packed tunnel. The dwarves, though, were taking the brunt of the assault and pressed on every side; the hret-dialt was already down to five dwarves standing, and though he couldn't be sure in the shifting skirmish, Joseph thought Tuvdahl had lost another man as well. Trolls were fighting to get into the fray, driving the defenders together. Joseph could see only one hope of making a hole through the mass of enemy bodies.

He pointed and gave a one-word order. "Badger."

The elves slipped between ranks and set to work clearing off the badger on the left side of the scrum. The hret-dialt was on that side and saw Joseph's play, wordlessly pushing the trolls back and forming a bulwark between the badger and the enemy. Seconds passed, then the badger was free, surging up and savaging the trolls weighing down his partner. Joseph's heart broke at the mass of wounds covering both his flanks; there was no hope he would survive the day, but his life would be purchased at a heavy cost to his enemies.

"Tuvdahl," Joseph shouted, "look. Get ready." He knew that any more complicated order would be lost in translation in the head-spinning rush of battle.

Apparently the dwarf understood, for he managed to form up with his men on the right side of the badgers.

With the elves' help, the first badger rescued his companion from the weight of trolls in a matter of moments, spitting some with his claws and slamming them to the stone floor, snapping limbs or heads off others without discrimination. Alas, this badger's wounds looked at least as bad as the first's, but he, too, paid them no heed as the pair lunged forward, their flanks and rear now protected by two legged warriors of every race.

As the badgers pushed, the party followed, step by agonizing step through the horde of trolls to the far side of the intersection, clawing their way out of the lethal pincer. Pikes and halberds held the enemy back at either side, and at last two of the elves had room to stretch their bows, helping Dorav cover their backs until the badgers had pushed far enough forward to allow the dwarves to turn from flanks to rear. Half the hret-dialt had fallen, and Tuvdahl had lost two. Given the hardiness of dwarves, Joseph doubted they were dead, but there was no way to retrieve the wounded without sacrificing the lives of every man there.

Adrenaline flagging, Joseph choked back a sob as he saw the badgers turn to face the trolls once more, beautiful in their unbridled fury, fur streaked with blood both red and black and murder in their eyes. Their roars shook the very stones, driving the trolls to throw clawed hands over their bat-like ears as elf and dwarf pulled back to the edges of the tunnel, opening room for their charge. The badgers launched themselves into their enemy, pounding into them in a display of ferocity that beggared anything Joseph had seen. Sparing no time for further admiration or gratitude, the party ran.

"They can't hold for long," Joseph shouted then noticed Tuvdahl had fallen behind and was kneeling on the ground. For a moment he thought the rover was wounded, and all things considered he probably was, but that wasn't why he knelt. Joseph saw him remove from his belt pouch a metal disk, no larger than a whetstone, with a crank handle on one side. Tuvdahl turned the crank, and sparks shot out of a slot on the side of the disk. A moment later some of those sparks caught on a fuse, and as Tuvdahl stood, he held his powder keg under one arm. Joseph thought the dwarf would heave it behind them until he saw Tuvdahl's left arm hung limp at his side, and the keg looked too heavy to roll or throw one-handed.

Joseph turned away and re-doubled his speed as the rover began his sprint back toward the trolls, but even the extra distance wasn't enough. Joseph was thrown forward by the force of the blast as his ears were smote by a noise like the boom of lightning hitting a nearby tree. He only just managed to get his forearms under his face so it didn't smash into the stone of the tunnel floor, but even then the wave of force disoriented his every sense. It may have been seconds or minutes when he finally rolled over and looked back to the tunnel crossing, his ears still ringing like the inside of a temple bell, and saw nothing of Tuvdahl or the badgers or even of the trolls, only a wall of rubble and shifting scree.

For several minutes the whole band just sat. Had all the trolls of the subterranean world come and assailed them at that moment, even still they could not have moved. Weariness and pain and deafness oppressed them, holding them in place without mercy or release.

Tes'sael was the first to speak. "Ten'marden, how is your arm?"

To Joseph, it sounded like his voice came from far off, or through a heavy door. Ten'marden appeared not to hear him at all until Tes'sael moved right next to him and repeated his question.

"On fire," the younger elf answered. "I have bandages in my—I lost my pack."

"It's alright," Tes'sael reassured him, "I have more than enough."

Slowly, Joseph's hearing was starting to clear, along with his wits, and the conversation to his right became less and less dreamlike as it progressed. He looked over at the pair to see Ten'marden looking pointedly at Tes'sael. "Am I going to lose my arm?" he asked.

Tes'sael offered no false hope. "Maybe," he replied. "I'll do my best for you."

Ten'marden nodded, and Tes'sael went to work.

"Dorav," Joseph called, not yet spotting him.

"I'm here," the dwarf called back, some distance farther up the tunnel and on the other side.

"Do we have any more of that blasting powder?"

Dorav spoke in dwarven, and Joseph assumed he was repeating the question to the last pair of Tuvdahl's men. "No," Dorav finally replied. "There was one more keg, but..." The dwarf looked toward the pile of rubble, and Joseph understood—the second keg was buried along with the dead. "There's the rest of my blast rope. Better than nothing, but not the kind of boom we really want, at least not without a couple hours of breaking open all the charges."

"Time we don't have," Joseph confirmed, standing up with a painful grunt. "Alright," he continued as he picked up his gear and started surveying the damage to his elves, "let's assume the Baron beats us to the Well, which seems inevitable at this point, and let's assume he resurrects some long-dead creature. How did Dalvinav kill the thing last time?"

Dorav scratched the back of his neck. "I don't know," he finally said. "The legends only say that he did it, not how."

Joseph looked around at the gathered elves and dwarves. He had no authority here, and yet even the remains of the hret-dialt seemed to be looking at him for some kind of ruling. What did they expect him to say? He didn't know how to kill the Baron, or rather destroy him, since he was already dead. He had no proof of his belief that the Baron's master was an ancient dragon, powered by the Hoard of Dalviir, or the plan was to resurrect it, but if that wasn't the case it was certain to be something at least as bad. And if something did come out of the Well, Joseph had no idea how to kill that either. He met the gaze of each of his charges in turn, then gave his verdict.

"We run."

Dorav turned his eyes to the ground, and Tes'sael looked shocked, even hurt. "Joseph," the elf protested, "if we go, there'll be no one to stop—"

"To stop what?" Joseph challenged. "We don't even know what we're dealing with."

"Joseph is right," Dorav said, looking up. "You've got your own people to think about. We're likely, certain even, to fail, and who will warn the Windriders of what's coming at them if we do? You should go. I'll take the dwarves on and do what we can."

"Dorav, no," Joseph protested, "you should all come back with us."

"That's not our home, Joseph. Our homes are gone. There's nothing left for us but to see this through."

"If Dorav is determined to go," Tes'sael said, "then I won't leave. The Baron slaughtered half our people, including my own family. 'A wise man feeds on peace while a fool starves for vengeance,' but now that same villain has visited the same evil on another people, and plans to do the same to still more, and someone has to answer it. You say we have no chance. I say none has a better."

Joseph's face was grim. No matter what he did, all he built, or tried to, was snatched away from him. He'd never wanted to be anyone's hero. Even now he wanted only to go back to his new home and his new wife, to find some secret place where danger could never reach, to live and hunt and be content. These men before him were determined to go on, though, and if they had precious little hope even with his leadership, then surely without it they had none.

"Very well," Joseph said at last. "I will go to the Well. We will see what chances present themselves. But if none do, I will not throw our lives away hopelessly. I'm a scout, not a soldier; given the chance, I will always choose to live to fight another day. If any of you will not flee with me in that moment, then your blood is on your own hands."

Tes'sael and Dorav nodded their agreement.

~ * ~

Their forward progress was slow. The way was clear, but they were weary from the sudden battle, and Tuvdahl's blast had battered their very bones. After only two hours, Joseph could see that Ten'marden was suffering greatly from the wound in his shoulder. The temperature this far underground was constant and comfortable, but the wounded elf was sweating more than their moderate pace would explain, and even in Dorav's dim light his face looked pale. While they walked, Joseph's mind churned on any way they might thwart the Baron or his master, whoever or whatever that was. Nothing he considered could be tried with any confidence, and all for one simple reason: magic.

Joseph hated the stuff. During the war, men he'd respected had told him of the good they'd seen it do. He took them at their word, but in his experience it was evil men who seemed to favor it most. Joseph's principal complaint, though, was that it was so damned unpredictable. Every wizard was a power unto himself, and the spells and abilities of one gave no clue as to the behavior of another. Men trained in such things were said to detect subtle differences in words or gestures that could point to a sorcerer's capabilities, but few had such training and Joseph, to be sure, had none.

He could only draw from what he'd seen directly, and that was enough to inspire rational fear. Neither piercing with arrows nor smashing with tons of rock seemed to do any permanent damage to the Baron's health, and he could break locks and ribs alike with unseen hands of great strength. Joseph remained convinced, however, these abilities were not the Baron's own but flowed from the unknown power Joseph had speculated, and which was now confirmed by the Baron's statement about his 'master.' Could there be some way to sever that link? Last time he'd faced Baron Turov, the man had been equally impossible to kill, but in that instance Joseph had shot a magical artifact, one piece of the Hoard, out of his hand, causing him to stumble and fall into the Well. In the end, that had not turned out for the best. The arrows did still sink into him, so it was possible to damage his body. Maybe they could cut off his head?

Joseph shook his own head in frustration at himself. He was grasping at straws, and he knew it. He needed to stay focused on the tunnels around them; they could not survive another ambush.

~ * ~

Rook was nearing the capital. The system of footpaths and dray oxen used to pull barges upriver was refined, and the punters poling the barges upstream where needed were born and bred to it. Even still, three days had come and gone before the barge passed through the great portcullis into the southern docks of Onderburg. The only enemy Rook had seen on the voyage was boredom, and she had sparred unsuccessfully with that particular menace for days.

She debarked on the east side of the river and began making her way down the narrow streets and back alleys toward the hovel she and Adler shared. Night lay heavy on the city. The midnight hour had long since passed, and even in the more raucous taverns, by now most of the revelers had surrendered to drunken sleep or the touch of a lady of the night.

Now Rook faced the most dangerous leg of her entire journey, and she neither missed nor appreciated the irony that it should come at the very end, so close to her goal. Here all her enemies would be alert for her, and as she had speculated almost a fortnight ago, there was no chance the Wolfsguard would be unprepared for the magical power she now held. King Dieter had sages to spare and enough wizards to put their research into actual use. A protection against the necklace could take any number of forms, from an amulet worn, and potentially disguised, somewhere on the body to a potion or spell that, once applied, would become completely undetectable. Even still, Rook felt the necklace was her strongest chance, and taking it off would buy her little, since by now her description was no-doubt known to any who hadn't seen her themselves. She clutched at the jewel adorning her chest, reassuring herself of its power, a move which had become as natural to her as breathing.

Rook was halfway home and turned down an alley behind a brothel. Several patrons deemed too rowdy for the establishment had been rousted into the alley to sleep off their intoxication; they now lay about the space, propped up against the walls or stacks of crates, some snoring. A handful of mangy dogs lazed about, their quest for scraps abandoned for another night.

Wood scraped on stone behind her, and Rook turned halfway around, expecting only to see a drunkard stirring in his inebriated sleep.

Instead Rook was confronted by a hulking shadow, a man as large as any she'd seen and shrouded in a charcoal cloak, his face invisible in the umbra of its hood.

"Get back!" Rook shouted. The dogs started up, and even some of the drunks began to awaken with lolling heads.

Rook could feel the cold weight of the silver chain on her neck, but despite its presence and her clear order, the mass before her advanced. "Stop!" she screamed, drawing her knives.

With a gauntleted hand the man before her, if man it

was, batted both of her blades to the ground in a single, mighty sweep. Rook tried to dart to the side, but the shadow loomed before her as if it filled the entire alley, sucking in the meager light from nearby windows and turning all to darkness. Suddenly a meaty hand was around her neck, lifting her off the ground as easily as a sack of feathers.

"Put me down," she managed to gurgle, grabbing the man's arm and pulling upward to take some of the strain off her throat.

Defiant, her attacker slammed her against the nearest wall, pinning her against it with his gauntlet, pressing against her chest like a ram. He let go of her throat, but now that her windpipe was open, still the force on her ribs prevented proper breath. Now the free hand reached behind Rook's head and grasped the necklace chain, yanking it roughly over the top of her head. The removal of the artifact struck Rook harder than any physical assault the man had made, and she cried out, using the last of her air and finding to her horror she could draw no more in. In another moment the hooded man had thrown her over his shoulder, pinning her in place with the same arm as he stalked out of the alley. Rook struggled at first, but the blows she rained on his back and the knees she tried to press into his ribs met the resistance of a cold, steel breastplate, and bruises were all she earned for her trouble. Screaming would do no good, not at this time of night in this quarter of the city, and might even lure the jackals of the darkness, men as bloodthirsty as any Wolfsguard and owing allegiance to no master but their urges. Finally, the girl relaxed, turning her mind to more useful pursuits: counting turns and craning her neck to see landmarks, running her hands with the deftness of a skilled pickpocket over her handler's back and belt in the hopes of finding some clue explaining his immunity to the necklace.

Suddenly a dog barked and an alley cat snarled, prelude

to a stack of crates smashing to the ground in the darkness and a cacophony of answering calls from the neighborhood strays. Rook winced at the noise breaking the thick blanket of silence, their volume almost impossibly great against the quiet, then noticed the man carrying her had not so much as flinched. Given all the power and mystical knowledge of the kingdom, she had to smirk, in spite of herself, at the simple genius of the man's immunity. Her captor was deaf.

~ * ~

In time Rook stopped counting the turns and feigned unconsciousness; there were too many to track, and anyway she had quickly realized where the massive man was taking her. They were headed straight back to King Dieter's castle. She noted with interest the hidden entrance on the rear wall the Wolfsguard used then abandoned any hope of using it as an escape route when she saw the small army, or so it seemed, of cloaked and armored men inhabiting the room inside. It could only be a Wolfsguard barracks, a room full of the most vigilant and deadly men in the kingdom. Given the need for those in their profession to work at all hours, she doubted there was any time of day or night she could pass through the chamber unnoted. She had barely eased her eyelids open a hair, and even still she was almost certain one of the men had caught her glance.

Minutes passed, and Rook knew they were heading into the bowels of the castle, where surely the dungeons must lie. The cut stone blocks gave way to tunnels, and the light grew dim as regular candelabrum and oil lamps were replaced by widely-spaced, guttering torches. As last the Wolfsguard stopped and dropped Rook onto the hard ground. She looked sidelong as he reached for a rope hanging to his left and gave it three sharp tugs, causing a small, unseen bell to ring nearby. Out of the deeper gloom came two smaller men, dressed in the colors of King Dieter's army but displaying none of their usual grooming; they were ill-shaven and gap-toothed, and one of them had a milky eye.

Rook tensed her muscles, hoping against hope her original captor would leave so she could evade the two lesser jailors and escape into the surrounding shadows, but the giant Wolfsguard stood like a statue above her as the other two grabbed her by the arms and began hauling her upward. Rook went immediately limp once again, allowing herself to be dragged into a lightless cell. The heavy wooden door slammed shut, and she heard the bolts shoot home.

~ * ~

Rook woke sometime later to a scraping sound from the door of her cell. A small slot had opened at floor level, permitting a dim glow of torchlight. For all of a second she cast her eyes about her cell, desperate to confirm what she had learned pacing out the cell before she'd slept and to spot any details she had surely missed.

What appeared in the orange glow was not originally a cell, but a natural cavern of irregular shape. Still, apart from a recess about two feet wide and deep in the back wall, it was six feet across, more or less, however she sliced it, and perhaps twice that high. Part of the right hand wall, as she faced the door, and the wall containing the door itself were constructed of stone blocks, skillfully mortared into place. The only feature of the room not a permarent part of its construction was a small wooden bucket she had half tripped over the night before.

"Bucket?" came a voice through the door.

Rook worked out the connection and answered, "No. Not yet."

"Suit yourself." A farl of bread and a strip of dried meat were slid through the slot, directly on the floor, then it closed.

The thief moved over to the food, wary of any trick and not yet hungry enough to be desperate. She sniffed at the bread and jerky then ate a tiny piece of each. Afterwards she set them aside to determine if they caused any ill effects. She was suspicious of their quality; the bread was no more than two days old, and any kind of meat in a dungeon was unheard of. Her principal need at the moment, however, was water, the one thing her jailers had not provided. After several minutes, though, she heard a trickling sound from the back of her cell and felt her way toward it. A tiny stream of water flowed down the rock wall of the recess and filled a shallow depression at its bottom. Rook lay down on her belly and sucked at the puddle. The water tasted flinty but was cold and drinkable.

Once her thirst was satisfied, Rook set the bucket upright near the door and relieved herself then set to work. The water had to get in somehow. Once a cup's worth or so had flowed into the bowl in the floor, the trickle had stopped, so she drank the rest and slid into the recess, which formed a three-sided chimney leading to the ceiling of the cell. It was so narrow Rook had a hard time applying any outward force, but by bracing her hands and feet on the opposite walls of the recess she was able to inch her way upward.

She fell twice, but it was a short drop and there was nothing else to occupy her time, so she persisted. At last her head bumped the ceiling in the blackness, and she quickly shifted her position, pressing her shoulders into one corner to free a hand to explore the rock above. In a matter of moments her deft fingertips found traces of moisture, and she followed these to an aperture in the stone, then cursed aloud in frustration. The hole was barely large enough to permit her little finger, and to the depth of that digit, limited though it was, the stone was solid all around.

Rook's next goal was to get an eye under the tiny hole to see if any sense of distance or light could be gathered, but she had selected the wrong side. Groping blindly, she found a handhold then shifted her feet, twisting her body into the opposite corner of the chimney. It took only a moment to feel the water hole again, then she stretched her neck upward, pressing her face against the stone with one eye directly under the hole. Sure enough, she could see a faint red glimmer above, as if she looked into a room lit by torches. The light bounced off the rough sides of the tiny shaft and came diffuse to her eye. Even had something passed directly over the hole, she doubted she could have made it out, but a rough estimate of the length of the tube she looked through suggested the stone was at least a foot thick. Probably more.

Defeated, Rook slid back down the recess, laying down across the cell floor and stretching her muscles. After a few minutes she crawled to the door and felt for the slot that had opened earlier. At the time, she had been more focused on using its light to see the cell and hadn't carefully noted the dimensions of the slot itself. She reasoned it must be tall enough to permit the bucket, which was a bit over a gallon in size, and she confirmed this assumption once she felt the edges of the opening. Next she measured the width with her hands and found it to be about as wide as her shoulders. A person of average size could never fit, unless perhaps they were a skilled contortionist, but Rook knew she could wriggle through easily if she could only get the outer door out of the way.

She pressed around the edges of the slot door and felt the wood give slightly in some places but not at all in others, and by this she determined the door was hinged at the top and latched on both edges. A few solid kicks might break it loose, but a quieter method would be better. Rook's attire fit her form and left little space for concealment, which was perhaps why her captors had not searched her before dragging her into the cell. They had left her dagger belt, so she had a buckle and two rigid sheaths of wood and leather. Better yet, strapped to the small of her back were two layers of supple suede between which she kept the tools of her larcenous trade: a few lock picks, a pair of thin files serrated for cutting on one edge, a few feet of wire in a thin coil, and a slim mirror of polished silver. All she needed was the door to go unwatched for a time, and she would be out.

Chapter Thirteen: Fire

Joseph's second day of travel from Glowing Rocks was nearing its end when Dorav came upon a side passage that would lead them through the rear entrance to the chamber of the Well. This was the same entrance they had used last fall to take the Baron by surprise. Another hour they pressed on until finally Dorav signaled that the door was just ahead, around two more bends in the tunnel. Joseph took stock of the band. The hret-dialt were beginning to fray around the edges, and Ten'marden was now shivering with fever, though he had kept the pace during the march.

Fifty yards ahead they crept, Dorav and Joseph going in front and peering around the corner while the hret-dialt protected the party's rear. As soon as the human and dwarf poked their heads around the bend in the tunnel, it was clear something was wrong. At the next bend some hundred yards distant, instead of a murky tunnel lit only by the steady blue-green radiance of Dorav's bowls of lichen, the walls reflected an orange, flickering firelight. Confirming the immediate stretch of tunnel was clear, Joseph motioned the rest of the party forward as he and Dorav continued on to the next bend.

Looking around this next, and final, corner, Joseph's fears were confirmed. The rearward door to the Well stood wide open, and the Baron stood on the other side of the yawning pit, looking at the open doorway as if expecting someone to appear, his one-eyed gaze fixed on he and Dorav's position. Aside from the patch over his eye, the rest of Turov's features were now restored, the scar tissue and missing hair replaced by the face he had worn in life.

Suddenly the ground shook, and Joseph heard cries from the rest of the party behind them. A deep cracking sound echoed overhead, and Dorav threw Joseph forward only just in time to avoid the slab of rock that crashed down from the tunnel ceiling. Around them, the rest of the band was likewise issuing into the chamber as rock and dust cascaded from above them, choking the rear tunnel within moments.

"Your arrival is well timed," the Baron announced. "The rituals are all but complete, and the master's heart needs but one thing to be reunited with him."

Joseph pressed off the stone floor, moving from a prone position to a crouch, his weight on the balls of his feet and ready to shift. As he moved, he saw the stone heart sitting at Turov's feet, still pulsing with an internal glow. The Baron had ended his statement with a pregnant pause, but Joseph wasn't about to give him the satisfaction of asking him to continue. He looked to the left, where the rest of his companions were scattered. Ten'marden inched toward Joseph, but Tes'sael was leading the others around the rim of the Well, trying to flank the Baron. The main, and now only, entrance to the chamber was in the same direction, which Joseph thought was fortunate, the need for flight being far more likely than any opportunity to attack.

"You see," the Baron continued, "those who have grown wise in the deeper ways of the world understand that there has ever been but one true currency. So it is today and ever shall be. Only one commodity is placed above price by mortals, and thus is it the only coin worthy of commerce: Life."

Baron Turov glared at Joseph with his single eye, and Joseph couldn't help but lock with it. Even over the hundred feet of the Well between them, the hunter felt suddenly sick. He had never struggled with heights, spending most of his youth and adulthood climbing up and between trees, but in that moment he thought he understood the queasy dizziness of people who did, the inexplicable sense of falling even though his feet were braced on solid stone. Though he was ignorant of such things, he felt sure this was no spell; it was the result of seeing into the depths of a dead man's eye.

Joseph clenched his jaw and took a slow breath through his nose, steeling body and mind for whatever assault was sure to come. The hunter caught a flash of movement out of the corner of his left eye, then everything happened at once.

The Baron flicked his hand out toward Joseph, and a bolt of crackling darkness sprang forth from the stone heart and headed straight for him. Tes'sael and the elves nocked arrows and shot with lighting speed. Dorav threw something, and in a dim corner of Joseph's mind he was aware it was his blast rope still in a coil, with one end burning. Joseph lunged to his right, but the dark energy arced in midflight, continuing its bearing toward him. The elves' arrows struck home, piercing the Baron and driving him a step to Joseph's right. The blast rope landed between the Baron and the stone heart. Joseph, horrified that the bolt of darkness seemed to be following him, reared back in surprise, rising from his crouch into a half-standing, half-stumbling posture. Suddenly, Ten'marden slammed into Joseph, bowling him out of the way with his shoulder. Had they been of like size, perhaps his momentum would have continued and carried him clear, but knocking the larger human aside left him hanging with his back to the Baron and directly in the dark bolt's path. Joseph watched the energy strike the elf and lift him from the ground, a white light coursing back up the bolt's path to the stone heart. The hunter could see in Ten'marden's eyes a blankness he had scarcely seen since the war. All life had left him in an instant. The Baron howled in frustration at the sudden change in his sacrifice as he stepped toward the blast rope, poised to kick it into the Well.

The rope exploded. As Dorav had predicted, it was not the staggering blast the powder keg had yielded, but it was enough to fling Baron Turov back against the nearest wall. The pressure of the explosion hit the stone heart and moved it, half-sliding half-rolling, to the very brink of the Well. It teetered crazily on the edge for a moment. Joseph scrabbled for his bow, but Tes'sael was already shooting, hitting the dense stone once, twice, thrice in rapid succession. Then it was too late. The stone was too heavy, and Tes'sael's angle too shallow. The heart slid off the ledge and fell.

The cavern was suddenly silent. None could say exactly how long they stood there, transfixed by terror and a sick fascination with what would happen next. The Baron stood, grinning wolfishly. Then the heart must have hit the bottom, or whatever served for one in the Well. A low roar, something like a storm gale mixed with war drums, echoed up from the depths. At last Joseph began to move, running toward the rest of the band. "Go!" he cried. "Go!"

A rushing column of fire, as wide as the Well itself, shot upward from it, blasting the whole cavern with searing heat.

Joseph was driven back, his arms covering his face, as the flames battered into the chamber ceiling a hundred feet above, scorching the very stones. The flames cooled over seconds, but their roaring rush was replaced by another sound, a cry Joseph could neither reckon nor describe. Something between a roar and a wail, it rose from the Well's depths and clawed at Joseph's heart, twisting inside him like a thousand knives as its volume rose enough to batter his ears, nearly as loud as Tuvdahl's explosion and rolling on without end. To Joseph it felt as if every moment of fear or pain in his entire life was being dragged out of the depths of memory and driven into his conscious mind, overwhelming him with feelings of rage and hatred and despair. He had no idea how long the cry went on. A second? A year? More? When finally it did recede, he noticed a renewed wailing in his ears and pain in his throat, and only then did he realize he was screaming. He was not alone.

As the band fought to remaster their wills, the one sound running constant above their screams was the Baron's cruel laughter. He made no move toward them, only standing and roaring in sadistic mirth. Though the flames were gone, the light flickering from the Well remained brighter than ever, lighting the face from below with hellish radiance. "Crawl away, worms," he finally taunted. "Crawl, run, fly if you can, for all the good it will do you. There is no longer any hope in flight or in hiding. My master's mind reaches to all corners of creation. Run, sheep! Malice is returned to the world, and the meek shall *burn*!"

They ran. The weaker of their party gave no heed to anything but flight, and even the most stouthearted kept only a dim sense for holding the group together. Their fear would not be left behind.

As their wits returned, Dorav took the lead once more, urging the shattered band to follow him to the surface. Only a few more minutes went by before a horrid screeching and pounding of feet sounded behind them. His heart still twisted by the terrors that had touched his mind, Joseph nearly dropped to the floor and wept, giving up life along with hope. The thought of facing more trolls was more than he could bear.

It seemed he was not alone in this. Indeed, *facing* any more trolls appeared not to be the plan for any of the elves or dwarves as each redoubled the speed of their mad retreat. Joseph ran until he thought his lungs would burst then finally halted, the rest, as by some unspoken agreement, stopping as well. He dropped to the stones, and Stitch and Yowler loped over to him, licking at his hands and face. Their tongues were dry, and he spared a little water for them to drink from his cupped hands.

Suddenly Dorav and the hret-dialt's dhor-zabh were yelling at each other in dwarven. A few phrases passed back and forth, then Dorav growled and threw up his hands, his expression of surrender, not challenge.

"Dead men," he grunted, turning to Joseph. "The hret-dialt will go no farther. They insist on holding the tunnel so we can escape."

Joseph looked at the flagging dwarves then spoke to Dorav. Knowing some hret-dialts, those whose patrols covered the exits to the surface world, could speak human tongues fluently, he kept his voice low. "Look at them, Dorav. It isn't a matter of choice. They can't run anymore. We've picked up some ground on the trolls, but you can hear them gaining now. Let them have this. After all they've suffered, let them die with some meaning."

The dwarf's all-black eyes sparkled, and his face betrayed that he already knew everything Joseph had told him and only feared to admit it. Dorav nodded, then set about the grim work of helping the hret-dialt redistribute their supplies to the rest of the dwindling band.

In a few minutes they were moving again, not fleeing in a headlong dash this time but making steady, jogging progress they could sustain for a period of time. Dorav seemed to be leading them to the tunnel Joseph and Kaillë had used to exit the dwarven lands after their last subterranean excursion, and if that proved true, Joseph remembered it was about a day to the open air. The trolls seemed to have spent much of their energy as well, and as Joseph and the rest trudged on, hour after monotonous hour, they heard no more sign of them. Joseph hoped the hret-dialt had turned them aside, spending their lives to convince the savage beasts to throw their fury someplace else, but he secretly feared they had just gone silent, creeping up in the darkness to launch an attack at any moment.

~ * ~

Hours passed, and Joseph was sure they must be nearing the surface. Their pace on his last trip had been more sedate, and even then a bit over a day had brought them into the light. The temperature seemed to be rising as well, heralding a warm spring day not too far ahead. Joseph wondered if his mind was playing tricks on him, the way men in the desert were said to see water in their desperation.

Suddenly the troll-sounds returned, still at the edge of their hearing but completely different in character. Their shrieks and snarls were not now of anger or bloodlust, but of panic, or else Joseph was no judge of animals. The noises gained at a great speed; something was driving them into blind flight.

Joseph and the band increased their pace as much as they could manage in their present state of weariness, and soon the human was sweating through his clothes. In his exertion, it took him a few extra moments to realize the tunnel had now grown hot, and it was a dry, roasting heat, not the humid warmth of spring in his woods. He hazarded a look over his shoulder, down the long, straight section of tunnel behind them, and in the farthest distance he spied a flickering orange light bouncing off the tunnel walls, the forms of dozens of trolls scampering ahead of it.

Joseph thought to urge the party to greater speeds, but he had neither the breath for a warning nor the energy to go any faster. They continued their dogged pace, desperate to make the surface before they became overwhelmed by the wave of fire and beast behind them, closing the gap at an alarming rate.

"We're almost there," Dorav, still in the lead, called back. "Half a mile, maybe."

Joseph looked over his shoulder and gauged their speed against that of the oncoming conflagration, the distance between them against the half-mile goal. It would be close.

Five minutes later their shadows now ran ahead of them, fleeing the burning light rushing up from behind, and Joseph saw the shadows turn and climb a sheer wall ending the tunnel before them. Behind them Joseph could now make out the features of individual trolls, backlit though they were, perhaps a hundred feet behind, perhaps less. Dorav placed his hand on a spot on the end-wall of the tunnel, as featureless as any of the rest of it to Joseph's eyes, and a moment later the undetectable door swung outward.

The band slipped through into a narrow cave. "Close it!" Joseph shouted. The elves did not wait for any of the dwarves to find the inexplicable closing mechanism and threw their weight directly against the stone portal, throwing it shut with ease by virtue of its excellent balance and hinges.

As the door slammed home, the cave went pitch dark. Dorav had long since stowed his lights when the fire glow overtook them, but no glimmer filtered into the cave from outside. The wind howled against the rocks. Suddenly, they were blinded by a blue-white flash as thunder smote their ears. Whether it was night outside or the storm clouds were so thick as to banish all light, Joseph could not be sure. The panicked screech of troll could now be heard through the door, even over the wind howling and rain lashing the rocks, and Joseph turned away in disgust. The creatures must be roasting alive inside, and for a moment he pitied even such savage creatures that horrible fate. Their screams were as much like the terror of dying horses as the wails of men.

Joseph walked down the curving length of the narrow cave, turning in the last twenty feet into the face of the gale outside. The storm pounded against the mountain slopes, its thick clouds hiding any moonlight, for Joseph was sure now it was night. Flashes of lightning illuminated rain coming down in thick curtains and the trees lashing back and forth in the erratic wind. "I'm not fond of the idea," Joseph called back to his men over the wailing of storm and troll, "but I think we'd best stay in the cave while the storm lasts. As long as that door holds, we're safer in here than out there."

Dorav had his hand against the stone of the door. "Safe so far," he decided, "it's still cool. We should stay as close to the surface as we can, though, in case something happens. The rovers will take turns keeping the watch."

Joseph was too weary to argue, and he could see his remaining elves were likewise. He hunkered down in his cloak, far enough from the cave entrance to keep out of the rain but close enough to feel the fresh air on his face. His conscience gnawed at him. Now one more elf under his care would not be coming home, and just as before he didn't even have remains or possessions to bring to his loved ones. Some hero he turned out to be. Perhaps if he knew the elves would hate him for his failure, he could take that as punishment and thereby forgive himself, but that wouldn't be the way of it. They would still love and worship him despite all he had lost.

Joseph chided himself for falling so easily back into old habits. When his mind was clearer he would consider his choices, whether he might have done anything better, but mere recrimination would not bring back the fallen or prevent future losses. He longed to be back home with Kaillë; she was wise despite her youth and would have words not only of consolation, but also of use. The dogs curled up near him and slept fitfully as Joseph watched the storm.

~ * ~

Joseph woke sometime later to the sound of Dorav shouting, "Wake up! Wake up! Out, out of the cave!"

Trusting the dwarf's expertise, Joseph didn't pause. He grabbed his pack and ran out into the ghostly dawn. The lightning and wind seemed to have slackened, but the rain still came down steadily, pelting Joseph with fat, cold drops. The dogs seemed to have wandered off someplace, but the elves and dwarves followed him out of the cave, Dorav bringing up the rear. The rover was waving his hands to the left and shouting in alternating languages to get away from the cave mouth, not to stand in front of it. Again, Joseph did as he was told, herding the elves ahead of him before running around the shoulder of the rock.

No sooner had he cleared the path to the cave than a searing heat washed over his back, and a great gout of flame launched out of the cavern, sizzling the rain to steam and blasting the trunks of nearby trees. Their vision began to fill with thick fog and smoke, and within moments the nearest trees were crackling and glowing. Still the flames erupted from the cave, impossibly far from any source of fuel or air. Joseph shrank back, but not from the heat. There was something else in the flame, some echo of the horrid sound that had assailed him the day before at the Well, some unspoken menace that shaded his heart. Without delay, he urged the rest of the band away from the rock wall where they sheltered. The forest would be blazing within minutes. Their safest course was to head to higher ground, get above the tree line, but that would do no good for the Windriders. Against a normal blaze, the damp of spring would choke out any chance of spreading, but this fire was anything but normal; it spread where it should not and consumed what it touched without regard.

"Come on," Joseph ordered, motioning the men downslope. The elves must have guessed his purpose, for they did not argue as he led them into thicker trees, and the dwarves faces showed only bewilderment at what they saw. At least the thick clouds shaded their eyes from facing the full sun so soon after they breached the surface. They hiked down, taking the fastest route Joseph knew back to the Windrider village.

If the damp brush didn't stop the flame altogether, it did seem at least to slow it, or perhaps it was the force of life and nature itself that resisted whatever magic of hatred and hopelessness was in the blaze. Soon the party had left the fire behind, though if they looked back they saw the thick, white smoke rising skyward through every break in the trees. Any hope Joseph had held that the fire might soon burn itself out was squelched when they climbed to the top of a bald hill to survey their surroundings. From that vantage he could see the fire spreading downslope from the cave, and rushing jets of flame issued from the larger limbs of charred and burning trees, expanding the fire's grip in all directions at once.

The desperation of the moment had occupied Joseph's mind since the first trees were kindled, but now he had a moment to reflect on the extent of the damage. His forest was burning—not the cleansing fire of a lightning strike or even the natural fire of a careless traveler, set to burn itself out and leave the wood to heal itself. This fire had an evil will behind it, spreading and growing with intent. In days his home would be utterly gone: the shell of the house where he'd been born, the trees and defiles where he sheltered after his parents' death, even the charred husk of the house he had shared with Delia, which he had broken and fired in his wracking grief. And the Windrider village. There was no chance it would escape the flames. All their hard work preparing lumber over the winter, all their frenzied building throughout the early spring, all was now for naught, and the Windriders were homeless again as surely as if the fire had already consumed them. In the end, it would have been better if they had fled from the trolls over a week ago and avoided all this. His involvement had accomplished nothing except the deaths of more elves.

"Hai, Joseph!" Dorav called. "Eyes to the ceiling."

Joseph squinted in puzzlement before realizing that Dorav was telling him, as a dwarf would, to look up. He did so, and circling high above was a winged silhouette against the gray of the clouds. Joseph cupped his hands around his mouth and called upward, then waved his arms at the owl above, but its keen-eyed rider was already guiding the bird down in tight circles to the top of the hill.

"It's Tes'voran," Tes'sael said when the owl was a bit lower. "No one else rides so recklessly."

It was true, the descent was perilously quick, and in a few moments the owl landed with a pair of hops and much flapping of wings. Tes'voran leapt lightly from the saddle and first traded informal salutes with Tes'sael, his peer in the Windrider command, before bowing to Joseph. "We received Ten'venni's report two days ago, and Tal'onë has been widening the patrols by degrees ever since. We have seen no more trolls coming in our direction. I caught site of the smoke and came to investigate. Little surprise that I would find you in the thick of things, and gathering more dwarves, I see."

"How are things in the village?" Joseph asked.

"Uneasy, but safe. Kaillë is well. Joseph, what is that hellish fire I saw from the air? What burns trees in the height of spring?"

"The end of many things we thought we knew, I'm afraid," Joseph said. "I don't know rightly what it is, but it is something very powerful, loosed from the depths of the earth."

"I was afraid you would say so, or something very like it," Tes'voran grimaced. "Kaillë may be able to say more."

"Kaillë?" Joseph argued. "If she knew anything more of this, she would have told me months ago when we were so near it, and when I feared more than coincidence in our travel after the Hoard."

"We've had a visitor while you were away. 'Chance meeting brings strange tidings' runs more fluid in the elven, but it's true in this case no matter the tongue."

"Who?"

"Best Kaillë tells you that," Tes'voran replied. "Shall I bring owls?"

"Bring five to carry our people back. Fresh scouts and supplies will help us heavier folk to move more quickly with less fatigue." Joseph usually had little to say once orders were given, and he had trained the elven guard not to wait around for elaboration, so he wasn't surprised when Tes'voran turned away. Joseph called him back. "The danger you saw from above is real. Give this message to Kaillë and Tal'onë, and only to them: The Windriders have to move, and quickly. Tell them to prepare only what they can carry, as many weapons and provisions as they can manage. If the danger passes, we can come back, but better we lose our homes than our lives."

Tes'voran's expression was stunned, but he spoke no word before jumping back onto his owl and taking off.

"Joseph," Tes'sael said, beginning the statement the hunter had been expecting, "we don't want to be sent back."

"I know, but I need you to *go* back. Without your report, some on the council may argue for waiting to leave, and precious time will be lost. And Tal'onë will need all the help he can get to order the evacuation. If you think you're being sent back to rest and ease, you're wrong."

"What now, Joseph?" Dorav asked.

"The owls will be back in a couple of hours, and this is the easiest spot nearby for them to land, so Tes'sael and the elves will stay here. We'll take some food and rest before we set out on foot."

For half an hour the party sat and ate what was left of their provisions, not speaking. Joseph was numb, and when his mind occasionally clawed its way to any kind of feeling, he decided that, for now, the numbness was better. As the food neared its end, Joseph heard Dorav conversing with the two other rovers, but they didn't share their discussion.

~ * ~

Two hours later, Joseph and the dwarves were working their way down a game trail Joseph believed crossed with a stream course farther down that would serve as a quick route back to the village. Dorav approached Joseph and spoke low. "The rovers are nervous, Joseph. They don't know what they're supposed to do now. For that matter, neither do I."

"I know this isn't the life you want," the hunter replied, "but you're welcome to travel with the Windriders for as long as you like. We would be honored to have your axes and hammers in our clan."

"It's appreciated," Dorav said. "We'll be looking to get

back to what is left of our own clans when we can, but we don't know when that may be."

Suddenly one of the rovers cried out in alarm, and Joseph looked toward the sound to see that several elven scouts had dropped out of the trees onto the path. Joseph was sure that to the dwarves' eyes, they had simply appeared from thin air. Despite the dire situation, Joseph smiled. "Yeah, they do that," he chuckled. The elves stood at arms' length from the dwarves, surveying them with awe.

Without introductions, the band started moving again. Joseph heard shouts and owl cries from overhead, and he knew the owls that had dropped off their new scouts had been led to the hill where the elves were waiting and started the flight back to the village.

The wind shifted, blowing out of the north, and Joseph realized there may have been another cause for the shouts from above apart from simple greeting. The north wind brought the smell of heavy smoke, inciting a feeling of regret over the time they had spent resting on the hill. Joseph wasn't sure he'd ever been so tired, at least not since the war, but he hitched his pack and started moving again. The elves knew their jobs, disappearing into the woods to scout the path ahead. Joseph led the dwarves forward with confidence, knowing no danger would fail to reach his ears well before he could stumble into it. One foot in front of the other, the smell of smoke growing thicker with each step, they made their way back to the village.

~ * ~

Joseph half-expected to find the village in chaos when he returned, but he should have remembered who he was dealing with. Many elves had arrayed on the green, their belongings packed and sitting next to them. Others moved to and fro, but their actions were ordered and calm. Joseph spied Tal'onë on the far side of the green, helping arrange provisions on a pair of handcarts. He looked up and caught Joseph's eye, then turned his head right, toward the stream. Joseph followed his gaze and saw Kaillë there, drawing water to fill three nearby barrels. She moved to pour a gourd and happened to flick her eyes across the place where Joseph was standing. For a moment she started to pour, then dropped the gourd in the barrel as she charged away from the stream, her bare feet dimpling the springy turf as she ran, her golden hair flowing unbound behind her, her blue dress blown against her shins. In a few seconds she had reached Joseph, and she leapt upon him, heedless of his exhaustion or bloodstained clothes. Joseph had let his pack slip from his shoulders as she ran, and now he wrapped his arms around her, his aching muscles forgotten. She kissed him, and he returned it, fierce and lingering. He had known he missed her during his journey, but only upon seeing her again did he understand how sharp the longing was, how completely he had come to rely on her presence.

Moments passed and Kaillë pulled away, her locks fallen forward like a hood around their faces so only Joseph could see the flush of her face, the sudden hunger in her eyes. He had chased her frightening world away for a moment, and the knowledge made him proud. Sadly, the dangers had been dispelled only from her thoughts; the reality would not be denied for long. Already a keen eye might notice the haze of smoke catching in the light of the setting sun.

Joseph set his wife down on her feet. "I have been to hell and back," he whispered, "and I'm afraid I've brought it with me. I'm sorry for all of this. I'm sorry your new homes are likely to be destroyed."

"*Our* homes," Kaillë corrected him, "and they are not our homes, only our houses. Home is wherever we can be together. Not just you and me, but all the Windriders.

Sometimes the winds are the winds of fate, and we will ride these as well."

"Is everything ready?"

"It will be. We have scouts aloft, reporting on the movement of the fires. These winds are working against us, but even still we seem to have a couple of hours left before we have to depart."

Dorav and the dwarves had gone to a slight remove, shifting their feet and looking about. A few members of the council had gathered, and Kaillë gave instructions to see to the needs of their new friends.

"Couple of hours?" Joseph confirmed. "I wish it was more, but I'll take it. I need sleep."

"Soon," Kaillë said, looking up into his eyes, and Joseph saw a hint of their fire rekindled. She took him by the hand.

Joseph smiled and allowed his wife to take him to bed.

Chapter Fourteen: Escape

"**J**oseph, wake up," the hunter heard Kaillë say. He reached to either side of him on the mattress, but she wasn't there. Their time together had been brief but passionate, then Joseph sank almost immediately into the oblivion of sleep. He opened his eyes and saw the inside of their house, lit by a single lantern, and Kaillë dressed for travel.

"How long was I asleep?" he asked as he rose from the mattress.

"More than an hour, but not much. I knew you'd want to oversee final preparations."

Joseph began to dress then paused. "Do I have time for a wash?"

"Go quickly, but yes."

The hunter pulled on his breeches and threw his cloak about him, then headed down to the stream. Once there, he threw his clothes on the ground and plunged into the cold water, wading to the center which, swelled by the spring rain, ran almost to his chest. He scrubbed furiously at himself, letting the brisk water carry away the sweat and grime of his travels. For a moment, he was self-conscious that he had lain with Kaillë in such a state, then remembered how the passion of that moment had driven any concerns from his mind, and seemingly from Kaillë's as well. He couldn't suppress a smile at the memory. Then he looked to the northeast at the fire glow on the underside of the night clouds and cursed his lapse in focus. He turned back to the streambank, and there saw Tal'onë holding out his cloak.

"Thank you," Joseph said as he took it and wrapped it around himself, grabbing his breeches and walking back toward the house. "How are you faring with this?" he asked his elven friend.

"As well as any, I guess," Tal'onë answered. "And you?"

"It galls me to leave all this behind, but I'm more worried about what we do afterward. Tonight we have to take the shortest route out of the forest but from there...?"

"Has Kaillë spoken to you about events while you were away?"

"No. I meant to ask her, but—"

"Youth is as youth does. Say no more. But you should ask her, Joseph, before we set out, or very soon thereafter."

"I will. Thank you, Tal'onë."

The elven commander nodded his acknowledgement then left Joseph at the bottom of the ladder up to his dwelling.

Once inside, Joseph found Kaillë had laid out his spare set of traveling clothes on their mattress, and underneath all was spread a new cloak, pieced together from dark brown and green fabric patches into a serviceable camouflage. The clasp was a simple loop and knot of cord, but around the neck and the opening of the hood the cloak had been embellished with quillwork in red, orange, and yellow like the turning of the leaves at autumn.

Joseph pulled on his clothes before holding up the cloak to admire it, then turned to Kaillë with questioning eyes.

"A gift from the widows of the clan," she explained. "Think of it as a wedding present."

Joseph settled the cloak on his shoulders then Kaillë reached up to clasp it.

"We need to talk soon," Joseph said. "Twice now I've heard of things transpiring while I was underground."

Kaillë nodded. "It wasn't my intention to delay the telling. That was just...an unavoidable consequence." Her eyes beseeched him, and he bent down to kiss her. "We'll talk once we're underway."

They stood for a moment, letting their eyes linger on the space where they had spent such a brief but pivotal time. Joseph looked with dual purpose, to imprint the memories of the place on his mind and to look for anything they couldn't afford to leave behind. They had few possessions, and Kaillë's preparation had been thorough, so on the latter point there was nothing to see.

Satisfied, Joseph turned away, Kaillë blew out the lamp, and they both left the house.

~ * ~

The evacuation was orderly. The Baron's attack the previous fall had taken its heaviest toll on those least able to flee: families with young children, the elderly, women in the latter stages of pregnancy, to say nothing of the warriors who fell trying to protect them all. Now there were few in the clan without the discipline and endurance to make a second flight. A few women had borne children late in the winter or early in the spring, and one more was near her time, but elves remained active practically to the point of delivery, barring illness or complications. The few older children and adolescents were old enough to master their fear and play their part by helping the remaining elderly and generally doing as they were told without argument. The dwarves, seeing an opportunity to do their part, insisted on pushing the pair of hand carts the elves had laden with tools, water, and bulk supplies, bringing up the rear. The owls with their riders went ahead and on the flanks, scouting for trouble.

Over a hundred souls made their way into the forest, cloaked in the night under a hazy moon, employing the usual elven stealth but without the usual elven speed. But for the dwarves pushing carts at the back, any observer watching this exodus would likely believe himself in a waking dream as a procession of somber specters passed him in the night traveling from invisibility to invisibility at the edges of his sight, vanishing forever from the realm of human memory.

Joseph had told the elves all along they might come back once the danger had passed, but he'd never believed it to be likely. Two hours after their departure, he passed a high fir with sparse needles and widely spaced ranks of limbs and scrambled up. From its lofty crown he could see back to the highest trees of their village, and he gazed on with grief as they kindled. The owl riders must have seen as well, but they didn't react, and he was sure they wouldn't spread the word beyond a report to their superiors, trusting Kaillë or Tal'onë to give the elders the news when the time was right, assuming any of them lived that long.

A few minutes later Joseph caught up with the head of the trudging column where Kaillë and Tal'onë marched.

"We're well underway," Joseph said. "What do I need to know?"

Kaillë and Tal'onë told Joseph the tale of Rook's arrival, the knowledge that had been gleaned thus far from her book, and the appearance of the Blood Clan elves.

"Blood Clan?" Joseph asked. "I've never heard of elves

so warlike. Do you know of them?"

"Only rumors," Tal'onë replied, "and even then not by name. From time to time clans come to internal quarreling and splinter, and an arrogant ruler sometimes decides that stealing from his neighbors is easier than working for their livelihood. Nothing like that has happened in these parts in many generations, but it's said that in the south, where the land is gentler, the clans sometimes outgrow their territories and come to strife. Some can't turn their back on such a life, once they've had a taste of it."

Joseph grimaced. He had known such men during the war. In the worst of cases they were little better than animals, useful when restrained to a purpose but not to be trusted to their own devices. Most lost the ability to trust other men or work in teams to any great effect, making them easy to put down when necessity demanded, but elves were cut from different cloth. If such men in their society banded together, they could be formidable. In any case, there was little to be done about it now, and all these interlopers had sought to raid was now burning to ash.

"Show me this book," Joseph said, changing the subject.

Kaillë reached into a pouch on her belt and drew out the small volume, handing it to Joseph. "It seems to have been rebound," she said. "All the pages inside are in the old script that we still use, and they show signs of long wear, but the cover is newer and has more modern characters on the spine."

Owing to the band's natural abilities, or long-trained ability in Joseph's case, there was just enough light for slow travel, but nowhere near enough for reading. Joseph ran his fingers over the cover, finding it smooth, and along the spine. He could feel the characters there, but their stamping was too shallow to make out by feeling alone. "What does it say?" he asked.

Kaillë's reply was grim. "Malice."

Joseph shuddered, almost dropping the book, and even in the dark Kaillë noticed. "Joseph, what's wrong?"

"The last thing the Baron said before we were forced to flee and all this started." He waved his hand behind them to indicate the fire. "He said that 'Malice' had returned to the world. At the time I thought he was speaking generally...but now it seems that our enemy has a name."

"Does that help us?" Tal'onë asked.

"I suppose not," Joseph admitted, "but maybe it will give me something to fix on other than that horrible scream in my mind if we need to speak about the thing we're fleeing."

For several more minutes they walked in silence, then Joseph conferred with Kaillë and decided to call a brief halt. There were many miles yet to go, and it would do no service to the clan if the weaker members collapsed for want of rest or water before they left the forest.

~ * ~

Assuming food was brought every twelve hours, Rook had been in the dark cell for two days, and she was going out of her mind. Hour after monotonous hour she spent with her ear pressed against the inner door, but there was always somebody, some worthless, mouthy sonnofabitch, on the other side. The guards would go quiet for a few minutes at a time, but no more than that, then conversation would resume, or rolling dice or shuffling cards or utensils scraping on plates and bowls. The first time she heard the telltale sound of someone urinating in a metal bucket she knew escape would take far longer than she had hoped; they didn't even leave to use the damn latrine. Near as she could tell there were three guards working in twelve-hour shifts; every four hours one guard would leave when a new one reported for duty. She did overhear one start to snore once, but the other two remained alert and woke him almost immediately. After the first few hours of listening and recognizing the uphill challenge before her, Rook tried plying the guards with coquettish talk; trying, without overselling it, to lure one of the men to open the door, but they laughed. The bastards actually laughed!

Rook had been in several dungeons in her time, and so far none had held her, but she was quickly losing confidence in her ability to escape any prison, namely the one she was now in. She had worked her way out of restraints far more elaborate, but her current cell was a jailbreaker's nightmare; a combination of extremely simple measures executed extremely well: stout walls, solid latches, and, worst of all, disciplined guards. A deeper part of her mind raged against the loss of the necklace even more than the incarceration. Without it she felt helpless, almost sick. Without thinking she knew its recovery would become her immediate goal if ever she could escape.

Nevertheless, by probing with her picks over the course of her imprisonment, she had managed to suss out the configuration of the latches on the slot door and was confident in her ability to pop them when the opportunity presented itself. She had even widened her access by sawing at the inner surface of the door, working with painstaking slowness to remain silent, and so far the guards taking her bucket and bringing her food hadn't noticed.

Now she sat, half in a doze, propped against the door, still listening, when a new sound suddenly pealed out. A bell rang twice, a crisp, clear sound, the same bell the Wolfsguard had rung when he delivered Rook to the dungeon. She heard chair legs scraping against stone as guards moved, but even still one stayed behind; she knew this because it was the guard that had a habit of drumming his fingers on the top of their table.

A voice echoed from somewhere to the left. "Fawkes,

get over here. This guy's huge." Another chair scraped back, and footsteps hustled away.

Rook's heart raced as she sprang into action. With a file in each hand, she slid them into the divots she had created in the wood, shoving back both of the latch bolts at once. Laying out straight before the slot, she pushed it open with one hand until that arm was straight above her head, out of the cell up to the elbow. With the movements of a skilled treasure hunter she slithered forward, passing her head out the slot door and dipping her shoulder for the one, hard push that would have her through. She shoved. Her shoulder popped out the slot. She wriggled forward, her first arm now back and bracing against the door to pull her through more quickly. Her second arm was out past the elbow.

The guards came back. All three of them stared down at her, their expressions impressed but not in the least concerned. Between them they dragged a large, unconscious man with a swollen, purple bruise covering half his face.

Rook stared back at them, hopeless but not completely able to deny the amusement she saw creeping into the guards' faces. "Hello," she said after a moment.

"You want I should shove her back in?" one of the guards asked.

"Nah, we were about to take her out before this big fellah got dropped off. Let 'er get out and stretch 'er legs. Even if she bolts, she can't get far."

The string of profanity that passed Rook's lips would have shocked a sailor. "Are you *serious*?" she ended.

"Sorry," the guard apologized as he pulled Rook the rest of the way out of the door slot and helped her stand. Damned if he didn't actually sound sincere too. "It was a good effort, but there was really no getting loose. There's only two ways in or out, and locked gates with three more guards on both of them. Not to mention one leads through the Wolfsguard barracks and the other through the regular cells, with all the regular gates and guards that way."

"I hate your dungeon," Rook said.

"Thank you. It's not a prestigious job. Like the Wolfsguard, not many even know we exist. But that doesn't mean we don't take pride in our work."

Rook was blindfolded and led on a baffling array of turns for what felt like ten minutes. Along the way were checkpoints where she heard gates being unlocked and twice there were long stairs leading upward. Now she heard a heavy door being opened, and the smells of subterranean air were replaced by the stench of squalid habitation. Rook surmised she had passed into the "regular dungeon" the guard had spoken of.

Two or three minutes of walking, a sharp turn, and Rook was assailed by jeers and catcalls from both sides, at her level and from at least one above. She made out the specifics of a few crude remarks, and given the more tepid reaction her appearance usually garnered from men, she gathered she was being led through a row of long-term inmates, men who hadn't seen a woman in a long time. Was that to be her fate, then? A lifetime of anonymous imprisonment?

"Apologies, miss," one of the guards muttered. "These animals have no decency at all."

A few more minutes, two more checkpoints, another flight of stairs, and somewhere along the line the reek was left behind. A heavy door, another, and Rook felt the hands that had led her on her path slide up to her shoulders and guide her to sit on a chair. It was hard wood, but after two days in a cell with no furniture, it was luxury.

Someone removed the blindfold, and Rook blinked at the sudden brightness of oil lamps. Once her vision resolved, she realized she was in a room of cut stone blocks probably four times the size of her cell. She must have faced the back of the room, for she had no door in her field of vision, but she didn't turn her head to see more, for she had been set down facing a standing man whose gaze bore into and held her. It was the eyes alone that kept her thus, for his looks were unassuming. The man was perhaps forty, but his face was worn and aged by worry. He had dirty blond hair that receded over a high forehead. His nose was small, his jaw squarish and adorned with an expertly groomed goatee that was darker than his hair, save that it was flecked with white. The eyes were wide but strangely hard, steel gray and they looked deep, past Rook's own eyes and into her secrets. She felt naked.

"Do you know who I am?" the man asked.

"Yes...Your Majesty." Rook looked down as she spoke the title. It was true; she had been brought into the presence of King Dieter himself. He wore no regal robes, dressed instead not unlike one of his guards, but she had seen his face twice before, albeit from a distance, and she knew it to be the face now before her.

"And I'm told you are called Rook. Your reputation names you the best thief in Onderburg. Is that true?"

"No," Rook answered levelly. "I'm the best thief in all Ondravia, and many other kingdoms besides."

King Dieter smiled. "You are wise to be honest. A good place to begin. Before we go any further, though, I must explain to you that I am not a cruel man by nature. Some say I am too soft to be king, but I only know that I derive no personal pleasure from cruelty, and in the long run I've never known anyone to gain anything by it. Do you understand?"

Rook nodded.

The king continued. "Apart from the aggression necessary in your capture, have you been mistreated in any way? Have you been denied food or water, or otherwise abused?"

"No," Rook answered, realizing only upon prompting that her captivity had not been unnecessarily harsh.

"Good." The king turned to a tall, well-groomed man in red and yellow robes that Rook only then realized was standing in the corner behind the king. "See that the prisoner's statements are noted in the guard captain's report." He turned back to Rook. "I choose not to enforce standards of appearance for my secret jailers since no one sees them anyway, but their looks don't reflect their character. Some men are beasts, but I do not tolerate them in my employ. I put such men *in* prisons, not in charge of them. All this said, you are a known criminal, an infamous one in fact, though I may be the first in authority to have both a name and a face to match to your many deeds. I've only allowed a few of my most trusted nobles to learn of your apprehension, but of those many are crying out to have your hand chopped off. I don't intend to do that, but it is within the bounds of our law if I chose to.

"You are here now because I believe you can be of use. At the very least, you have information that I need. At this point, I assume you are marshalling your resolve, swearing you won't tell me anything, and so on. I invite you not to waste your time or energy on such games."

The king motioned behind Rook, and a guard paced into her peripheral vision and handed something to the robed advisor in the corner. The guard moved away, allowing Rook full view of a wooden stand under a bell-shaped cover of glass, and within that cover was the necklace, now restored to its original case. It took all her will not to leap for it.

"Do you have any idea how dangerous it was to put this on?" the king asked. "Magical artifacts are not to be trifled with; it might have killed you, or worse. We didn't even clearly know what it did until my men saw how you used it. Now we do know what it does, and we know you do as well. You understand with this object I can get anything I want from you, information or otherwise, without struggle."

King Dieter paused for a moment, seemingly changing the subject. "It may interest you that there are two types of cells in my Wolfsguard dungeon. You have seen one, meant only for short-term holding. The other kind is a trapdoor cell, whose residents are thrown in and, apart from being lowered food and water, forgotten forever. Since stays there are permanent, they are larger than the cell you visited and have three other amenities: a canvas cot, a wooden chair, and, in a corner far from the trapdoor, a noose. As I said, I am not cruel. You do not want to go into one of those cells. I do not want to be forced to put that thing on to get the truth out of you," the king continued, pointing at the necklace. "Do we understand each other?"

Rook nodded. She was as stubborn as anyone she'd met, but she could see when she was licked. The authorities had all the cards, and they had *her*, dead to rights. On some level she knew this moment was inevitable from the first job she pulled, and now it was here.

"Where is the book you stole?" the king demanded.

"I left it with friends."

"Why?"

"They could read it," Rook answered, "and I thought they'd know the right thing to do."

"And who are these friends?"

"I'd rather not say."

"I'm sure you wouldn't," the king pressed. "I've made your options clear."

"They're elves," Rook relented, the thought of being driven to suicide by darkness and isolation demolishing what was left of her will, though her eyes left King Dieter's and strayed lustfully to the necklace. "They're called the Windriders, living right around where your agents lost me in the forest. Though I would have thought the fabled Wolfsguard would have figured some of that out on their own."

"And did these Windriders learn what was in the book?"

"Some. Something to do with an ancient power that incited wars and eventually got imprisoned underground."

"Nothing else?" the king insisted.

"Not that I knew. Things got hot and I got gone."

"What do you mean, 'things got hot'?"

"We got a report that the Baron... You know what? This is going to be a long story."

King Dieter narrowed one eye and regarded Rook for a moment. "I have time."

The thief revealed the previous year's events as succinctly as she was able, glossing many details but essentially admitting her involvement with the Baron in the search for the Hoard of Dalviir and her subsequent journey underground with the Windriders. She ended with the report of the Baron's resurrection.

The king's eyes were skeptical. "That's quite the story."

"I know. I wouldn't believe it myself if I hadn't been there."

Dieter looked to his advisor, who gave a slight nod.

"It does seem to fit with the knowledge we've gleaned from other sources," the king admitted. "I notice your tale was bereft of names. I respect your loyalty and won't ask you to reveal any of your compatriots, save one. You have said the leader of your expedition was a human hunter. I would have his name."

Rook scowled at the demand but knew she could not refuse. "Joseph," she spat.

King Dieter's eyes flinched to his advisor, and the surprise on both their faces was plain to read. When he spoke again, the king's words were quicker, more urgent. "This Joseph, was he tall, dour, as good with a bow as you've said?"

"He was."

"And you could locate him, or arrange a meeting with the elves he's with?"

Rook had no idea why the man was so important to a royal, and she didn't care, for in a flash the situation had changed. Now Rook had a card. Only one, it was true, but if she'd read the king's tone right, it was a big one. Possibly the only one she'd need. "I might," Rook answered after a pause. "If it was worth my while."

"Our agreement—"

"Has changed," Rook finished, brushing aside the realization she had just interrupted a king. "Sure, you could put the necklace on, force a location out of me, throw me in a cell. But what good would that do you? These are elves we're talking about; telling you a spot in the forest doesn't get you to them unless they want to be found, which they don't. It isn't as though there are passwords or secret handshakes you can force me to give up; they're a close-knit community who know each other's faces and allow entry based on trust, not procedures. Now you don't just need what's in my head. You need *me*. And you need me cooperative.

"We both know you could give the necklace to one of your agents and keep him on me all the way there and back...or could you? Are you sure the necklace can work for that long on one person, especially one who knows what it does? Even if it would, what if your agent slips up in any of a hundred ways and I manage to escape? What if the elves spot us...let me rephrase that. *When* the elves spot us in the forest, what if they perceive somehow I'm being controlled and perforate your man with arrows before he even knows they're there? What if Joseph doesn't like the way things are being handled and your man has to continuously control *both* of us to get him back? That's a lot that could go wrong, and that just off the top of my head. And in every case, you're left with nothing."

It was the king's turn to scowl. "You never miss a turn, do you?"

"Can't afford to," Rook countered.

For a long moment there was silence between Rook and King Dieter, a silence thick with striving wills. As the silence drew on, Rook began to doubt herself; she could read in the king's expression that his eagerness to know Joseph's whereabouts was urgent, but she didn't know the cause for it. Was the card she had played as powerful as she'd initially thought?

"What do you want?" Dieter finally asked.

Rook betrayed none of her doubt as she answered. "If I succeed in bringing Joseph to you, I don't ever want to see the inside of a cell again for any crimes I've allegedly committed up to that moment."

"Granted, barring murder and high treason. Those are beyond my authority to pardon."

Rook considered her brother's condition and how near the solution had seemed while she still possessed the power of command. Her eyes bored into the king's. "I want the necklace back."

~ * ~

The king agreed to Rook's terms, at least for the duration of the mission, but in order to ensure she remained focused on the task and didn't try to flee, two Wolfsguard would accompany her. Two deaf Wolfsguard. Her daggers had been collected from the alley where she was taken, removing any trace she'd been there, and these were now returned to her, though she knew they would do no good against her captors.

By way of a briefing for her mission, Rook was able to

gather a few bits of the larger situation that had somehow come to form the framework of her life. It seemed early in the year King Dieter's sages had detected some other-than-natural cause behind the growing conflicts. They had no idea what that cause might be, but Dieter trusted their conclusions and set resources to the task of unraveling the mystery. By a combination of magical means and a careful reading of what various nobles had said in council meetings, and as many private conversations as the king's agents could report upon, Dieter's men traced the warmongering agenda, at least on their side of the borders, to a handful of nobles and court officials. At some point in their surveillance they learned of a theft commissioned from those quarters, at which point the object of that theft and its precise recipient came to be of great interest.

Rook had less success in determining the king's interest in Joseph, save to infer his role in the wars years back had been more influential than anything the hunter's own words had given her reason to believe. The piece of information that gave her the gravest concern was a word she overheard the king's advisor use in a murmured conversation, and by all evidence he must have been speaking of Joseph. The word Rook heard, though, wasn't "hunter" or "scout." It was "assassin."

By mid-morning, preparations to set out had been completed. Once again, Rook headed south, once again looking for Windriders. The principal difference was this time, her captors were in plain sight.

Chapter Fifteen: Loss

The long night march let the Windriders outrun the flame but taxed their speed thereafter. Two days of marching with all the haste the slower members could manage had carried the clan a mile or more into the plain. Joseph was exhausted, having been moving and fighting for over a week without reprieve, so the morning was wearing on when he woke on the third new day of their flight. He'd completed most of the work of repacking and restocking his gear before Kaillë awoke. She looked up at him with eyes as tired as they were somber. "Where do we go now, Joseph? We've been so focused on escaping the flames, as we had to, I've given little thought to what happens after that."

"I've been pondering that myself," Joseph replied. "Considering Rook's report, both from her own eyes and via the Blood Clan, we know the north and south are embroiled in war, or soon will be. Seems our only choice is to go west, make for the coast, perhaps find a way to charter passage on a ship that will take us far from here."

"What about to the north? You have allies there, don't you?"

"None who's help would come without a high price. West is the better option."

"Better for whom?" Kaillë pressed.

"What are you getting at, Kaillë? Better for us, for all of us."

"Meaning all of the Windriders."

"Of course." Perhaps somewhere deep down Joseph anticipated Kaillë's meaning, but he chose not to acknowledge it.

"And what about everyone who is not a Windrider?" Kaillë's eyes were stern.

"You can't be serious," Joseph argued. "You surely can't want me to go headfirst into all that."

"Want? No. And *you*? No. But do I believe the right thing to do is for *us* to get involved? Yes."

Joseph's stomach twisted at the thought of facing war's desolation again. The skirmishes he'd suffered over the last six months had been bad enough, but in many ways they paled in comparison to a full confrontation. True, his role in the wars had been primarily as a scout, so if he did his job correctly, the enemy never even knew he was there. In that sense, his recent fights had been more immediately dangerous than most of his time serving Dieter's army. What horrified him now were the memories of the constant background inhumanity of war, of being constantly surrounded by the starving, the sick, the dead, and the dying. Grown men sobbing for their mothers, the constant reek of sweat, blood, and rot, the screams of dying horses. At times going on a mission was a welcome relief, despite the danger, just for the opportunity to get away from the camp where the atrocities' effects were so densely packed. The idea of the innocent Windriders subjected to such conditions was too much.

Joseph fixed Kaillë with a hard stare. "I know you're trying to do the right thing, and I admire you for it...but you don't know what you're asking."

"That's true, but you do. If in the end we can't run, it is you who must prepare our people to face what you have faced. In this even Tal'onë cannot teach them."

Joseph noted the "if" in Kaillë's answer and the tacit agreement to his plan it implied. There was no need to speak of it further. The hunter walked to the stream by which they'd camped to prepare himself for the day and looked back to the east. They had only just broken from the wood the evening before, so much was hidden behind the first ranks of smaller trunks and the canopy growing denser by the yard, but the heavy pall of smoke over the forest was unmistakable. Everything in the world he'd ever loved, save only Kaillë and her people, was being consumed. How could she ask him to expose these last remnants of his life to a different, no less ravenous conflagration?

He turned back west and let his eyes roam over the camp. The going would get more difficult as they continued onto the flats. They had allowed the owls to rest in the nearby trees, but by the next night's camp they would be forced to nest on the ground. It wouldn't do them any harm, but they didn't like it, regardless. By the following day, even at their slower pace, they would reach the river. There were no bridges, so they would somehow have to negotiate ferry trips across. Between the river and the coast were several days' worth of travel through barren lands that would yield little in the way of water or forage. Joseph only knew the region by reputation, but what he did know was discouraging. Their hasty departure had been no way to begin a migration of this magnitude, but there hadn't been another viable choice. Bad as these prospects were, they were a damn sight better than marching the Windrider clan into a war zone. Joseph finished his morning ablutions and found Tal'onë to prepare the Windriders to move.

Half an hour went by, more or less, before all the tents had been struck and the camp broken, but without further delay, the Windrider column was on the march once more.

~ * ~

Mid-morning had come and gone when Tal'onë came to Joseph with concern furrowing his brow. "Joseph," he said, "we are being followed."

The owls were largely ranging free and riderless to conserve their energy for the long journey, but two riders were aloft and on the lookout for trouble. Joseph supposed this was the source of Tal'onë's news. "Is it this Blood Clan you told me about?"

"By the rider's description, I think so."

"How many?"

"A dozen he could see. Maybe more in concealment of brush."

Joseph was exhausted and sick of being chased from pillar to post. He was fed up with every living thing trying to kill him and the ones he loved. He was disgusted at this clan of murderous parasites who called themselves elves. A rage burned in his gut.

He looked down at Tal'onë with embers in his eyes, and the elf stepped back a pace. Joseph pulled his bow from his back and began to string it. "Get me Dorav and Tes'sael. Tell them to bring the rovers and our ten best fighters."

"Ten, Joseph? Are you certain? After our recent losses—"

"I'm certain," Joseph growled.

Tal'onë jogged off, and Joseph finished stringing his bow and adjusted his long knife on his belt. Only a minute or two passed before his team had assembled.

"What are we doing, Joseph?" Dorav asked.

"Hunting." With that, Joseph sprinted east.

On the flat plain, they spotted the enemy at several hundred yards, but Joseph didn't stop. A red wrath was upon him, and he rushed to the battle with an eagerness he seldom felt. At a furlong he knew the Blood Elves had seen them, too, and were also on the charge. The distance was now closing rapidly, and at last Joseph slowed. "Rovers, pike wall. Tes'sael, leave two archers then skirmish."

The rovers formed up in front, as did an elf on either side. Tes'sael took the rest in a wide loop to the left preparing to flank. The Blood Clan carried thick, round shields, but their holding was lax. Joseph took aim at the lead runner and stretched his bow with a roar. His target was knocked clean off his feet with Joseph's arrow through his sternum. The rest were given pause, slowing now and holding their shields forward.

Arrows whizzed from the bows to Joseph's sides, one thudding into a shield but the other piercing a Blood Elf's calf. They were now close enough for Joseph to clearly hear his cry of pain, close enough for Joseph to see their eyes over the rims of their shields. He stretched his bow again, and one of those eyes was obliterated. Two more arrows from the Windriders and two more leg wounds. Tes'sael's squad now shot on the run, peppering the Blood Clan's unprotected flank. Some turned in their direction, indecisive, and Joseph knew if their leader was still alive, he was no less flatfooted than his men.

"Press," Joseph growled to the rovers, and they moved forward with their pikes at a hustle toward the enemy, now less than thirty yards away. Joseph and the elves continued to loose arrows.

The Blood Clan made a final charge, desperate to close the range with foes who had them in such deadly peril from a distance. A few came at the pikes, but the rest turned their charge to Tes'sael's band. Everyone clashed at once. Their training having focused on trolls, the enemies' shields were a hurdle for the rovers, but only briefly, their superior reach and strength making the difference. Now that they were close, these stout, black-eyed men must have appeared as monsters to the Blood Elves. Joseph, tall and grim-faced, could scarcely have appeared any less frightening as he stretched his bow with ruthless constancy.

Tes'sael and his elves, forced to go hand-to-hand, set to work with knife and ax. They held their own, but the enemies' superior armor gave them the advantage; they would have been hard-pressed were it not for the relentless press of the rovers and withering arrow attacks from behind them.

The Blood Clan fighters were now hemmed in from both sides, half down or dead and half the rest wounded. On those faces he could see, Joseph saw eyes on the verge of surrender, but the rage had not lifted from him, and he had no intention of granting quarter to these men who had been intent on killing him only moments before. "Joseph," called the elf to his left, "look to the stream."

Joseph looked, and from the bank on their left another half dozen Blood Elves had broken cover and were charging to the rescue of their embattled companions. They were but thirty yards distant and threatened to catch Tes'sael's group in a pincer. Joseph backpedaled to get a clean shot, and his archers followed him; the rovers with their pikes were more than enough to keep the remaining foes at bay. He loosed three arrows as he moved, but these newcomers had seen the previous fight and were prepared, ducking low and overlapping their shields as they marched forward, denying any clean targets.

Joseph's wroth still burned, and he charged as he shot, piercing one through the foot and another, adjacent, in the face through the tiniest chink in the overlapping shields. These two elves fell, opening a gap in the shield wall.

Joseph shot one more time, felling another elf, then dropped his bow and hit that gap like a thunderbolt, his long knife flashing in the sun. The Blood Elves were strong for their size, but they were no match for Joseph's speed and reach. He stabbed one in the throat and relieved him of his ax, then planted it into the face of the next one in line. At some point the two elven archers joined in the fray, and within a few seconds the enemy's reinforcements lay on the ground, all slain save one.

Joseph's chest was heaving, and he was covered in blood, as Dorav and Tes'sael brought their men over to his side, their bloody work also finished. The elves seemed loath to approach the hunter in his current state. "Joseph," Dorav said, "we left three enemy wounded in our mob. They're not fit to walk. What do you want us to do with them?"

"Let the plains have them. How is our side?"

"Two wounded, nothing we can't bandage," Tes'sael reported. "What about that one?" Tes'sael was pointing to a Blood Elf on the ground, his left arm shattered above the elbow and bleeding from an ax wound. With help standing, he could likely walk, and though the arm was a loss, his chances for survival were good if he got the proper care.

"Him we leave alive," Joseph explained. "We want him to carry news of their defeat to the rest of his people, explain that the Windriders are not the easy pickings they thought us to be." Joseph walked over to the ground where he had dropped his bow and retrieved it. "Start mending the wounded and gathering up arrows; we can't spare them. Dorav, see what—" Suddenly Joseph whipped an arrow from his quiver and shot his bow back toward the surviving Blood Elf. The man screamed in fresh pain as Joseph's arrow ripped through his hand and pinned it to the ground, just an inch away from the throwing knife for which it reached. Joseph's feet pounded the ground as he stormed over to where the elf lay, put one foot on his trapped wrist, and ripped the arrow back out, eliciting another scream. "I should stab your feet and make you *crawl* back to your people," he bellowed, "like the worm that you are! Murderer, raper, preying on the weak and the innocent. Curs like you are why I spurned the world of men, and now here you are in the wilderness. I won't have it! How I wish my forest hadn't burned so we could have fought you from the trees; we'd have slaughtered every worthless one of you. Now you're going to—"

An owl shriek pierced the warm air, drawing everyone's attention upward. A rider had put his bird into a steep dive, opening its wings at the last second in a slowdown that jolted the rider in his saddle. "Joseph," the elf cried out as he put his owl into tight circles over their heads. "We are attacked!"

Joseph cursed himself. "Get the riders aloft, all of them, shoot from the air."

"But Joseph," the rider called back, "then there will be too few to protect—"

"Do it now! Go!"

Bird and rider sped off to the west, and Joseph rallied the men to run back to the main group with all speed. He looked briefly to the surviving Blood Elf, looking for some smirk or indication of victory, but the man seemed to recognize he'd outlived his usefulness; his face was blanched. It was well for him, for he would not have survived any other expression. Joseph turned and ran.

As he sped back to his people, his stomach knotted and rose into his throat. How could he have been so foolish, his attention so lax? It was impossible to know whether the men behind them had been meant to lure warriors away; in fact he doubted it, but of course the enemy would have other watchers concealed nearby, ready to send word to their main force when Joseph left with so many of their guards. He cursed his lapse in discipline as he ran, mentally scourging himself for giving in to his anger. He was lower than a beast.

He had learned over the months to slow his sprints when he traveled with the elves, for though their endurance was unmatched, their legs were simply too short to hold pace with him stride for stride. In that moment he left them behind, desperate to reach the battle, dread fueling his speed.

Joseph's worst fears were made flesh when he came within sight of the main Windrider body. The chaos and distance were too great for a precise count, but his experienced eyes reckoned the entire Blood Clan had joined the attack en masse. Joseph redoubled his speed as he continued to survey the situation. The women and very old had fled into the streambed and were shepherding the young farther to the west. Joseph noted they were unencumbered, then spotted a knot of Blood Elves picking through a pile of packs at the edge of the stream where the fleeing Windriders has ostensibly thrown them away. Another handful of enemies, seemingly confident in the battle's outcome, stood a little distance to the south rifling through the contents of the hand trucks.

Amidst all this the Windrider guard, along with every male of fighting age, were engaged in a fighting retreat at the stream's edge. It wasn't the Windrider way to be so static in a fight, but the Blood Elves had forced them to mount a hard defense of the non-combatants.

Only two things worked to their advantage. The Blood Clan did not seem to favor bows, and those archers they had were beggared in skill by even novice Windriders. Also, many riders had managed to get aloft as Joseph had ordered, and even now they harried the Blood Clan from the sky, distracting the enemy and providing crucial, if marginal, respite for the defenders on the ground.

Joseph had reached his effective range, and the plain provided a gentle rise from which to attack. Taking his stance, he launched arrow after arrow, spreading his attacks about so as not to draw unwanted attention. In a minute's time he had emptied his quiver, and he did not miss.

The elves and dwarves, led by Tes'sael and Dorav, caught up to Joseph, their faces grim. Just then, Joseph spotted a dozen Blood Elves fording the stream, skirting the Windrider rear guard. "Dorav, bring your rovers, we need to catch them," Joseph ordered, pointing. "Tes'sael, get into range and soften them up."

The band charged forward, bellowing a battle cry the enemy couldn't help but hear. They turned toward Joseph and the dwarves and, left with no other choice that didn't present an ideal target to their new attackers, charged back. Again, their lack of discipline proved their undoing. Heedless, it seemed, of Tes'sael's archers in the distance, their shields were slung, and Joseph heard the whine of Windrider arrows on either side as they let loose with their volleys. Many found their mark, and Tes'sael and his elves did more than their share in weakening the Blood Elf band. By the time the two sides met, Joseph and the Rovers had merely to mop up what was left.

Joseph turned and saw Tes'sael had wasted no time in turning his archers to the main body of the Blood Clan assault, though he knew their quivers must be getting light. Still, Joseph's pinpoint attacks had opened gaps in the enemy ranks that only redoubled the airborne archers' effectiveness. The Blood Clan's numbers were beginning to noticeably thin, and though it broke Joseph's heart to see it, as yet their inferior archers had only brought one owl down from the sky.

The appearance of a dozen more warriors was too much for the opportunistic raiders. A horn blew, and the enemy began their retreat. A few tried to make off with the handcarts, but Joseph and the dwarves, along with Tes'sael's last few arrows, convinced them otherwise. Above, Joseph saw Tes'voran gathering the riders into formation and leading them in pursuit of the Blood Clan, adding to their losses and, with any luck, convincing them not to return. It was the order he would have given himself.

The hunter immediately began to take stock, urgently seeking to assess their losses and see to it the wounded received care. First and foremost, he had to locate his wife. "Kaillë," he shouted, suddenly filled with fear. "Kaillë!" He ran to the Windriders, asking who had seen her, but everyone he approached only shook their heads, their expressions numb. Joseph's eyes went wild as he turned, looking in every direction.

"Joseph!"

The human turned toward the stream and saw Kaillë running through the shallows to approach him, hurrying back from where the women and children had been fleeing. She came to Joseph and pressed against him, heedless of the blood spattering his body, and laid her face against his chest. Her story tumbled out in a frantic rush. "I didn't want to leave, but Tal'onë ordered. Someone had to lead the innocent away, and so I went with them. I wanted to stay and fight, but there were so many, and it was terrible, and the children were screaming..."

Joseph held her and stroked her hair, urging her to be calm. "It's alright, Kaillë. You did right; I was the one who failed. I never should have left, I should have been patient and sent scouts. I failed our people." He cast his eyes around the carnage of the battlefield. "Some of our people are dead because of me."

Kaillë pulled away only far enough to look into his eyes. "I know better than to try to talk you out of these tempers. I only remind you of this: Even if you were right that *some* are dead because of you, *all* who live are alive because of you, and twice over."

Joseph's self-recrimination was too black to be dissuaded, and in any case he hadn't the time to argue the point. Now satisfied Kaillë was unhurt, he turned back to the task of ordering the Windriders into care for the wounded and regathering their scattered supplies. Already Kaillë was beset with questions from half a dozen elves, and if leadership was not given soon, they would be overwhelmed.

Joseph separated from Kaillë. "To our tasks, Chieftain," he said, bowing his head. She nodded to him and set about her work. Joseph needed help. Tes'voran was still off driving the Blood Clan south, and likely would be for some time, and Tes'sael had already started at the eastern edge of the battlefield and, with his elves, began the search for wounded. Joseph returned to the main band and looked for Tal'onë. Not locating him quickly, he called the captain's name.

"Joseph," came Tal'onë's voice from a few yards away. The call was hoarse and ended with a wet, bubbling cough.

Joseph looked to see the elf lying on the ground, propped up on one elbow, surrounded by half a dozen dead Blood Clan elves. Joseph took two steps before gasping in horror at the broken spear through Tal'onë's abdomen. He sprinted the last few strides and dropped immediately to his knees at the captain's side. "No, no no no no no," he muttered. Closer now, he could see the blood on Tal'onë's lips. Tears sprang to his eyes. The elf clung to life, but Joseph knew nothing could be done for him. He looked into Tal'onë's face and saw the elf knew it too. He propped his friend's head in his lap, his tears falling freely now, and held his hands, no words adequate to his pain. "It's my fault," he finally choked.

"True enough I was stabbed from behind," Tal'onë whispered, "but a moment later I saw his face. He's over there somewhere." He gestured with his head to the dead foes surrounding him. "I'm quite sure it wasn't you."

Joseph tried to chuckle, for Tal'onë's sake, but he couldn't manage it. His first instinct was to tell Tal'onë not to try to talk, but even that was pointless, and he knew it. If the elf had words, Joseph would hear them. He coughed past his tears. "Is there anything I can do for you? Anything you want, a message, or...?"

Tal'onë reached up and put one hand on the back of Joseph's neck, his grip still strong. "Yes, a message. And it's to you I give it. The day we met one of my elves died, and you blamed yourself. I told you it wouldn't bring him back. That hasn't changed. Do you understand? *My* path led me to this. You did not blaze it for me. You aren't so damned important as all that." He coughed, and blood splattered from his lips. His grip on Joseph's neck weakened. "Run all you want from prophecies, but never run from being Joseph." He drew a deep breath through his nose, but even this seemed not to fill his lungs. His words grew weaker. "You are a good man, my friend. Be that man. Love her, love her with all you have and help her lead our people. *Our* people, Joseph. Our people. You are a Windrider, always... A Wind—"

Tal'onë's labored breathing slowed, then he choked and convulsed. Joseph had seen it a hundred times. In the minstrel's songs a bold warrior died in a final moment of peace, but there was no truth in them. The last moment was always of pain and fear. His friend kicked one last time as his body fought for air that wouldn't come, and to the last second Joseph held his eyes, refusing to let him go, refusing to free himself of the burden of Tal'onë's death, carrying him with his eyes to his final second of life. And then he saw, with a wrenching heart, that Tal'onë looked no longer into his eyes, but past them, gazing with a stare that fixed on eternity. Joseph reached down and closed his friend's eyes, then sat for a few moments, looking at his bloody face. At last he lay Tal'onë's head on the ground and gentled his repose as best he could, then stood, leaning his head back to the sky. He didn't know how long he stood there, staring into the high, blue nothing. A wordless scream of rage and pain welled up from deep inside him, but it died before it reached his lips. He was too exhausted even for his grief, too numb for his feelings of murder toward the Blood Clan to find any purchase in his thoughts.

Somewhere in the midst of it all he felt an arm about his shoulders and looked over to see Kaillë. Her head and arm were higher than they should have been, and only in that instant did he realize he was no longer standing but sitting, his knees drawn up before him as he sat upon the blood-slicked earth, whether open-eyed in sleep or utterly thoughtless in waking he couldn't rightly say. "Tal'onë," he managed to mutter.

"I saw," Kaillë said. "After, I mean. I saw you were with him and so continued on helping the living."

Joseph rubbed at his face. "You're right, I'm sorry, I should have—"

"No," Kaillë interrupted. "You were doing exactly what you should. He deserved to have you there at the end, even if that cost you too much to help elsewhere It was right."

Joseph looked again at his wife. "I love you. I know I don't say what...the things a woman wants to hear. Not much. But I do. If you'd been lost, I... I don't..."

"I know. It's alright. I wasn't lost. We are here. And the Windriders are here. We had losses, but less than we might have."

"Am I needed? Should I be..."

"Not right now. Everything is being tended, and when all else was in motion, the people insisted I go and see to my husband."

Joseph nodded. For all his instincts to be useful, he was

relieved by Kaillë's report. The whole world felt like a strange dream, and he was glad of a chance to simply sit awhile longer, even in such gruesome surroundings. He leaned against Kaillë, looking down and realizing she was as bloody as he was, but her covering came from saving the wounded, while his was born of inflicting the wounds. Slowly his thoughts cleared and recent events began to solidify in his mind. "I need to find my bow," were the next words that found their way out of his mouth.

"Tes'sael picked it up where you dropped it. He has it in safekeeping."

Joseph nodded. "Is Tes'voran back yet?"

"Yes. He doesn't believe the enemy will return. They made off with some of our supplies, but we've already started gleaning what we can from the field. We'll certainly have great store of weapons, perhaps enough to barter with when we reach the river."

Joseph's next words were raw, but living with elves for so long had influenced him to work past his pain to the needs of the moment. "We will need to appoint a new guard captain. I don't know whether Tes'sael or Tes'voran is more—"

"No," Kaillë said. "Both of them, and Tal'onë and I, decided weeks ago who would take Tal'onë's place if the worst should happen."

Joseph looked to Kaillë, puzzled. "No elf is more qualified than either of them."

"And no elf will take Tal'onë's place. You will."

"Kaillë, how could I? I'm not—"

"You are a Windrider," Kaillë proclaimed, emphasizing each word. She spoke in that moment with the boldness she showed when addressing her people as their chieftain. "You are the greatest warrior and the most decisive leader in the clan. It would be a disservice to my people to choose anyone else."

"But I cannot train the fighters in elven ways."

"Which is precisely why you will have two experienced lieutenants in Tes'sael and Tes'voran. You will lead the guard, but you need not lead it alone. Just as I have never needed to lead our people alone, not from the moment you rescued me stumbling through your woods." She smiled and touched his cheek.

Joseph could not bring himself to smile back. The elves had their way, but he had his, and his pain was still too fresh.

"I will make a formal announcement later, but for now, by my authority as chieftain of the Windrider Clan, I name you Tal'Joseph."

"Thank you," Joseph replied, though what he felt was not gratitude but burden, and he was sure Kaillë knew it. He would feel honored later. "Can I ask you a favor?"

"Of course. As Kaillë or as Chieftain?"

"As Chieftain. Can you find Tes'sael and Tes'voran and send them to me? By your leave, I recommend that we move the people no farther tonight than we must to get clear of the carnage. They have had too hard a day, and there will be more than an afternoon's work in continuing to gather useful things from the field." Had Joseph led a human clan, he would have spoken of burial, but such was not the way of elves, or of Windriders at any rate. "That said, there is no cover here, and we must be alert. I do not believe the Blood Clan will come back, but believing is not knowing, and there may be other threats."

"I will. In the meantime, Tes'voran has already set patrols, so you may consider a short walk upstream to wash while you wait for them." Kaillë gave Joseph's knee a pat before standing to go to her errand and her myriad other duties.

Joseph stood and turned toward the stream, but before he could look away, his eyes fixed on Tal'onë's body for a long moment. He knew the captain's loss would be acute, a hole that would take long to fill. He had known the elf only half a year, and yet in that time they had forged a brotherhood he had seldom known even with humans. Joseph's eyes misted over anew as he walked to the water, and his tears flowed softly.

He spread his clothes to air out on the bank as he waded into the water; there would be no time to wash them properly, and he had no idea where his spare sets of clothing had ended up after the fighting. He had retrieved a bar of rough soap and a pumice stone from his pack, and he worked at stripping the blood from his skin. He hadn't bothered to go as far upstream as he should, but as he washed he saw Windriders pulling bodies from the water and up onto the bank, and little by little the water ran less riled and bloody and more clear. Tes'sael and Tes'voran found him as he was finishing and waited on the bank in quiet conversation. They kept their eyes averted until the hunter had dried and dressed, then turned to salute. "We are honored to serve you, Tal'Joseph," Tes'voran said as Tes'sael handed Joseph his bow.

Joseph's first instinct was to refuse the title, but he dared not. From the lowliest Ten to the most respected Tal, a man's name changed when he joined the guard, and that could not simply be put off. In this he could only bow to the Windrider custom or face the risk of insulting them. Slowly he reminded himself that these customs must now become his, for he could no longer deny that he was a Windrider, by choice, by marriage, by title, and by unspoken oath to a respected friend now gone. "I have advised Kaillë not to move the people any farther than we must today. Setting the guard will be vital. Tell me your thoughts."

The two lieutenants laid out their plans to their new captain. Joseph made minor adjustments and explained them, then sent the two elves off to execute the plan.

Chapter Sixteen: Crossroads

The Windriders moved half a mile onward. It took them downstream, but to move toward cleaner water would have forced them to cross the battlefield again in the morning, so they relied on their water stores until the stream flowed completely clear once more. The fallen Windriders, twelve all told, were laid in rows on the plain across the water from the battle, naked as the day they came into the world, and the words of parting were spoken over them. Heirs of the fallen received their belongings, and the possessions of those without surviving kin were presented to Kaillë to be distributed for the good of the clan. Had there been enough fuel for a fire, the Blood Elves would have been burned to remove their wickedness from the cycle of renewal, but that wasn't possible. Instead the bodies were stripped of all useful goods, including armor and clothing, and collected into a heap in more or less the center of the battlefield. As the sun set over the burning hills, Kaillë announced to the people that Joseph was now Tal'Joseph, and the members of the guard bowed and placed their right fists over their hearts in salute. No greater ceremony was required.

Joseph walked the edge of the camp, feeling strangely rested in the twilight. Kaillë was near the stream, discussing their situation with the council, and Joseph had said all he meant to and been excused. Reconstructing the day's events, he estimated he had sat by Tal'onë's body for just over an hour, but once the initial shock had passed, he felt as though his heart had slept a lifetime in that hour. His limbs were still weary, but his mind was clear. The challenges that had so daunted him even that morning had not changed, indeed they had grown with their losses save for the acquisition of Blood Clan gear to use as trade goods, but he was prepared now to take them as they came and face them, one by one.

As Joseph neared the eastern end of the camp, two elves approached him, Ten'daren and another he knew less well, though the name Ten'cavel came to his mind. "Tal'Joseph," Ten'daren began, the use of Joseph's new name easy on his lips, "we were just about to find Tes'sael to give a report. The outer pickets have sent word of travelers approaching along the stream, a small woman and two large men."

Joseph had seen many coincidences in his life, but he had also learned not too quickly to pass strange events off as such. "How small?" he asked.

Ten'daren's face was perplexed. "Tal'Joseph?"

"The woman. How small is she?"

Ten'daren looked to Ten'cavel, who answered. "No larger than Kaillë, or close enough as to make no difference."

Joseph raised his eyebrows, shooting the pair a wry look. "Rook," he said.

The elves both sighed as if they should have considered it sooner.

"Ten'daren, take the report to Kaillë. I'll go investigate myself. Ten'cavel, with me."

The two of them moved east, passing over the plain like moon shadows. After the best part of a mile, they passed the outer picket line and spotted the travelers. Joseph watched their movements and was convinced the woman truly was Rook. He had never seen the two men. The hunter led Ten'cavel on a looping path away from the stream, approaching the trio from behind. At about ten yards distant, he called out, "Hold there. No quick moves. Rook, are these men threatening you?"

Rook, for indeed it was she, held up her hand, and the men stopped. "Save your threats, hunter, they can't hear them. And to answer your question...it's complicated."

"Tell them to show their hands, unless you vouch for them."

"I do, damn it all. They're not here to hurt anyone." Joseph relaxed, if only slightly, and approached. He noticed Ten'cavel remained on alert and didn't discourage him. "Why are you here, Rook?"

"We're here for you, big man." She turned to one of the cloaked men and waved her hand in front of his face, then pointed to Joseph. "There's your man," she said, louder than normal and moving her mouth more slowly.

The large man looked at Joseph, then back to Rook. He pointed at Joseph and arched his eyebrows in question. Rook made an exaggerated nod and all-but shouted, "Yes, that's him, I just said that."

Joseph observed Rook's antics and grasped her previous statement that the men couldn't hear his threats. "Rook, these men are deaf?"

"Yes," she answered, exasperation obvious in her voice.

"Then what good does she think yelling will do?" Ten'cavel asked in elven.

Joseph laughed, which earned a scowl from Rook, but

she didn't ask what was said. Meanwhile, the man Rook had spoken to held one hand up and reached slowly with the other into his cloak. With it he produced a rolled piece of parchment, stamped with a wax seal. He handed the scroll to Joseph with his head bowed.

Joseph took the parchment, though the light had grown too dim to read. He needed to produce a light, and he chose not to do that so far from the safety of the camp. "Come on," he ordered, leading the three forward as Ten'cavel brought up the rear. Joseph conducted the travelers safely through the pickets and returned to the eastern edge of the camp, where he found Kaillë waiting.

"My invitation was sincere," the chieftain said to Rook, "but I didn't expect you back so soon."

"Seems your man is a bigger player up north than he let on," Rook answered, but she said no more.

Joseph asked for a lamp, and in a moment he had enough light to read by. His customary frown deepened when he recognized King Dieter's seal in the wax, but he broke it without further reaction, unfurled the scroll, and began to read.

Joseph,

I offer my sincerest greetings and warm wishes to you and your household.

Matters in the north are once again moving quickly toward war. My sages agree that some unknown power is at work, and based on the report of the woman, Rook, it appears you have stumbled into the thick of it.

I have no right to ask your help. When last we parted I offered you any boon, up to half my kingdom, and all you asked was to be left alone. It was a promise I fully intended to keep. Even now I offer no order or threat, though some in my council would inveigh upon me thus. Instead I only beg your help on bended knee, as it were; my pride will not come before the lives of my people. I need every good man I can get, and you are among the best. To learn that you may have some knowledge in the face of this threat is a hope un-looked-for. Even had you not, I would not have passed an opportunity to seek your help when it fell into my lap.

It would do the court's heart glad to see you again. Though I respected your wishes, I was grieved when you refused my offer of ennoblement. Another man of integrity on my council of vassals would go far. I digress. Please come to Onderburg with all haste. I ask not for me or my kingdom, but for the innocent lives that will be lost if I cannot find a way to prevent these conflicts from igniting into open war.

So speaks Dieter, son of Wolfgang, Warden of Onderburg and King of Ondravia from the Mountains to the Sea

Joseph handed the letter to Kaillë, and she skimmed it quickly. "Joseph," she said, "I knew you fought for your king, but...you *knew* him?"

"It's a long story," he replied. "The summary version is that I may have saved his life once...or twice. After that my name started to come up when they needed work done behind enemy lines."

"Work," Rook broke in. "Is that a nice way of saying murder?"

Joseph glared down at her. "Sometimes," he shot back, his tone curt. "A man who fights fair is fighting to lose. A king is no different. I did things that had to be done, that other men couldn't do. You think I'm proud of it? There's more than one reason I didn't stay."

Rook and Joseph's eyes were locked, but Kaillë broke the stare-down. "Perhaps if there were not so many dangers surrounding us, a discussion of history or morality might prove interesting. As things stand, I think we'd best keep our focus on the present."

Joseph looked down at his wife, and if there was any surprise at Rook's accusation or his admission, she didn't show it. Though Joseph had told her little of his time in the war, he had never doubted her ability to read between the lines. He also knew she was no hypocrite, and his ability to inflict violence at need had saved her life and that of her people.

"What are we going to do, Tal'Joseph?" Kaillë asked, her use of his new title making plain he was being asked for a decision, not an opinion.

Joseph looked around at the assembled Windriders, the majority of the clan now awake and arrayed in row upon row back to the stream. He didn't doubt their courage, but they were a simple clan. If more than half of them really understood the magnitude of their peril, he would be surprised. He grieved for the horrors that would be inflicted on the people in the north, but they were not his people.

"Please give the king my apologies. I have enough innocent lives on my hands right here."

"Joseph," Rook hummed, looking sidelong at the Wolfsguard, "I have a lot riding on your sense of duty here..."

"Not my problem, Rook."

"It's too dark to travel now, anyway," Kaillë interjected, to Joseph's surprise. "Give us until the morning to change our minds."

"Kaillë," Joseph began, but her eyes warned him not to continue.

"Tes'sael," Kaillë ordered to the nearby lieutenant, "please see to what accommodations we can afford our guests." After Tes'sael led the humans away, the other elves began to disperse, leaving Kaillë and Joseph to confer.

"Joseph," Kaillë began, "I'm sorry to second-guess you."

"You're the chieftain," Joseph replied, chagrined.

"I know I have the authority in matters of the clan," Kaillë clarified, "but I shouldn't have asked for your decision in front of the clan, and then failed to support it. It isn't good for us or for the Windriders. I had meant to accept your decision, but something held me back. My heart misgives me. Give me the rest of the night in council and with the book."

"You have to do what you think is right for our people. I know that. I only wish our first disagreement as man and wife wasn't a matter of life and death for all of us."

Kaillë smiled a mirthless smile. "It was certainly not what my mother told me to expect when I became a bride." Even the mirthless smile faded. "Joseph, if I do decide to go north, I will not hold any obligation over your head. I will not order you back into war."

The image of Tal'onë's lifeless eyes flashed through Joseph's mind, and the elf's final words echoed in his ears. "I am a Windrider," Joseph replied, drawing himself up, straight-backed. "In our household, I am your husband, but in the clan, you are my chieftain. Where you lead, I follow."

Kaillë touched his arm. "Thank you. Go then, and rest. You shall need it. It pains me to spend another night apart, but I will attend to my other pressing duty and have an answer in the morning. I will speak to you again before I declare anything to the clan."

"Send for me if you need anything?"

"Of course."

Joseph admired her strength and allowed himself the luxury of embracing and kissing his wife before letting her go. Afterwards, he sought his bedroll, eager for the rest Kaillë had ordered.

~ * ~

"Joseph, wake up," came a voice above him, and he felt himself being gently shaken. Joseph looked to the sky and saw that dawn was still an hour off, perhaps more. He looked up at the voice and saw Rook's shorthaired silhouette kneeling above him. Something at her throat glinted in the moonlight.

"Rook?" Joseph asked. "What's going on?"

"Get up and grab your gear. We've got to go."

Joseph nodded his assent and stood, casting off his cloak, which he'd spread over him as a blanket, then flipped it around to put it back on his shoulders and clasped it. He stepped over to his things and donned his quiver, then picked up his pack and bow. Rook walked toward the edge of the camp, and he followed. There was a circle of yellow light some fifty yards away where Kaillë still sat with her council, but the rest of the encampment was lit only by the moon.

They were skirting the camp on the western side and halfway to the stream when Joseph asked, "Where are we going?"

"Back to Onderburg. You have to answer the king's summons."

"Alright," Joseph answered, still following Rook.

A few moments later, Rook held up her hand for a halt. "We'll try to avoid the sentries, but you'd best go in front in case we're spotted. If you're questioned, say we're just going a little way away to talk in private."

Joseph nodded and took point. They were almost to the stream when an elf whispered in the night. "Tal'Joseph, is everything alright?"

"Fine," Joseph replied, his tone easy. "Rook and I just need to discuss the situation in the north, and I thought it best we get out of earshot of everyone trying to sleep."

"Would you like an escort?" the elf asked. "There might still be Blood Clan about in hunting bands."

Joseph considered for a moment. He was known for self-sufficiency, so it may not arouse suspicion if he declined, but then again it may, for he was equally known for prudence. Regardless, it wouldn't do to have elves following them as they absconded from the camp. He wondered what Rook would consider the best ruse, but then she spoke on her own.

"Just let us pass, please," Rook said. "We don't need any help."

"As you wish," the elf answered, his outline in the night moving aside.

Joseph hoped no one had seen the exchange; it would be immediately suspect to any onlookers that an elf of the guard had taken direction from Rook without getting Joseph's confirmation first.

Suddenly Joseph heard the creak of a bow being pulled and Tes'sael's voice from behind them. "Speak one wrong word and you die, Rook. Whatever bewitchment you have him under, release him now, before my fingers get tired."

Rook raised her hands out from her sides and sighed. "Forget my orders, Joseph," she said. "Do what you want."

Joseph turned around so he was facing Rook, took a step forward, and slapped her, hard, across the face.

"Ow!" Rook screamed, though she had rolled with the slap to avoid the brunt of the force. Joseph looked down at his hand, shocked and confused.

Rook put a hand on her cheek and glared at Joseph. "I guess now I know what you really think of me."

"I never realized it was any secret," the hunter answered, still confused by his sudden attack on Rook. It hadn't been entirely unpleasant, but it wasn't his way to strike anyone, especially a woman, that wasn't an immediate threat.

"I always wondered what would happen if I tried to

drop control on purpose," Rook grunted.

"What are you talking about?"

Instead of answering, Rook unclasped a necklace from around her slender neck and looked toward Tes'sael. "How did you know?" she asked.

"I doubt there is anyone alive who could change Tal'Joseph's mind about anything," the elf replied, "but if such a person does live, she is Kaillë Windsong, not you. Your whispers at Joseph's side might as well have been shouts on a night as quiet as this. The nearest sentry overheard and alerted me." Tes'sael went on, seemingly pleased with himself, in a rare display of pride at his deduction. "Since I saw the aggression and brutality of the Blood Clan this morning, I had been puzzled by Tes'voran's story of your having gotten information out of them without being harmed. Your exchange with Ten'raldi," he motioned toward the sentry by the stream, "was the last straw."

"So," Joseph put in, "*that's* how you got yourself into trouble with the Wolfsguard."

"Wolfsguar— You knew?"

"Not right away, but yes. They have a distinctive air about them, sort of brooding and overly alert. Once I knew they were on an errand from King Dieter, I figured it out."

"How did you even know they exist?" Rook asked.

"How do you think?"

The gears clicked over in Rook's mind. Secret missions, working directly for the king, a brooding air... "No. You were *one of them*?"

"No no," Joseph assured her, "but I might as well have been after Dieter learned what I could do. We did a lot of the same work; I even had a few with me on assignment a time or two." Joseph recalled his previous interactions with the secret agents of the king. In truth, despite their reputation, he had found their attitudes and personalities as varied as any other men. Their air of menace was cultivated as a powerful tool of the trade. Once Joseph had been allowed to see past that shell, he'd discovered the things that made them truly frightening, skill and discipline creating capabilities rarely to be found in lesser men. They were the most dangerous people Joseph knew, and if they doffed their black cloaks and scowls no one would ever mark the threat.

"Secrets on top of secrets," Rook muttered, shaking her head. "As it happens," she continued, coming back around to Joseph's prior comments as she held up the necklace in her fist, "*this* is not how I got into trouble with them. That damn book is what really put me up to my hips in all this. The necklace is just an added complication, as though I needed one."

"You're very lucky Tes'sael stopped you when he did," Joseph said.

"How's that?"

"Because if we'd made it out of the camp, then I'd have been missed in the morning. The Wolfsguard would have caught up to you by then, and Kaillë never would have believed I'd leave her behind of my own will. She'd have had me tracked, and Tes'voran would have led a wing of owls. Seeing me with the three of you, they'd have assumed I was under some kind of duress and shot you all down like dogs before you had even half a chance to use that magic trinket of yours."

Rook's horrified expression was plain even in the moonlight, and she looked over at Tes'sael. The elf nodded quickly in confirmation.

"I'm going back to sleep," Joseph announced. "Tes'sael, have someone keep an eye on her. If she tries to put that damn thing on again in the camp, shoot her."

"Understood, Tal'Joseph."

"Bastard," Rook muttered, though there was more

frustration at being beaten than actual anger in her tone.

Joseph walked away without answering, though he could think of a few words that would do. His order to Tes'sael was not entirely in jest, since in the event Rook did try anything he expected it to be carried out, but nor was it entirely serious, since he strongly doubted Rook would try to manipulate anyone again. As he paced back to his bedroll, he was suddenly glad Rook had kept her eye on the long-term goal and not been distracted by the desires of the moment. There had been no feeling of dominion in Rook's control, nothing for his own will to recognize as unnatural and fight against. Quite the opposite in fact; her commands had seemed right and sensible at the time, and he remembered well her unveiled advances from the previous autumn. Had her orders now been of a carnal nature, he knew he would have followed them just as naturally, and he did not relish the thought of explaining such actions to Kaillë, though they would not have been his to control.

~ * ~

The sun was over the mountains when Joseph awoke. Without delay he sought out Kaillë near the center of the camp where she had sat in discussions with the council. When he arrived, he saw the debate had ended, but only recently. Some of the elders were nodding off where they sat; it seemed they had worked through the night. Kaillë saw Joseph approaching and rose to meet him.

"We worked most of the night finishing the translation," she said, holding up the book, or what was left of it. The once-trim volume was now a disheveled sheaf of uneven paper with the leather cover fighting a losing battle to hold it all together. Joseph correctly surmised that Kaillë had disassembled the latter two-thirds of the book and pieced the pages out to anybody on the council who could read the ancient text.

"What did you learn?" he asked.

"We learned how to kill Malice," Kaillë answered, her tone weighty.

Joseph raised an eyebrow. "Just like that?"

"The sages who imprisoned Malice centuries ago predicted that, were he ever to escape, much of his power would have to be vested, at least for a long while, in a subordinate. Not a vessel, strictly speaking, more an intermediary or a conduit. It seems he even tried it once on some subterranean creature, but with his true being still imprisoned, he could only extend his influence to the nearby trolls, savage enough to begin with, and not to the dwarves, nor any farther than his immediate environs."

Joseph considered the news. Certainly the tale seemed to fit perfectly with the legend of Dalvinav and the dragon. "And so he sat," Joseph theorized, "watching, until he learned of the Hoard of Dalviir and all its power, then bent all his will toward finding and luring someone that would bring it to him. Then the Hoard gave him enough power to fan the flames of war abroad and send the Baron to bring about his release."

"By returning to Malice the last thing he needed," Kaillë picked up the narrative, "the piece of himself he had lost in his prior, failed attempt: the essence poured into the stone heart of a dragon. That was our best theory as well. Had the dwarves found a way to destroy that, there's a chance Malice would have been killed, or at least lost all hope of escape, for the book explains that as the means of ending him. While he regathers his strength from the effort required to escape his mystic dungeon, clinging to this subordinate as an anchor for his power, his existence even, kill the subordinate and Malice will be forever dispelled."

"So, this subordinate or conduit or whatever you call

it...must be the Baron."

Kaillë nodded.

Joseph smirked, the sort of smirk that caused Kaillë to frown and knit her brows. "So, your solution on how to kill an unkillable thing," Joseph clarified, "is to kill a *different* unkillable thing?"

Kaillë's frown became a scowl. "There is just no pleasing you, is there? I thought you'd be glad."

"I wish I was," Joseph answered, "but I don't see how we're any better off now than we were last night."

"Because," Kaillë said pointedly, her tone now that of the chieftain and not the wife, "Malice has no body, nothing for you and your warriors to shoot at. The Baron, though, the Baron is *flesh*. Flesh now sustained by enchantment, yes...but enchantments may be broken."

"We have no wizards."

"No. But King Dieter does."

Joseph was silent for a handful of long moments. "So, you're determined to go north," he said.

"I am, and so is the council...on one condition."

"What condition?"

"The council will not endorse the plan over your objection," Kaillë answered.

"Do you *need* their endorsement?"

"By our law, no. But this matter is life and death for the entire clan. In this I will not overrule them."

So once again, though all his life he had tried in vain to avoid leading, the final decision would be his. Joseph looked deep into Kaillë's eyes. Every time he did he saw something new there. This time, though, he saw something old, the same eyes he had seen when Delia had urged him to go to war. Her reasoning had been simple, and though she had stated it with more crystal beauty, as was her way, it boiled down to this: If men like Joseph did not make a stand against evil, what hope could there be for the world?

"I withdraw my objection."

"Joseph," Kaillë started, "I don't want you to feel coerced—"

"Kaillë, you know I've always tried to do the right thing. I've also gone far out of my way to stay out of the troubles of other men. You know my past and what I've done. I care nothing for honor; I prize my life too highly for that. But you have believed from the beginning this wasn't a threat we could outrun, and you were, you *are*, right. Even if we made it to the sea, what then? To be uprooted again and again, always running from the next war, the next Baron, the next Blood Clan? Even here in the wilderness we sought only to run and were met with brutality, losing many loved ones. No, sooner or later we should be forced to make a stand, and so I say, as you have said, that if we must make a stand we make it now, on our own terms, or as close to them as we're likely to get. We continue on to the river. Then we go north."

Joseph's voice had risen as he spoke, and the elders had gathered nearer, as well as a growing band of other Windriders. Rook and the Wolfsguard were there, too, the latter standing out starkly from the crowd by their height and heavy, black cloaks. Now in the light of day, the men could read Joseph's lips, and they nodded to him.

"Even if *you* changed your mind," Kaillë said quietly, "I thought you'd try to leave us behind."

"You would follow me, though, just as you did last fall, only this time you would bring all your people. Besides, how could I leave? I rejected the name of Azrith, but the name Tal'Joseph I have accepted. I may have little honor, but I don't shrink from duty."

Kaillë frowned again. "I think you parse words, husband."

Joseph considered all the things he had been forced to do in the name of survival or of duty, things outside any reasonable definition of "honor" that he knew; the distinction he made was real, but he valued Kaillë's innocence in disagreeing. "I hope you never have reason to think otherwise," he replied.

By that time Rook had made her way through the surrounding elves to look up at Joseph. "I know my fate played no part in your decision, hunter," she said, "but I benefit just the same...so thank you."

"There you're wrong, Rook. It's true my motivation had nothing to do with rescuing you from trouble of your own making, but your fate, or your future, anyway, was on my mind, to keep war from your doorstep. And your past fate as well, for I hope to keep many people from having to suffer as you and your brother have suffered."

Kaillë looked around her. "The decision is made. Strike the camp."

Chapter Seventeen: Commitment

$\mathfrak{T}$raveling with the king's agents proved a useful advantage. The Wolfsguard stowed their cloaks and armor and instead donned uniforms and sigils marking them as royal couriers. They further carried writs of appropriation, allowing them to commandeer vessels and equipment with relative impunity. The Windriders spent a day camped outside the nearest river town while the Wolfsguard, with Joseph and Rook ostensibly acting as their interpreters, made arrangements for the travel. In reality, hunter and thief did the actual negotiation while the king's agents stood by to lend authority, and not just a little menace, to the enforcement of their writs.

At last the elves were traveling upriver, spread across three vessels. The humans conveying them spent all of the first day dumbfounded every time they laid eyes on Windriders. All of them had seen elves from time to time as they came into the towns and villages to trade, but so many in one place, and undertaking such a long voyage, was an oddity outside even tavern tales.

Normally boat travel made Joseph restless, but unbeknownst to him a few of his warriors had negotiated a private berth for their chieftain after the barge had been chosen. The room was barely large enough for a cot and two large trunks, but it was, indeed, private, and the newlyweds found ways to fill the time, though after Joseph's long travail, more of the time was filled with sleep than some might have presumed.

Still, Joseph could see the elves going slowly mad with the confinement once the initial excitement wore off. The vessels made brief stops at the docks along the way, but as the Windriders had no knowledge of city life, Joseph thought it best to order them sequestered lest they get into trouble with the notoriously rough humans that lived and worked around the docks. They knew the discomfort was temporary and bore it with characteristic grace, but by the time they reached Onderburg, stir crazy had long-since become an understatement.

Once near the city, Joseph ordered the vessels' captains to put in at a quay that served nearby villages, about a mile south of the city walls. The docks were small, and it took two hours of jostling and bumping before all the elves and their goods were unloaded. With that the barges continued north into the city, their captains eager to cash in the treasury vouchers the Wolfsguard had given them for their trouble and find a contract on any kind of cargo so as not to waste the return voyage.

Joseph was just seeing to the ordering of the camp under the late afternoon sun when a detachment of soldiers in King Dieter's livery approached. Their captain was perhaps five years Joseph's younger, and his well-trimmed blond hair and beard exuded all the signs of social privilege. He carried his gold helmet under his arm, its red plume sticking up before his shoulder. Joseph noted their approach but thought nothing of it until they stopped at the edge of the camp, where the young captain began gesturing and giving orders. Even from thirty yards away, it was clear to Joseph the man was setting up guard positions. He stood from the tent stake he was driving and approached the soldier.

"What do you think you're doing here, Captain?" Joseph asked before the man could introduce himself.

"We're here on orders from His Majesty, King Dieter. Do not interfere."

"I'll do a damn sight more than interfere if you don't answer my question," Joseph growled, glaring down the three inches of height he had on the captain.

The shorter man was undaunted, clearly used to giving orders, not answering questions.

"I'm to present myself to one called Joseph, a hunter from the eastern forests. I'll explain nothing to you."

"I'm the man you're looking for."

The captain looked up and down Joseph's travel-stained garb. "I think there's some mistake."

"You were sent to find a hunter, not a prince. This is what we look like." Joseph held the man's eyes for a long moment.

"I'm sorry, sir," the captain said, his back suddenly straightening as he threw a salute and adopted the unfocused stare of one addressing a superior. "You weren't...that is to say..."

"You were expecting someone taller?" Joseph quipped. "And drop the 'sir.' I'm no knight."

"Of course not, s— I only meant to show respect. My father fought in one of the armies you scouted for. He spoke very highly."

"Who's your father?"

"Sir Wilfried of Usselrich. And I am Sir William, Captain of the Fourth Guard Company of Onderburg."

"I'm sorry, but I don't remember your father, sir. No disrespect, but I didn't spend a lot of time with the armies I scouted for. Now, since we've accomplished the pleasantries, will you answer my question? What are you doing here? How did you even know I'd be here?"

"The king's couriers sent riders ahead three days ago; they beat you here by more than a day."

Damn Wolfsguard, Joseph thought.

"King Dieter ordered me to deploy some of my men to ensure your people's safety, then we are to escort you, the couriers, and a woman called Rook to an audience with His Majesty."

"A suspicious man might think your men are here to keep tabs on my people, not protect them."

"I assure you we are here only to help," the captain replied, his tone only a little affronted.

Tes'voran was nearby, listening in on the conversation. The owls had shadowed the boats all the way upriver, but knowing they couldn't hope to find concealment too near the city, the lieutenant had been on the lookout for somewhere they could shelter. The day before, a small wood had approached nearly to the eastern riverbank, and Tes'voran had sent a rider up to corral the owls and bring them down to the trees to roost, leaving a pair of Windriders behind to tend to them. Since then, his duties had been much reduced.

Now Joseph motioned the elf to his side. "Tes'voran, these guards are here to keep our people safe in this place that is strange to them. If you need anything, you should expect these men to provide reasonable assistance. They are not to hinder or harm any Windrider in any way. If they do, I expect to hear a full report. Understood?"

Tes'voran nodded, then answered with a question of his own in elven. "Should we fear these men, Tal'Joseph?"

Joseph replied in the elven tongue as well. "I don't think

so, but keep a sharp eye. Also, go collect Rook and her escorts, and request Kaillë's presence as well. The king will want news of what's in the book, and it will be best that he get it firsthand."

Tes'voran left to complete his assignments. While they waited for Rook and the Wolfsguard, Captain William made an attempt at conversation. "You seem very well acclimated to these elves."

"These are my people," Joseph replied. He glanced down at the captain, deciding how much to say. "I never meant to have people, but now I do. I was not cut out for the lands of men. Particularly their cities and castles."

"Onderburg is a beautiful citadel," the captain replied.

"A merchant for the city, a plowman for the field, and a hunter for the forest," Joseph answered. "I am no merchant or plowman."

"Each to his own, then."

"Tell me of the situation here. The rumor in the south is that Ondravia is on the cusp of war with her neighbors to the north and east."

Captain William averted his eyes and shifted his feet uneasily. "King Dieter intends to brief you on the situation. I will not supersede him."

"Of course not," Joseph answered, but his eyes narrowed.

By then Rook had arrived with the Wolfsguard, and Kaillë was with them. Dorav had seen the gathering and elected to present himself as well.

"At this time, the king has not extended his invitation to anyone but those I named..." the captain hazarded, eyeing Kaillë and Dorav.

Joseph believed Captain William to be a good man, but his hard adherence to the rules of court wore thin. "I don't go without them. Decide quickly; if you want to go to the palace for more orders, we'll be gone by the time you get back."

The captain scowled. "The king did warn me you were too wild for the city."

"Like I said," Joseph replied, "I'm no merchant."

~ * ~

Half an hour later, the group was walking through the streets of Onderburg. They had avoided the traders' entrance by the docks and instead walked out of their way to the main gates where wealthier merchants, travelers, and dignitaries made their ingress. Joseph noted, however, the usual well-dressed crowds were all but absent, and instead soldiers were everywhere. Even more telling, once they passed the gates, Joseph could see that timbers and planks were being stockpiled at the base of the wall: the hoarding was going up in anticipation of a siege. Captain William may have stayed tightlipped, but his city spoke volumes.

Joseph saw Rook in her element for the first time, every nuance of her body language exuding confidence and ease. The Wolfsguard played their parts perfectly, taking on the hurried but efficient gait of royal couriers with somewhere to be. Kaillë's eyes roamed up and down the high buildings, and Joseph saw wonder there, but she kept close to his side, and he sensed the press and bustle of the manmade structures made her feel small in a way even a towering pine on a mountainside never would. Joseph kept his arm around Kaillë, but where she seemed overwhelmed, Joseph felt utterly on edge. In the forest, the background sounds were innocuous, and noises, or their lack, warning of danger were obvious to any who knew how to listen. In the city there was no such distinction, at least not that he understood. The prevalent noises were a jumble of voices, slamming doors, creaking cart wheels, and clopping hooves, every one of which in its own way could foretell an enemy growing nearer. The smells were even more disconcerting and a strong contributor to Joseph's desire to live as far from cities as he could.

After several minutes, a glance down at Kaillë revealed to Joseph her eyes were no longer on the buildings, but on the faces of all the people they passed. Her brow was furrowed with concern. "What is it?" Joseph asked.

"Listen to the background voices, Joseph, and look in the eyes of the people, only not too directly. Tell me what you see, what you feel?"

Joseph followed his wife's instructions, setting aside his unease enough to sift the details of what he heard and saw rather than simply cataloging them all as dangerous. In a few moments he understood what Kaillë had already seen. "Anger," he answered.

"From everyone," Kaillë confirmed. "Are human cities often like this?"

"I'm not the one to ask, but not that I've known. Events can make the people of a city angry, even enraged, but not like this, not so uniform. Nobody's arguing about something that's happened or an edict that's come down, they're just...mad."

"So, this is Malice's work. Do you feel anything?"

"No more than I'd expect in a place like this," Joseph answered.

"Nor I. So, the influence must take time."

"When we finish with the king, we should move the Windriders farther from the city, just to be safe. Unless there's an army within a day or two, I think we have as much to fear from the citizens reaching a breaking point and going into a riot."

~ * ~

Despite the undercurrent of anger running through the

populace, the group reached the palace without incident. They noted a few scuffles in side alleys outside taverns, an oddity so early in the day, but if any ill intent was focused on the group, the city colors on the guards' uniforms and royal livery on the Wolfsguards' held it at bay.

Soon they were ushered into the vestibule to King Dieter's throne room. A herald took their names, then entered before them.

"Your Majesty," they heard the herald call on the other side of the partially opened door, "one of your commanded audiences has arrived, escorted by Guard Captain William of the Fourth Company."

For the first time in many long years, Joseph heard King Dieter's voice. It sounded no older, strictly speaking, but more tired. "Clear the room," it said.

Joseph and the rest of the group moved aside to make way for the parade of people exiting the throne room, but those filing past were not dignitaries and courtiers, but knights and generals. Once the last one had exited the vestibule, the herald resumed his introductions. "Majesty, I present free woman Rook of Onderburg, freeman Joseph of the eastern forests, Dorav, a dwarf of the Ninth Clan, and Kaillë Windsong, Chieftain of the Windrider Clan." Captain William led the group forward to enter the chamber.

King Dieter's throne room left no doubt a visitor had entered the center of power in Ondravia. It was not ostentatious, but the sheer scope of the chamber spoke to wealth and authority. Thirty feet across and four times that long, the room occupied the center of the palace's highest floor. Granite columns supported the ceiling on either side of the chamber every ten feet, the facing pairs of columns alternating between a jade green and dusky rose. Their bases butting against the walls, the columns created alcoves out of the way of foot traffic to and from the throne without screening off any significant portion of the room from the sight of guards. Tapestries hung flat against the alcove walls, the hangings depicting the history of Ondravia back to King Huscal I who had wrested power from the Fifth Dynasty and founded Ondravia as a sovereign state. From the ceiling hung three great chandeliers of polished wood and brass, though the candles stood now unlit while the sun shone down through two glass skylights overhead. At the far end of the room five steps led up to the dais where the throne sat, a chair of carven wood stained almost black. On either side of the dais was a hearth, though in the spring warmth no fire burned in either one.

At each of the two front corners of the platform stood a sword-bearing guard with a red tabard over his armor and a white cape at his back. These men wore no scabbards. On Joseph's first visit to the throne room this uniform of the king's personal guard had been explained to him. The guard always stood facing away from the king, protecting him against threats from any quarter. Should an attack come, wounds the guard suffered would be invisible on their red garments, but were the king somehow wounded behind them, any spattering blood would be obvious on their white capes, alerting them immediately to their master's peril. Joseph had been in battle enough to know blood spurted and spattered where it liked, but he respected the intent behind the symbolism just the same.

Joseph was halfway down the aisle when King Dieter came down from his throne and hastened forward, meeting the hunter some feet before the dais. He was shorter than Joseph by almost a head, and as he neared, his gaze was forced upward at an ever sharper angle to meet Joseph's eyes. Rook lowered to one knee, at which Kaillë began to do likewise, but a look from Joseph held her still. Dorav seemed indifferent to the entire affair.

"One kneels before the king!" Captain William hissed.

"This one does not," King Dieter answered before Joseph could make any reply, grasping the hunter briefly by the shoulders before drawing him into an embrace that Joseph returned but lamely. After releasing him, the king spoke again. "Joseph, in return for his exemplary service, is no longer counted the subject of any man. He lives on my land not by my leave, but by unbreakable decree.

"And this," the king continued, moving to stand before Kaillë, "can only be Kaillë Windsong. No elf owes me fealty, nor any dwarf either," he added with a nod to Dorav. "My father taught me, just as his father taught him, that elves come and go in the land like the seasons, and any attempt to stay them is as foolish as ordering the stars to different courses. In every history and legend I know, those who presume to roust them from their forests meet with a bad end."

"King Dieter," Joseph broke in when the ruler finally paused. His tone offered none of the supplication of a subject, but all the respect the hunter would offer to any good man. "We appreciate your greeting, but we've traveled far, and we would not have come if the need wasn't so great. I've seen the preparations being made throughout the city, so I guess the need is even more urgent now than we knew when we set out."

The king turned to Joseph and stepped back. "You're right. All the counts granted fiefdoms in King Ludvarch's former lands have declared war on one another, and the two on our northern border are in open revolt and send their levies against us. My agents have also sent reports that the north tribes living in Oskar's Gap are marching this way to war, though none can be sure which side they'll join, or if they just mean to pick through the spoils after we've all done killing one another. The rider my couriers sent has informed me of the conflicts breaking out to the south. We are beset on all sides, and my own counselors are showing signs of unwarranted aggression, insisting on first strikes where consolidating our defense is clearly the stronger option."

"We're too late," Kaillë muttered.

"Never," King Dieter reassured. "Where there is life, there is hope, it is said, and so far the lives lost have been few. Tragic, to be sure, but few. We have only now to set ourselves to the task of stopping this peril before it grows."

"What did the rider tell you?" Joseph asked. "Whether by choice or impairment, your...couriers...are silent, so we have no idea what they've shared."

"They told me enough to know you were coming and what they learned from you of the disposition of things to the south. They told me nothing that was better kept secret."

"In that case we'd best start at the beginning," Joseph said.

The Wolfsguard were dismissed, and Joseph, Kaillë, Rook, and Dorav were escorted to a private chamber behind the throne room. The two guards accompanied them, never leaving the king's side.

The band recounted the story Rook had already given in summary to King Dieter, filling in missing details and offering alternate perspectives, as well as framing the events in the context of the knowledge they had since learned from the book. Afterward they continued with a report of what transpired after Rook left the king's presence and more information on what they'd learned from the Blood Clan than the Wolfsguard had been able to provide by way of a brief dispatch. Joseph and Dorav recounted the horrors they experienced with the Baron underground, then finally Kaillë ended with her revelations from the book of Malice and the possible method for his destruction.

The king pondered for a few moments then spoke. "Though I realize time is pressing, Joseph, first I must offer my deepest sympathies. My heart breaks for your loss. I wish I might have met your wife before she passed; I'm sure she was a wonderful woman."

No one had said anything of Delia's death in their tales, but Joseph was not surprised King Dieter had deduced this on his own by Delia's conspicuous absence from the stories and Joseph's familiar body language with Kaillë. He nodded his thanks. "What now?" he asked.

"Now that we have a better understanding of this Baron's role, perhaps my sages can stop their arguing over why Onderburg has been so much less affected than our neighbors. A man matching the Baron's description has been seen going to and fro in the warring kingdoms, but those reports had only just reached me, and I wasn't sure what bearing they had on events until your tale made that clear. Recent news suggests he is heading in this general direction but taking his time, stopping off in smaller fiefs along the way. No doubt he is continuing to spread his master's seeds of rebellion and war.

"Kaillë, let me ensure I understand your proposal. You suggest I send wizards, those skilled in the breaking of enchantments, against the Baron in the hope of destroying him, and that in turn should destroy Malice?"

"I believe it to be our best chance, King Dieter."

"I believe you're right, and pray that we both are. I have two wizards suited to the task, and I have in mind to send Wolfsguard along as bodyguard. Joseph...you're the best tracker on the continent, and you've faced this revenant before. Will you go with them?"

"I don't know that my prior results against the Baron recommend me, but I will go," Joseph answered. "I wouldn't miss the chance to see Turov die, permanently this time."

"I'll second that," Dorav piped up.

Joseph turned to Rook. "What about you? Planning to

follow along and check the body for artifacts?"

Rook's expression was blank. "I need to see to my brother. By now he probably thinks I'm dead."

"Very well," the king said. "Rook, you have honored your half of our bargain. You have my pardon and my leave to go. I even grant you leave to keep the necklace, save that you use it only to compel such services as you need to continue in your quest to heal your brother. That is a wrong even I would see righted, and for many other men besides if you can find the way. Do no harm with this boon, and do not give me cause to regret my magnanimity. If you do, it will be the Wolfsguard for you again, and you *will* die in the sort of cell which this time you've avoided. Is that understood?"

"Yes, Majesty. Thank you."

Joseph looked sidelong at Rook, his instincts on alert. In his brief association with the thief, he'd found when she became too agreeable, it was because her mind was already gnawing on some other plot. Unfortunately, he hadn't time to keep watch on her. He looked over at Kaïllë and saw her eyes were already on him, and he guessed she was thinking much the same thing.

"The hour is grown late," the king began again, "and we have all missed our suppers. I'll order food to be brought at once and guest chambers arranged for each of you. Preparations for the mission will be made through the night, and you can set out at first light. Joseph, since you've agreed to go, I place you in command of the expedition. None I can send would be more suited."

"In that case," Joseph spoke up, "with your permission I will bring some of my elves to assist in the job. I need the Wolfsguard focused on protecting the wizards, and the more eyes and bows the better on this hunt."

"If they're good enough for you, they're more than good enough for me," the king confirmed.

"King Dieter, may I ask a boon?" Kaillë said.

"Of course."

"Can a courier be sent to our camp to explain where we are? We didn't warn our people that we might be gone through the night, and in a strange place they will worry."

"No sooner asked than granted." King Dieter motioned to one of the guards. "Sir Erik, you know what orders are required for all the preparations. Communicate them to my steward now."

The guard bowed and left.

Supper was brought to the small audience room in short order, and the travelers set to with abandon, having lived on nothing better than trail rations for well over a week. Soon thereafter they were shown to well-appointed quarters, left to trust the king's men to make ready for the mission.

~ * ~

Rook awoke in the night and immediately felt under her pillow for the necklace. She considered putting it on, but in the castle the risk was too great. King Dieter had not earned her trust, and he might misconstrue anything she said or did if she wore the artifact within the castle itself. Instead, she got up and pressed the jewelry to her heart for a moment before placing it in her belt pouch, then began packing her things. The king's mistrust galled her, as had Joseph's in the camp. She did all she was asked and more, and all she received in return were threats, being put on notice like a naughty child. It crossed her mind to put the necklace on just for the spite of it, and she chafed at the thought of being denied the use of something that belonged to her.

In a few moments she was slipping out her chamber door, easing the oak timbers closed behind her. The group's guest chambers opened onto a continuous balcony that overlooked a courtyard. The moon was shining, and the sound of crickets filled the warm night.

"Good evening, Rook."

The voice was soft, but to Rook's ears it was like thunder, and she jumped with a gasp. Dorav stepped forward from the shadow of a pillar, and only then did she see the sparkle in his black eyes. Before that he had stood so motionless as to be indistinguishable from the stone behind him.

"Dammit, Dorav," the thief hissed. "What are you doing up?"

"I could ask you the same, but I'll go first. I haven't slept well since I came to the surface. Certainly, the light and dark that seem so important to surface-walker habits mean nothing to me. And I think I hear too much to sleep in a castle like this. Too many night noises, all too different from a dwarf city. I thought since I'm stuck in this new world, I might as well try to appreciate it's differences, so I came out onto the balcony to see all the green, growing things in the moonlight. I've given my answer; your turn."

"Same as you, just needed some fresh air," Rook answered.

"And is it normal for humans to take all their things along when they're just getting some fresh air?"

"What I do with my things, or what I do at night, are really none of your business, Dorav."

"That's true enough," the dwarf assented. "It's never been my habit to stick my nose in other people's affairs, or even to give advice when it isn't asked. If I was going to break my rule, though, it might be for your sake, because I think you need help."

"Help? I've never needed anybody's help."

"Maybe you've never *accepted* anybody's help, or admitted to it, but that's not the same thing as never needing it. I think you're lost."

"*I'm* lost?" Rook spit back. "I'm the only person around here who really knows what they're after."

"You want to heal your brother, of course. Do you really know why?"

"What kind of question is that?"

"A simple enough kind," Dorav said. "Why do you want your brother to walk again? Is it for his sake, or your own?"

"It can't be both?"

"No, not anymore it can't. Maybe once, in the beginning, but you've taken it too far for that. When you leave a crippled brother alone for weeks at a time to fend for himself, can you really say you're doing it to help him? Or are you just running away from things as they are?"

"It so happens I was just on my way back to see my brother before you sidetracked me with this sermon," Rook shot.

Dorav nodded in the dark. "You sure that's where you're going, Rook?"

Rook looked down into the courtyard and realized she wasn't sure. Certainly, that's what she'd told herself when she left her room, but now she wasn't satisfied that's the course she was truly about to take. Everything else the dwarf said had no impact but to put her on the defensive, but that simple question had given her pause. The Baron was close now, if reports could be believed, and something was keeping him alive. A piece of the Hoard was still the most likely explanation, and surely a power that could give life to the dead could easily give healing to the crippled.

After waiting a few moments for her answer, Dorav continued. "We have a saying underground, Rook. We say, 'Not all tunnels lead to where you're headed, and some that do take a harder way around.' I think you picked your tunnel a long time before we met, but if you've thought about turning around and picking a different one, you should know it's never too late...until it is. I hope you realize it before you cross that line 'cause I don't think the tunnel you're walking now leads anyplace good."

Rook looked back at Dorav in the dark. "I'm not giving up on him. Not now, not ever."

"Best decide what that really means before you make your next move, then. I've done enough talkin' for a week now. Good night, Rook."

Dorav went back into his room, and Rook stayed awhile looking out into the moonlit courtyard. She pictured a simple life, living with her brother, busking for coins while he worked for the carpenter until they could save enough for decent rooms someplace. She imagined meeting a boy in the streets, maybe another performer, a young man with fierce, hungry eyes and a passion for life rivaled only by his passion for her. Together they could see her brother was cared for, and from there, who could guess? Children, maybe? Or she and her love could join a troupe and have Adler as the manager; he had a good head for that kind of thing, and you didn't need legs for it. Maybe when they got too old for tumbling they could take over as leaders of the troupe, introducing acts and running things.

She smiled, but after a few minutes the visions grew blurry and burned away like morning fog. The world did not send you good things, and life offered no solace. Anything you wanted you had to take for yourself. The dwarf's words had been convincing for a moment, but at a second look he was just one more trying to get in her way, though he barely even knew her. What was it to him what she did with her life? His veneer of caring was as flimsy as the "walls" around Adler's room. Rook had known since her brother came back broken what she wanted, and she had the means now to take it. The wise and powerful were hers to command, and no rover or hunter, or even king, could stop her. How could she even consider abandoning her goal now, when she was so close?

Rook turned from the balcony and cinched up her pack. She slipped one hand into her belt pouch to make sure the necklace was where she'd put it, then took a step, heading deeper down the tunnel.

~ * ~

Joseph awoke before dawn, his muscles bunched and cramped all over. The down mattress had seemed comfortable at first, but how folk slept on such beds he had no idea; he felt like the mattress was trying to wrap around him and swallow him whole. He considered that he'd passed more restful nights wedged between the boughs of an oak tree, then paused for a moment to wonder what that said about his life. Kaillë was pressed up against his side, as had become her wont, her lithe body matching the contours of his chest and hip with one leg draped over his. How hard it had been to choose this life, and now that he had it, he seemed destined to be dragged away from it time and again. He started to move, and Kaillë woke. "You have to go?" she asked.

"Soon."

Kaillë slid on top of him, her elven frame seeming feather-light as she laid her head on his chest. "How long do you think you'll be gone?"

"Not long, I hope. A few days to track the Baron down, then only a couple back, if it's true that he's already heading this way. A week at most, then all our problems will be over." Joseph wondered if he sounded as unconvinced as he felt.

"Except for being homeless again," Kaillë answered.

"Elves can make a home anywhere, anywhere with trees and game, anyway," Joseph said, shifting his weight, hoping to signal his intention to get up and start preparing for the journey.

Kaillë ignored his motion and settled in with a contented sigh. "How long is 'soon'?"

~ * ~

Joseph was briefly delayed in his arrival at the meal the king had ordered laid out for their departure. He and Kaillë entered a small dining chamber off the main banquet hall to find Dorav already there, as well as five other men all dressed in travelers' garb. Two of them were younger than he'd expected, both dark-haired and sharp in features. The elder looked less than twenty and the other only on the cusp of manhood, sixteen perhaps. When he entered, the younger looked up from his plate of eggs. "Is that him, then?" he asked. "I don't see why he's in charge." His words were not quiet.

The elder of the pair, sitting next to him, cuffed the younger sharply on the back of the head. "Because he's Joseph, stupid. Hunter of the eastern hills, hero of the battle of the north downs, greatest scout ever to live in Ondravia, *that* Joseph. You'd best watch your mouth or he'll likely leave you behind."

"So, you're brothers," Joseph said.

"I'm Axel," the elder answered, standing and extending his hand, which Joseph shook, "and this whining reprobate is my younger brother Olaf. We can just leave him here, if you like, I'm more than enough wizard to get the job done."

"Really," Joseph challenged. "You both seem young to have mastered much of anything, much less magic." Joseph had harbored misgivings about relying on wizards for the job, necessity aside. What he'd seen so far had done nothing to reassure him.

"We're good enough for you, old man," Olaf scoffed. He waved his hands and whispered, and suddenly a spot on the breakfast table beneath a bowl of fruit began to glow with a blue light. The bowl slowly sank through the tabletop as it might have sunk in porridge.

Axel smacked his brother again, and the magic stopped, leaving the bowl embedded a few inches in the table. The elder brother snapped his fingers while extending his hand in the direction of the bowl, and it sprang back into its previous position with a *pop*, jostling the fruit within.

"Forgive Olaf; he was born obnoxious. He's right about our skills, though. We are young for our profession, but we were born to it. Our father was Albert the Arcane, sensed our potential even from the womb. We were apprenticed in King Dieter's stable of wizards not long after we were weaned, so we've been learning magic since we learned walking and talking. Enchantments are our specialty, making and breaking."

"What about in a fight?" Joseph asked.

"Hide, mostly," Olaf said around a mouthful of eggs. "Enchantments take a calm mind, you know."

"Don't worry, Captain," one of the three men at the other side of the table spoke up. "We'll keep them safe." There was an edge of confidence in his voice, and next to him on the table sat a wide belt holding a long and short sword.

Joseph moved around the table to get closer to the speaker. "Who are you?" he asked.

"You can call me Wolf, and those two are Falk and Dachs."

Joseph raised his eyebrows. "Wolf?" He had learned during the war that the Wolfsguard were given new names at some point in their training. Only the most capable and deadly were granted the name "Wolf;" it was a sign of great authority among them.

The man nodded once, his voice level and showing no bravado. "Wolf."

"Do these two boys know what you are?" Joseph asked. Knowledge of the Wolfsguard was restricted to a trusted few.

"Special agents of the king," said Falk, nodding. He was a wiry man with an alert posture. "They know." His choice of words and look to Joseph revealed that the brothers, in fact, did not.

Joseph looked to Dorav. "Where's Rook?"

"Gone," the dwarf replied, shoveling the mixed contents of a plate into his gullet; two more, emptied, sat in front of him.

Joseph and Kaillë looked at each other with dread. "Where?" Kaillë asked.

"If she took my advice, back to her brother to live a long, satisfying life. So, since it's Rook, straight into the middle of one kind of trouble or another, I expect."

"Should I send trackers to try to find her?" Kaillë looked up at Joseph.

"Your decision, Chieftain, but I don't recommend it. Picking up her trail in this city is a different kind of tracking than any of us know, and it's too dangerous to send our people out with war on every border."

"She's being watched," rumbled the hulking man called Dachs.

"Only until she decides different," Joseph replied. "It doesn't matter. Our course is set. After I've eaten, we go south to the camp of my people. We need to escort Kaillë home and pick up two men I want to accompany us. After that we'll head northeast, where the king's men here can begin gathering fresher information on where the Baron is likely to be found. Easy enough?"

Everyone nodded, but Axel, nearly as tall as Joseph, came close to speak privately to him. "I was only half joking about leaving my brother behind. I really do think I have the power to complete this mission without him, and it's too dangerous for one so young."

"The danger is exactly why we have to have him," Joseph answered, feeling heartless. Axel gave him a questioning look, so the hunter clarified. "In case you get killed."

Chapter Eighteen: Betrayal

An hour later, Joseph and Kaillë were back in the Windrider camp, meeting with Tes'sael and Tes'voran. "If this doesn't work," Joseph said, "you'll have to decide the wisest course. No heroics; the survival of the clan comes first. It might be that flight is the best choice, or you may have to join the fight. I can't predict that. If you can't run, try to get into the city walls, but it will be a mad dash if the danger is realized too late. I wish I could tell you more. These kinds of battles aren't much my strength, but they're even less yours."

"We'll be alright, Joseph," Kaillë answered.

"You don't know that any more than I do. I wish Tal'onë was here."

"We all do," Tes'voran replied.

Joseph chose Ten'daren and Ten'vahlë to go with him. They had been with him in the race for the Hoard, and only Tes'sael and Tal'onë had earned his trust in greater measure. The trio rejoined the others, who waited some distance away with horses for the journey. They had smaller steeds for the elves, who took to horseback riding almost immediately after years of riding owls, though even the relatively smooth gait of the horses they'd been given was jarring by comparison. Dorav protested at riding for the sake of the back of any creature forced to bear him, but his animal was a stout, short-backed tournament charger accustomed to bearing a heavy man in armor. Joseph was concerned for the shorter dwarf's ability to get into the saddle, but Dorav was only a couple inches shorter than some of the stouter knights, and a lifetime of scrabbling through caves had granted him incredible strength. After several minutes of acclimation, and ultimately a decision to hand the reins off to Joseph to be led, the band was ready to set out.

~ * ~

North central Ondravia, the region surrounding the capitol, was a land of rolling hills and meadows. Small woods and thickets dotted the lowlands, but all in all the terrain was too open for Joseph's liking. For two days they travelled, stopping at every farmstead and hamlet on the roads to the northeast in search of news, but all they got of the Baron, which was little enough, was repeated rumors from farther away.

Near the end of the second day they sighted a stone keep on a low hill, lit in red by the westering sun; the Wolfsguard identified the place as Helmuthall, seat of Duke Helmut V of Estony. They hastened through the surrounding fields and townlands to reach the main gate before total nightfall. They arrived at the steep ditch surrounding the keep just as the drawbridge was being pulled up for the night and hailed the wardens in the gatehouse. Wolf invoked King Dieter's name, which was enough to earn them a brief conversation with half a dozen guards who came out the postern and crossed the drawbridge, pikes in hand. Even then they would likely have been forced to wait until morning when the duke could receive them, but Wolf also carried sealed letters from the king himself, and one of these was enough to gain them an immediate audience.

The band was conducted to the throne room, which by that hour was empty of courtiers, those having already been ushered to the great hall where supper was to be set at any minute. Duke Helmut V was a burly man, certainly bear-like in his youth but now showing a gut that hung over his belt and an extra roll of flesh around his neck. His greeting was cordial, but Joseph sensed he was displeased at being kept from his dinner.

"Quite the strange band that comes before me," he rumbled after initial introductions had passed. "Two elves, and a human dressed like one, and a dwarf besides, which none of our people have seen in many long ages. You say you hail from Onderburg, but as likely it seems you march up from fables and children's songs."

"I know our appearance is unusual," said Falk, the spokesman of the Wolfsguard trio, "but these are perilous times, when even strange friends might prove best, if they are trusty. We know our unplanned intrusion must be disruptive to your household, so we will be brief with the king's business, then leave you to your own.

"We seek news of a tall, dark-haired man, dressed usually in purple and with a patch over one eye. His manner may be grim or arrogant, in turns, and he would seek to speak to those in power. It is said he has been making his way to these parts. Have you heard any news of such a man?"

"Interesting," the duke replied, stroking his course, graying beard. "One of my vassals, Lord Sigmund to the northwest, has only this day sent a courier inviting me to a banquet in his demesne, and when plied for rumor later on this courier spoke of a man having arrived there the day before who exactly matches your description. Thinking nothing of it either way, I had agreed to attend this banquet, two days hence, as Lord Sigmund's keep is just a little distance. Perhaps now I should send my regrets? It seems this man is not altogether safe, to have so many on his trail."

"It may be best that you stay at home, sir," Falk replied, "but we beg you not to send news of your changed plans. To keep this man where he is, awaiting your arrival, will be of great benefit to your king."

"Very well. What other service may I offer to the king's representatives?"

"None, Duke Helmut. By your leave, we will go."

"Nonsense," the duke said expansively. "The hour is too late to travel now, and your destination is but half a day's journey away, though you have nearly two days to get there if you wish them. Stay, stay, I insist. For the integrity of your mission I will not present you in the main hall, but if you take the servants' stairs to the back of the chamber, there are rooms near the kitchens where you may eat in privacy while I have sleeping quarters prepared for you. The king's work demands full bellies, does it not?"

Falk accepted the Duke's invitation, and guards conducted them to a back stairway that led into a corner of the main hall, screened from the eyes of the guests by hanging tapestries. Joseph could smell bread and meat wafting down a short length of hallway that radiated warmth, and in the left wall of this short passage were two doors. The guards opened the nearer one and ushered the band inside, where they took their seats around a table large enough to sit half again more than their number. The guards left and closed the door behind them.

Then the sound of a lock clunking into place and a heavy bar thrown down pounded through the wood.

Joseph's mind leapt to action. "We are betrayed," he said. "We need to get out of here."

"How can you be sure?" Axel asked. "The duke may just want to verify our story before giving us the run of the place."

"If he doubted us, he would have left us outside or kept us detained while he took a second look at the king's letter," Falk reasoned. "It wasn't until after he found out *why* we're here that he decided to lock us up. That does not bode well for his faithfulness."

"Meaning that we don't know where the Baron really is," Joseph added. "He may well be here now, or even have been here and gone, but what's certain is that if the duke is in league with him, then he may have a way to get him word. By the presence of Dorav and the elves alone, he's likely to realize who we are, and that will surely pique his interest. He's a dangerous thing, and for this plan to work, we need to confront him on our terms, not his."

Olaf was picking something out of his fingernails. "So it's an escape you want, old man? Why didn't you say so?" He began chanting and waving his hands.

Axel kicked over his chair. Olaf grabbed the table to keep from falling, but it interrupted his motion. "Just hold on, idiot," the elder brother ordered with a sigh. "Did you hear the guards march away after they barred the door? No? That's because they didn't. You might maybe want to work with the group to decide what the plan is before you start casting spells, don't you think?"

Olaf scowled at his brother but stayed silent as he retrieved his chair and sat back down with a huff.

"It would be best if we could see out," Wolf observed. "Axel, is there any way you can let us see through the door without letting the guards see in?"

"Tricky, but yes, I think I can." Axel moved to the door and placed his hands against it, then his ear, then finally his whole body. His eyes were squinted, and the muscles of his jaw bunched and relaxed in exertion. Suddenly, his eyes snapped open. "Got it!" He pounded the door three times with his fist and stepped back, then the surface of the timbers seemed to shimmer and ripple like water. After a moment Joseph could see out into the hallway as through a filmy piece of glass. Two guards were there, one at either side of the door, and one was just turning toward the barred portal.

"Hey, you lot, stop that pounding in— What the hell?" His eyes were fixed directly on Axel.

"Dammit!" the wizard cursed.

Olaf wasted no time. He jumped to his feet, his chair clattering once again to the floor behind him, and waved his hands toward the door with a rolling chant. Through the now-transparent barrier, Joseph could see the heavy timber bar at waist height dissolve into sawdust and ash. Apparently Dachs saw this too, for in the same instant he hit the door like a ram, shattering the lock and slamming the door into the guard looking in at them. The second, who had just started to turn toward his partner's confusion, managed to dodge away at the last second. Dachs recovered from his slam against the door and grabbed the guard's pike before he could lower it, then out of nowhere Falk was on him with a dagger, punching it repeatedly into the guard's exposed throat.

Wolf shoved his way past the confrontation and took point, heading the party through the kitchens. Joseph urged the brothers and his elves forward as he strung his bow, then along with Dorav brought up the rear with an arrow nocked. Screams broke out from the kitchen as Wolf charged in with a blood-spattered Falk right behind, but the only aggression the servants showed was to one another as they fought to get out of the way. As expected, the kitchens had doors to the outside, and soon the group had burst out into the humid night air of the keep's baily.

"How are we going to get out of here?" Joseph growled. "The keep is secured for the night; we'll need to take the gatehouse, but it'll be a deathtrap if we don't get the portcullis and drawbridge opened fast." He saw a crossbowman spanning his weapon on the wall top to the right and loosed an arrow that shredded his right shoulder and drove him, screaming, against the parapet. He continued to act as rearguard as they all moved toward the gatehouse.

"Joseph, we have wizards," Wolf reminded. "They can breach the defenses. Right?" he added, looking at Axel.

Meanwhile, Olaf gestured toward the back of the keep and let out a long, warbling whistle, and only a moment passed before a great cacophony of neighs and crashing sounded from the stables.

"We can breach," Axel confirmed. "Just keep us covered. We'll need to focus."

As they rounded the corner of the keep, several guards from inside were exiting the main doors. Joseph dropped two before archers above demanded his attention; even with Ten'daren and Ten'vahlë covering the walls, the foes' advantages of elevation and numbers were enough to require three good bows.

Wolf drew his blades and threw himself at the guards. Falk ranged to the right and harassed their flank while Dachs dodged a pike thrust then relieved the smaller man of his weapon, which looked almost toy-like in his brawny hands. Dorav, his feet shifting with uncertainty against human opponents, hung back to protect Axel and Olaf from any foes that made it past the Wolfsguard. The party wheeled toward the gatehouse so that Joseph and his elves were now in front with the Wolfsguard engaged in a fighting retreat as more guards joined the battle. Joseph saw archers now moving into the guard towers at the corners of the wall, and though he stopped as many as he could he knew some had reached cover. The open baily was about to become lethal.

The riot Olaf had started in the stables had boiled over, and with a noise like thunder the horses came bounding from behind the keep, not only those of Joseph and his band but seemingly all the others in the stables, reins trailing from those that hadn't been unsaddled.

In a flash Joseph was transported back in memory to the previous autumn and his rescue of the Windriders, though in that case he had employed a ruse to ensure the drawbridge would be down. Now he was forced to rely on two wizards, the most unpredictable men he knew of. Joseph urged the band toward the cover between the gatehouses, but not before arrows whistled down one after another into their midst. He saw Olaf now chanting and gesturing, and the horses charged into the flanks of the guards on the ground, then started a running circle around the group, providing some cover from the archers.

Axel passed by Joseph and the elves to reach relative safety, his eyes bent on the portcullis. His charges now safely in cover, Dorav joined the Wolfsguard in holding the line. Axel's outstretched palms, pointing toward the barrier, vibrated almost to a blur, and within seconds the iron banding had begun to glow red hot.

Joseph cast his eyes upward. The guardhouses, one on either side, were two stories, but fortunately there was no covered walk linking them through which stones or boiling oil could be dropped. Large windows were on either side, and a crossbowman appeared at one, but Joseph shot him dead, and after he ordered his elves to keep watch on them, the shutters were rapidly closed. Their horses had now left the mob and stood calmly in the space between the guardhouses while the rest formed a milling, ill-tempered barrier between the enemy and the company.

Axel grunted and thrust his palms forward. The smoldering portcullis creaked but didn't visibly budge. "Olaf," he grunted, "I need your help."

"What about the horses?" the younger brother replied, his voice distant.

"Leave them, dammit!"

"We're ready," Wolf announced, Falk and Dachs standing on either side of him with Dorav on the far right, prepared to hold off the guards as soon as the cover of the horses was lost. Satisfied his elves had the upper stories covered, Joseph also set up a few paces behind them.

Olaf let out a cry, and the wall of horses almost immediately scattered. No sooner had they done so than Joseph began loosing arrows between the Wolfsguard and into the oncoming soldiers, holding them back as best he could alone. From the corner of his eye he saw the brothers shoving their hands toward the portcullis in unison, and the noises from it grew louder with each onslaught as smoke billowed from the dense wood.

The guards clashed with Wolf and his men, and Joseph refocused on the battle, looking for shots of opportunity and taking them as he could.

Axel growled so loudly Joseph thought he would lose his throat, then an explosive *boom* sounded from behind him. Joseph looked over his shoulder just in time to see the portcullis shatter and slam into the drawbridge, tearing it free from its upper mounts to fall with a slam across the moat. Dorav felled the guard he was fighting with an ax to the knee, then turned and made a break for his horse. The Wolfsguard, long on discipline, didn't turn but seemed to understand the way was now clear, pressing one final assault to give themselves room before jogging backwards toward the drawbridge.

Joseph knew they would have no cover but the night once they reached the bridge, so speed was their best defense. "Mount up," he yelled to the main band before shouting to his archers to provide cover. The three of them shot indiscriminately at every moving shape in the twilight, pressing against the walls of the gatehouses to offer minimal targets to any with the temerity to shoot back.

"Joseph, come on!" Wolf shouted.

He ordered the elves to move, then turned and ran toward the horses, which were already heading away at a trot. As soon as their backs were turned, Axel threw something over their heads that exploded in the night like a sun, bright enough to blind anyone looking in their direction. Joseph and the elves mounted their horses on the run, then all were spurred to a gallop, their hooves thundering over the ruined drawbridge before clattering on the cobblestones of the surrounding village.

They rode on for a mile before turning from the road and sheltering in a thicket. Joseph sent Ten'daren and Ten'vahlë on foot back along their path to watch for pursuit, though given the displays Axel and Olaf had just provided, he doubted any of the duke's men would have the courage to come after them until sunrise at the earliest.

"Falk didn't have to kill that first guard," Joseph murmured to Wolf. "We might have gotten out with less frenzied pursuit if he hadn't. The man was just following his duke's orders."

"And we follow our king's. We didn't have time to reason with him, and you know as well as I do fighting to subdue takes longer. Suppose the Baron was just upstairs; we didn't have time to spare."

Joseph nodded, though in the dark Wolf probably didn't see the scowl that went along with it. He couldn't argue with the man's tactics, and had he been standing where Falk had been he probably would have done the same, but those compromises were exactly what he hated about living in the lands of men in general, and fighting in their wars in particular.

"I could use a hand," Dachs rumbled, and in the gloom Joseph could see he was clutching his right shoulder with his opposite hand.

"What the hell happened to you?" Falk asked.

"I got shot."

"What? When?"

"Sometime during the battle," the large man answered, his tone betraying he considered this a fool question. "Wasn't really time to mend it, so I snapped the shaft off and went about my business."

Joseph felt around the wound, which forced a grunt of pain from Dachs. "This is a barbed arrow, and it's bleeding pretty bad. We need to make a fire."

"Fire, are you insane?" Wolf protested. "Duke Helmut could have men after us any second."

"I know that, but if I don't dig that arrowhead out, he's likely to bleed to death. I need light to see and heat to cauterize the wound. Or you can watch him die."

"Axel, Olaf," Wolf hazarded, "anything you can do here?"

"Not us, boss," Olaf replied, his voice weary.

"We're spent," Axel concurred. "We're enchanters by specialization; what we needed with those gates was outside our skills. Brute force sufficed, but it emptied us out for a while."

Joseph heard a rough, striking sound and saw sparks off to his left. "Dorav?" he asked.

"The way I remember hearing it, you're in charge of this rove, Joseph. I didn't reckon you were fixing to change your mind." In a few moments Dorav had a blaze of kindling going, then proceeded to feed it with deadwood from the thicket. There were no logs for a proper burn, so the fire had to be constantly refreshed, but Dorav saw to that while Joseph pulled a sharp skinning knife and set to work on Dachs' shoulder.

The man was a titan when it came to resisting pain. Unbidden, he grabbed a woody vine from the ground, doubled it over, and set it between his molars. Joseph worked quickly and as cleanly as he could, though he was no surgeon and knew it. Still, Dachs had done much of the work of clearing the barbs by continuing to fight after taking the arrow. The meat of his shoulder was well shredded, so a pair of quick cuts and the arrowhead came out.

Joseph cleaned the wound as best he could, but the profuse bleeding made sight impossible. He held it open and dumped a canteen of water over it, then took the red-hot chisel Dorav had placed in the fire. The wound was deep, and Joseph heard the wood in Dachs' teeth snap when he drove the chisel in, but when he removed it the bleeding had slowed almost to nothing. The big man spit the wood from his mouth and leaned his head back; Joseph was reasonably sure he'd passed out. The outer layers of the wound he left open and packed with one of his poultices, then bandaged it while Dorav improvised a sling from a spare cloak. As soon as the work was done, they doused the fire.

"What's our next move, Joseph?" Wolf asked.

"Well," the hunter responded after a moment's pause, "If the Baron had been in Helmuthall, he'd already be here, more than likely, so we can assume he wasn't. It's possible Helmut was giving us just enough truth to hide his treachery when he said the Baron was with Lord Sigmund, but I don't think so. Imprisoning representatives of the king, without cause, during times like these could be counted as treason, so it seems Duke Helmut is sold out to the Baron's cause, which points to a personal visit."

"So we assume the Baron had been to Helmuthall and moved on," Wolf surmised.

"Right. You know the roads and settlements hereabouts, and the road we took to reach the Duke. Where might the Baron have gone that we could have missed him on the way?"

Wolf pondered this for several minutes. "We came up the King's Highway from the southwest," he finally said, "but suppose the Baron has assumed Onderburg would be too tough a nut to crack. They're already preparing for a siege, and all of King Dieter's wizards are there."

"Then he's not heading for Onderburg at all," Joseph reasoned. "He's circling it, inciting an attack from all sides."

"That's my belief...and my fear," Wolf confirmed. "If that's the case, then the Baron's departure from Helmuthall was likely due south, down the old forest road to Suftondell, Lord Tobias' holding."

"Would he have made it there by now?" Joseph asked.

"The old forest road isn't in the best repair; it's more than a day on foot, and so far none of the reports have the Baron using any magic openly while he travels. Without knowing when he left Helmuthall, though, it's impossible to be sure."

"Alright. My elves are still standing sentry, and Dachs is out. Everybody else takes a one-hour watch in the usual turns. Get some sleep; at first light we'll strike out overland to the east until we reach the old forest road. From there, we'll see what we see."

~ * ~

Rook had eyes on the Baron. Before leaving the city, she had tapped her criminal contacts. None of them would have dealt with her after rumor of her being dragged into the castle had spread, but the necklace overcame that obstacle. Preparations for war were lucrative, and such preparations seemed to follow the Baron in his travels, so there was no shortage of information regarding his movements and location if one knew who to ask. Some of that information was even accurate. The thief had moved quickly, driven by obsession to reach the Baron and take what magic she could from him. Joseph's reports of the undead noble's power were frightful, but she had the necklace. She needed nothing else.

Leaving the city had proven more difficult than Rook imagined. Losing the men King Dieter sent to follow her had been easy, but mastering her heart had been hard. She had even gone to Adler's room before leaving and stood outside, her hand on the latch. Part of her wanted to go in, but another part misgave her. Her mind was made up to leave again; if she saw Adler first, he would just try to convince her to stay, and they would fight. It was a common pattern. Why put either of them through the exercise one more time? In the end she had crept inside, silent enough not to disturb her brother's slumber, and left a black feather on the table, adorned with leather thongs and beadwork. It would be enough to convince him she had been there, that she was still alive. Then she left.

Now she lay in the shadow of a black alder, peering out at Baron Turov himself, who sat on the ground next to a lantern, a flickering light illuminating a circle just a few feet across in the darkness. A walking staff leaned next to a tree within arms' reach. It was strange to see him that way, sitting passively, and it troubled Rook when finally she spotted him. It seemed to her the lantern had only just been lit as she paralleled the road coming up from the south, and now that she could see the object of her search, he sat with his head cocked to the side as if listening for something. His posture suggested he waited for someone as well. Still, if he had heard Rook somehow, he showed no sign of it.

Faintly, the sound of hoofbeats ran down on the wind, approaching from the north. The Baron seemed satisfied somehow and stood, facing that direction. Rook watched and waited.

After a few minutes a rider came into view, picking his way along the lapsed road in the moonlight. He held a staff out before him with a lit lantern hanging from a crook on its end, allowing him to guide his horse around the worst of any dangers. Soon he had come near the Baron, and Turov called out to him. "I believe you bring me news," he said.

"I do," the rider answered, "a report from Duke Helmut. He has detained a party of men asking after your whereabouts. They were on errand from King Dieter, and their group was of odd configuration. Several humans, but also two elves and a dwarf."

This news seemed to take even the Baron by surprise, though he recovered quickly and rubbed his hands together with unabashed glee. "This is worth a brief detour," he told the rider. "Go ahead of me and inform Duke Helmut of my coming. I will interrogate the prisoners and determine what King Dieter now knows. I hope very much that securing their cooperation requires force."

Rook had heard enough. She stepped from her hiding place with both daggers drawn, the ruby of the necklace gleaming like blood in the lanternlight. "Stop," she ordered. "Turn around."

The Baron turned toward her and locked her up and down. "Rook," he said, again surprised. "I never expected to see you again. I thought after I threw you in my dungeon that our association was at an end."

"Tell me how Malice is keeping you alive," Rook ordered, no patience for banter. Suddenly she felt a great pressure in her skull, like a wave rebounding from a cliff face was washing over her brain. All the sensations of struggle she'd expected to feel when using the necklace to dominate another's will, which in fact had been utterly absent, she felt now more deeply than she had imagined.

The Baron looked into her eyes, his own eyes wide, and Rook knew the Baron was not completely immune to her control, that he felt the same pressure she did. "What...?" he gasped.

The duke's courier turned and fled, and Rook made no move to stop him. Instead, she pierced the Baron's gaze with her own and bent all her focus to overpowering him. She could feel her thoughts sliding over the tower of his guarded will, looking for any seam or chink where they might get purchase. The Baron took a halting step toward her, and his defense seemed to slip just enough for her to feel his desperation. Perhaps he could feel this threat, for suddenly his defense was redoubled, and Rook's assault was thrown down. She reeled back three steps, her dagger guard lowering, but the Baron was driven down to one knee by the force of their mental clash. Rook pressed forward again, seeing in her mind's eye something with the seeming of a crack in the Baron's psychic wall. She threw her weight against it, peering in even as she pounded her fists against it in attempt to pull it wider.

Through that crack she became suddenly aware of another mind, another consciousness, hovering somewhere in the Baron's thoughts. It was deep and cold and terrible, but worst of all it was inevitable, it's victory as certain as that of death itself. It inspired no fear; rather, it urged her to cast aside all fear, all restraint, to see herself as powerful, a conqueror, a force of terror among the unjust and protection to the weak, savior of a thousand cities. Too late, she realized it was Malice.

Too late, for only in that instant did she understand the chink in the Baron's defenses had not been made by her assault, but by this entity from within, and now it held her, as curious as it was confident, regarding her from every angle. As strongly as this body of thought urged her to lord her power over the world, to claim her rightful place as a goddess among worms, just as strongly it held her cowed, unable to meet the mental gaze of this titan of chaos, older than history and greater than thought.

A thousand years might have passed as she remained there, naked and helpless, examined and appraised in every detail, her every thought and experience laid bare. In a rush she relived her life, each moment and sensation and emotion stacked one upon the other in lightning succession, each regarded and appraised by the blazing fire commanding her thoughts. Its awareness touched on the necklace, on the power to command thought and action, and though Malice had guarded its own mind from hers, for a moment she could sense its hunger, and from that hunger grew a redoubling of all its promises to power. Rook saw her brother strong and hale again, performing in the perfect world she would create, earning the applause of gathered thousands made equal by her wise power, king and commoner alike in dignity.

Then suddenly she was cast out from its presence, cast out from the Baron's mind, and the walls of his will were slammed shut before her once again. The battle was over; the necklace would not work. As fearful as Malice's mind had been, now that she was cut off from it, she felt empty and insignificant, desperate to contact that raw power once again. Still one thought hammered at her brain like a sledge swung in endless repetition. *Baron Turov has to die.*

The Baron stood but slowly, as if struggling under a weight. "Master?" he called, as though expecting Malice to be physically present nearby. His confusion was almost childlike, but Rook felt no pity. With a growl she charged at him, her daggers held high.

Turov thrust his hand forward with a snarl while Rook was still yards away, but when nothing happened he wailed in anger. Just then Rook noticed his face was no longer pristine; half his hair was burned off, and on that side his features were replaced by a mass of shiny scar tissue. The Baron reached out toward the ground where he had sat, and the lantern and staff flew into his hands just in time to meet the thrust of Rook's knives. With one hand he slammed the staff into her wrists, driving her back, then swung the lantern at her face.

It connected, and she screamed as the hot glass sizzled against her skin. The light was no weapon, though, and the body of it came apart, dumping oil onto the ground that ignited as the burning wick fell. The Baron dropped the remains of the lantern and took the staff in a two-handed grip.

Rook's searing face fueled the hatred in her heart, and she attacked once more, this time less recklessly. The end of the staff thrust forward and forced her back, it's head following her every move. She stabbed at the Baron's forward hand, but he sidestepped and rammed the stave into her gut, doubling her over. The other end whipped upward and slammed into her jaw with a *crack* that split the woods, sending her reeling.

Stars danced in Rook's vision as she gave ground, the trees spinning around her. For a moment she circled, avoiding the Baron's follow-up attack as she waited for the world to hold still. At last the night settled, and the Baron was now just steps away, silhouetted against the burning lantern oil. Relentlessly he lured her into his longer range while still keeping well clear of hers.

Rook's head hammered with pain, sharp and burning on one side, low throbbing radiating from her jaw. The Baron jabbed forward with the staff, and she slipped the strike by the barest margin; Rook knew another solid hit would put her down, and then the Baron would kill her, beating her to death or slitting her throat with her own daggers. She worked to get inside, but the Baron, while clearly no expert fighter, seemed to know the value of reach and used it well.

Rook launched several quick thrusts at the Baron's face; he was still well out of her range, but the instinct to protect his remaining eye was strong, and she watched as the quarterstaff rose higher and higher by degrees in his guard stance. She hesitated for a split second, and the Baron drove his weapon forward at her face. With the speed of a lightning bolt she fell to the ground, tucking into a somersault that brought her almost to the Baron's feet. She drove her toes into the ground to stand completely inside his reach, driving both of her daggers into his belly as she did. The Baron's good eye went wide with pain and terror, and Rook drank in the sight without mercy. One by one she pulled each dagger out and plunged its point back into the Baron's chest, angling upward between his ribs.

He tried to gasp, but his lungs no longer worked, and the quarterstaff slipped from his limp fingers. Rook tore her knives free and shoved Baron Turov backward into the oil flames on the ground. His legs kicked as the fire ignited his robes, but he no longer had the wherewithal to roll out of danger. Rook watched him burn for a few moments but found her hatred was not slaked by the sight. Avoiding the heaviest of the flames, she knelt by the Baron's head. His eyes followed her as she moved, and she was glad to realize he still lived. With calm precision she reached down and laid both daggers across his neck, then pressed hard as she pulled both hands outward to slit his throat. The first spurt of blood sprayed her face, but after that there wasn't enough pressure in his veins to reach her.

Rook stood and watched the life drain from her enemy's eyes as blood dripped from her hands. She looked down and remembered a time when much less blood had driven her to panic, but the memory seemed long ago, more like a story she'd heard than something that had happened in her own life. Suddenly remembering her purpose in being there, she put a boot under the Baron's hips and rolled his corpse out of the blaze. She stomped on it until the fire of his clothing had been put out, then set to searching the remains for a glowing orb, a piece of the Hoard of Dalviir. When she found nothing out of the ordinary, she expected to be disappointed, but with a distant sense of surprise she realized she wasn't. The Hoard had only ever been a means to an end; what she really needed was power. Power. *Now* she had it, and she knew how to get more.

Rook turned down the firelit road and started walking south, into the darkness.

Chapter Nineteen: Promises

Joseph was up with the dawn, rousing his company from uneasy slumber. Ten'daren and Ten'vahlë had just returned, reporting no pursuit. Joseph found this strange, unless it was because Duke Helmut had sent word to the Baron and planned to await his return. Dachs' arm was swollen and throbbing, but it appeared Joseph's ministrations had staved off the worst of any infection. The hunter cleaned the wound again, reapplied the poultice, and rebandaged the shoulder before they set off. Axel and Olaf also seemed much better for their brief rest, a fact upon which Joseph questioned them aggressively.

"If all goes to plan," he told them, "we will confront the Baron *today*. If you aren't up for your part, I have to know now."

Olaf was unusually silent, his face serious. Axel spoke for them both. "We're rested, Captain, and as ready as we can be. Get us to the target; we won't let you down."

Preparations were completed in haste, then the band set

off overland, due east. They pushed the horses as hard as they dared, but the terrain was easy and streams were plentiful. After several uneventful hours, they struck the old forest road and turned south into the trees.

The sky was clear, and their mounts were sure-footed, allowing them to make good time toward Lord Tobias' manor. The sun was westering, casting the wood into a golden, mote-filled light, when Joseph, out in front leaning down over his horse's neck to examine hoofprints in the mud between jutting roots, called a sudden halt. Up ahead, he saw the dead leaves and loam of the path scorched in a wide arc, and nearby a singed body with a single crow pecking at its hair. On a closer look, Joseph realized a second, crossing arc he'd at first taken for more burnt ground was, in fact, the stains from a great spurt of blood. Signing for caution, he dismounted and crept toward the scene of violence. At ten paces out, he recognized the color of the robes between the charred places, as well as the strap of an eyepatch running around the back of the head. Joseph moved forward with greater haste, though he remained wary. The crow flew off with an indignant call. Joseph's knife was in his hand as he made the final approach to the body, then nudged it with his foot.

Nothing happened. Joseph's fear of some trick began to dissipate when he realized the body was stiff in death. He motioned the rest of his band forward, trusting his elves to keep their eyes on the trees in case of ambush, while he heaved the body over onto its back.

The first thing Joseph noted wasn't the corpse's identity but the way its neck yawned open where the throat had been deeply cut. Next, he noted the face itself, clearly recognizable as Baron Turov, the rapid exsanguination from the throat seeming to have reduced the swelling and discoloration from pooling blood. Finally, his eyes rested on the abdominal wounds, caked with dirt and crusted gore.

"It's him," Joseph confirmed as Wolf approached, "or seems to be."

"How long, do you think?" the Wolfsguard asked.

Joseph took a second look at the body as he considered. He had seen more than enough dead bodies in his day to make an educated guess. "Not long. Less than a day, I think. I can't understand it. I saw this body survive being crushed in a rock fall. Even if he avoided that somehow, my elves and I made him a pincushion with arrows, and it didn't so much as slow him down. How did a few stabs and a slit throat do him in?"

"Axel, Olaf, time to earn your keep," Falk broke in. "This doesn't sit right with me, either. Is there magic at work here, some illusion?"

The brothers dug into their packs and each produced an implement, Axel, a pair of crystal spectacles as the old were known to wear for reading and Olaf, an eyepiece that looked like a jeweler's loupe. Both dismounted and began a survey of the body, mumbling chants as they went.

Several minutes passed before they looked up from their work, putting away their talismans and blinking as if in a struggle to refocus their eyes.

"Well?" Wolf asked.

"There's *something* of magic lingering around the body, but not of the sort you asked about. No illusion, that's for sure," Axel replied.

"No transformation, either," Olaf confirmed. "If that isn't the Baron, the body was made to look like him by purely natural means."

While the brothers had worked, Joseph had taken a closer look at Turov's face. "No, it's too exact a likeness, and no tampering that I can see. The old burn scars even match what I saw the first time he appeared, though those seemed healed later. It doesn't make sense they'd be back now."

"It might," Axel broke in, "at least as much sense as the rest of it. We can't account for how this form was remade at all. There are echoes of a powerful regeneration spell on the body, powerful enough even to replace dead flesh from next to nothing, though the process would be slow. And painful. That kind of magic doesn't exist, or shouldn't, but even so it must have limits. There could be other scars beneath his clothing."

"How does that explain the wounds coming and going?" Joseph asked. "Or why I saw a skull when he used magic against me, but now I see flesh on his head you say is no illusion?"

"Because something changed not long before death…or whatever you call this. Regeneration restored the body as far as it could but left scars, and I sense a vital spark was withheld as well. The flesh was preserved but remained dead; perhaps the skull you saw was a shadow of that truth. Over that was a binding spell of some kind, holding in the spirit to animate the corpse."

"But I know you didn't miss all those enchantments ending," Olaf prodded his elder, "or the surge of power along with it."

"No, I didn't. It's almost as if—"

"As if that 'vital spark' was finally provided," Olaf finished. "Malice made Turov mortal."

Axel nodded. "And revoked access to his magic, leaving the Baron only with his own talent, which wasn't much, not enough to mask the scars of his remaking. The only outside spell I sense working all the way up to the point of death was a powerful mental guard, more powerful than I've seen."

Joseph looked at Wolf, and the experienced agent looked back at him with a similar expression. "It explains the how," Joseph agreed, "but not the why. I don't like this."

"Why don't we like this?" Dorav interrupted. "Baron's

dead, however it happened, and that means Malice is destroyed and everyone is saved. Doesn't it?"

Wolf raised an eyebrow at the dwarf, clearly perplexed that a seemingly shrewd man could fail to grasp their concerns.

"Magic isn't his strong suit," Joseph explained, "or even his weak suit, for that matter. What the Brothers Enchanter are saying, Dorav, is that all signs point to Malice withdrawing his magic from the Baron willingly...*letting* him die. I don't know why that might happen, but it doesn't make sense for Malice to do that if it meant his own death."

"We still have too many more questions than answers," Wolf said. "We need to get back to Onderburg and make our report to the king."

"What about the body?" Dachs asked.

"If we don't bring it back for the sages to study, we'll never hear the end of it," Falk answered.

"That's what I was afraid you'd say," Joseph added with a grimace.

"Never figured it'd go any other way," Falk replied, untying a rolled up sailcloth from the back of his saddle bag and unfurling it toward Joseph. "No need to field dress him, hunter, just bag 'im up."

"You're forgetting one thing," Joseph said, kicking the sack back in Falk's direction. "I'm in charge of this mission. *You* 'bag 'im up.' Anyway, I'm not done searching."

Joseph paced out the scene, noting the broken lantern and discarded quarterstaff. On closer examination he saw the staff bore gouges as from a deflected blade, probably two of them by the varying angles of cuts. The staff and lantern pieces he placed in the bag with the Baron's corpse before it was tied shut. After that he walked back and forth, keeping to the brush at the edge of the path so as not to disturb the shallow prints. He had noted the hoofprints on his way down the old road, a set moving southward at a careful pace, then heading back north with more reckless speed. This now made sense. He had at first assumed the southbound prints were from a messenger sent by Duke Helmut, but he couldn't guess what message the Baron might have requested sent back that had urged the courier back in such a hurry, most likely still in the dark of night. Now Joseph speculated the rider had either seen the Baron dead or had seen whatever killed him, either one being enough to send him back to his master in terror.

Baron Turov's killer remained a mystery. The prints of the fight were jumbled, but apart from the Baron's, those he could make out were small and light, so much that he took them for elf prints, though he didn't know how that could be. It would not be unheard of for a Windrider to strike out on his own in the hopes of eliminating a threat to his people, but none of them had any knowledge of magic or any leverage he could imagine that would persuade Malice to drop his protections. He had neither seen nor heard news of any other clans in the area, and even if there were, the same questions would apply. Ruling out elves for the moment, the prints could only come from an older human child, or perhaps a small, young woman. A thought flashed through Joseph's mind, but he dismissed it as quickly. The tracks left the scene of the fight heading south down the forest road, but they were quickly lost on a stretch of hard-packed earth, and Joseph knew following them that way down the rough path would take long hours.

After several minutes of surveying the scene, he picked up the approaching prints and backtracked them to the cover of a nearby alder. It was possible he could continue to follow the trail back the way the killer had come, but he couldn't be certain the signs would remain visible as the path left the woods. Worse, if at any point the tracks joined a road or village, which seemed more than likely, he was almost certain to lose them; there was little, if anything, to be gained in tracking and precious time to lose.

Joseph returned to the group and found the elves had arranged to ride double so a single horse could bear the corpse. The others had worked the stiffened body into as balanced a load for the animal as they could manage, then tied the burden to the front and back of the saddle and ran a rope all the way around the horse, positioning the cord over the girth strap to help reduce it rubbing. It remained an awkward load, but manageable. They retraced their steps northward along the old forest road until Joseph found a game trail leading back to the west that he thought would take them out of the trees. The company turned down the narrow path and started the journey back to the capital.

~ * ~

Joseph's band rushed on the return trip to Onderburg, traveling overland westerly until once again striking the King's Highway at nightfall. Axel and Olaf worked together during the ride to magically arrest the Baron's decay, ostensibly to preserve the specimen for study, but more probably to spare their noses the stench, which was just as valid a need in Joseph's book. Once darkness fell, they made camp a stone's throw from the road, resuming a normal rotation of watches after Joseph redressed Dachs' arm and satisfied himself it was healing properly, despite their rapid pace.

Joseph was up before dawn, as usual, and urged the party on as soon as they could be roused. Ever since the brothers had declared the dissolution of the Baron's magic a willful event, Joseph's heart had fallen deeper and deeper into dread. Olaf had surmised the day before that perhaps Malice had not survived his escape from the Well and, hence, the magic sustaining the Baron had simply faded, but Joseph knew how empty that hope was. Olaf had not seen the flames erupting from the earth and consuming an entire forest in the damp of spring; he did not know Malice's power.

Two hours into the ride, the party was making good time when Ten'vahlë alerted Joseph to a disturbance behind them. On the very horizon, a great cloud of dust rose up from the road to the northeast. Only one thing Joseph knew made such a storm: an army on the march.

"Go quickly," Joseph ordered as he turned his horse about.

"Joseph, what are you doing?" Wolf asked.

"Someone has to find out if they're friend or foe, don't they?" the hunter answered. He rode back up the highway until he could just see the front ranks of the marching column, then concealed his mount in a nearby ditch and approached the army on foot. He only needed to get close enough to see their colors to have his answer—they were Duke Helmut's banners. Moving alongside in smaller numbers were horsemen wearing a different shield, a rampant griffon on a vert and sable field. Joseph noted the coat of arms and made his way back to his group.

Wolf scowled when he took Joseph's report of the advancing horde, especially his description of the other riders. "Those are Lord Tobias' cavalry," the agent explained. "If the Baron fell before he got there, then why are some with Helmut now? They'd have had to move fast too."

"Let's not speculate," Joseph replied. "Our task hasn't changed."

By afternoon the walls and towers of Onderburg were within sight. The hoarding was up, and the city was readying for a fight. Wolf insisted on reporting to King Dieter immediately, but Joseph was equally insistent on a detour to the Windrider camp to ensure his wife and people were safe. In the end the band split up so the Wolfsguard could make their report without delay.

Joseph, along with Dorav and the elves, headed south to the Windrider camp; however, when they arrived, they found the area deserted. Merchants and drovers moved through the countryside in panicked trips to and from the outer docks, but of the elves there was no sign. Joseph was growing worried when Sir William rode up to the band on the plain.

"Sir Joseph, please report to the palace at once. Your people are safe; they were moved inside the walls the day before yesterday."

"What do you mean *were* moved? On whose order?"

"King Dieter's."

Joseph spurred his horse toward the city and quickly left his friends behind, and William as well. The guards had been instructed to expect him, so his passage through the gates was expedited. Once inside, he saw the enraging influence he and Kaillë had seen a few days prior had only grown worse in his absence. Harsh yells and shoving matches were the norm, and Joseph saw city guardsmen breaking up or joining in scuffles several times on his ride to the palace. He felt his temper rising several times when smaller or weaker citizens seemed to be the victim of unwarranted violence, but he kept his focus on his path and drove his horse forward. He had frustrations enough without going to find more.

Once at the palace, the hunter was admitted without argument, and a stable boy led his horse away as soon as he jumped from the saddle. His feet pounded the earth as he crossed the green to the great front doors and stomped through the halls to the throne room. The herald approached him just outside with his usual obsequious stance, but Joseph shoved him aside and threw open the doors. "How dare you, Dieter? How dare you give orders to my people and force them into this seething prison?"

"How dare *I*?" King Dieter shouted back, looking up from his conversation with the Wolfsguard and enchanter brothers. "You storm into my hall unannounced and speak so to a king. I should have you flogged!"

Joseph lost all patience. "You're welcome to try." His voice dripped venom, and his hand was on his knife.

Wolf drew his swords, and the king's personal guards strode forward with their naked blades in their hands.

To Joseph's shock, it was Olaf who kept things from bloodshed. "Stop, stop!" he cried, placing himself in front of the guards. "Majesty, please, you know what this is. Joseph is a trusted friend, not an enemy, and you are never so quick-tempered. Can you even recall the last time you ordered someone flogged over an insult?"

The king un-balled his fists and ordered his men to stand down. For several moments he closed his eyes and was silent, visibly fighting to master himself. Finally, he spoke again. "Do you not feel it, Joseph? How easily rage comes in this place, always just below the surface?"

Joseph took deep breaths. "I feel it. I saw it in the streets, thought I was on my guard, and even still it overwhelmed me. I *am* sorry, Dieter. Yet still I ask on what authority you ordered the elves into the city." Joseph worked his jaw as he fought to stay calm.

"I only thought to keep them safe. My scouts reported enemies growing near. I knew they would not flee before your return and had no idea when to expect you. I feared they would be shut out or killed in the rush if they waited until the last moment to seek refuge. I swear to you, unless Sir William is a liar, they came willingly and are quite safe."

"That seems wise," Joseph assented, "save that I'm not sure it's any safer in here. As we've just seen."

"I know," Dieter answered, his voice weary. "I have

wizards doing what they can to keep the effect at bay, but they say the influence is more primal than magic, at least as we currently understand it. They do their best, but conditions worsen by the hour. I'm glad to have my two young prodigies returned unscathed." He nodded to Axel and Olaf.

"Shall we join the others now, Majesty?" Axel asked. "I don't believe there's anything more we can add to the report."

The king nodded and bade them go.

"Can I ask a question?" Joseph asked, going out of his way toward civility to curtail the aggression he could still feel roiling beneath his thoughts.

"Of course," King Dieter answered as Wolf finally sheathed his weapons.

"What do Helmut and Tobias seek to accomplish? They couldn't hope to take Onderburg with ten times their number."

"They don't have to," Wolf answered. "All they have to do is choke the large gates and blockade the river until we feel the slightest thirst or hunger, and the whole city will boil over with this building rage. We'll tear ourselves apart from the inside.

"Neither are they alone," the king added. "All the lands I spoke of before you left are reported to be on the march, and even the free cities to the west have raised a militia and sent boats down the tributaries to assist with the siege."

Falk, perhaps the craftiest of the gathering, added his thoughts. "Since Ludvarch's fall, Onderburg is the greatest power in the region. It only makes sense that Malice would agitate for our destruction. The ensuing chaos will be ripe for his influence."

"Is there a plan?" Joseph asked.

"Not as yet," the king replied. "You should go see to your people, Joseph. I gave them the tournament fields just northeast of the palace to make camp. If Kaillë or her elders can think of any other insights, please return with the news."

As Joseph turned to leave, King Dieter spoke up again. "And Joseph, if you can think of anywhere else your people might be safe, even for a little while...get out while you can."

Joseph bowed, not to the title, but to the man, and hurried to rejoin his people.

~ * ~

On the way out of the palace, Joseph heard a gruff voice shouting his name. He turned to see Dorav, Ten'daren, and Ten'vahlë sitting beside the street. "We were close enough on your heels to convince the guards at the city gate we were with you," Dorav explained as they closed the distance then pointed to the royal guardsmen at the gate Joseph had just exited, "but these palace men weren't having any of it."

"I found out where everyone is," Joseph said. "Let's go."

They reached the Windriders on the parade green of the tournament fields and broke up to their respective corners just as the sun began to set, the elves to their lieutenants and Dorav to his rovers while Joseph sought out Kaillë. As he went, he cast an eye to the city wall to the north, separated from the tournament green by only a couple rows of houses. If the enemy built siege engines, the Windrider camp would be vulnerable to any missiles shot with a high trajectory. Still, there were few other places within the walls large enough for the Windriders to camp, and others were more closely surrounded by residents growing more dangerous by the day.

Joseph was quickly directed to where Kaillë worked directing the assessment of their current supplies. She embraced him as he approached, but layers of fear replaced the passion she had displayed at their last reunion. "How long have you been back?" she asked.

"A couple of hours."

"What happened?"

Joseph related the entire tale, giving special attention to the unexpected discovery of the Baron's corpse and the analysis provided by the Axel and Olaf. "What do you think?" Joseph asked at the end.

Kaillë's voice was level. Joseph wondered if she felt the same anger and agitation he did from Malice's influence and merely did a better job keeping it in check. "Let's consider the possibilities. One, that all has proceeded as the book suggested, the Baron's death did kill Malice, and it simply takes time for his influence to dissipate."

"Not likely. The effects on the city haven't just continued since the Baron died, they've gotten worse."

"Agreed," Kaillë responded. "Two, the Baron was not the conduit, either because we were wrong in identifying Baron Turov or because the sages were wrong, and Malice needs no such conduit at all."

"I think the evidence that Turov was acting in that capacity is too strong to ignore."

"Three, the Baron *was* a conduit for Malice, but killing him had no effect."

"Yet," Joseph answered, strongly feeling Kaillë was leading him down the path of conclusions she had already made, "if we still believe that a conduit is needed, then losing it would have to be a major blow, even if not fatal, so why let the protection magic fade?"

"Which leaves option four," Kaillë finished. "It's possible, under circumstances we don't yet understand, for Malice to break his connection with one intermediary and bond with another."

"That does seem to explain the presence of Tobias' cavalry with Helmut's forces," Joseph concurred, "as if someone took up the baton after the Baron's death and ran it ahead on the same course. But where does that leave us?"

"Much worse off, I'm afraid," Kaillë answered. "Killing Malice by severing his link to the world, killing the conduit, still seems our best hope, but clearly it's more difficult if Malice has this power. And now we have no idea who this new vessel might be."

"The Baron seemed invulnerable to anything we could do to him," Joseph added. "Axel and Olaf implied it was because the Baron's body didn't function like a living thing, just a corpse animated by Malice's magic. Suppose Malice's new servant is a living, breathing person. Wouldn't that make him far more vulnerable?"

"Possibly," Kaillë concurred. "And if that's true, what could have tempted Malice to make that sacrifice?"

That had been exactly Joseph's concern, and he was quiet for a time as he considered their danger. "King Dieter said we should get out of town if we had anyplace safe to go."

"Do we?"

"...No. I haven't changed my mind. Sooner or later we'll have to make a stand, so I say let's make it right here."

"In that case," Kaillë replied, "then stand we must, not kneel and cringe. Tonight we will organize and tomorrow morning return to the king, not as Joseph his former servant, but as Tal'Joseph, a man who offers the king for the defense of his city a company of the best archers in the world. I will go as well, for those who cannot shoot can dress wounds or run messages or bear water. And we can scout from the air."

"Reveal the owls?" Joseph asked. "Are you sure?"

"These are desperate times. To keep the secret would be to hold something back for a future we may never see. You were right before when you said I didn't know what I was asking in leading us back here, that I didn't understand how terrible war is. I still don't. But I've seen the slaughter of my family and many of my people, and I've gone into danger in the depths of the earth, and I'm afraid...but not too afraid to fight. Windriders have no love for battle, but when we must, we fight with everything we have and everything we are. You know this, Joseph. You've seen it."

Joseph allowed himself a rare smile, though a slight one. "I understand, Kaillë...but I was really only surprised about the owls."

Kaillë lowered her eyes. Joseph thought she was about to speak but didn't want her to apologize for her passion, so he pulled her close. For a few brief moments, twilight and quiet reigned over the camp, as if the night had paused, shunning the drums of war to wrap it's summer arms around two lovers whose desire for a simple life was too fragile for their perilous circumstances. Just as suddenly the moment passed, the night withdrew its cloak, and reality crashed back in like a storm against the mountainside.

"I'll send Tes'voran with a picked force to bring back the owls," Joseph said, releasing Kaillë.

"And I'll finish directing the stock of supplies and begin making assignments for the noncombatants."

They both set about their respective duties, praying to survive to a time when such partings were no longer necessary.

~ * ~

Joseph and Kaillë were back in the palace with the dawn awaiting an audience with King Dieter. Joseph assumed the king was only recently awake, but when after half an hour they were admitted to the throne room, he saw that wasn't the case. The king did not appear to have slept, and instead of an empty throne room or perhaps an advisor, the king was accompanied by half a dozen rough-looking men in uniform and a knight still wearing his chainmail and greaves, sweaty as from a hard ride.

"I'm sorry to keep you waiting, Joseph," King Dieter said after the hunter was announced. "The wizards have managed to keep the palace civil now that Axel and Olaf are returned, but apart from that it has been a dire night. Our enemies stole a march on us; they arrived two hours before dawn and are massing on the plain outside the main gates. If you'd had to travel any farther across the city to get here, you'd have probably heard the news on the way. Now, I'm sorry to be blunt, but what brings you here? Good news, I hope."

"Probably not the kind you were looking for, but better than nothing." Joseph outlined Kaillë's plan, offering the services and bows of the Windrider clan. King Dieter was pleased, but Joseph interrupted his gratitude. "We do need one thing in return."

"What do you mean?"

"We have some other resources to offer, but...we'll need to take over the tops of your guard towers. They need to be cleared in half an hour."

~ * ~

The king agreed to Joseph's terms, but the owls couldn't be hidden for long. Rumors flew, and before long their presence began to cause quite a stir. Fortunately, the news was generally a boon to morale within the city, and by midday the common tale in the taverns and around the docks was that an army of griffons had arrived from some far off land and would break the siege before it got underway. The following day the king requested Joseph and Kaillë to appear, and they delegated their duties so they could comply. The throne room had been converted into the king's war room, with knights and generals coming and going at all hours, to say nothing of the couriers and other underlings at the periphery of the major planning. Hostilities hadn't yet begun in any meaningful way, but Dieter planned for Onderburg to hit the harder when they did.

Joseph and Kaillë entered the chaos of the room unannounced, the herald having long since given up his efforts to keep any intelligible track of who was coming and going. After several minutes the king looked up from his map of the city and the general he was conversing with and spotted the pair of them waiting to be acknowledged. They watched as the king excused himself from his conversation and hurried to their side, ushering them to an empty space between the pillars on the left side of the room.

"Are your people in position?" he asked.

"Ready and waiting," Joseph answered.

"Good, good." The king paused, and Joseph knew they hadn't been summoned for a situational update. Still, Dieter's body language didn't suggest bad news, but rather a sense of melancholy. After a few moments the king spoke. "I've had the sages working their research while the military prepares the city. So far they haven't come up with anything that might defeat Malice or even strike a blow against what's happening. I've kept that knowledge as quiet as I can, but I thought it best you knew the truth. I have no idea if any of us will survive this." The king paused again, then his countenance lifted, if only slightly. "You've placed yourself in harm's way, though, and without anything here worth fighting for, at least not for yourselves. Don't misunderstand, it's admirable that you sacrifice for right, for your fellow men, but I've always found the people fight best when they have a home to protect. I understand *your* home has been utterly destroyed."

Kaillë and Joseph nodded silently.

"There is an ancient forest a day northwest of here, four hundred square miles no ax or saw has ever touched. King

Ludvarch used it as a private hunting ground, and since the war I haven't had the chance or inclination to do anything with it. Smaller than you're used to perhaps, but large enough to support your people, I think. If we survive, it's yours, until the end of Ondravia or you decide to go elsewhere. None will enter without your leave. Tell your people. I want them to know what they're fighting for." The king clapped Joseph on the shoulder and turned to leave before even receiving their thanks.

Joseph looked down at Kaillë. "Do you think the Windriders will accept it?"

"It isn't normally our way...but we've been on the run for months, and the loss of the new village has cut them deeply, though they don't much show it. The idea of home..."

Joseph heard the longing in Kaillë's voice when she used the word, a sense of contentment that remained out of reach.

"Home," Joseph repeated. He put his arm around Kaillë, and they left the throne room.

Chapter Twenty: Partings

A week passed. The Windriders responded well to the promise of a new home, and word filtered back to Joseph's ears that after a few days they had even named it: Windhaven. Kaillë's estimation of her people's desire had not been too great.

More enemies arrived on the plain every day. Probing attacks at the gates began, but all were repulsed. In this the Windriders proved their worth and more. Launching arrows from the cover of the hoarding on the walls, their accurate range proved to be at least fifty yards farther than the enemy had anticipated, and within hours of the first attack they had redeployed their entire camp for the fear of them. The owls flew high, too high to be seen as anything unusual from the ground, but the keen eyes of their riders noted everything, from the banners of those joining the battle to the logging operations at nearby copses in preparation for building siege engines. After two days of such intelligence, the king used them to move messages out of the besieged city, sending word to the vassals that remained loyal and coordinating a counterattack on the enemy as soon as their position around the city became complacent.

Malice's influence kept the city on edge, but the threat outside was enough to prevent a mass riot. Still, the guard were spread thin breaking up fights, and murders were on the rise as evidenced by the bodies that had to be fished from the river at the outflowing gate. Any pressure would likely spark exactly the conflagration they all feared, but Onderburg proved a difficult city to besiege. The river provided a constant source of water and flowed too fast and deep to be dammed or poisoned without a mass and concerted effort. Food would become a problem eventually, but King Dieter's stewards were skilled at their craft, and rations were stocked and distributed throughout the city.

The shadow of Malice still hung heavily over the leaders of the defense. For every short-term victory or lucky break the defenders enjoyed, the answering fact remained unchanged: even if the city survived this siege, for as long as the real enemy remained, the war would never end. Kaillë convinced King Dieter of the probability that Malice had formed a link with a new conduit, but his wizards remained unable to locate or identify him. The sages and wizards completed a detailed, magical examination of Baron Turov's corpse, but though they learned much that allowed them to attempt spells of location, they found nothing that could guarantee success.

~ * ~

Joseph rested on the tournament green that had been converted into a temporary field hospital, though so far it had seen only minimal use. Still, it had been a trying day. The enemy had sent repeated assaults at the main gate, and a minor riot had broken out near the docks. To discourage continued violence, the king had responded in kind on both fronts. Guards had been sent in force to put down the riot with extreme prejudice, and a cavalry squad made their way out a sally port for a hit-and-run charge against the enemy camp.

Many of the injured had been borne in on litters an hour before, and now the walking wounded were filtering in a few at a time. Joseph had visited to ensure that Kaillë had everything she needed, especially enough guards to discourage any flare-ups as increasingly mobile and potentially violent victims began to populate the hospital.

Joseph stood and headed to the north wall to take a report from Tes'sael. Suddenly a great roar sounded from the east, then heavy crashes shook throughout the east and south quarters of the city. Joseph looked toward the sounds in time to see another wave of stones hurtling over the walls, by what engines he had no idea. From his position he could just make out the northern end of the east wall as a lower trajectory shot shattered a ten-foot section of hoarding, sending splinters and chunks of timber flying into the air as cries of pain and fear lofted faintly to Joseph's ears.

With the frequent attacks of the day, troops had been rotated frequently to stave off fatigue; he couldn't be sure whether any Windriders were working that corner of the wall. Joseph readied his bow and sprinted to the north to find out. A glow at the right edge of his vision caught his attention, and he looked to see another salvo of catapult shot arcing over the walls, this time burning and trailing flame and black smoke. It seemed the first two bombardments had satisfied the enemy of their range, and now the most lethal artillery was being unleashed. The missiles crashed into streets and buildings screened from Joseph's view, but the intensifying glow and columns of smoke were evident, even in the light of day. He maintained his course but redoubled his speed, desperation fueling his legs as another fusillade of smaller stones obliterated more of the hoarding on the east wall with uncanny accuracy.

Joseph was a hundred yards from the wall steps when he saw Dorav charging back toward him. There was no sign of any Windriders, but the other two rovers were just a few paces behind the dwarf. Dorav was shouting, but a general clamor had arisen throughout the city, and his words were lost in the din. Joseph cupped his hand to his ear in sign, and Dorav shook his head and ran faster. They met in the middle, and Dorav took a pair of breaths as the rovers caught up before he spoke. "They're digging," he said. "Fast, impossibly fast."

"How do you know?" Joseph asked.

Dorav simply looked at him with a scowl and pointed to his ears and feet.

"Right," Joseph realized. "Where?"

"Right here. They're—" The rovers shuffled their feet and looked down, then toward Joseph, then beyond him. "They're passing under our feet right now, toward the palace."

At once they turned and ran the other direction, Joseph now following the dwarves and their vibration-attuned senses. "Will they breach the palace?" he shouted.

"I think they'll stop short," Dorav hollered back over his shoulder. "They went under the foundations of the wall rather than mining it for collapse; however it is they're digging so fast, I don't think it works through solid stone, and the palace sits on bedrock."

They ran for a few more seconds, then the ground a furlong from the palace exploded in a shower of dirt and rocks. For a moment Joseph could only cough and shield his eyes from the debris, and when the air had cleared enough for him to see, the dwarves, undeterred, had gone well ahead of him. A great shout sounded from within the cloud of dust, and as the flame-fueled wind blew away the veil, Joseph saw dozens of warriors issuing from a sloped hole in the ground, heading away from him toward the palace. Not fifty yards to the right the main knot of wounded had been settled, and Joseph knew Kaillë must be working somewhere there. Fear and confusion warred in his mind. Kaillë's safety sprang foremost into his thoughts, but at the same time he couldn't understand why the enemy had launched their attack at the north side of the palace, the opposite side from the main gates. Even now they ran toward the rubble-strewn ditch at the base of the wall, though there was no hope of entry there without the ability to claw through stone.

Neither emotion stilled Joseph's bow; he shot as he ran in concert with the rovers forming up and charging into the enemy rear. Some turned to face them and managed to hold the dwarves back for a few seconds.

It was enough. At that moment the diggers emerged from the hole.

Joseph wasn't sure what he expected. His mind had raced too quickly to form any clear assumption about how the tunnel had been formed so suddenly and without fear of collapse. He was sure what he didn't expect was two men, their faces tattooed in the style of the northern tribes. Unlike their brethren, their heads were shaved, their clothing adorned with fetishes of bone. They carried no weapons, but wherever they moved their hands, the earth moved in sympathy, clubs and spikes of clay thrusting from the ground and battering their enemies. Joseph shot two arrows in quick succession, but one of the wizards seemed to sense the missiles' coming and went on the defensive, hurling up a shield of compacted dirt. Joseph was confident he could get through their defense with a few Windriders at his side, but alone he had little hope.

The sorcerers fixed their attention on the dwarves. The rovers seemed to sense attacks coming and dodged more quickly than any human or elf could do, but the offensive was a constant barrage that forced them completely to defense. The enemy rearguard, eager to leave the area of bucking earth, turned to rejoin their compatriots in the assault on the north wall, the target of which still left Joseph baffled.

Suddenly, a roar sounded from inside the ditch, and fighters from inside the palace fought their way out onto the plain, their presence just as inexplicable. Joseph continued to advance, skirting the earth wizards to the right, between them and wherever Kaillë stood among the wounded, and now he was close enough to see the palace fighters in some detail. Most were guards, even a few of the king's personal bodyguard, but by their arms and livery Joseph knew some of the fighters were dismounted knights. In coordination and tactics they couldn't match a dwarven hret-dialt, but as individual warriors their skill in melee was unrivaled. Hammer and sword struck the enemy with brutal power, and the tide of the attack began to slow.

Then the enemy wizards redirected their attention, and chaos suddenly reigned through the palace guard, fighters stumbling and falling where not impaled outright. Joseph shot where he could without hope of making any meaningful change in the outcome of the battle. Then from the right corner of his eye he saw a small contingent of knights and king's guards breaking away from the battle, skirting its west side as if making a play for the mages where they sheltered behind their own lines. They moved in a knot, protecting something or someone at their center, and Joseph paused in his attack long enough to see what it could be. In an instant he caught the eye of Axel, tall and dark above the heads of most of the defenders, then glancing between the outer ranks he saw Olaf as well. Axel raised his hand in salute, acknowledging Joseph was there, then turned his eyes significantly toward the wizards and back again. Joseph nodded back and readied his bow, one arrow nocked and another held against the bow in his gripping hand. He kept his eyes on the brothers just long enough to see Olaf begin his hand waving while Axel, with his smaller movements, pointed his palms toward the enemy mages.

A long moment passed. The earth wizards turned toward the incoming warriors, but the band continued to advance at a steady pace that did not disturb their own sorcerers. Joseph saw the enemy become more labored in their movements, then all at once the earth stopped shaking. The wizards' shield of earth dissolved into blowing dust. Joseph loosed his first shot, but before he could nock his second, a hail of arrows thudded into the enemy from his left.

"For Windhaven!" came a shout.

The two wizards fell dead, bristling with arrows as Joseph looked to see Tes'sael leading his Windriders from the defense of the north wall.

A great cheer went up from the palace guards as they regrouped and pressed their momentary advantage. The earth wizards' assault had thrown them into disarray but at the same time denied that strip of ground to the attackers, so their momentum had remained neutral. Now the tide turned, and the defenders pushed them back in great surges, pikes and shields driving against them. Tes'sael arrayed his elves in preparation for a ranged attack at the enemy rear.

"Joseph."

The hunter turned toward the call of his name to see Kaillë running toward him. "Kaillë," he shouted, "what are you doing? Get back!"

By the time she was close enough to be heard over the noise of battle, there wasn't much ground left to cover, and so she finished the distance. Joseph kept on the alert and shielded her from the general direction of the nearest violence, but catapult shot still rained down to the east, and the fire was spreading.

"I saw Dorav and the rovers earlier but lost track of them in the dust, then Tes'sael coming across the green. I have stretcher bearers right behind; we'll take the wounded as soon as we can—"

The wind shifted, and a sudden chill ripped through the green. For half a heartbeat all movement stopped, and the only sound was the roar of the fires. Then around the hole the enemy had rent in the earth were a ring of fighters in armor, perhaps two dozen, their breastplates and helms blackened with soot. They carried shields with spears held across them that they beat together in a perfect rhythm. Joseph had no clear memory of their emergence from the ground; one moment they were not, and the next moment they were, and the change felt as inevitable as the setting of the sun. Joseph's heart quailed at the sight of them, but he could pinpoint no clear reason why; certainly he had faced more terrifying foes and numbers, and he had a few arrows in his quiver with heads that, at this range, would punch through their breastplates like paper. Still he stood transfixed, grappling with his inexplicable fear.

The black-clad soldiers began a steady march outward, and as their ranks opened Joseph could see that someone stood behind them, on the side of the hole's rim nearest him, one small figure standing motionless with daggers in her hands. The soldiers took two more steps, and Joseph could see the figure was Rook, the necklace she had used on him pulsing with a bloody glow. The face and form were the same, but the look in her eyes was one he did not recognize. Suddenly the light footprints at the scene of the Baron's death were clear, though now, as then, Joseph's mind rebelled against the thought. Joseph had only to see her eyes, though, to know the woman now before him was capable of that brutality.

She flicked her eyes to Joseph's left, where Tes'sael stood with his archers, and in an instant they were shooting, their arrows arcing high over the enemies' heads to fall mercilessly into the palace guard. Joseph heard Axel and Olaf chanting, but Rook waved a dagger in their direction, and they fell silent. Joseph turned his bow on the circle of men defending them. He didn't know why he was doing it, didn't want to do it, but knew he had to. On the other side of the ring of armored warriors he saw Dorav and the rovers turn ax and hammer on one another, and Kaillë began a dead sprint toward Rook. A distant part of him was horrified for her safety, but he felt the release of endless burdens in the knowledge that it didn't really matter. All he needed do was keep loosing arrows at the men before him, and his heart, his very soul, was content.

Beyond his targets, he saw the defense of the palace wall collapse and the enemy attackers surge into the ditch, and somehow he knew it was good.

"Joseph! Joseph, help!"

The scream was Kaillë's, and the first syllable had barely reached his ears when his will flooded back into him in a noisy rush, the din of battle and roar of flame sounding in his ears again. The elves didn't shake off the control so easily, but their chieftain's scream had not failed to move them, and their attacks faltered and became sporadic.

Joseph turned toward the horrible sound and saw Kaillë standing in front of Rook with her back to the thief, facing him. Rook had a fistful of Kaillë's hair in her left hand, pulling the elf's head back to expose her throat.

Time slowed to a fraction, lifetimes passing between heartbeats. Rook's guard took another step forward, clearing Joseph's view of the horror before him ever so slightly. He pivoted his body toward the threat as Rook laid the dagger in her right hand across Kaillë's throat.

Joseph had no arrow in his hand. He reached over his shoulder, knowing he couldn't hope to move faster than Rook's blade.

A cry of rage and pain ripped free from his open mouth as his fingers found fletching and nock and drew forth an arrow. Rook's silhouette was completely hidden behind Kaillë's struggling form; even as he nocked the arrow, he knew he had no shot, could see the dagger's edge pressing into the skin at Kaillë's throat.

Joseph stretched his bow, then immediately lost all will to shoot it. He stood motionless, helpless, his mind still his own but his body no longer following its commands. Frustration and fear surged within him. A tear pooled in his vision and forced him to blink, though he dreaded what might pass when he did.

Then Rook did something strange. She kept her grip on Kaillë's hair, but rather than cut, she kicked the elf's legs from behind, forcing her to her knees. Joseph's vision cleared as he pinned his eyes on Rook's chest and throat, his shot as clear as he could want if he could only force his fingers to release the string. He saw that Rook was looking directly at him, and he met her gaze. Gone were the hatred, the bloodlust he'd seen earlier. Now he saw only shame and terror. The elves stopped shooting. The rovers stopped fighting. Rook's eyes on his were beseeching and her head shook in a nod so subtle it was almost invisible.

Then in an instant her eyes changed. Everything evil was back in them, and a sneer spread across Rook's lips as her grip on the dagger tightened. Joseph fought down the shake of his shoulders and focused all his will on three fingers of his right hand. He drew a breath. His heart stopped.

He shot.

Again. Again. Again.

The dagger fell from Rook's fingers, and she dropped to her knees, then slumped sideways, four broadhead arrows through what was left of her heart.

A wail keened from the very air all around them, a sound as full of rage and hatred as the roar Joseph had heard at the Well, but without its force, instead laden with fear and pain and impotent frustration. The sound clawed at his heart and mind but found no purchase there as the power drained out of it, receding into the upper airs where at last it died.

Joseph found he was running toward Rook's fallen form, and already Kaillë was leaning over her, feeling for breath. He knew by his wife's posture her action was motivated more by duty or habit than any real hope of finding life. Joseph had done his bloody work too well.

He slowed to a walk the last few paces, Kaillë's slack face casting away all doubt there might be any use in haste. His shadow fell over Kaillë and Rook's body as he came close, and tears were in Kaillë's eyes. Rook's were closed, and the expression of hatred was gone from her face. But for her wounds, she might only have been sleeping beneath the spring sun. Perhaps Malice had pulled her pain out of her as he went, but to his surprise all Joseph saw in Rook was peace, and the minstrel's could not have sung it any better.

"She was our friend," Kaillë said, her tone almost confused, the words unable to put any sense to what they had just witnessed.

Joseph only nodded. He had no words at all.

"What do we do now?"

For an instant Joseph was struck by how many times in the last few months someone had asked him that question, or one just like it, he who had been responsible for none but himself for so many years. It was his lot, he supposed, one he had fled awhile but could never really escape. He looked down at Kaillë and saw her focus had risen from Rook's body and back to him, and perhaps for the first time he understood the weight of her question. His answer wouldn't take away her grief, but it could alleviate for a time the weight of decision that was the young chieftain's ever present burden. He could grant a direction that would provide room for his wife's emotions to run their course and find a place within her memories.

Joseph looked and listened to the battle that still raged around them. If Malice truly commanded the wills of men, as Rook's necklace had, then perhaps his destruction would have brought an instant end to the battle, but that wasn't the way of it. As it was, the ancient enemy's defeat could no more end this battle than a peace treaty signed in some far-off capitol could end a battle in any of the countless wars men had fought. His gaze was still on Kaillë. "First," he finally answered, "we survive. Then...we find her brother."

~ * ~

Later they realized Rook's personal bodyguard in their blackened armor had been under her direct control and had thrown down arms at the moment of her death. The rest of the battle died down after a few more hours as the leaders realized their folly. By the time King Dieter's loyal vassals arrived the next day to break the siege, it was already over.

Dieter had the best wizards in the kingdom, so they should have detected the spells of concealment that had been placed around the siege engines the enemy had transported and brought suddenly to bear, but all their attention had been absorbed in keeping a lid on the insatiable aggression Malice had sowed through the city. Only at the last moment had Olaf sensed the power of the approaching earth wizards and warned the king. Dieter had learned of the secret tunnel Rook had used to enter the palace, but he couldn't spare the workers to seal it. Since he couldn't know who else was aware of it, as soon as Malice's unrest had stirred in the city, Dieter had placed a large force of guards around the tunnel, so they were quickly deployed to the defense. Only later, after learning Rook was the mastermind of the whole attack, did Dieter realize that very entrance had been their objective in the first place, likely to make an attempt on his own life.

Axel had been wounded by Joseph's forced arrow barrage, taking a hit meant for his brother, but with rest he was expected to recover. As the experts in making and breaking enchantments, the brothers were tasked with the responsibility of destroying the power of the necklace before it could do further harm. They did so after a careful study of it, and in the end speculated it as the reason Malice had chosen to abandon the Baron in favor of a more vulnerable form. After countless millennia influencing the minds of men, the power to control them outright must have been irresistible, and Axel speculated the Baron, being a thing of undeath, probably could not have used it, or at least that Malice believed so. The vast amplification of the necklace's domination in the final battle, and leading up to it, as reports from the other side would eventually reveal, they attributed to Malice's considerable power working in concert with the necklace's capabilities.

At first Joseph was too glad to be alive for questions about how he had resisted Rook and Malice's powers at the end, but after a time he had to know. He proffered the theory that his bond with Kaillë was so central to his identity that her peril allowed him to resist, but Axel responded with doubt. "Poets may tell of such things, but I think it more likely Kaillë's screams touched something deep in Rook's conscience that weakened Malice's influence for a few key moments. In that instant she could

see only one way out, so she fought to allow you the
window to do what needed to be done."

Joseph wasn't wholly convinced, knowing how sharply
his focus had returned the instant he knew Kaillë to be in
mortal danger, but for Rook's sake he hoped Axel was right,
that she had found a way to atone in her last moments, the
only way she could.

~ * ~

As in Joseph and the Windriders' home forest, fire
ultimately did more harm than any other tool of warfare
Malice had agitated men to employ. Long after the battle
ended the citizens of Onderburg fought the blazes, and
flare-ups in hot spots would remain a danger for days.

While Kaillë continued to tend the wounded and
Tes'voran directed owl riders in carrying messages
between crews fighting the fires, Joseph took stock of their
people. The non-combatants had all been spared, but
amongst the archers were four wounded and one dead.
Dorav had taken several flesh wounds when the rovers
were ordered to fight one another, and one of his fellows
had lost a hand, but they had all survived. They planned to
remain with the Windriders until the clan was settled in
their new home, then make the trek east to the tunnels of
the Eleventh Clan.

Through the Wolfsguard, King Dieter knew where
Rook's brother, Adler, could be found, and Joseph insisted
on the duty of informing him of his sister's death. Two days
after the battle, he and Kaillë stood in the room where he
made his home, looking into the eyes of a young man who
had no doubt how this story must end.

Joseph explained the existence and powers of Malice as
succinctly as he could and shared Axel's educated guess of
how Rook had fallen in league with him. At the end, he

would not shy from the reality of his own actions. "I killed Rook. At the time, I couldn't see another choice. Letting her live would have cost Kaillë her life, and probably many others. I won't apologize for what I did...but I am sorry for what it means for you, for the pain I caused."

Joseph expected Adler to be outraged, or at least shocked, but instead the man was quiet. After a few minutes he looked up. "Rook didn't talk much about her...work, but she did speak of you. She wasn't one to offer respect, at least not by any usual definition, but I know she thought well of you. Now I see why."

Joseph and Kaillë traded glances, and he could see his wife was thinking the same thing he was, that Adler must be in shock.

"Is there anything we can do?" Kaillë asked. "I know this news must come as a terrible blow."

Adler's face was sad when he spoke. "The truth is, I hadn't seen my sister in weeks. It isn't the first time she'd disappeared, but she always gave some idea of when I should expect her. Until she left me this two weeks ago," he said, holding up a beaded, black feather, "I'd started to think she must be dead. I told her many times she'd come to a bad end if she didn't give up what she was doing. I'll admit this isn't what I expected, and there will be raw nights ahead, but...I've been preparing myself for this a long time."

The room was silent for a few minutes, then Kaillë spoke their last piece of news. "King Dieter has invited you to the castle as his personal guest. In fact, he's rather insistent. He's done his best to keep things quiet, but it's only a matter of time before word of Rook's involvement with the battle gets out, and some may look to her friends and family for retribution. The king would prevent that but doesn't feel confident he can keep you safe outside the palace."

Joseph saw Adler begin to object and cut him off. "He's also asked for your help. One of his advisors recently retired and left the king in need of an expert to arrange for entertainment at holidays and feast days. It would be a considerable service to your king if you accept."

Adler gave a half-smile, and Joseph saw that Dieter's ploy did not go unmarked, but the younger man looked interested despite himself. "As long as I can be of use," he replied, "please tell His Majesty I accept."

"You can tell him yourself when you arrive," Joseph answered, opening the door to show the royal coach that had drawn up outside while they spoke.

Adler had few possessions, and Kaillë and two of King Dieter's manservants gathered them while Joseph carried the former acrobat to the coach and set him inside. Adler looked surprised when Joseph closed the door without first entering himself. "You aren't coming?"

"No. I've said such goodbyes as I need to already, and if I never see the inside of another castle, it'll be too soon. Besides...you're not the only one with a new home to go to."

~ * ~

The next day the Windriders assembled outside the city gates an hour after dawn. The way to Windhaven was easy, and two of Dieter's huntsmen had laid out the route for them in detail, sparing no landmark or bearing. Joseph had convinced the king not to come in person to see them off, feeling the ceding of so much territory to an elven tribe would cost the king enough friends and support without adding a royal appearance during such a continuing crisis. Dieter did, over Joseph's objections, send a company of royal cavalry to escort them to their new home, the horsemen following at a respectful distance to provide support in case of trouble without appearing to move the Windriders where they didn't want to go.

The elves had much to mourn but as much to celebrate, and they focused on the latter as they travelled to Windhaven, passing the days at an easy pace and enjoying the new sights and sounds and smells of a region none of them had ever before visited. The future lay before them, uncertain as days yet-to-be always are, but with more promise than they'd felt since their perils began months before. They sang and laughed, choosing to leave their sorrows behind with the miles.

The sun was high on the second day when they reached the eaves of Windhaven. As a body they turned and raised their hands in salute to their escort, then turned and walked ahead, vanishing completely in the shadows of the trees, leaving the cavalry to wonder at their stealth. The only sounds that reached their ears were those of Dorav and his rovers navigating their unfamiliar terrain.

Once inside, elf and dwarf alike dispersed to explore, Stitch and Yowler bounding around with them, leaving Joseph and Kaillë alone in a clear space with wildflowers growing around the edges.

"Will you be happy here, Joseph?" Kaillë asked.

"For as long as we can have peace, together, I will be happy."

"No misgivings this time?"

"None," Joseph answered after a pause, and he laughed a clear, contented laugh as he realized how long it had been since he could say so. He smiled at his wife, drinking in the sight of her beauty in the dappled sunlight, the sound of a brook he hadn't yet sighted, the smells of the flowers and damp earth on the late spring air. "So, my chieftain...what do we do now?"

"Now?" Kaillë responded. "Now we do whatever we like. We explore and hunt and build and sing and dance. We race the wind through the woods and stay up naming every familiar star in our new sky. We tell our new stories around the campfires, remember our fallen and rejoice for tomorrow. We love, Joseph. And we live. We *live*."

And Joseph, the Spirit of the Trees, lived with them.

About the Author

Shane L. Coffey lives in Colorado with his wife and the multitude of characters trying to fight their way from his brain to his computer screen. He is a man of simple tastes, inexpensive hobbies, and little travel...but if anybody starts making plans for an expedition to Mars or Rivendell, he'll be very interested to know whether they require any skillsets he possesses (...or could convincingly fake).